Living]

Living Fiction

Reading the British Novel from Daniel Defoe to Julian Barnes

WILLIAM HUTCHINGS

First published 2014 by
PALGRAVE MACMILLAN

Palgrave Macmillan in the UK is an imprint of Macmillan Publishers Limited, registered in England, company number 785998, of Houndmills, Basingstoke, Hampshire RG21 6XS.

Palgrave Macmillan in the US is a division of St Martin's Press LLC, 175 Fifth Avenue, New York, NY 10010.

Palgrave Macmillan is the global academic imprint of the above companies and has companies and representatives throughout the world.

Palgrave® and Macmillan® are registered trademarks in the United States, the United Kingdom, Europe and other countries.

ISBN 978–1–137–29834–8 hardback
ISBN 978–1–137–29833–1 paperback

This book is printed on paper suitable for recycling and made from fully managed and sustained forest sources. Logging, pulping and manufacturing processes are expected to conform to the environmental regulations of the country of origin.

A catalogue record for this book is available from the British Library.

A catalog record for this book is available from the Library of Congress.

Printed in China

For Shelagh

Contents

Principal Novels Discussed   viii

Timeline of Selected Significant Novels, 1719–2012   x

1   Introduction   1

2   Describing People   4

3   Describing Places   37

4   Presenting Action   65

5   Speaking   104

6   Commenting   134

Notes   180

Index of Literary and Grammatical Terms   185

General Index   189

Principal Novels Discussed

Jane Austen:	*Emma*
	Mansfield Park
	Persuasion
	Pride and Prejudice
Julian Barnes:	*The Sense of an Ending*
Arnold Bennett:	*The Old Wives' Tale*
	Riceyman Steps
Anne Brontë:	*Agnes Grey*
Charlotte Brontë:	*Villette*
Anita Brookner:	*Hotel du Lac*
Frances Burney:	*Cecilia*
Joseph Conrad:	*Lord Jim*
Daniel Defoe:	*Moll Flanders*
	Robinson Crusoe
Charles Dickens:	*Great Expectations*
	Hard Times
George Eliot:	*Middlemarch*
Henry Fielding:	*Joseph Andrews*
	Tom Jones
Ronald Firbank:	*Valmouth*
Penelope Fitzgerald:	*The Blue Flower*
Ford Madox Ford:	*The Good Soldier*
E. M. Forster:	*A Room with a View*
Elizabeth Gaskell:	*North and South*
William Golding:	*The Spire*
Henry Green:	*Living*
	Nothing
Thomas Hardy:	*The Mayor of Casterbridge*
	Tess of the d'Urbervilles
	The Woodlanders
Eliza Haywood:	*The History of Miss Betsy Thoughtless*
B. S. Johnson:	*Albert Angelo*
	House Mother Normal

Samuel Johnson:	*Rasselas*
D. H. Lawrence:	*The Rainbow*
Charlotte Lennox:	*The Female Quixote*
Ian McEwan:	*Saturday*
George Orwell:	*Coming up for Air*
Ann Radcliffe:	*The Mysteries of Udolpho*
Samuel Richardson:	*Clarissa*
	Sir Charles Grandison
Laurence Sterne:	*Tristram Shandy*
Jonathan Swift:	*Gulliver's Travels*
Anthony Trollope:	*Framley Parsonage*
Evelyn Waugh:	*Men at Arms*
	Unconditional Surrender
P. G. Wodehouse:	*The Code of the Woosters*
Virginia Woolf:	*Mrs Dalloway*
	To the Lighthouse

Timeline of Selected Significant Novels, 1719–2012

1719	Daniel Defoe, *Robinson Crusoe*
1722	Daniel Defoe, *Moll Flanders*
1724	Daniel Defoe, *Roxana*
1726	Jonathan Swift, *Gulliver's Travels*
1740	Samuel Richardson, *Pamela*
1742	Henry Fielding, *Joseph Andrews*
1747–8	Samuel Richardson, *Clarissa*
1748	Tobias Smollett, *Roderick Random*
1749	Henry Fielding, *Tom Jones*
1751	Henry Fielding, *Amelia*; Eliza Haywood, *The History of Miss Betsy Thoughtless*; Tobias Smollett, *Peregrine Pickle*
1752	Charlotte Lennox, *The Female Quixote*
1753–4	Samuel Richardson, *Sir Charles Grandison*
1759	Samuel Johnson, *Rasselas*
1759–67	Laurence Sterne, *Tristram Shandy*
1764	Horace Walpole, *The Castle of Otranto*
1766	Oliver Goldsmith, *The Vicar of Wakefield*
1768	Laurence Sterne, *A Sentimental Journey*
1771	Henry Mackenzie, *The Man of Feeling*; Tobias Smollett, *Humphry Clinker*
1778	Frances Burney, *Evelina*
1782	Frances Burney, *Cecilia*
1788	Charlotte Smith, *Emmeline*; Mary Wollstonecraft, *Mary*
1793	Charlotte Smith, *The Old Manor House*
1794	William Godwin, *Caleb Williams*; Ann Radcliffe, *The Mysteries of Udolpho*
1796	Robert Bage, *Hermsprong*; Frances Burney, *Camilla*
1797	Ann Radcliffe, *The Italian*
1800	Maria Edgeworth, *Castle Rackrent*
1811	Jane Austen, *Sense and Sensibility*

1813	Jane Austen, *Pride and Prejudice*
1814	Jane Austen, *Mansfield Park*;
	Walter Scott, *Waverley*
1815	Walter Scott, *Guy Mannering*
1816	Jane Austen, *Emma*;
	Thomas Love Peacock, *Headlong Hall*
1818	Jane Austen, *Northanger Abbey and Persuasion*;
	Susan Ferrier, *Marriage*;
	Thomas Love Peacock, *Nightmare Abbey*;
	Walter Scott, *The Heart of Midlothian*;
	Mary Shelley, *Frankenstein*
1819	Walter Scott, *The Bride of Lammermoor*
1824	James Hogg, *The Private Memoirs and Confessions of a Justified Sinner*
1831	Thomas Love Peacock, *Crotchet Castle*
1836	Frederick Marryat, *Mr Midshipman Easy*
1836–7	Charles Dickens, *The Pickwick Papers*
1837–9	Charles Dickens, *Oliver Twist*
1838	R. S. Surtees, *Jorrocks's Jaunts and Jollities*
1838–9	Charles Dickens, *Nicholas Nickleby*
1840–1	Charles Dickens, *The Old Curiosity Shop*
1845	Benjamin Disraeli, *Sybil*
1846–8	Charles Dickens, *Dombey and Son*
1847	Anne Brontë, *Agnes Grey*;
	Charlotte Brontë, *Jane Eyre*;
	Emily Brontë, *Wuthering Heights*
1847–8	William Makepeace Thackeray, *Vanity Fair*
1848	Anne Brontë, *The Tenant of Wildfell Hall*;
	Elizabeth Gaskell, *Mary Barton*
1848–50	William Makepeace Thackeray, *Pendennis*
1849	Charlotte Brontë, *Shirley*
1849–50	Charles Dickens, *David Copperfield*
1850	Charles Kingsley, *Alton Locke*
1851–3	Elizabeth Gaskell, *Cranford*
1852	William Makepeace Thackeray, *Henry Esmond*
1852–3	Charles Dickens, *Bleak House*
1853	Charlotte Brontë, *Villette*
1854	Charles Dickens, *Hard Times*
1855	Elizabeth Gaskell, *North and South*;
	Anthony Trollope, *The Warden*
1855–7	Charles Dickens, *Little Dorrit*

1857   Anthony Trollope, *Barchester Towers*
1859   George Eliot, *Adam Bede*
1860   Wilkie Collins, *The Woman in White*;
            George Eliot, *The Mill on the Floss*;
            Anthony Trollope, *Framley Parsonage*
1860–1   Charles Dickens, *Great Expectations*
1864–5   Charles Dickens, *Our Mutual Friend*
1866   George Eliot, *Felix Holt the Radical*;
            Elizabeth Gaskell, *Wives and Daughters*
1866–7   Anthony Trollope, *The Last Chronicle of Barset*
1868   Wilkie Collins, *The Moonstone*
1871–2   George Eliot, *Middlemarch*
1872   Samuel Butler, *Erewhon*;
            Thomas Hardy, *Under the Greenwood Tree*
1874   Thomas Hardy, *Far from the Madding Crowd*
1874–5   Anthony Trollope, *The Way We Live Now*
1874–6   George Eliot, *Daniel Deronda*
1878   Thomas Hardy, *The Return of the Native*
1879   George Meredith, *The Egoist*
1885   Walter Pater, *Marius the Epicurean*
1886   Thomas Hardy, *The Mayor of Casterbridge*;
            Robert Louis Stevenson, *Dr Jekyll and Mr Hyde*
1887   H. Rider Haggard, *She*;
            Thomas Hardy, *The Woodlanders*
1890   Oscar Wilde, *The Picture of Dorian Gray*
1891   George Gissing, *New Grub Street*;
            Thomas Hardy, *Tess of the d'Urbervilles*
1894   George Moore, *Esther Waters*
1895   Thomas Hardy, *Jude the Obscure*
1900   Joseph Conrad, *Lord Jim*
1901   Rudyard Kipling, *Kim*
1902   Arnold Bennett, *Anna of the Five Towns*
1903   Samuel Butler, *The Way of All Flesh*
1904   Joseph Conrad, *Nostromo*
1905   H. G. Wells, *Kipps*
1906   John Galsworthy, *The Man of Property* (first part of
            The Forsyte Saga, published together 1922)
1907   Joseph Conrad, *The Secret Agent*
1908   Arnold Bennett, *The Old Wives' Tale*;
            E. M. Forster, *A Room with a View*

1910	Arnold Bennett, *Clayhanger*;
	E. M. Forster, *Howards End*;
	H. G. Wells, *The History of Mr Polly*
1911	Arnold Bennett, *Hilda Lessways*;
	Joseph Conrad, *Under Western Eyes*
1913	D. H. Lawrence, *Sons and Lovers*
1915	Ford Madox Ford, *The Good Soldier*;
	D. H. Lawrence, *The Rainbow*;
	W. Somerset Maugham, *Of Human Bondage*;
	Dorothy Richardson, *Pointed Roofs* (first part of *Pilgrimage*, –1938)
1919	Ronald Firbank, *Valmouth*
1920	D. H. Lawrence, *Women in Love*
1922	James Joyce, *Ulysses*;
	Virginia Woolf, *Jacob's Room*
1923	Arnold Bennett, *Riceyman Steps*
1924	Ford Madox Ford, *Some Do Not ...* (first part of *Parade's End*, –1928);
	E. M. Forster, *A Passage to India*
1925	Ivy Compton Burnett, *Pastors and Masters*;
	Virginia Woolf, *Mrs Dalloway*
1926	Ronald Firbank, *Concerning the Eccentricities of Cardinal Pirelli*
1927	Virginia Woolf, *To the Lighthouse*
1928	Aldous Huxley, *Point Counter Point*;
	D. H. Lawrence, *Lady Chatterley's Lover*;
	Evelyn Waugh, *Decline and Fall*
1929	Henry Green, *Living*;
	J. B. Priestley, *The Good Companions*
1930	Wyndham Lewis, *The Apes of God*
1931	Virginia Woolf, *The Waves*
1932	Stella Gibbons, *Cold Comfort Farm*;
	Aldous Huxley, *Brave New World*
1933	Walter Greenwood, *Love on the Dole*
1934	Robert Graves, *I, Claudius*;
	Evelyn Waugh, *A Handful of Dust*
1935	Ivy Compton Burnett, *A House and Its Head*
1938	Elizabeth Bowen, *The Death of the Heart*;
	Graham Greene, *Brighton Rock*;
	P. G. Wodehouse, *The Code of the Woosters*

1939   James Joyce, *Finnegans Wake*;
        George Orwell, *Coming up for Air*
1940   Graham Greene, *The Power and the Glory*;
        Arthur Koestler, *Darkness at Noon*
1944   Joyce Cary, *The Horse's Mouth*
1945   Henry Green, *Loving*;
        George Orwell, *Animal Farm*;
        Evelyn Waugh, *Brideshead Revisited*
1947   Malcolm Lowry, *Under the Volcano*
1948   Graham Greene, *The Heart of the Matter*
1949   George Orwell, *Nineteen Eighty Four*
1950   Henry Green, *Nothing*;
        Doris Lessing, *The Grass Is Singing*
1951   Anthony Powell, *A Question of Upbringing* (first of
        A Dance to the Music of Time, –1975)
1952   Barbara Pym, *Excellent Women*;
        Evelyn Waugh, *Men at Arms*
1953   L. P. Hartley, *The Go-Between*
1954   Kingsley Amis, *Lucky Jim*;
        William Golding, *Lord of the Flies*
1955   Evelyn Waugh, *Officers and Gentlemen*
1956   Angus Wilson, *Anglo-Saxon Attitudes*
1957   Lawrence Durrell, *Justine* (first of *The Alexandria
        Quartet*, –1960)
1958   Iris Murdoch, *The Bell*
1959   Muriel Spark, *Memento Mori*
1960   Olivia Manning, *The Great Fortune* (first of *The
        Balkan Trilogy*, –1965)
1961   V. S. Naipaul, *A House for Mr Biswas*;
        Muriel Spark, *The Prime of Miss Jean Brodie*
1962   Anthony Burgess, *A Clockwork Orange*;
        Doris Lessing, *The Golden Notebook*
1964   B. S. Johnson, *Albert Angelo*;
        William Golding, *The Spire*;
        C. P. Snow, *Corridors of Power* (ninth of *Strangers and
        Brothers* series).
1966   Jean Rhys, *Wide Sargasso Sea*;
        Paul Scott, *The Jewel in the Crown* (first of *The Raj
        Quartet*, –1975)
1967   Margaret Drabble, *Jerusalem the Golden*

1969   John Fowles, *The French Lieutenant's Woman*;
        B. S. Johnson, *The Unfortunates*
1971   B. S. Johnson, *House Mother Normal*;
        Elizabeth Taylor, *Mrs Palfrey at the Claremont*
1973   B. S. Johnson, *Christie Malry's Own Double Entry*
1974   Beryl Bainbridge, *The Bottle Factory Outing*
1975   Malcolm Bradbury, *The History Man*
1977   Barbara Pym, *Quartet in Autumn*
1978   Iris Murdoch, *The Sea, The Sea*
1979   Emma Tennant, *Wild Nights*
1980   Paul Bailey, *Old Soldiers*;
        Anthony Burgess, *Earthly Powers*;
        William Golding, *Rites of Passage* (first of *To the Ends
        of the Earth* trilogy, –1989)
1981   Salman Rushdie, *Midnight's Children*;
        D. M. Thomas, *The White Hotel*
1982   William Boyd, *An Ice-Cream War*;
        Anita Brookner, *Providence*;
        Alasdair Gray, *Lanark*
1983   Graham Swift, *Waterland*
1984   Martin Amis, *Money*;
        J. G. Ballard, *Empire of the Sun*;
        Julian Barnes, *Flaubert's Parrot*;
        Anita Brookner, *Hotel du Lac*;
        Angela Carter, *Nights at the Circus*;
        David Lodge, *Small World*
1985   Peter Ackroyd, *Hawksmoor*;
        Jeanette Winterson, *Oranges Are Not the Only Fruit*
1986   Kingsley Amis, *The Old Devils*
1987   Margaret Drabble, *The Radiant Way*;
        Penelope Lively, *Moon Tiger*
1988   Salman Rushdie, *The Satanic Verses*;
        Alan Hollinghurst, *The Swimming-Pool Library*
1989   Martin Amis, *London Fields*;
        Beryl Bainbridge, *An Awfully Big Adventure*;
        Julian Barnes, *A History of the World in 10½Chapters*;
        Rose Tremain, *Restoration*
1990   A. S. Byatt, *Possession*;
        Pat Barker, *Regeneration* (first of trilogy, –1995);
        Penelope Fitzgerald, *The Gate of Angels*

1993   Sebastian Faulks, *Birdsong*
1995   Penelope Fitzgerald, *The Blue Flower*
2000   Zadie Smith, *White Teeth*
2001   Ian McEwan, *Atonement*
2005   Ian McEwan, *Saturday*
2009   Hilary Mantel, *Wolf Hall*
2011   Julian Barnes, *The Sense of an Ending*
2012   Hilary Mantel, *Bring up the Bodies*

1

Introduction

My principal aim in writing this book is to show that our appreciation and understanding of novels can be enhanced by according them the respect implicit in close reading. It is therefore intended as a companion volume to *Living Poetry*, in which I sought to demonstrate that poetry of the past can speak strongly and directly to present-day readers and can be discussed in a manner that is attentive but clear, informed but not pedantic.[1]

Close reading is fundamental to all understanding, interpretation and judgement of literary works and written communications of any kind. A novelist's choice of language, selection of details in a description or action and decision about the point of view from which to tell a story form the essential constituents of a narrative. The more attentive we are to these basic elements of writing, the more we shall be able to comprehend what is being said and why it is being said in the way it is. We shall be able to follow, and so to some extent engage in and share, writers' creativity. Why, for example, does Thomas Hardy describe the couple in the opening chapter of *The Mayor of Casterbridge* so minutely and yet omit such an obvious detail as their names (see Section 2.2)? Why does Jane Austen embed at the heart of her description of Fanny Price's room a sentence of immense complexity (see Section 3.2)?

An obvious problem with reading novels closely is their sheer length. It is one thing to examine intensely a lyric poem, which can to some extent be seen steadily and whole; it is quite another to approach *Bleak House* in the same spirit. I do not propose that we should read every page of a novel in the exhaustive way in which I analyse, say, the opening of Anita Brookner's *Hotel du Lac* (Section 3.1). *Ars longa vita brevis* ('art is long, life is short').[2] However, most novelists do spend a great deal of time and effort writing their books. Their aim is to use language creatively and expressively, just as poets seek to do. My proposition is twofold: (a) close reading of a section of a novel, whether a chapter, a paragraph or just a sentence, can reveal detail in a way that allows us greater comprehension and enjoyment; and (b) this increased understanding of parts of a novel can infiltrate and illuminate our reading of the whole. What we glean from attention to a short excerpt opens out into appreciation of the novel as a whole, and indeed novels in general and how they are written. For example, the linguistic and stylistic similarities between the two separate paragraphs of *Mrs Dalloway* discussed in Section 5.7 provide a fruitful way into Virginia Woolf's vision of existence as a texture of half-apprehended interrelationships transcending commonly accepted divisions, such as gender.

A book which looks at extracts from novels encounters a further problem: to do so is to remove them from their context. It is, therefore, often the case that my discussion of examples involves some degree of explanation of what has gone before or who a character is, in order that we can understand how the extract works. Novelists rely on readers to apply accumulated knowledge of the narrative to their reading. I have tried to steer a course between impoverishing our reading by ignoring context and losing sight of the extract in excessive plot-telling. At other times, my extension of the analysis to include material external to it – from elsewhere in the novel, other writings or even (more rarely) the author's life – is an attempt to show how wider knowledge can illuminate a short passage, and vice versa. I have also varied the intensity of my examination to explore how different degrees of analysis can produce helpful results. Throughout, my aim has been to help readers to enhance their understanding so that they can gain more pleasure from their own reading.

I have organized the book by dividing extracts into five principal narrative modes: describing people, describing places, presenting action, speaking and commenting.[3] Writers do not, of course, divide their books into such neat and separate categories. Paragraphs and even sentences are usually doing more than one thing at a time. For example, how characters speak is one element in describing them, and authorial comment may be implicit in how an event is narrated. There is therefore inevitably some degree of arbitrariness in my allocation of extracts to chapters. My criterion for the distribution of examples is to allot them to the mode that is arguably or evidently most significant at that moment in the novel. More importantly, the coexistence of different narrative modes within an excerpt demonstrates that good writers are creatively flexible, and that to live is to experience multiple sensations in close proximity to one another. As the elements of novels are commingled, so the creative act of reading looks from a variety of angles and encompasses a vibrant multiplicity of responses.

This book is not intended as a history of the novel, an undertaking way beyond its scope. However, I have chosen examples from the eighteenth, nineteenth and twentieth centuries in approximately equal numbers and have, when it seemed appropriate, indicated where novels fit in historical terms. The earliest extract is from Daniel Defoe's *Robinson Crusoe* (1719), and the latest from Julian Barnes's *The Sense of an Ending* (2011). There is no exact starting point for the novel as it is generally understood, let alone for prose fiction in general. *Robinson Crusoe* is as good and commonly cited a place as any to locate a beginning for the modern British novel. *The Sense of an Ending*, which won the Man Booker Prize in 2011, is a suitable place to end, although, like the novel form itself, Barnes's work defies any attempt at complete conclusions.

2

Describing People

2.1 Openings (first person): Daniel Defoe, *The Life and Strange Surprising Adventures of Robinson Crusoe of York, Mariner* (1719); Laurence Sterne, *Tristram Shandy* (1759)

I was born in the year 1632, in the city of York, of a good family, though not of that country, my father being a foreigner of Bremen, who settled first at Hull. He got a good estate by merchandise, and leaving off his trade lived afterward at York, from whence he had married my mother, whose relations were named Robinson, a very good family in that country, and from whom I was called Robinson Kreutznaer; but by the usual corruption of words in England, we are now called, nay, we call ourselves and write our name, Crusoe, and so my companions always called me.

'Where shall I begin, please your Majesty?' asks Lewis Carroll's White Rabbit. 'Begin at the beginning,' replies the King, 'and go on till you come to the end: then stop.'[1]

What, though, is the beginning? Robinson Crusoe is in no doubt. He begins as if filling out his own birth certificate: 'date of birth'; 'place of birth'; 'father'; 'father's occupation'; 'mother'; 'mother's maiden name'. Crusoe gives us the facts, briskly and with minimal elaboration. He is going to narrate his life story – his life and adventures, as the title of the novel says – and so starting where life begins, with birth, has a crisp logic consistent with his no-nonsense prose style.

Daniel Defoe opens his first novel by setting an individual human being firmly and unmistakably at the centre of the narrative. The first word is 'I': from the outset Crusoe's voice shapes and controls his own story. The paragraph's precision, concern with the facts and concentration on the self constitute a declaration on both Crusoe's and Defoe's behalf. Crusoe says to us that this is who he is, these are the facts that define him. Defoe, Crusoe's creator, says to us that this is what a narrative should be: spare, concise and about a person's life and experience.

Robinson Crusoe is a fictional autobiography, a form that has run through the history of the novel. *Robinson Crusoe* was so successful that Defoe, who had lived a varied and full life as a merchant, government agent, journalist, pamphleteer and prolific miscellaneous author before writing *Robinson Crusoe* at the age of 59, followed it up with a second part (*The Farther Adventures of Robinson Crusoe*) and then a series of lively narratives presented as the 'authentic' memoirs of a range of controversial figures. The opening of *Roxana* (or *The Fortunate Mistress*, as its primary title has it) strikes a note familiar from *Robinson Crusoe*:

> I was born, as my friends told me, at the city of Poitiers, in the province or county of Poitou in France, from whence I was brought to England by my parents, who fled for their religion about the year 1683, when the Protestants were banished from France by the cruelty of their persecutors.

Roxana may be a very different person from Crusoe but shares with him a desire to ground her story in time and place and to begin at the beginning: 'I was born'.

The apparent 'authenticity' of a Roxana or a Crusoe in these beginnings is a consequence of how they present themselves and their stories. They fix on certainties, the simple bare bones of their past. Their language is correspondingly spare, avoiding any surplus or extravagant terms. It is literal, devoid of metaphor. Crusoe's use of 'corruption' to apply to linguistic change hardly counts as a metaphor, despite its origins in physical breaking – Latin *rumpere*, 'to break' – as both Latin and English applied it to moral contexts from the outset. They appear as direct, straightforward reporters.

However, some explanation and elaboration have crept into even Crusoe's economical account of his origins. Co-ordinates of time and place do not emerge from nothing. How did Crusoe's father come to be in York? An answer requires a brief statement of where his father came from. Bremen, a commercial city in what is now north-west Germany, explains his father's occupation and how he came to Hull, whose trading links across the North Sea to northern Europe were well established by the seventeenth century. Success with his business affairs enabled him to move to York, where he married Crusoe's

mother, whose family name explains his forename. These are all facts,
but they also demand approbation. Crusoe's style is certainly lucid,
aimed at providing just the necessary information. There are only two
adjectives in the paragraph, but one of them – 'good' – occurs early
and is repeated twice. Crusoe is quick to tell us that he is 'of a good
family', a statement supported by the 'good estate' his father's trade
brought him and by the 'very good family' that his father married into.
Crusoe's genealogy contains both merit and, consequently, status.

Without any overt pleading or even argument, Defoe is using
his fictional autobiographer to represent certain attitudes which, we
know from his non-fictional writing, Defoe himself endorsed. Crusoe's
father gained his 'estate' – that is, his property and prosperity – 'by
merchandise'. 'Merchandise' as a noun meant the commodities of
commerce, the goods themselves that are traded, and the action of
trading, of engaging in merchant activity. Both senses are historically
original, dating from the thirteenth century, but the latter fell out of
use in the nineteenth century.[2] Crusoe's father did not inherit wealth;
he was not born into a landed family. He prospered by trade, by
engagement in the economic activity of seventeenth-century Europe.
Defoe was born in London, in 1660, the son of a tallow-chandler, that
is a man who lived by making and selling candles and soap. Defoe
himself traded in hosiery, wine and tobacco, where mercantile activities required extensive travel through Europe. Unlike Crusoe's father,
he did not always prosper and was declared bankrupt in 1692 for the
very large sum of £17,000.

When, in the late seventeenth and early eighteenth centuries, Defoe
took to making his way through the world by his pen – words becoming his merchandise, newspapers, journals and pamphlets the agents
of exchange – his subjects reflected his lifestyle. He set up and main-
tained a thrice-weekly journal called *A Review* from 1704 to 1713,
ranging over political and cultural topics, not least that of trade. In the
number for 3 January 1706, Defoe exalts its value as a means of
enabling all countries to thrive by exchange of the commodities and
products natural to their differing climates and customs. Trade, or merchandise, is 'certainly the most Noble, most instructive, and Improving
of any way of Life'.[3] Later, after embarking on his career as a novelist, Defoe wrote *The Complete English Tradesman* (two volumes: 1725
and 1727), an extensive advice manual about how to succeed in that
enterprise. 'Letter III' of the first volume is entitled 'Of the Trading
Stile' and recommends to tradesmen the use of 'a plain and homely

stile', of which they have no need to be ashamed since 'easy, plain, and familiar language is the beauty of speech in general, and is the excellency of all writing, on whatever subject, or to whatever persons they are we write or speak'.[4] Trade, for Defoe, is morally admirable, even divinely sanctioned (since it is a means of harmonizing nations), and it both necessitates and is enhanced by language of direct and unambiguous communication. Language is both how we trade and what we trade; and its value lies in its capacity to bring people and nations together. For Defoe, language is business, a means of livelihood, and an ethical duty.

The merchant's world is international, as shown by its linking the Germanic Kreutznaer with the English Robinson. Crusoe's name joins both nations and acclimatizes the German to English. Defoe had no time for theories of racial purity. Politically, he supported the governments of the Dutch William of Orange and, later, of the Hanoverian succession. One of his most scathing occasional writings is his verse satire, *The True-Born Englishman* (1701), aimed at those who vainly vaunt themselves as of 'pure' English pedigree when the English nation is historically the result of various invasions and waves of immigration. The poem exhorts its readers to treat foreigners – in particular, the Dutch who were bearing the brunt of anti-William III feeling in some quarters – as equals. In a preface, Defoe declares that England would not have achieved its present level of wealth and glory 'if the additions of Foreign Nations both as to Manufactures and Arms had not been helpful to it'.[5] Robinson Crusoe stands himself as a tribute to the English genius for welcoming the foreign and encouraging their mutual benefits. If we allow, for the moment, *Robinson Crusoe* to mark the beginning of the modern English novel, the 'I' that asserts its identity is the result of international co-operation. The novel is European. That simple adjective 'good' is Crusoe's direct means of asserting equal rights: his father's 'good' estate joins with his English mother's 'very good family' (from 'that country', in the sense of district, rather than nation) to form another 'good family', whose son he is.

Crusoe's rapid recourse to a brief genealogy entails his taking a step back from the date of his own birth. Any event, including a birth, actually implies events that have preceded it, without which it would not exist. Things do not just happen; they happen because of other things.

In 1759, another first-person narrator appeared in print, intending to present the story of his life and (in place of Robinson Crusoe's 'adventures') his 'opinions'. He, too, decided to begin at the beginning, but opted for an event earlier than birth:

> I wish either my father or my mother, or indeed both of them, as they were in duty both equally bound to it, had minded what they were about when they begot me; had they duly considered how much depended upon what they were then doing; – that not only the production of a rational Being was concerned in it, but that possibly the happy formation and temperature of his body, perhaps his genius and the very cast of his mind; – and, for aught they knew to the contrary, even the fortunes of his whole house might take their turn from the humours and dispositions which were then uppermost; – Had they duly weighed and considered all this, and proceeded accordingly, – I am verily persuaded I should have made a quite different figure in the world from that in which the reader is likely to see me.

Tristram Shandy, the fictional creation of Laurence Sterne, a Yorkshire vicar and a prebendary of the Minster in Robinson Crusoe's home city of York, does not share the capacity for brisk narrative seen in Defoe's character. Crusoe manages to convey at least four facts in his 33-word opening sentence. By the end of Tristram's 145-word sentence, we have learnt nothing about him. Yet, in another sense, we know a great deal about him: not when and where he was born, but the importance he attributes to the state of his parents when conceiving a child, and his view that his 'figure in the world' is the result of their failure to take their conjugal duties sufficiently seriously. The priority Tristram gives to these somewhat eccentric concerns tells us quite a lot about the quirky way he thinks. For Crusoe, language is a means of conveying a series of facts as clearly as possible. For Tristram Shandy, language is a tricky maze through which one threads one's way in pursuit of elusive ideas. His prose is addicted to qualifications and interpolations: 'or indeed both of them, as they were in duty both equally bound to it', 'for aught they knew to the contrary'. Such desire to explain everything, to cover all possibilities, entails a wordy and circuitous style. Tristram spends so long trying to explain the unpropitious circumstances behind his arrival in the world that contemporary readers had to wait until the second instalment (published in 1760) to read his account of the event itself. Crusoe is born in his first sentence and before long has told us about his first sea voyage and the violent storm he encountered. The epigraph Sterne chose for *Tristram Shandy* reads as a deliberate counter to Defoe's action-packed story: 'It is not actions, but opinions concerning actions, that disturb people.' This proposition is fundamental in the Stoic philosophy of Epictetus (whose original Greek Sterne cites). Human beings suffer not because of events but as a result of the thoughts they have about events. The proper philosophical response to the vicissitudes we encounter is to apply reason in order to distinguish between the things we can control and those we cannot and to train ourselves to accept and cope with the suffering consequent on our human condition. In *Tristram Shandy*, ideas and opinions so occupy the minds of people that action is continually deferred. For example, Tristram's father has such decided views on educating children that he sets about writing a manual called *Tristrapaedia*. Unfortunately, he spends so long writing it that Tristram grows up unnoticed by the obsessed author before it can be put to use.

The beginnings of *Robinson Crusoe* and *Tristram Shandy* point in different directions: one to an external world of events and facts, and the other to an internal world of ideas and opinions. A Cartesian dualism of body and mind opens up.[6] But, just as much eighteenth-century philosophy is about how body and mind are connected, so our two novels pursue the relationship between these 'exterior' and 'interior' states. Acting and thinking are not mutually exclusive. Much of *Robinson Crusoe*, especially when he is shipwrecked on an island, shows the hero taking mental stock of his circumstances, his hopes and fears. Conversely, most of the opinions in *Tristram Shandy*, whether Tristram's own (such as his conviction that a person's character depends on his or her parents' state at the moment of conception) or his father's (such as his theory that some names are favourable and some are not – Tristram is firmly one of the latter), are thwarted either by such events as do happen or by the lack of them.

With these contrasting yet complementary beginnings, the English novel is born. That, at least, is a common idea.[7] But it is equally common for historians to observe that there is no birth without an earlier cause, that mothers and fathers, whether or not they minded what they were doing, were responsible. But who? Thomas Nashe in the Elizabethan period? Aphra Behn in the seventeenth century? Or should its genealogy be pan-European? No earlier writer is more often acknowledged by eighteenth-century novelists than Cervantes. For example, the title page of Henry Fielding's first substantial novel (1742) is as frank as it is lengthy: *The History of the Adventures of Joseph Andrews, and of His Friend Mr. Abraham Adams. Written in Imitation of the Manner of Cervantes, Author of Don Quixote.* Where does the novel begin? Where does a person begin? As Tristram Shandy believes, one's birth is not actually one's beginning; a cause lies behind it. But, then, that cause will have had a cause. There is always something before, from which the present moment derives, out of which it is born. But we have to start somewhere, otherwise – like Tristram – we run the risk of never being born at all.

2.2 Openings (third person): Thomas Hardy, *The Mayor of Casterbridge* (1886); George Eliot, *Middlemarch* (1871–2); Arnold Bennett, *Riceyman Steps* (1923)

Robinson Crusoe is a first-person narrative. There have been occasional attempts at second-person narration. Here the narrator of B. S. Johnson's *Albert Angelo* (1964) describes his experiences as a supply teacher:

> You have a phone call from them this first morning. The woman at the office gives you directions to the school, and you look at it in your *A to Z* to make quite sure. You put in a briefcase those textbooks experience has suggested will cover most of the subjects you are likely to be required to teach.

This section of *Albert Angelo*, entitled 'Exposition', is narrated in turn in first-, second- and third-person singular (I, you, he/she) and first-, second- and third-person plural (we, you, they). The cumulative effect is of an exercise in narrative possibilities, an 'exposition' of form in the appropriate manner of a class learning the parts of a verb. It is characteristic of B. S. Johnson's novels that he is, at the same time, defiantly non-realistic in his overt pursuit of experimentalism and subtly expressive in matching form to content.

However, the other principal way of telling a story is in the third person:

> One evening of late summer, before the nineteenth century had reached one-third of its span, a young man and woman, the latter carrying a child, were approaching the large village of Weydon-Priors, in Upper Wessex, on foot. They were plainly but not ill clad, though the thick hoar of dust which had accumulated on their shoes and garments from an obviously long journey lent a disadvantageous shabbiness to their appearance just now.

> The man was of fine figure, swarthy, and stern in aspect; and he showed in profile a facial angle so slightly inclined as to be almost perpendicular. He wore a short jacket of brown corduroy, newer than the remainder of his suit, which was a fustian waistcoat with white horn buttons, breeches of the same, tanned leggings, and a straw hat overlaid with black glazed canvas. At his back he carried by a looped strap a rush basket, from which

protruded at one end the crutch of a hay-knife, a wimble for hay-bonds being also visible in the aperture. His measured, springless walk was the walk of the skilled countryman as distinct from the desultory shamble of the general labourer; while in the turn and plant of each foot there was, further, a dogged and cynical indifference personal to himself, showing its presence even in the regularly interchanging fustian folds, now in the left leg, now in the right, as he paced along.

The narrator of the opening of Thomas Hardy's *The Mayor of Casterbridge* looks at the young man and woman from the outside, describing their appearance and then, in some detail, the man's clothes and the manner of his gait. The characters make their way across the scene, absorbed in their own world and oblivious of the intense stare of the observer.

Such narrators – detached, describing characters and action from the outside – are commonly referred to as 'omniscient' (all-knowing). They are not limited to the perspective of one individual but see all the characters with equal clarity. They do not inhabit the consciousness of one character, identifying with her or him, but maintain an external stance. This third-person narrative view therefore comes across to the reader as objective, whereas a first-person narrative conveys the subjective vision of a single person.

But how truly 'omniscient' is Hardy's narrator? Compare this opening with that of another well-known nineteenth-century novel, equally celebrated as a major contribution to the tradition of omniscient narration, George Eliot's *Middlemarch*:

Miss Brooke had that kind of beauty which seems to be thrown into relief by poor dress. Her hand and wrist were so finely formed that she could wear sleeves not less bare of style than those in which the Blessed Virgin appeared to Italian painters; and her profile as well as her stature and bearing seemed to gain the more dignity from her plain garments, which by the side of provincial fashion gave her the impressiveness of a fine quotation from the Bible, – or from one of our elder poets, – in a paragraph of to-day's newspaper.

Like Hardy's beginning, this passage is strongly visual. It is about how Miss Brooke – the novel's heroine, Dorothea – looks, how she dresses and how features of her anatomy – her hand and wrist – appear alongside those clothes. The characters even, in one respect, dress similarly: Miss Brooke wears 'plain garments'; Hardy's figures are 'plainly but not ill clad'. But the narrators treat these sartorial details in very different ways. Despite her visual emphasis, Eliot is not describing what is actually there, immediately present to her eye or that of her assumed narrator. She is not taking a snapshot of the moment, as if Miss Brooke had just entered a room; rather, Eliot takes a more general view of how her character dresses. Miss Brooke's custom is to wear plain dress, notably different from the 'provincial fashion' of Middlemarch (located, as the name suggests, in the midlands of England). Her choice of clothes sets her apart, a distinction the narrator elaborates by means of religious and cultural analogies: the Blessed Virgin as represented by Italian painters and a biblical or poetic quotation in the humdrum context of a newspaper. The narrator is familiar with her subject and has thought carefully about her. She is able to draw some telling conclusions, as well as to assert that the plainness of Dorothea's dress actually elevates her. Eliot allows this paradox to sit quietly in the narrative, leaving it to the reader to wonder about the fine line between humility and pride. But this narrator is clearly thoughtful and observant not merely in a visual sense.

By contrast, Hardy's narrator is taking his first view of his characters. He inspects them as new creatures, setting down their features as they strike him at the moment of observation. He does not even know their names. They are 'a young man and woman', whereas the first words of *Middlemarch* are 'Miss Brooke', a third-person equivalent of *Robinson Crusoe*'s opening 'I'. This narrator has not had the time to get to know his subjects and so can make no judgements about them. The term 'omniscient' needs to be qualified. Hardy knows about his characters only as much as we would know about a couple we were seeing for the first time if we were as observant and careful as he is. Here he is not claiming privileged access to the thoughts and feelings of his creations, as many narrators do.

However, the narrator does possess some significant knowledge, which enables him to put his characters into context. He does know all about the world the young man and woman are stepping into. He knows where we are, the name of the village they are approaching and where that village is. The names Weydon-Priors and Upper Wessex lie somewhere not only between history and geography but also between topography and fiction. The idea of defining a region called 'Wessex' as the setting for most of his novels and many of his poems came to Hardy while he was writing *Far from the Madding Crowd* (published in 1874). The name Wessex resounds in history as one of the seven kingdoms of Anglo-Saxon England. Weydon-Priors shadows the real Weyhill (west of Andover and then the site of a fair and farm-sale) and evokes a generalized rural and ancient southern England.[8] Hardy's novels create a topography that is both invented and rooted in English history, rather as his characters (such as the hero of *Far from the Madding Crowd*, Gabriel Oak) are both fictional and redolent of a whole landscape and culture.

Hardy's narrator also knows when the action is taking place. The first sentence of the novel is carefully balanced between, on the one hand, an adverbial phrase ('One evening of late summer') and a sub-ordinate adverbial clause ('before the nineteenth century had reached one-third of its span'), which specify respectively narrow and broader moments of time and, on the other hand, a main clause ('a young man and woman . . . were approaching the village of Weydon-Priors, in Upper Wessex'), which provides the location. Together, the grammat-ical elements form a unit, defining the time and place of the novel's action. Hardy's description maintains a sense of the specific, a grasp on the actual, which is a key part of the texture of realism.

The description of the characters concentrates on specifics. The nar-rator observes deposits of dust on the couple's shoes and clothes and concludes that they have emerged into view after a long journey. He is here not all-knowing and godlike but more like another fictional, yet somehow real, figure who made his first appearance at the time of *The Mayor of Casterbridge*. Arthur Conan Doyle wrote *A Study in Scarlet* in 1886, and it was first published in *Beeton's Christmas Annual*, 1887. Like Sherlock Holmes, whose habit was to detect from a new client's clothes and complexion his or her background and cir-cumstances, Hardy's narrator subjects his characters to a systematic examination. He notes the man's facial qualities, in particular the way he holds his head erect. He describes in detail how the man is dressed, down to the buttons on his waistcoat and the covering on his hat. He identifies the tools the man is carrying, and describes his man-ner of walking, even how his level tread produces alternating folds in the legs of his breeches. All these details are presented in the precise and unfussy style of a lab report. Hardy's language is literal and definitional. It says what the eye sees: what material a hat or a button is made of, what colour a jacket is, how a basket is being car-ried. The narrator's account appears to be scientifically thorough. His gaze takes in the man from top to toe, from straw hat to shoes, and pretty well all points in between, his face, his jacket, waistcoat and breeches.

Like a detective examining a new case, the narrator brings to bear the knowledge he has accumulated from his experience. He is familiar with the ways of the country, so can identify the tools the man is carrying. From the handle of a knife – transverse like the head of a crutch – he recognizes its function. He knows a wimble when he sees one – a gimlet, that is, for boring holes – and what it is used for. These identify the man's trade: they are the tools of a hay-trusser. Further, the narrator understands the behaviour of country people. He can distinguish between the careful and regular walk of the skilled countryman and the lazier, less disciplined 'shamble' of the general labourer. Our narrator comes from, or is at least acquainted with, the world he describes, and is thus able to locate the man's position within the hierarchy of rural trades. The status his trade confers is reflected in clothes that, while being practical and plain, are also respectable ('not ill clad').

Close relatives of Hardy's narrator occur regularly in nineteenth- and twentieth-century realist fiction. Arnold Bennett's *Riceyman Steps* opens with this description:

> On an autumn afternoon of 1919 a hatless man with a slight limp might have been observed ascending the gentle, broad acclivity of Riceyman Steps, which lead from King's Cross Road up to Riceyman Square, in the great metropolitan industrial district of Clerkenwell. He was rather less than stout and rather more than slim. His thin hair had begun to turn from black to grey, but his complexion was still fairly good, and the rich, very red lips, under a small greyish moustache and over a short, pointed beard, were quite remarkable in their suggestion of vitality. The brown eyes seemed a little small; they peered at near objects. As to his age, an experienced and cautious observer of mankind, without previous knowledge of this man, would have said no more than that he must be past forty. The man himself was certainly entitled to say that he was in the prime of life. He wore a neat dark-grey suit, which must have been carefully folded at nights, a low, white, starched collar, and a 'made' black tie that completely hid the shirt-front; the shirt-cuffs could not be seen. He was shod in old, black leather slippers, well polished. He gave an appearance of quiet, intelligent, refined and kindly prosperity; and in his little eyes shone the varying lights of emotional sensitiveness.

Bennett adds a touch of self-consciousness about the act of observation ('an experienced and cautious observer of mankind…would have said'); but otherwise the characteristics of his narrative closely resemble Hardy's. The narrator is objective, looking on from outside the figure, and providing a very detailed account of his face, complexion, hair and clothes. The man is subjected to thorough scrutiny, like a specimen in a laboratory. The narrator is therefore not omniscient or godlike, knowing all about his character. However, he does know about the conditions in which the observation takes place. As in the opening of *The Mayor of Casterbridge*, the first sentence provides details of time and place. Bennett's setting, too, mingles topography and fiction: Riceyman Square does not exist, but Granville Square (upon which it is based) does, just off King's Cross Road in Clerkenwell. This narrator knows his London, as Hardy's knows his Wessex. He is also, like the potential observer he invokes, experienced in ways of seeing, so that he can come to some conclusions about this new, nameless subject.

Such description enables the reader to scrutinize characters along with the narrator. The novelists create an impression of thoroughness, every detail of their characters' physical appearance being rendered precisely. It may be that some of these details are 'surplus' in the sense that they are not necessary for the way the novel proceeds.[9] But, then, life itself is full of such surplus details, which simply make up the plenitude of perceptions that inform our experience. When we meet someone for the first time, we may – depending on the thoroughness of our gaze and the level of our perceptiveness – take note of many details of her or his appearance without, at that early stage, knowing how revealing of personality they are. It is the same with these descriptions. Does the neat suit worn by the man walking up Riceyman Steps, which strikes the narrator sufficiently for him to conclude that it must be folded carefully at night, tell us something about his social class and his scrupulous personal habits? Or does someone else fold it for him? But his shoes, though old, are well polished, so evidence perhaps grows for the former conclusion. On the other hand, it may be that the man's age – equally emphasized in the description – will prove to be more important. At present, we are accumulating elements of knowledge and beginning to fit them into a 'picture' of the man.

Such narrators soon begin to evaluate the evidence. By the end of Bennett's paragraph, he is commenting on the kind of person the man's appearance suggests he is. Hardy's narrator is able to apply local knowledge to an interpretation of what he sees, but he is also a student of human nature in a wider sense. He admires the man's 'fine figure', thus making a value judgement, and he proceeds to conclude the second paragraph with an extended reading of his character. This final sentence ('His measured, springless walk ... as he paced along') is by some distance the longest in the passage, its 64 words making it almost twice the average length of the earlier sentences. It has the weight of a concluding comment and an extension that enables a modulation

from narrator as knowledgeable countryman (the two types of coun-
trymen's walks) to – after the semicolon – narrator as interpreter of
character through action. The regularity of the man's stride – rendered
imitatively in the repeated pattern of 'now in the left leg, now in the
right' – is taken to reflect a particular quality of the man himself, 'a
dogged and cynical indifference'. In this context, those earlier observations of the man's 'stern' aspect and erect head perhaps begin a
process by which our narrator detects a character whose virtues, of
self-sufficiency and pride, may accompany related vices, of egotism
and pride (in a bad sense). As with George Eliot's opening description
of Miss Brooke, though by a different route, interpretation quietly
infiltrates description. The novel is on the move: the game's afoot,
Watson.

2.3 Describing through action: Thomas Hardy, *The Woodlanders* (1887), volume one, chapter eight

Novelists describe their characters by setting them in situations in
which they decide what to do and how to respond to what happens
as a result. We learn about characters from the care, or lack of it,
with which they deliberate on appropriate actions, from how they
conduct themselves and from the thought they give to consequences.
Defoe rapidly sets Robinson Crusoe on his first (and, given the sever-
ity of the storm he sails into, very nearly his last) sea voyage. The
impatience of the narrative to get Robinson to sea reflects and exemplifies his 'wandering inclination'. With equal speed, Hardy rushes
Michael Henchard, the young man at the beginning of *The Mayor of
Casterbridge*, into a dramatic scene, the consequences of which dominate the rest of his life and eventually destroy him. We are still in
the first chapter when, at Weydon-Priors fair, he sells his wife and
child – like livestock – as a result of a disastrous concoction of stub-
born bitterness and rum-fuelled rage. The egotistical pride that we saw
potentially in the narrator's opening description erupts into destructive action with a suddenness which expresses Henchard's volcanic
temper, fatal lack of self-control and self-obsession.

Hardy's next novel, *The Woodlanders*, begins in much less dramatic fashion, with a barber lost in deep woods where most of the
novel's action takes place. He is looking for a tiny village called Little
Hintock, which he manages to find thanks to a passing horse-drawn
carrier's van whose driver gives him a lift. The narrative quietly enters
a place so hidden away that even Mrs Dollery, the van driver, regards

it as the back of beyond: 'Now at Great Hintock you do see the world a bit'.

The actions of *The Woodlanders* inhabit a correspondingly quiet and secretive world. In the extract that follows, Giles Winterborne is planting young fir trees in ground cleared by woodcutters. This is work for which he has a special aptitude. He has, the narrator has told us, 'a marvellous power of making trees grow', a 'sympathy' between himself and the tree he is planting, such that its roots take hold of the soil in a few days – whereas a quarter of those planted by 'journeymen', despite apparently identical treatment, would die that summer. Giles is helped by a young woman called Marty South, whose job is to hold the trees upright while he arranges their roots and fills the holes with earth.

> The holes were already dug, and they set to work. Winterborne's fingers were endowed with a gentle conjuror's touch in spreading the roots of each little tree, resulting in a sort of caress under which the delicate fibres all laid themselves out in their proper directions for growth. He put most of these roots towards the south-west; for, he said, in forty years' time, when some great gale is blowing from that quarter, the trees will require the strongest holdfast on that side to stand against it and not fall.
>
> 'How they sigh directly we put 'em upright, though while they are lying down they don't sigh at all,' said Marty.
>
> 'Do they?' said Giles. 'I've never noticed it.'
>
> She erected one of the young pines into its hole, and held up her finger; the soft musical breathing instantly set in which was not to cease night or day till the grown tree should be felled – probably long after the two planters should be felled themselves.
>
> 'It seems to me,' the girl continued, 'as if they sigh because they are very sorry to begin life in earnest – just as we be.'
>
> 'Just as we be?' He looked critically at her. 'You ought not to feel like that, Marty.'
>
> Her only reply was turning to take up the next tree; and they planted on through a great part of the day, almost without another word. Winterborne's mind ran on his contemplated evening-party, his abstraction being such that he hardly was conscious of Marty's presence beside him.

The extract works largely through action and speech. Verbs dominate, usually active: 'they set to work', 'He put most of these roots'.

The speeches are mostly direct, conventionally set out with inverted commas and markers ('said Marty', 'the girl continued'). Hardy applies the procedures of drama to the novel form, so producing a 'scene'. This is one of the commonest methods of realist fiction. The novel in the nineteenth century often had an intimate relationship with the theatre: Hardy's own books were frequently adapted for dramatic versions. We shall look at some of the ways in which novelists handle actions and speeches in Chapters 4 and 5, respectively. Here, we are concerned with how these narrative modes contribute to the delineation of character.

Giles's actions reflect his rapport with the natural world, demonstrating that instinctive sympathy with his environment the narrator has told us about. Hardy's language emphasizes Giles's sensitivity. His touch as he spreads the roots is 'gentle', a 'caress' expressive of affection, of tenderness for the trees. His delicacy matches the fragility of the 'little' trees and is transferred as if magically ('a gentle conjuror's touch') to their roots, which lay themselves out in the most propitious way for growth, as though without any active interference from Giles. Man and nature act together, move in the same direction. Giles also possesses knowledge of the soil and weather conditions, and he is aware of the long timescale for the growing trees. He looks to the future.

Marty, by contrast, is taken up with the present moment in a way that baffles Giles. She notices the sound – 'soft musical breathing' – the saplings make when set upright. She employs anthropomorphic language, using the word 'sigh' three times. It was not until the nineteenth century that 'sigh' was used regularly as a noun to refer to the sound of wind blowing through trees (*OED* cites a line from Walter Scott's poem *The Lady of the Lake*), although the verb 'to sigh' had been so used from the mid-eighteenth century. The principal and original reference of 'sigh' was, and is, to human respiration suggestive of weariness or sadness. Marty explicitly takes up this transference of human emotion to the natural world with her rather portentous – or, at least, self-conscious – remark about the sigh of the trees being an expression of their regret in beginning life, a feeling they share with us. Her sentiments strike us, as they strike Giles, as at odds with her age – we have been told in chapter two that 'she was no more than nineteen or twenty'. Hardy here emphasizes the disparity between the world-weariness of her sentiments and her youth by using the word 'girl', which presents her as someone with her life before her, like the trees. He has already introduced a comparison between trees and people by relating their likely lifespans and by applying the word 'felled' to

the human figures. Marty's speech is a melancholic continuation of
the narrator's analogy. Giles's stern and rather condescending rebuff –
'You ought not to feel like that, Marty' – is followed by silence.

Hardy's plots often involve irony. Indeed, he gave the title *Life's
Little Ironies* to a collection of short stories. Giles has an instinctive
sympathy for the saplings, and he and nature act in harmony with
each other. But Marty observes what he does not: ' "Do they?" said
Giles. "I've never noticed it." ' His mind is elsewhere, with 'his con-
templated evening-party', so that he is not really with Marty and can
only respond insensitively, uncomprehendingly, to her fatalism. Giles
and Marty are working together at the beginning of the saplings'
lives; but they are, as people, apart. Giles's natural accord with the
trees does not extend to his young companion: the extract ends with
his losing consciousness of her very presence. The human sapling
that is the young girl, we know and sense from this passage, needs
the tender care Giles instinctively gives to his trees but withholds
from her.

The particular form of irony known as 'dramatic irony' refers to a
situation in which the audience (or, in the case of novels, the reader)
knows something significant that a character does not. Back in chapter
three, Marty overheard Mr Melbury, the village's chief businessman,
speaking of how he had promised his daughter Grace in marriage
to Winterborne. Marty realizes that 'Giles Winterborne is not for
me, and the less I think of him the better'. Frustrated in her love for
Giles, Marty sacrifices her abundant chestnut hair, her only beautiful
feature, to a wig-maker – the lost barber of chapter one.

Now Marty suppresses her true feelings for Giles and diverts them
into melancholy musing on life in general. Giles, unaware of her love
for him, lacks the means to respond to her hidden meaning. What they
say and do not say, what they do and do not do, tell us much about who
they are. Marty accepts her situation and translates it into fatalism.
Giles, blessed with a gift of tactile understanding of nature, is deaf
to human sighs. Characteristic of Hardy's fiction is one of life's little
ironies: the recurrent love of the wrong woman for the wrong man, of
the wrong man for the wrong woman.

2.4 Describing through other characters: George Eliot, *Middlemarch* (1871–2), chapter nineteen

One fine morning a young man whose hair was not immoderately
long, but abundant and curly, and who was otherwise English in his
equipment, had just turned his back on the Belvedere Torso in the Vatican

and was looking out on the magnificent view of the mountains from the adjoining round vestibule. He was sufficiently absorbed not to notice the approach of a dark-eyed, animated German who came up to him and placing a hand on his shoulder, said with a strong accent, 'Come here, quick! else she will have changed her pose.'

Quickness was ready at the call, and the two figures passed lightly along by the Meleager towards the hall where the reclining Ariadne, then called the Cleopatra, lies in the marble voluptuousness of her beauty, the drapery folding around her with a petal-like ease and tenderness. They were just in time to see another figure standing against a pedestal near the reclining marble: a breathing blooming girl, whose form, not shamed by the Ariadne, was clad in Quakerish grey drapery; her long cloak, fastened at the neck, was thrown backward from her arms, and one beautiful ungloved hand pillowed her cheek, pushing somewhat backward the white beaver bonnet which made a sort of halo to her face around the simply braided dark-brown hair. She was not looking at the sculpture, probably not thinking of it: her large eyes were fixed dreamily on a streak of sunlight which fell across the floor. But she became conscious of the two strangers who suddenly paused as if to contemplate the Cleopatra, and, without looking at them, immediately turned away to join a maid-servant and courier who were loitering along the hall at a little distance off.

Novelists can permit their characters to describe themselves in their own voice, can delineate characters from the narrator's standpoint (assuming various degrees of familiarity with their subject) and can reveal characters through their actions and words as though seen on a stage. The extracts we have taken from *Robinson Crusoe*, *The Major of Casterbridge* and *The Woodlanders* stand for very many examples. Most novels use the dramatic method to some degree, the difference between first-person and third-person narrative being the identity (and so, to an extent, the reliability) of the reporter of actions and words. A further significant method is to adjust the point of view to that of another character.

In our present extract from *Middlemarch*, the author whom we earlier (Section 2.2) found beginning her novel by assuming a considerable familiarity with her character allows the same woman to be seen by two, as yet unnamed, men. The 'breathing, blooming girl' is Miss Brooke – or, rather (an important rather), is now Mrs Casaubon. She is recognizably the same woman. The narrator in chapter one described how Dorothea's beauty is 'thrown into relief by poor dress' and selected for particular comment her hand and wrist as 'finely formed' against the barest of sleeves and her profile as enhanced by plain dress. Dorothea now wears what resembles the prim grey dress of a Quaker and has removed one of her gloves in order to rest her head on her hand in a pose which, unconsciously, presents the beauty of that hand to a viewer. A religious frame of reference, invoked by the narrator's comparison in chapter one of Dorothea to an Italian painting of the Virgin Mary, here modulates from the subdued adjective 'Quakerish' to the more striking comparison of her white bonnet to a halo, a powerful if again unconscious result of that hand gesture.

The lineaments of a resonantly visual evocation of Dorothea as set up at the novel's beginning are now given amplified expression in a setting that is dramatically appropriate. A woman whose beauty takes the narrator to Italian religious painting for comparisons is now herself in an Italian gallery – the Vatican galleries in Rome – where she is caught in a temporary 'pose', like a piece of sculpture, only one instinct with the breath of life. The intimate relationship between how the narrator sees Dorothea in chapter one and this elaborate scene is clinched by Eliot's subtle handling of the point of view.

The first paragraph is devoted to the two witnesses of the scene. They are also described in visual terms, though more briefly than Dorothea, who is the object of a leisurely and detailed gaze in the second paragraph. The 'dark-eyed' German who takes the initiative is himself an artist. In the paragraph before we join the novel, Eliot has set the scene by referring to 'certain long-haired German artists' who at that time (the action of *Middlemarch* takes place in the years leading up to the Reform Bill of 1832) were active in Rome. These were the 'Nazarenes', or the remnants of that group of German artists, which had by then largely split up. Our character is clearly one who has remained in Rome. Later, he will be named as Adolf Naumann, but for the present it is enough that he has the artistic sensibility of one who can view a woman as taking a 'pose'.

Naumann's English companion is described in terms that continue a subdued strain of parody in Eliot's characterization of the Nazarenes as 'long-haired' artists. Her depiction of him through his 'abundant and curly' hair will at once jog the attention of the alert reader. Back in chapter nine, a character has already been introduced to the narrative through his hair. There Dorothea, accompanied by her uncle and her sister Celia, visits the house and grounds at Lowick, the estate belonging to the Reverend Edward Casaubon, to whom Dorothea is engaged. He, an older man devoted entirely to abstruse studies for a great syncretic key to all mythologies, is reflected accurately in his dark and chill house. Dorothea finds the house suited to her serious and Puritanical outlook, a view not shared by her livelier sister. Celia it is who reports, with comic but innocent astonishment, seeing 'some one quite young' in the grounds: 'a gentleman with a sketch-book. He had light-brown curls. I only saw his back. But he was quite young'. (Her repetition is hardly tactful, but is ultimately not insignificant.) When, later, they come upon the young man, who is described as having 'bushy light-brown curls', Mr Casaubon introduces him as his cousin, Mr Ladislaw. Now, in chapter nineteen, Dorothea is married to Casaubon, and the couple have come to Rome on their honeymoon. For both Casaubon the ecclesiastic and Ladislaw the artist, Rome is a natural attraction. The Vatican galleries, the intersection of both aspects of Roman culture, are the very place for their paths to cross again.

Soon after the paragraphs we are reading, Eliot confirms the identities of the two men; but, for the moment, she is more concerned with their observation of Dorothea. The narrative incorporates the men's vision into its description of Dorothea, so itself 'seeing' her along with the two actual observers. Eliot thereby combines a dramatic incident in which the two men briefly gaze at the static 'figure' of Dorothea with omniscient narration.

The narrative's temporary conversion of Dorothea into a work of art is further confirmed by its precise location. Eliot first refers to two sculptures in the gallery: the Belvedere Torso from which the Englishman has just turned away, and the Meleager the two men pass by. These are both male sculptures: one of a headless, muscular trunk, the other of a Greek mythical hero. The context for the scene is the art of a pre-Christian era, art that proffers a vision different from the religious associations of the Vatican and Mr Casaubon's status.

Dorothea herself is posed beside a female figure. As Eliot tells us, this had long been referred to as an image of Cleopatra, but had by then been identified as a reclining Ariadne, a sleeping figure robed in a chiton (a Greek tunic). Eliot's description of the sculpture stresses its sensuality ('the marble voluptuousness of her beauty'), its dress ('drapery') and its gentle naturalness ('a petal-like ease and tenderness'). Dorothea is positioned in explicit comparison with the Ariadne. She is standing, not reclining, and her dress (Eliot confirms the comparison by repeating the word 'drapery') evokes puritanical reserve rather than classical sensuousness. So far, the two figures are contrasting, nineteenth-century female modesty versus antique display of beauty. But Dorothea's long cloak, fastened demurely at the neck and hiding her form rather than – as the Ariadne's chiton does – folding 'around' her, leaps into life at the vigour of 'thrown backward from her arms'. One part of her body is unclothed: her 'ungloved' hand, 'beautiful' as the 'marble voluptuousness' of Ariadne's 'beauty', and pillowing her cheek as if gently sustaining her sleeping face and attracting attention to the colour contrast of her white bonnet and dark-brown hair.

Dorothea may be viewed by the narrator and the two men as a beautiful sculpture, but she herself is not looking at her fellow work of art. As the curly-haired Englishman turned away from a torso to look out at the view beyond the galleries, so the dark-haired Dorothea gazes at a 'streak of sunlight' falling across the floor. Art is central to the intensely visual sensuousness of the scene and yet is not, ultimately, its point of repose. Suddenly, in the final sentence of the extract, the artistic spell is broken. Dorothea awakens from her dream-like state, conscious of the stare to which she has been subjected, a gaze in which the reader, like the narrator, has collaborated with the two men. She does not return the look, but turns away to rejoin her group in a direct echo of the man we guess to be Ladislaw turning his back on art.

People, even in novels, do not stay still for ever: movement is the central quality of their living, breathing being. Description gives way to action. Dorothea steps away from her accompanying sculpture, back to her human company. She is not a sleeping Ariadne, a beautiful nymph in Greek myth deserted by the god Theseus and left to wait for rescue by a new god, the young and vital Dionysus. However, there is truth in description. For an instant of time, the static moment in which Dorothea is illuminated by the joint gaze mediated through Eliot's descriptive language, she is that figure of dream-like suspension between the restriction of her dress and the beauty of her form.

When Dorothea has departed, Naumann and Ladislaw argue about the relative merits of pictorial art and language. Naumann views the posed Dorothea as a model for a painting, one which would represent 'antique form animated by Christian sentiment', 'sensuous force controlled by spiritual passion'. Ladislaw, unaccountably irritated by his friend's observation that the minister of religion with whom he had earlier seen Dorothea resembles an uncle rather than a cousin, objects that painting is ultimately a restrictive and limiting medium. Visual art can represent only the 'coloured superficies' of a woman, whereas her existence lies in 'movement and tone' and in her capacity for changing from moment to moment. How, for example, he asks, would you paint the voice of the woman we have just seen? And yet her voice is 'much diviner than anything you have seen of her'. How does Ladislaw know this? Back at that first meeting in the grounds of Lowick, he exclaimed to himself that her voice was 'like the voice of a soul that had once lived in an Aeolian harp'.

The scene in the Vatican galleries looks back to that earlier occasion when the paths of Dorothea and Ladislaw crossed, and its description of Dorothea echoes the narrator's observations about her in the novel's opening paragraph. Neither the narrator nor Ladislaw can forget her striking and particular beauty. The scene also looks forward in two ways. First, its language and images are reflected in specific reminiscences. For example, in the following chapter the narrator, reflecting on Mr Casaubon's withdrawal into the restricted world of his antiquarian studies, observes that the habitual presence of the artificial light of a candle in his study has rendered him 'indifferent to the sunlight'. She goes on to recall that 'streak of sunlight' on which Dorothea's eyes were fixed, and informs us that the real object of her inner eye was 'the light of years to come in her own home'. Secondly, the scene reaches out suggestively to the wider pattern traced by the novel's action. Hints of the unsatisfactory nature of Dorothea's marriage leaving her as it were a sleeping nymph, and Ladislaw's insistence that her beauty is not static, like the sculpture, but living and breathing – these lie within the texture of a novel which, as it proceeds, folds images over on themselves while still moving them on in time. Scenes do not just anticipate the future or recollect the past: prolepsis and analepsis (to give anticipation and recollection in narrative their technical names) reinforce each other in ways *Middlemarch* shows to be complex, profound and even discrepant.[10] For example, a narrow streak of sunlight expands into the potential 'light of years to come'. And Ladislaw's objection that painting cannot represent sound picks up on his earlier comparison of Dorothea's voice to an Aeolian harp, a stringed instrument on which air 'naturally' plays to create music, but whose name is yet another of those classical references (to Aeolus, the god of the winds) enshrined in the abiding power of classical art.

The form of *Middlemarch*, both linear and a complex interfolding of motifs, allows Eliot to have it both ways. The essence of the novel is forward movement, reflecting a living experience of changing from moment to moment. But it also pauses, fixes moments of stasis, which give shape to a detailed picture. Ladislaw and Naumann are both right. The full truth requires a wide sympathy which can encompass the dense intertexture that is *Middlemarch*'s, and life's, pattern. George Eliot, in her essay 'The Natural History of German Life', defined her vision in inclusive terms. 'The greatest benefit we owe to the artist, whether painter, poet, or novelist, is the extension of our sympathies,' she wrote. 'Art is the nearest thing to life; it is a mode of amplifying experience and extending our contact with our fellow-men beyond the bounds of our personal life.'[11] That we, Naumann, Ladislaw and the narrator are all included in one of the novel's moments of stasis – its vision of Dorothea in the Vatican galleries – is itself an aspect of, and representation of, the impulse to inclusion defined in the word 'sympathy': the capacity to feel with others.

2.5 Unreliable narrator: Ford Madox Ford, *The Good Soldier* (1915), part one, chapter three

And now you understand that, having nothing in the world to do – but nothing whatever! I fell into the habit of counting my footsteps. I would walk with Florence to the baths. And, of course, she entertained me with her conversation. It was, as I have said, wonderful what she could make conversation out of. She walked very lightly, and her hair was very nicely done, and she dressed beautifully and very expensively. Of course she had money of her own, but I shouldn't have minded. And yet you know I can't remember a single one of her dresses. Or I can remember just one, a very simple one of blue figured silk – a Chinese pattern – very full in the skirts and broadening out over the shoulders. And her hair was copper-coloured, and the heels of her shoes were exceedingly high, so that she tripped upon the points of her toes. And when she came to the door of the bathing place, and when it opened to receive her, she would look back at me with a little coquettish smile, so that her cheek appeared to be caressing her shoulder.

I seem to remember that, with that dress, she wore an immensely broad Leghorn hat – like the Chapeau de Paille of Rubens, only very white. The hat would be tied with a lightly knotted scarf of the same stuff as her dress. She knew how to give value to her blue eyes. And round her neck would be some simple pink, coral beads. And her complexion had a perfect clearness, a perfect smoothness...

Yes, that is how I most exactly remember her, in that dress, in that hat, looking over her shoulder at me so that the eyes flashed very blue – dark pebble blue...

In August 1904, at the fashionable German spa resort of Bad Nauheim, John Dowell, a wealthy American, and his wife Florence meet an Englishman, Captain Edward Ashburnham (the 'good soldier' of the novel's title) and his wife Leonora. Both Florence Dowell and Edward Ashburnham supposedly suffer from a heart condition, for which they take treatment at the spa baths. The two couples form a friendship, and meet every summer for nine years, making what John Dowell, who narrates the story, calls a 'four-square coterie'. Just before describing the first meeting of the couples in the dining-room of the Hotel Excelsior, Dowell presents this striking memory of his wife as he used to escort her from the hotel to the baths. Did I say that, on the night of 4 August 1913, Florence ran back to her hotel room, past a startled Dowell, and was found dead on her bed?

What are the outstanding qualities of this passage? What do they suggest to us about Dowell himself? He writes in a familiar manner, as a man talking to someone reflectively. He engages directly with his audience: 'now you understand that', 'yet you know'. He is repetitive, corrects himself ('I can't remember a single one of her dresses. Or I can remember just one'), searches his memory ('I seem to remember') and confirms his recollections ('Yes, that is how I most exactly remember her'), as would an impromptu speaker looking back on an event. He takes his time as if a man gradually reconstructing his memory, and yet the details he describes are intensely visual and clear. He appears both a little vague, as one might be about what happened some years ago, and yet at the same time very precise and detailed in his description of Florence's appearance.

He keeps on beginning his sentences with 'and', just as we're told at school not to. Of the ten sentences in the first paragraph, five begin with 'and' – and, for good measure, one begins with another conjunction, 'or'. Two more sentences out of the five in the second paragraph also begin with 'and'. This stylistic habit, a combination of what is technically known as polysyndeton (the repetition of conjunctions) and anaphora (beginning successive sentences with the same word or phrase), recurs throughout *The Good Soldier*. Indeed, the paragraph following our extract starts 'And, what the devil!' Dowell is particularly drawn to such sentences when summing up difficult or significant memories, as if reaching out for them. For example, the entry of Ashburnham into the dining-room and Dowell's life is so rendered: 'And then, one evening, in the twilight, I saw Edward Ashburnham lounge round the screen into the room.' Such dramatic effects are matched by anti-climaxes: 'And it occurs to me that some way back I began a sentence that I have never finished.'

Other words are used reiteratively. In the first sentence of the extract, 'nothing' is repeated for emphasis. Successive sentences pick out Florence's talent for making 'conversation', an ability to talk about anything, which accompanies her walking 'very lightly', as if skating delicately over the surface of life. Not surprisingly in a passage so much concerned with recollection, Dowell repeats the word 'remember' four times, in two sets of pairs. The first pair expresses correction: 'I can't remember a single one of her dresses. Or I can remember just one.' The second modulates from uncertainty to certainty: 'I seem to remember . . . . Yes, that is how I most exactly remember her'. These stylistic effects reinforce the impression Ford gives that Dowell is talking his way through his efforts to remember, building up his picture of the past slowly, sometimes unsteadily.

Other repetitions, such as that of 'dress', reflect Dowell's focus on Florence's visual appearance, the substance of the passage. His description of her develops from rather vague, general statements to a highly specific and detailed picture. At first there is nothing very precise, just a series of approving adverbs: 'her hair was very nicely done', 'she dressed beautifully and very expensively'. That last adverb diverts Dowell to a rather fussy, defensive comment: 'Of course she had money of her own, but I shouldn't have minded.' Indeed, there is something rather comically finical about Dowell's manner up to this point, particularly his remark about obsessively counting his footsteps. This effect is stronger in context. The preceding paragraph concludes with a demonstration of how exactly Dowell got to know the townscape of Nauheim:

> From the Hotel Regina you took one hundred and eighty-seven paces, then, turning sharp, left-handed, four hundred and twenty took you straight down to the fountain. From the Englischer Hof, starting on the side-walk, it was ninety-seven paces and the same four hundred and twenty, but turning left-handed this time.

We certainly have no difficulty in believing Dowell when he says he had nothing to do and suspect that Florence's entertaining conversation was not quite matched by her husband's. There is also something odd about Dowell's pedantic, indeed pedestrian activities. He says you had to turn left-handed 'this time' when he has already described a left turn from the Hotel Regina. Is he aware of his error? Do we

care enough to worry about it? And when Dowell, as he frequently
does, queries the accuracy of his own memory ('the reddish stone of
the baths – or were they white half-timber chalets?'), do his questions
amount to anything more than comical confessions of inadequacy?

But, suddenly, with his description of Florence's Chinese-pattern
dress, Dowell's memory and his prose wake up. The details now have
a vivid immediacy. Florence's hair is no longer simply 'nicely done',
but 'copper-coloured', the metallic analogy just right for combining
vibrancy with brittle superficiality, in accord with the high heels that
have her tripping along rather than being more solidly (but less inter-
estingly) flat-footed. It is as if her blue dress has made Dowell newly
alert to colour, to fine detail and to action. Colour takes us through
Florence's white hat to her 'blue' eyes, 'pink' bead necklace, returning
emphatically to the reiterated 'very blue – dark pebble blue' of her
eyes. That final qualification, or rather intensification, of the colour –
'dark pebble-blue' – both draws us in to something deep and keeps
us on the shiny surface of another mineral. This is a strongly pictorial vision, as is reinforced by Dowell's reference to Rubens's famous
'Chapeau de Paille', his portrait of his sister-in-law wearing a hat
which looks, notwithstanding the picture's familiar title, to be of a
soft material such as felt. Dowell's picture of his wife entices, but ultimately excludes the viewer. For whose benefit, Dowell asks, did his
wife dress and look as she did? 'For that of the bath attendant?'

This portrait of Florence Dowell takes its place amid a series
of intensely descriptive yet strangely superficial images in *The
Good Soldier*. For example, later in this chapter Dowell describes
Ashburnham's eyes. They, like Florence's, are blue. Indeed, pretty
well everyone in the novel seems to have blue eyes – everyone, that
is, except Dowell, the colour of whose eyes remains unknown to us.
We can't see our own eyes when we're looking through them. Like
Florence's, Ashburnham's blue eyes are set off by contrasting pink,
though in his case the pink of his complexion. The effect, Dowell
writes, is of 'a mosaic of blue porcelain set in pink china': attractive,
even delicate, yet fragile and skin-deep.

These portraits suggest something impenetrable. However, they
possess a sharp precision, which provokes a response, even from
a narrator of Dowell's limitations. Ford Madox Ford held strong
views about how novels should be written. He objected to intrusive
authorial voices that interpret action and direct a reader's response.
Henry Fielding's *Tom Jones* (see Section 4.3) he picked out as especially guilty for popularizing such a narrative method, which he

saw as all too common in nineteenth-century novels. George Eliot's
Middlemarch (see Sections 2.2 and 2.4) would be one example. *The
Good Soldier* is Ford's riposte to this, as he saw it, lamentable tradition. By making Dowell the narrator of his own story, Ford excludes
any external narrative, whether or not omniscient. When we read *The
Good Soldier* we are entirely reliant on Dowell for our information.
But Dowell makes mistakes, seems to lack certainty of recollection
and, moreover, keeps on telling us that he does not understand the
people and events he is describing. 'I know nothing – nothing in the
world – of the hearts of men', he has told us in the opening chapter.
Dowell is not just an unreliable narrator; he is pitiably, sometimes
comically, aware of his unreliability. The wise sympathy of a George
Eliot standing above the action she describes is replaced by the limited vision of a puzzled participant in his own story. What, after all,
do we know of our fellow human beings? We are not blessed with
godlike knowledge of their intimate feelings and deepest motives.
So a novelist who seeks to represent truly the experience of living with people should not allow unfounded certainty into his or
her work.

But there is another, equally important, aspect of Ford's theory
of the novel. This he called 'impressionism': the presentation of
people through perceptions, descriptions, actions or speeches that
fix their character with indelible clarity. In one of his essays on
'Impressionism', Ford quotes (not accurately, but imaginatively) an
example from the French novelist and short-story writer Guy de
Maupassant: *C'était un monsieur à favoris rouges qui entrait toujours
le premier.* Ford comments:

> Maupassant's gentleman with red whiskers, who always pushed in front
> of people when it was a matter of going through a doorway, will remain,
> for the mind of the reader, that man and no other. The impression is as
> hard and as definite as a tin-tack.[12]

Dowell's impression of Florence in her blue silk dress and broad hat,
smiling back at him as she enters the baths and passes beyond his
vision, is as hard and as definite as a tin-tack. His adjective 'coquettish'
may appear lightweight in the context of the repressed but inex-
plicable passions, which lie beneath the superficially serene habits
of a rich, leisured class in pre-war Europe and suddenly erupt with
destructive force. Did I mention that, when Dowell is summoned by
the Ashburnhams to visit them at their Hampshire estate, he learns
of Edward's series of affairs, including one with Florence Dowell,

whose death was not accidental but suicide? But 'coquettish', with its connotations of self-consciousness and superficiality, does capture precisely the quality of a 'pose', of a forming oneself into a picture, which Dowell's description of Florence so memorably fixes. In the passage from *Middlemarch* we discussed in Section 2.4, the narrator, Naumann and Ladislaw see Dorothea's moment of abstraction as unconsciously forming a 'pose' within a sculpture gallery. Dorothea soon breaks free: *Middlemarch* is centrally about the will to live. Florence Dowell ostentatiously presents herself to her husband as an image, teasing and tantalizing. John Dowell records this indelible image with a clarity that reflects its power as both visually arresting and seemingly motiveless. Dowell both sees clearly and yet sees – understands – nothing of what is really going on in the hearts of women and men. 'My wife and I knew Captain and Mrs Ashburnham as well as it was possible to know anybody, and yet, in another sense, we knew nothing at all about them', Dowell writes in the novel's first paragraph.

Our extract's combination of dull confusion and sharp vision exemplifies and expresses this paradox. Dowell's memoir is repetitive, self-contradictory and confused. 'I have', he later confesses, 'I am aware, told this story in a very rambling way so that it may be difficult for anyone to find their path through what may be a sort of maze' (part four, chapter one). And he nearly forgets to tell us about the book's supposed climax, the suicide of Edward Ashburnham. So he adds it at the very end, like an afterword. And the picture he presents may, like that of the mad Nancy Rufford, Ashburnham's last passion, be 'without a meaning' (part four, chapter six). But are pictures of other people all we have of them? And is a narrative which winds its way uncertainly and repetitively a truer reflection of the human mind than one that maintains a clear, linear direction? And are we ultimately left with questions, not answers?

2.6 Describing people through a third party: Jane Austen, *Pride and Prejudice* (1813), volume three, chapter one

'He is the best landlord, and the best master,' said she, 'that ever lived. Not like the wild young men nowadays, who think of nothing but themselves. There is not one of his tenants or servants but what will give him a good name. Some people call him proud; but I am sure I never saw anything of it. To my fancy, it is only because he does not rattle away like other young men.'

'In what an amiable light does this place him!' thought Elizabeth.

'This fine account of him,' whispered her aunt, as they walked, 'is not quite consistent with his behaviour to our poor friend.'

'Perhaps we might be deceived.'

'That is not very likely; our authority was too good.'

On reaching the spacious lobby above, they were shown into a very pretty sitting-room, lately fitted up with greater elegance and lightness than the apartments below; and were informed that it was but just done, to give pleasure to Miss Darcy, who had taken a liking to the room, when last at Pemberley.

'He is certainly a good brother,' said Elizabeth, as she walked towards one of the windows.

Mrs Reynolds anticipated Miss Darcy's delight, when she should enter the room. 'And this is always the way with him,' she added. – 'Whatever can give his sister any pleasure, is sure to be done in a moment. There is nothing he would not do for her.'

Elizabeth Bennet has rejected Mr Darcy's proposal of marriage on the grounds that his manners and behaviour have shown him to be arrogant, conceited and lacking concern for the feelings of others. In a letter to Elizabeth, Mr Darcy has frankly given his reasons for interfering in the developing relationship between Elizabeth's sister Jane and Darcy's friend Bingley and has explained his antipathy to Mr Wickham by means of an account of Wickham's true character, with particular reference to his near-seduction of Darcy's then 15-year-old sister, Georgiana. This letter has caused Elizabeth to revise her views and question her previous confidence in her discernment of the merits of other people. Glad to have the opportunity to distance herself from scenes of embarrassing events, Elizabeth accompanies her uncle and aunt, Mr and Mrs Gardiner, on a tour to Derbyshire. Mrs Gardiner's proposal that they should visit Pemberley House, Mr Darcy's home, distresses Elizabeth, until she is assured that the family is not at present in residence.[13]

Mrs Reynolds, the housekeeper of Pemberley, shows the party round the house. Her account of Darcy draws a portrait of him which runs counter to the impression he originally made on Elizabeth, and on Mrs Gardiner, who still believes that Darcy has behaved badly to Wickham ('our poor friend'). Mrs Reynolds has spoken warmly of her master's good nature: 'I have never had a cross word from him in my life, and I have known him ever since he was four years old.'

Our extract begins as Mrs Reynolds continues her praise of Darcy. We learn from her that he is a responsible landlord; that the pride some people see in him is, in her opinion, a reputation gained only because he is more reserved and less loquacious than other young men; that he has arranged for an upstairs sitting-room to be furnished in a more elegant and lighter style than the lower apartments, such as the dining-room earlier viewed by the party; that this redecoration has been carried out because Georgiana Darcy – who we later learn is now little more than 16 – took a liking to the room when last there; and that such concern to please his sister is characteristic of his regard for her.

Within the context of *Pride and Prejudice* as a whole, and of this visit to Pemberley in particular, certain words resonate to provide a texture of significance. The most obvious of these is 'proud', a keynote in the novel from the moment when, in the third chapter, Mr Darcy is rapidly 'discovered to be proud' by everyone upon his arrival at Netherfield with his friend Mr Bingley. Jane Austen decided to make 'pride' the first word a reader encounters when picking up the novel. We know that it was a considered decision because her working title was 'First Impressions'. 'Pride' is a complex word covering a range of meanings, from a 'high or overweening opinion of one's own qualities, attainments, or estate, which gives rise to a feeling and attitude of superiority over and contempt for others' (*OED* B1) to 'consciousness or feeling of what is befitting or due to oneself, which prevents a person from doing what he considers to be beneath him or unworthy of him' (*OED* B3). In simplified form, there is 'bad' pride and 'good' pride. Mr Darcy has gained, as we have seen, a reputation for 'bad' pride from people who have just encountered him. Mrs Reynolds, a woman who has known him since he was four years old and remains in his service, refutes this character description on the basis of long experience. In the following chapter, Elizabeth meets Darcy's sister. Elizabeth has heard that Georgiana is 'exceedingly proud', but 'the observation of a very few minutes convinced her that she was only exceedingly shy'. Alerted by Mrs Reynolds's careful discrimination, and herself an intelligent and perceptive observer when not distracted by the novel title's other abstract noun, prejudice, Elizabeth is rapidly able to see through to the real cause of Georgiana's demeanour. Perhaps she now begins to suspect a family trait.

The relationship between brother and sister is prominent in Mrs Reynolds's speeches. His delight in making his sister happy cannot but resound strongly in the mind of Elizabeth, who has only recently had her opinions of Darcy and Wickham profoundly shaken by the former's account of his fortunate discovery of Wickham's designs on Georgiana. Elizabeth's own earlier attraction to Wickham, which lies unspoken beneath Mrs Gardiner's whispered reflection about 'our poor friend', adds to her confusion.

Our passage sets up another linguistic pattern, which points to the moral issues at the heart of the narrative. Mrs Reynolds's comments about Darcy and his sister are prompted by the party's observation of the light 'elegance' of the decoration and furnishings of the upstairs sitting-room. Earlier in their tour, Elizabeth observed that the main rooms were handsomely fitted out:

> The rooms were lofty and handsome, and their furniture suitable to the fortune of their proprietor; but Elizabeth saw, with admiration of his taste, that it was neither gaudy nor uselessly fine; with less of splendour, and more real elegance, than the furniture of Rosings.

The word 'taste' here reflects an idea recurrent in the eighteenth century: that there exists a profound correlation between ethics and aesthetics, between our response to how people behave and our response to objects of beauty. Our revulsion at acts of moral depravity and our disgust at exhibitions of aesthetic vulgarity operate in spheres which are, in reality, cognate. Both reflect feeling, an immediate reaction to what we perceive. For philosophers such as David Hume, ethics and aesthetics are at root the province of feeling, not of reason.[14] Actions (such as the attempted seduction of a 15-year-old girl) and artefacts (such as a newly furnished room) cause us to react with repugnance or attraction. These responses we trace back in our judgement to their causes, the characters of the people responsible for them. It is in the would-be seducer and the interior designer that we locate the underlying principles, moral and aesthetic. In both areas, we are concerned with the effects of actions on a wider society, whether a relatively narrow group, such as a family, or a potentially wider group, such as tourists visiting country houses.

Among the virtues we recognize as having a beneficial effect on society is generosity. Jane Austen sets her guided tour of Pemberley in a chain of ethical significance through a network of incidents interconnected by the narrative, by key words and their moral implications. The 'elegance' Elizabeth perceives in the rooms brings to her mind the contrasting 'furniture of Rosings'. Rosings is the home of Lady Catherine de Bourgh, aunt of Mr Darcy and patron of the Reverend Mr Collins. Elizabeth has built up quite an impressive experience of rejecting marriage proposals. One of *Pride and Preju-dice*'s funniest and most celebrated scenes is her refusal of Mr Collins. Nothing daunted, Collins has turned his attention to Elizabeth's friend Charlotte Lucas, who – to Elizabeth's confusion and disbelief – has accepted him. While visiting her newly married friend at Collins's parsonage, Elizabeth is invited with the party to dine at Rosings (volume two, chapter six). Her experience of this stately home sets up a significant contrast to Pemberley. The enraptured Mr Collins counts the windows in the front face of Rosings and informs the party how much money the glazing had cost Sir Lewis de Bourgh. Lady Catherine's behaviour is correspondingly concerned to impose on her guests a sense of her superiority: 'Her air was not conciliating, nor was her manner of receiving them, such as to make her visitors forget their inferior rank.' The independent-minded Elizabeth is not cowed by Lady Catherine's aristocratic vulgarity: she observes in Lady Catherine no 'extraordinary talents or miraculous virtue, and the mere stateliness of money and rank, she thought she could witness without trepidation'.

Later in her stay with Mr and Mrs Collins, Elizabeth is invited to visit Rosings when Lady Catherine's nephew, Mr Darcy, is present (volume two, chapter eight). Music is the topic of conversation, and Jane Austen, with fine irony, has Lady Catherine raise the issue of 'taste'. With splendidly characteristic conceit, she declares that there are few people in England 'who have more true enjoyment of music than myself, or a better natural taste'. The first irony here is to do with good manners: if you openly pride yourself on your good taste, you simply demonstrate your lack of it. The ironies double up, as Lady Catherine adds: 'If I had ever learnt, I should have been a great proficient.' If you are going, however tastelessly, to claim taste, you should have something to prove it. Lady Catherine is really demonstrating her proficiency in tasteless egocentricity, which reflects an absence of social and personal understanding. As we read, we react against Lady Catherine's demonstration of snobbery and arro-gance, and our judgement traces this back to the moral nature of the character.

Lady Catherine then turns to Darcy and asks him how Georgiana is getting along with her piano-playing. His reply shows that his aunt's solecism has not passed him by: 'Mr Darcy spoke with affectionate praise of his sister's proficiency.' His picking up on her word 'profi-cient' is pointed; and his praise for his sister acts as a counter to her egotism and as a reflection of his contrasting sympathy for others.

Now, during the tour of Pemberley, Mrs Gardiner's attention is taken by a series of miniatures above a mantelpiece. Mrs Reynolds points out an eight-year-old Georgiana:

'And is Miss Darcy as handsome as her brother?' said Mr Gardiner.

'Oh! yes – the handsomest young lady that ever was seen; and so accomplished! – She plays and sings all day long. In the next room is a new instrument just come down for her – a present from my master; she comes here tomorrow with him.'

Darcy's generosity towards his sister is here expressed in a gift, which sets itself against his aunt's arrogance and self-obsession. Moreover, his generosity is not just one of sentiment: it manifests itself in deeds. Darcy's practical virtue exemplifies another keyword in Elizabeth's praise of Darcy's taste. The furniture Elizabeth sees is 'neither gaudy nor uselessly fine'. Just as we judge people by their actions, so we look to virtue to demonstrate its usefulness. Whereas Lady Catherine claims a proficiency which does not prove itself by actions, Darcy, by providing for his sister a piano and a room refurnished for her pleasure, demonstrates in deeds, not words, his affection for her. Whereas Wickham acts solely out of self-interest – Georgiana's sexual attraction ('the handsomest young lady that ever was seen') enhanced by her fortune of 30,000 pounds – Darcy acts discreetly but effectively to protect the vulnerable. The novel's climax will be precipitated by actions that bring together the fortunes of the Darcy and Bennet families. Wickham will succeed in his elopement with Elizabeth's younger sister Lydia (whereas he had failed with Georgiana Darcy thanks to Mr Darcy's intervention). Darcy's discreet actions will then remedy the situation, as far as it can be, given the current social stigma of such an elopement. Lady Catherine then makes her own intervention: a rude, vulgar and arrogant lecture demanding that Elizabeth should promise never to enter into an engagement with Darcy (volume three, chapter fourteen). Lady Catherine's actions are the opposite of discreet and reflect her social snobbery and absence of sympathy for the feelings of others. The moral geometry of *Pride and Prejudice*'s narrative is precise and unerring.

The ethical pattern Austen creates demonstrates what David Hume calls 'the nature and force of sympathy'.[15] 'Sympathy' – the capacity to feel with others – is a central term in Hume's study of the causes of moral behaviour.[16] Mr Darcy's sympathy for his sister gains the approval of Mrs Reynolds, which in turn further impresses Elizabeth. Hume writes: 'The minds of all men are similar in their feelings and operations; nor can any one be actuated by any affection, of which all others are not, in some degree, susceptible.'[17] Human beings operate within communities: families, domestic estates and society in general. Darcy's virtues have effects, are profoundly useful, unostentatious and praiseworthy, within his immediate family, within the grand household that he has the good fortune to inherit and within wider society – notably the Bennet family with which he will ultimately ally himself. At a still further level, novelists and their readers take their place within this pattern. George Eliot, herself an admirer of the novels of Jane Austen, declared that the principal aim of the novelist is to enlarge the sympathies of his or her readers (see Section 2.4). Jane Austen's attractive portrayal of her hero and heroine guides readers towards an appreciation of their fundamentally moral character.

In our example, the key role in this transference of sympathy is taken by a 'minor' character, Mrs Reynolds the housekeeper. Further in that chapter, the narrative identifies itself with the thoughts of Elizabeth (see Section 5.6 for free indirect style):

> The commendation bestowed on him by Mrs Reynolds was of no trifling nature. What praise is more valuable than the praise of an intelligent servant? As a brother, a landlord, a master, she considered how many people's happiness were in his guardianship!

Elizabeth recognizes the intricate forms of social organization, and the responsibility accompanying such a structure. Novels, too, contain their hierarchies, as reflected in our tendency to judge characters as 'major' or 'minor'. Of course, in the overall narrative of *Pride and Prejudice*, Elizabeth Bennet is a 'major' character, and Mrs Reynolds plays a role, that of tour guide and 'intelligent servant', only within this one incident. But, in the society of a novel, all are part of a wider whole. Jane Austen decides, at this key part of her work, to make Mrs Reynolds the agent of character description. It is a third party – neither the narrator nor one of the principal figures in the novel (as, in *Middlemarch*, is Ladislaw, one of the witnesses of Dorothea in the Vatican galleries) – who crucially defines Darcy for Elizabeth and for the reader. This description is at a further remove: Darcy is absent, so that the account of him is indirect. It is in the effects of his actions as shown to her by Mrs Reynolds that Elizabeth and the reader see him anew. Minor characters can have major impact.

3

Describing Places

3.1 Opening: Anita Brookner, *Hotel du Lac* (1984)

From the window all that could be seen was a receding area of grey. It was to be supposed that beyond the grey garden, which seemed to sprout nothing but the stiffish leaves of some unfamiliar plant, lay the vast grey lake, spreading like an anaesthetic towards the invisible further shore, and beyond that, in imagination only, yet verified by the brochure, the peak of the Dent d'Oche, on which snow might already be slightly and silently falling. For it was late September, out of season; the tourists had gone, the rates were reduced, and there were few inducements for visitors in this small town at the water's edge, whose inhabitants, uncommunicative to begin with, were frequently rendered taciturn by the dense cloud that descended for days at a time and then vanished without warning to reveal a new landscape, full of colour and incident: boats skimming on the lake, passengers at the landing stage, an open air market, the outline of the gaunt remains of a thirteenth-century castle, seams of white on the far mountains, and on the cheerful uplands to the south a rising backdrop of apple trees, the fruit sparkling with emblematic significance. For this was a land of prudently harvested plenty, a land which had conquered human accidents, leaving only the weather distressingly beyond control.

Environment reflects, influences and, some would say, perhaps even determines human action. Novels, in common with other forms of literature, return again and again to a sense of place as a key element of their created world. Writers for whom location is a dominant factor may declare their hand at the outset. Joseph Conrad's *Nostromo* (1904) begins with a chapter describing the harbour of Sulaco, a fictional South American town, which plays a major role in the novel's tragic action. Thomas Hardy, whom we have seen opening *The Mayor of Casterbridge* by setting character in place (Section 2.2), starts *The Return of the Native* (1878) with a celebrated chapter describing Egdon Heath as, in effect, a character whose influence will be felt throughout the course of the novel.

Both Hardy and Conrad establish their keynotes with a grand, dramatic sweep. Anita Brookner opens her fourth novel, *Hotel du Lac*, winner of the 1984 Booker Prize, more modestly, with just a single paragraph preceding the entry of her main character, whose name begins the second paragraph. But, as in *The Return of the Native* and *Nostromo*, the descriptive opening of *Hotel du Lac* is no mere incidental scene-setting. Quietly, as is Brookner's habitual style, this description of Lake Geneva in autumn (the location is specified by Brookner's reference to the Dent d'Oche, a mountain in Haute-Savoie overlooking the towns of Evian and Thonon) lays down the contours that her narrative will slowly and undemonstratively follow.

The paragraph modulates from a short opening sentence of just 14 words, through increasingly longer sentences of 64 and 118 words and back to a shorter final sentence of 23 words. This rise and fall in length is, not unnaturally, accompanied by an increasing and decreasing complexity of sentence structure. The inner, complex sentences explore a landscape whose existence is only 'supposed'. The first, very simple, sentence blots out the scene to anything but imagination and the novelist's eye; while the fourth sentence balances the richness of the landscape as described to us with a final brief return to the weather, which at this season renders it invisible to any present, actual observer. From an assertion that there is nothing to describe, the paragraph opens up, like drawing of curtains, to reveal light and vitality before closing down again in deference to a force which exists 'distressingly beyond control'.

Brookner's flat opening sentence is emptied of all human agency by its passive voice ('could be seen'), just as what it describes is drained of all activity. This is a 'window' onto not a world but blankness. But, as far as the paragraph as a whole structure is concerned, two keywords have already been planted. 'Grey' is the more obvious of the two, since Brookner at once enforces its significance by simple repetition, turning the initial general noun into specific adjectives: 'grey garden' and 'grey lake'. These phrases share the de-energized quality of the first sentence: the passive voice continues in 'It was to be supposed', and the lake's existence is assumed but not actively experienced.

The participial adjective 'receding' matches the lack of vitality of this opening by setting up a semantic field of departure. Again, the second sentence follows this up not only by its lack of any human agency but also by a sequence of words indicating absence: 'anaesthetic', 'invisible', 'silently'. Most descriptions are of what the eye can see or the ear can hear: Brookner's tells us of what we cannot see or hear. It is a reverse description, negating the facile temptations of an idealized travel advertisement. The landscape might be true in the sense that it is 'verified' by a brochure, but it is not real in the sense of being present.

The third and longest sentence is the climax of the paragraph. It begins by explaining what has gone before in terms that continue the idea of 'receding'. It is out of season, not only September, but late September: the month and the year are running down. Tourists 'had gone', the pluperfect (or past perfect) tense rendering departure with particular finality, and the town is as depressed as the weather. In this context, even Brookner's statement that the hotel rates were 'reduced' seems less an enticing invitation to a good-value holiday than a further acknowledgement of the dreariness of the place.

Then, roughly half-way through this sentence, the descriptive language changes as suddenly as a lifting cloud. We plunge into a renewed world 'full of colour' rather than monochrome, and full of incident rather than uneventful. The participles shift from 'receding' to active: boats are 'skimming on the lake', the landscape is a 'rising backdrop' and fruit is 'sparkling'. Brookner gathers these words and phrases into a list which, in a manner not uncommon in realist narrative, mingles habitual detail with dynamic detail.[1] The elements of the description occupy different time spans: the castle is static and ever-present, whereas skimming boats are temporary and fast-moving. An observer of the scene will always, given fair weather, be able to see the castle, while boats will move in and out of view. However, as we read such a description we hardly notice this compression of timescales, nor that the details are heavily selective. We accept the 'picture', as frozen in time as a painting in which movement is perpetually suspended. Nothing seems discordant, for each individual item is acceptably 'real' (so does not appear artistically chosen) and is juxtaposed as if randomly with other items. It is only when the eye, or inner eye, senses an overload of data that we notice the actual artificiality of what the writer is doing. Those paintings that cram every corner with multifarious details, such as a Canaletto view of a Venetian regatta or a Frith scene of Derby day, provide a sensation of teeming life, of an excess of events concentrated into a single vision. That is their point: to evoke a dizzying plenitude, an impression of a social event which, in its surplus detail, reflects a centrifugal energy. The whole of Venice appears animated by one event. A more restrained canvas of, say, an impressionist seaside scene is closer to the kind of realist description Brookner presents. It is selective in the way that memory is selective: we think of the past as constructed out of striking and recurrent images which define and sum up the feelings we associate with the experience. Brookner's description of a colourful and lively lakeside scene is the possible alternative to the present grey blankness, one verified by experience rather than brochures.

The description, however, strikes a further note, which Brookner holds back until the very end of the long third sentence. Apples sparkling in the sun naturally suggest light, vitality and, of course, fruitfulness. Such associations are readily transferable to human emotions, so that a narrator does not need to push the point. But Brookner does: she self-consciously adds that there is 'emblematic significance', at least in the fruit. Why does she do this?

We have noted Brookner's use of the passive voice in the early stages of the paragraph. As well as conveying absence of action, the passive voice obliterates a subject. The entire paragraph omits one important piece of information: who is actually looking out of the window of this sad hotel? For the answer, Brookner makes us wait until the second paragraph, which begins like an alternative opening: 'Edith Hope, a writer of romantic fiction under a more thrusting name, remained standing at the window'. The observer is herself a novelist, a writer of genre fiction of the sort one associates with love and, after appropriate difficulties to be overcome, happiness. At least, that is what one hopes such fiction means: that trees will bear fruit, that – as Jane Austen described her *Pride and Prejudice* – all will be 'light and bright and sparkling'.[2] Having tantalizingly pointed to the possible 'emblematic significance' of her description, Brookner comments a shade sardonically on her fictional novelist. Romantic fiction demands a more positive name than Hope. She then teasingly keeps us waiting for Edith's *nom de plume*.

We shall learn that the present moment, the 'receding area of grey', is an exile into which Edith has been driven after her embarrassing and shameful lapse from seemly behaviour in leaving her fiancé Geoffrey without warning, if not quite at the altar, then at the registry office door. Everything in the hotel, we discover, matches Edith's present mood of grey hopelessness. The carpet, curtains and counterpanes in her room are 'veal-coloured'; the hotel is apparently deserted, having but few guests, and is soon to close for the winter. On the other hand, though not exactly welcoming, the quiet hotel offers her 'sanctuary', a private space where she can try to come to terms with her desertion of Geoffrey and her now empty life.

Edith is actually offered two proposals for a comfortable, love-less marriage. One is narrated in retrospect as the cause of her exile, while the other is from one of the few guests she meets at the hotel, a Mr Neville. Geoffrey offered her the respectability of a London flat in Montagu Square, where her life of writing would be super-seded by one of 'ordinary' wifely activities. It was only when, as her car approached the registry office, she saw 'in a flash, but for all time, the totality of his [Geoffrey's] mouse-like seemliness', that Edith changed her mind and asked her driver not to stop. Mice are grey. Only, she reflects, in her romantic novels does the 'mouse-like unas-suming girl' get the hero. That is what fiction means. Mr Neville is, at least, a shade more colourful, despite the grey suit he is wearing when they first meet. He offers her, frankly, an arrangement of shared self-interest, but with a fine Regency house and his collection of *famille rose* Chinese porcelain. But, if well off, he is also shady. She breaks from him when she sees him emerge in the early morning from the hotel room of another guest, Jennifer, who is staying with her elderly mother.

Throughout her stay at the Hotel du Lac, Edith writes a series of letters, none of which she actually posts, to her lover, David, a mar-ried man whom she sees once or twice a month. He is her real distant beloved, the figure outside the window of her empty life. Her last let-ter to David, in which she tells him of her intention to marry Philip Neville, is her final expression of longing, her real romantic fiction. In it, she asserts that her profession of romantic novelist is not, as everyone else assumes, adopted with cynical detachment, but reflects her true belief. It is on her way to get a stamp from the night porter that she observes Neville's treachery and realizes that the open cool-ness of his offer of a mutually selfish arrangement would reduce her to an object, to stone, to an item in his china collection. Edith tears up her letter, and instead sends a telegram to David, containing one word, which is the last word in *Hotel du Lac*. It is a present participle, 'returning', a counter to 'receding' in the book's first sentence. The ebb tide of her time at the hotel – a place of temporary stay – gives way to the flow that returns her to home and her existing relationship. Her position as David's occasional mistress may be unsatisfactory in many

ways, but it represents feeling, her true self as she herself expresses it
in her last, unsent, letter: 'You are the breath of life to me.'

Edith finally accepts her status as eternal romantic. Her pretensions
as a serious writer are comically, but ruthlessly, undercut in Brookner's
narrative. Edith prides herself on her physical resemblance to Virginia
Woolf, but reminds a fellow guest (Jennifer's mother) of Princess
Anne. Her *nom de plume*, we eventually discover, is Vanessa Wilde:
'VW', combining the first name of Virginia Woolf's sister with the
surname a Brontë-style writer might have had but which belongs,
in fact, to the witty and cynical creator of Miss Prism, another fictional romantic novelist whose lost three-volume novel ('of more than
usually revolting sentimentality', according to Lady Bracknell) was
written according to the principle that the good end happily and the
bad unhappily ('that is what fiction means'). Edith herself can manage
only to write novels with titles such as *The Sun at Midnight* and – her
present venture – *Beneath the Visiting Moon*. She puts what talent she
has into her books, but her life is scarcely a work of genius.

The opening paragraph of *Hotel du Lac* may not sparkle, its depiction of human vitality and natural fecundity being retained as only a
possibility obscured by autumnal grey, a world receding and preparing to close for the season. But it does have 'emblematic significance',
as the phrase ruefully confesses. Even a land of 'prudently harvested plenty' must acknowledge its impotence to control the weather.
Edith's lover David is an auctioneer. When Edith goes to a sale at his
auction house, the painting he is selling is entitled 'Time Revealing
Truth'.

3.2 Views with rooms (1): Jane Austen, *Mansfield Park* (1814), volume one, chapter sixteen

The aspect was so favourable, that even without a fire it was habitable in
many an early spring, and late autumn morning to such a willing mind
as Fanny's; and while there was a gleam of sunshine, she hoped not to
be driven from it entirely, even when winter came. The comfort of it
in her hours of leisure was extreme. She could go there after anything
unpleasant below, and find immediate consolation in some pursuit, or
some train of thought at hand. Her plants, her books – of which she had
been a collector, from the first hour of her commanding a shilling – her
writing-desk, and her works of charity and ingenuity, were all within her
reach; or if indisposed for employment, if nothing but musing would
do, she could scarcely see an object in that room which had not an
interesting remembrance connected with it. Everything was a friend, or

bore her thoughts to a friend; and though there had been sometimes
much of suffering to her – though her motives had been often misunderstood, her feelings disregarded, and her comprehension under-valued;
though she had known the pains of tyranny, of ridicule, and neglect, yet
almost every recurrence of either had led to something consolatory; her
aunt Bertram had spoken for her, or Miss Lee had been encouraging,
or what was yet more frequent or more dear – Edmund had been her
champion and her friend – he had supported her cause, or explained her
meaning, he had told her not to cry, or had given her some proof of
affection which made her tears delightful – and the whole was now so
blended together, so harmonized by distance, that every former affliction had its charm. The room was most dear to her, and she would not
have changed its furniture for the handsomest in the house, though what
had been originally plain, had suffered all the ill-usage of children – and
its greatest elegancies and ornaments were a faded footstool of Julia's
work, too ill done for the drawing-room, three transparencies, made in a
rage for transparencies, for the three lower panes of one window, where
Tintern Abbey held its station between a cave in Italy, and a moonlight
lake in Cumberland; a collection of family profiles thought unworthy of
being anywhere else, over the mantel-piece, and by their side and pinned
against the wall, a small sketch of a ship sent four years ago from the
Mediterranean by William, with H.M.S. Antwerp at the bottom, in letters
as tall as the main-mast.

'How we live measures our own nature', grimly observes Philip
Larkin of the 'hired box' with thin and frayed curtains which was
Mr Bleaney's room and is now his. The East room at Mansfield Park
formerly served as a school-room for Fanny Price (the novel's heroine) and her cousins Maria and Julia, lapsed into disuse when their
governess Miss Lee departed and gradually came to be considered
Fanny's as it served more and more as a space for her possessions.
Jane Austen's description displays the contents of this room with
what Henry James called 'solidity of specification', reflecting Fanny's
collection of objects that measure her nature.[3] The room's interior
is designed to express her experience and, increasingly, her moral
clarity.

Within the precise economy of the novel's architecture, Fanny's
room represents a microcosm of the larger action. Maria and Julia
vacate the space of education, leaving emptiness, which Fanny quietly and gradually fills as her own small world. In the wider novel, the
older generation vacates the space of the whole house – Sir Thomas
Bertram, the owner, literally leaving for Antigua, Lady Bertram and
her sister Mrs Norris present physically but in terms of moral authority

vacant and inadequate. In their places, Maria and Julia are given
the freedom to express their tendency towards egocentric and competitive behaviour. Outsiders – the Crawfords, Mr Yates – initiate a
physical transformation of the house into a theatre, an ironic reverse-
image of Fanny's transformation of the East room into an authentic
representation of her mind, feelings and experience.

The room is Fanny's refuge, her 'comfort' and 'consolation' from
'anything unpleasant below', a euphemistic phrase which withdraws
delicately from naming anything or anyone specifically – retreating
as Fanny herself shrinks sensitively from it – while, at the same time,
suggesting in its very vagueness some of the pain she has endured.

The contents of the room form Fanny's real response to pain and
assert her identity. It is not just an escape, but a means of positive
self-expression. This is a vital stage in the gradual growth of her significance as a counterweight to the events that threaten to engulf
Mansfield Park. Her plants are the first item listed. Herself a sensitive
plant, the nurturing of plants is her first care. She has a silent sympathy with the natural world, which will later find vocal expression when
she and Mary Crawford walk together in the Grants' shrubbery (volume two, chapter four). And sympathy with the natural world is part
of, and also indicative of, a capacity for a wider humane sympathy.

Her books are next in the list. The discovery that Fanny has been
for some considerable time building herself a library reveals intellectual and cultural strength, reflected in the word 'commanding'
(a departure from the defensive language so far allocated to her).
This is a young woman of quiet self-determination. She does not
merely occupy a deserted school-room but transforms it into a place
of mature study and learning. She is, in microcosm, acting as a responsible owner of any respectable house would: building up its cultural
and intellectual holdings, which in this house are neglected. Houses
are places for living and growing – as children, as plants do – but also
for reading, thinking and judging.

Next comes her writing-desk, the literal support for the expression
of thought in language. Fanny is, in her early years, generally inar-
ticulate as a result of both her character and her circumstances. But
she has, right from the outset, found private correspondence a vehicle for self-expression and communication. When her cousin Edmund
encounters the young Fanny, recently brought to Mansfield from her
parental home, crying on the attic stairs, he soon discovers that her
earnest desire is to write to her brother William. Writing letters is an
expression of human sympathy and engagement. Edmund's provision

of the means of communication – the first act of kindness she receives at Mansfield – also communicates his sensitivity and sympathy.

The final item described in the room is from William, his sketch of HMS *Antwerp* with his immature writing (he is just one year older than Fanny). This response to her communications with him is William's expression of his identity (as a professional sailor) and is displayed as visual enactment of their sister/brother affection. In a novel where marital relationships are not universally successful and other sibling relationships (Maria and Julia) strained, the strength of Fanny's love for William is both constant and a significant adumbration of an eventual marriage between cousins.

At the heart of the paragraph lies its most complex sentence, the kind Jane Austen writes when she has something particularly powerful and significant to say:

> Everything was a friend, or bore her thoughts to a friend; and though there had been sometimes much of suffering to her – though her motives had been often misunderstood, her feelings disregarded, and her comprehension under-valued; though she had known the pains of tyranny, of ridicule, and neglect, yet almost every recurrence of either had led to something consolatory; her aunt Bertram had spoken for her, or Miss Lee had been encouraging, or what was yet more frequent or more dear – Edmund had been her champion and her friend – he had supported her cause, or explained her meaning, he had told her not to cry, or had given her some proof of affection which made her tears delightful – and the whole was now so blended together, so harmonized by distance, that every former affliction had its charm.

The sentence is organized by means of balanced pairs and groups of three. Its long middle section balances two sets of syntactic triads. Three subordinate clauses beginning 'though' define the difficulties Fanny has endured during her time at Mansfield. They are answered by the conjunction 'yet', which introduces matching consolations for the difficulties in three people: her aunt Bertram, Miss Lee the governess and, the most significant of these, Edmund. The pre-eminence of Edmund in her memory is marked by the emphatic rhetoric of two matching pairs of clauses: 'he had supported her cause, or explained her meaning, he had told her not to cry, or had given her some proof of affection which made her tears delightful'. The language in which Jane Austen describes Edmund picks up and exemplifies the beginning of the sentence, where she describes how memory works through objects gathered around Fanny: 'Everything was a friend, or bore her thoughts to a friend'. So Edmund 'had been her champion and her friend'. The balanced 'or' pattern – 'Everything was a friend, or bore her thoughts to a friend' – expands into those matching pairs in the list of Edmund's affectionate and charitable actions towards Fanny. This section on how Edmund's kindness transformed sorrow into joy ('some proof of affection which made her tears delightful') is a preparation for and explanation of the sentence's powerful conclusion, which is about reconciliation, bringing together what at first produced Fanny's feelings of isolation: 'the whole was now so blended together, so harmonized by distance, that every former affliction had its charm'.

Step back from the whole sentence, and we see how it is blended together, harmonized by Jane Austen's powers of composition. It is itself a small-scale demonstration of the power of language to bring balance and order to what have been difficult experiences. The sentence works its way from suffering to reconciliation, at each stage subsuming disorder (words such as 'ridicule', 'neglect') in the order of balanced syntax; and weaving through it the language of moral action (such as friendship), which transforms unhappiness to happiness. Its complex but well-regulated syntax enacts the power of human affection and sympathy to heal what is broken, to resolve affliction. Edmund and time ('so harmonized by distance') combine to smooth over the disturbances of day-to-day experience. This is a testimony to the healing power of time and of the associations of memory brought by time; and a testimony to active virtue, the perception that ethical human agency is characterized by capacity to sympathize with another human being and to convert sympathy into positive acts of kindness. As is so often the case in Jane Austen's novels, aesthetics are at one with ethics. The rhythmic elegance with which language and grammar are gathered into a whole stands as a representation of the attractive ethical process by which acts of sympathy reconcile and harmonize human feelings. Edmund is here at one end of a spectrum whose other is complete egocentricity, absorption in the self, of which the starkest exemplar in the novel is Mrs Norris.

This complex sentence represents the process of the book as a whole. Fanny Price begins as a disregarded, inferior inhabitant of Mansfield Park, but gradually, and after much suffering, grows into its strongest moral voice, the woman looked to by others for support and guidance. Friendships (particularly those of William and Edmund) and time (for example, the time it takes for her suitor, Henry Crawford, to reveal publicly his moral weakness by running off with the married Maria) are the agents of a transformation in

Fanny's position within the house and the novel. The room prompts this weighted microcosm of the novel's ethical process because it contains the material objects that, for Fanny, represent those agents. The sentence and the room both give solid specificity to the novel's vision, Jane Austen's narrative voice inhabiting the one as creatively as Fanny does the other.

3.3 Views with rooms (2): Virginia Woolf, *To the Lighthouse* (1927), part one ('The Window'), chapter seventeen

Novels in the realist tradition commonly use the natural or built environment to express in material terms the temperament or character of those who live in it. Mr Casaubon's house in *Middlemarch* is 'in the old English style, not ugly, but small-windowed and melancholy-looking' (chapter nine). Inside, carpets and curtains have 'colours subdued by time', bookshelves in the library are predictably 'dark'. The house's pinched, restricted and sombre aspect both suggests and reflects the nature of its owner, congenial though it all is to Dorothea at this early stage of her dream of life as consort to a great scholar. The irony of Eliot's comment that it is the sort of house that needs children and open windows to make it joyous will only later become apparent.

Modernist novelists may, in broad terms, be defined as those who set themselves against the Edwardian tendency, as represented by such writers as Arnold Bennett and John Galsworthy, to dwell on the surface of objects. In her essay 'Modern Fiction', Virginia Woolf calls these writers 'materialists'. They write of 'unimportant things', the 'trivial' appurtenances of everyday life, rather than the experience of living. 'Because he has made a house,' Woolf writes of Bennett in another essay, he tries to persuade us that 'there must be a person living there.'[4] It is, however, easy to exaggerate the differences between such modernist writers as Woolf and their predecessors. For one thing, they were doing what many artists do: clearing the ground for their own art by knocking down what had gone before. Woolf's object is, in any case, not the entire realist tradition. She called *Middlemarch* 'one of the few English novels written for grown-up people'; and knew well enough the value of trivia to praise Jane Austen for her capacity to offer the reader what may seem at first sight a 'trifle' but is really 'composed of something that expands in the reader's mind' and 'endows with the most enduring form of life scenes which are outwardly trivial'.[5] Woolf's quarrel is with writing that, in her view, restricts itself to the level of the trivial and does not expand.

To the Lighthouse illustrates both what Woolf shares with her predecessors and what she brings that is her own. The scene in the first
part of the novel is the Ramsays' holiday home on the Isle of Skye.
They have assembled a house party of diverse guests: a young student Charles Tansley, a scientist William Bankes, an artist Lily Briscoe,
a poet Augustus Carmichael, young lovers Minta Doyle and Paul
Rayley. Mrs Ramsay strives continually to create harmony among
these different and often conflicting personalities. The long chapter
seventeen, describing the company assembled for evening dinner,
is the culmination of her effort, her arrangement of their places
around the table a physical representation of her attempts to organize their lives and feelings. Events at dinner continue to thwart her
best endeavours. Tansley's disdain for 'silly women', her husband's
scarcely repressed anger at Carmichael's daring request for a second bowl of soup, these evoke Mrs Ramsay's efforts to subsume male
social intransigence which, at the same time, fatigue her.

But now the narrative takes a step back, pauses to 'compose' a scene
in which no individual people are named:

> Now all the candles were lit, and the faces on both sides of the table were
> brought nearer by the candle light, and composed, as they had not been
> in the twilight, into a party round a table, for the night was now shut off
> by panes of glass, which, far from giving any accurate view of the outside
> world, rippled it so strangely that here, inside the room, seemed to be
> order and dry land; there, outside, a reflection in which things wavered
> and vanished, waterily.

During the meal there have been awkward conversations and difficult silences, while Mrs Ramsay and – responding to Mrs Ramsay's
silent entreaties for help – Lily Briscoe have desperately tried to hold
the group together. Their struggle is now suspended in a moment of
strange visual description of the room. The room takes over from the
people in it, gathering them together as 'a party round a table' and
bringing them nearer by the force of candlelight.

Throughout the meal, Lily, the painter, has been working through
the composition of the painting on which she is currently engaged, and
which she will complete only at the very end of the novel. Her painting
and Woolf's writing move gradually towards convergence. Lily uses
the trivial materials of the dining-table to trace her action of com-
posing. Deciding to move a tree nearer to the middle of the canvas,
she picks up a salt cellar and, as a reminder, places it like a miniature lighthouse on a flower in the patterned tablecloth. She keeps

looking at this salt cellar, holding on to its inner meaning in spite of the discord around her. Art gives shape to a fragmented world: 'that matters – nothing else', says Lily in her interior voice. Like a painting, this instant of lighting the candles arranges the fragments of the scene. The separate actions of the guests cease, time pauses in favour of an essentially visual moment. In the novel as a whole, the second part ('Time Passes') moves ahead with destructive rapidity (the deaths of Mrs Ramsay and two of her children, Prue and Andrew, are reported in parentheses). In the third part ('The Lighthouse'), Lily Briscoe replaces Mrs Ramsay as centre of consciousness and, while Mr Ramsay leads his children on a trip to the lighthouse, as a deferred counterpart of a journey frustrated by bad weather in part one, she finishes her temporarily suspended painting. As their journey to dry land is achieved, Lily accomplishes her 'vision' (the last word in the book): the novel is complete.

In our paragraph, Woolf composes language into a moment of vision. It is one complete and complex sentence, whose movement is as assured and significant as that written by Jane Austen to represent the meaning of Fanny Price's room for her moral consciousness (see Section 3.2). Woolf begins with three co-ordinated clauses, each linked by 'and': 'all the candles were lit', 'and the faces on both sides of the table were brought nearer by the candle light', 'and composed . . . into a party round a table'. The second and third clauses state consequences of the first, so that the first 'and' has the force of 'and so'. The remainder of the sentence, from 'for the night' to the end, consists of a series of subordinate clauses, which are dependent on those co-ordinated main clauses. 'For the night was now shut off by panes of glass' provides a cause of the composed effect of the tableau: darkness excludes the outside, forcing the interior scene to close in upon itself. 'Which . . . rippled it so strangely' renders the watery effect of the panes of glass. 'That here, inside the room, seemed to be order and dry land; there, outside, a reflection in which things wavered and vanished, waterily' describes the effect of the rippled light, conveyed in an antithesis between the clarity of the candlelit room and the diffracted darkness seen through the windows. So the hinge of the sentence is the twin verbs 'were brought nearer' and 'composed'. They are the consequence of the simple main clause ('Now all the candles were lit') and they generate the rest of the sentence. The appearance of security is created by chiaroscuro: a contrast between interior light, drawing the group together, and exterior, unsettling darkness. The scene is 'composed', shaped into a picture.

Woolf's sentence is as carefully constructed as Jane Austen's. The difference between them is that Jane Austen's points of reference are firmly external and real. The idea that Fanny Price's growth to maturity of vision has been nurtured by human contact and friendship is located in particular people and objects which recall them to her mind. Friendship has been demonstrated by specific actions, particularly the support and comfort of Edmund. The sufferings that Fanny has endured are also specific (motives misunderstood, feelings disregarded), and, although in the sentence culprits' names are discreetly and generously withheld, the events of the novel make evident to the reader the true sources of her pain. Fanny lives in a clear and distinct world of social and familial relationships. This is the world that Jane Austen's novels describe, illustrate and explore.

Virginia Woolf's sentence, by contrast, is depersonalized, devoid of human agency. No one appears to light the candles: they 'were lit'. The faces are not identified. Woolf's emphasis is on dissolving individuals into a 'party', a group. The effect is analogous to painting, but a particular kind of painting. In his preface to the catalogue of the second post-impressionist exhibition he curated in London in 1912, Roger Fry wrote of the artists' desire not 'to imitate form, but to create form; not to imitate life, but to find an equivalent for life'. In a later essay, Fry described the relationships between the lines and colours of an artist's vision as taking on the dominant role within a painting:

> In such a creative vision the objects as such tend to disappear, to lose their separate unities, and to take their places as so many bits in the whole mosaic of vision. The texture of the whole field of vision becomes so close that the coherence of the separate patches of tone and colour within each object is no stronger than the coherence with every other tone and colour throughout the field.[6]

Virginia Woolf was, as a member of the famous Bloomsbury group, intimately acquainted with the artistic, aesthetic and philosophical ideas being circulated, discussed and implemented in that vibrant community. Her sister, Vanessa Bell, was one of the artists whose work was shown in the second post-impressionist exhibition. Her depiction of the composed room blends elements into a coherent mosaic conveying a feeling of process, a movement towards harmony and intimacy. Conversely, the objects in Fanny Price's room represent her own achieved state of harmony, but retain their distinct individuality, with a force as strong and clear as those tall letters in which her brother

William has spelled out the name of HMS *Antwerp*. The objects do not disappear but rather emerge in strong clarity.

Our paragraph in *To the Lighthouse* constitutes a moment of stasis within a larger narrative. In that narrative, objects and characters maintain an entirely traditional distinctiveness. The 'candles were lit', but the reader already knows by whom. Mrs Ramsay, fearing that her daughter Rose and son Roger will begin to laugh at the sight of Mr Ramsay's frustration over Mr Carmichael's second helping of soup, has told them to light the candles. The paragraph that follows describes a 'change' going through the party, which takes specific forms. Mrs Ramsay herself feels her uneasiness about the absence of Minta and Paul turn to expectation, and at once the lovers do come in, apologizing for their lateness and explaining that Minta had lost her brooch. Woolf's novel moves in and out of direct action, ebbing and flowing like waves. Later novels, in particular *The Waves* (1931), will push further the abstract quality of her writing; but here, in *To the Lighthouse*, that writing is as balanced as the ending of the novel, where Mr Ramsay leaps from the boat onto the solid 'rock' of the island even as Lily Briscoe draws the final line in her post-impressionist painting.

3.4 Describing views (1): Ann Radcliffe, *The Mysteries of Udolpho* (1794), volume two, chapter one

The nineteenth-century novel as often plunged its characters into the untamed world of wild nature as it seated them decorously in manageable rooms and houses. Indeed, when we think of novels such as Emily Brontë's *Wuthering Heights* (1847), the landscape – those intimidating but thrilling Yorkshire moors – may reverberate in the mind along with its impassioned, selfish inhabitants. Often, landscape became so dominant that it has seemed to many to take on a life of its own, as a – or even the – protagonist. The Egdon Heath of Thomas Hardy's *The Return of the Native* (1878), say, has furnished many a weary examiner with an obvious essay question: ' "Egdon Heath is Hardy's principal character." Discuss.'

The sources of fictional environmentalism lie earlier, however. It was in the eighteenth century that increasing opportunities for travel among a growing leisured middle class (as well as the privileged aristocracy) combined with Rousseauesque theories of natural virtue and such practical developments as better roads to open up landscape, both at home and abroad, to British travellers. Ann Radcliffe, whose romantic novels cast such a spell on many more readers than the susceptible Catherine Morland of Jane Austen's *Northanger Abbey* (1817), was not among them. Domesticity and poor health were the determinants of her quiet life. It just goes to show what a strong imagination and lots of reading can do.

Emily St Aubert, a young French woman orphaned by the death of her beloved father, is left in the care of her aunt, who marries an Italian nobleman, Signor Montoni, owner of a remote castle called Udolpho. It comes as a surprise to no one except Emily herself that dark secrets and frightening experiences await her at Udolpho. But first comes a journey across the Alps and a series of descriptive passages as extensive and dizzying as mountain views:

> Emily, often as she travelled among the clouds, watched in silent awe their billowy surges rolling below; sometimes, wholly closing upon the scene, they appeared like a world of chaos, and, at others, spreading thinly, they opened and admitted partial catches of the landscape – the torrent, whose astounding roar had never failed, tumbling down the rocky chasm, huge cliffs white with snow, or the dark summits of the pine forests, that stretched mid-way down the mountains. But who may describe her rapture, when, having passed through a sea of vapour, she caught a first view of Italy; when, from the ridge of one of those tremendous precipices that hang upon Mount Cenis and guard the entrance of that enchanting country, she looked down through the lower clouds, and, as they floated away, saw the grassy vales of Piedmont at her feet, and, beyond, the plains of Lombardy extending to the farthest distance, at which appeared, on the faint horizon, the doubtful towers of Turin?

> The solitary grandeur of the objects that immediately surrounded her, the mountain-region towering above, the deep precipices that fell beneath, the waving blackness of the forests of pine and oak, which skirted their feet, or hung within their recesses, the headlong torrents that, dashing among their cliffs, sometimes appeared like a cloud of mist, at others like a sheet of ice – these were features which received a higher character of sublimity from the reposing beauty of the Italian landscape below, stretching to the wide horizon, where the same melting blue tint seemed to unite earth and sky.

> Madame Montoni only shuddered as she looked down precipices near whose edge the chairmen trotted lightly and swiftly, almost, as the chamois bounded, and from which Emily too recoiled; but with her fears were mingled such various emotions of delight, such admiration, astonishment, and awe, as she had never experienced before.

The first and second paragraphs are parallel in their structure. The first contains two sentences of roughly similar length, describing in turn alpine scenery and a contrasting vista of the Italian plain beneath. In the shorter second paragraph, the same pattern is concentrated into a single sentence, with a dash separating the two components. The longer paragraph describes the landscapes from Emily's personal point of view, while the shorter applies to the same contrast the language and attitudes of general aesthetics.

Emily sees a world of elemental extremes. The language is pitched at the level of hyperbole. Clouds are not lonely, but crowd into 'billowy surges'; cliffs are 'huge'. Features of landscape are not rivers but 'torrents', not just 'precipices' but 'tremendous precipices'. Earth, air and water are all present, either literally or metaphorically, as with the 'billowy surges' of clouds. All is in a state of violent activity: the surges 'rolling', the torrent 'tumbling down'. The forces of nature are in control. This is not scenery disposed by human hands to accommodate moderate pleasure; this is landscape and skyscape responding to laws beyond our control. As part of the scene, Emily, 'among the clouds', experiences vitality and freedom all the stronger when contrasted with the threatening human forces lying in wait for her. Although hints of fear lie in the language (as with the adjective 'tremendous', which literally means 'making tremble'), the chief qualities in Emily's responses are a quasi-religious 'awe' (that is, reverential wonder) and 'rapture'. The description moves from violent action to the distant stillness of the view of the plains of Lombardy, from vertical extremes of rocky chasms and precipices to horizontal extension, from vivid immediacy to a 'faint horizon', so suggesting a pattern of calming, of containment of energy within quiet. Emily is not in real danger here: nature is powerful but ultimately restorative. It is human beings who are the real enemies of her well-being.

The second paragraph continues with extremes of language, sometimes direct repetitions ('precipices', 'torrents') and sometimes such new words within the same semantic area as 'towering', 'headlong' – the latter being the Anglo-Saxon equivalent of the Latinate 'precipice' (Latin *praeceps* from 'prae caput', or head-first). Such repetitions and synonyms are partly due to the limited range of hyperbolic rhetoric. Previous paragraphs have, indeed, also contained their fair share of 'torrents' and 'precipices'. Radcliffe's language, rich and voluminous as it is, can tend towards the repetitious. But this is not being entirely fair to her. Hyperbolic language is, after all, appropriate for extreme situations, and this alpine landscape is nothing if not staggeringly impressive. Further, the repetitions tie together the two paragraphs, just as the pattern of movement from grandeur to distance ('faint horizon', 'melting blue') is reflected from one to the other. The terms of the description need to chime in order to demonstrate the intimate connection between personal response and the same landscape rendered into aesthetic terms. The crucial words in the second paragraph are 'sublimity' and 'beauty' – the key terms of Edmund Burke's highly influential treatise, *A Philosophical Inquiry into the Origin of our Ideas of the Sublime and Beautiful* (1757). Partly a synthesis of earlier ideas from writers such as Joseph Addison, Burke's treatise advanced analysis of sensory apprehension and artistic representation by giving full value to the psychological dimensions of experience. Sublimity and beauty are not just categories, boxes in which to slot ideas, but reflect potent contrarieties within our minds. Emily responds in a manner consistent with profound philosophical attempts to establish, and define the sources of, human responses to the world. Radcliffe's descriptions search for a vocabulary which combines the particular and the general: not so much imaginary as imaginative.

Radcliffe was writing at a significant time for literary environmentalism. *The Mysteries of Udolpho* appeared four years after a young William Wordsworth and his fellow student Robert Jones went on a walking tour during which they crossed the Alps, and four years before Wordsworth began writing his autobiographical poem *The Prelude*, which contains an extensive account of that crossing. Like Emily St Aubert, Wordsworth created in personal experience a landscape of sublimity (for example, 'torrents shooting from the clear blue sky'[7]) which formed an important stage in his development. For the point of landscape lies ultimately within the human capacity to respond to, and feed from, experience. Emily's profound reactions are the subject of the third paragraph of our extract, set up by contrast with her aunt's shallow response to (again) 'precipices'. Like the two preceding paragraphs, this one is divided – here by a semicolon and 'but' – as a register of demarcation. Both Emily and Madame Montoni feel fear, but, where the latter 'only shuddered' without taking further steps in aesthetic awareness, Emily's emotions broaden out – like a vista of a distant plain – into 'delight ... admiration, astonishment, and awe' (the last word repeating the first emotional and reverential term in the passage). We are in a different type of environment from that of Jane Austen's Pemberley (see Section 2.6), and this is reflected in the vastly different kinds of language used by Radcliffe. But there is, at root, a similarity. The tastes might differ, but 'taste' is still the touchstone of a person's nature. Landscape is not merely background – it also, to the extent that it evokes the sensibilities of the character, both represents and validates her humanity.

3.5 Describing views (2): E. M. Forster, *A Room with a View* (1908), chapter six

Landscape description as it appears in Ann Radcliffe's novels could be regarded as a study in the relationship between aesthetic theory and individual experience. In nineteenth-century novels, such as Charlotte Brontë's *Jane Eyre* (1847) and Emily Brontë's *Wuthering Heights* (1847), the tendency is for the personal to take precedence over the aesthetic. Indeed, the power of such novels lies to a large extent in the subjection of all other parts of the narrative to the dominant psychology of the individual – of, in the case of *Jane Eyre*, the narrator herself.

The association of nature with passion, with the capacity or potential of the individual for self-expression, thus became a staple of novels through to twentieth-century writers such as D. H. Lawrence. Conflict between emotional repression and fulfilment figures largely in this kind of fiction. In the novels of E. M. Forster, young men and women commonly experience frustration or puzzlement as they struggle to understand their own feelings within a social environment which operates along straight and rigid lines. In his more complex novels, *Howards End* (1910) and *A Passage to India* (1924), the interplay between social codes and individual self-determination results in ambiguous and sometimes destructive outcomes. Forster's earlier novels, including *A Room with a View*, trace a simpler pattern in which impediments to self-fulfilment are encountered but overcome. The narrative takes on the air of a fable, a progress from dark to light, from uncertainty to clarity.

In the first chapter of *A Room with a View*, Lucy Honeychurch and her chaperon, Charlotte Bartlett, arrive at a *pension* in Florence to discover that their rooms face north when they had been promised south-facing rooms with a view. The unconventional Mr Emerson, also staying there with his son George, offers to exchange their rooms, much to the consternation of Charlotte, for whom such informality among strangers is unacceptable. Under pressure, Charlotte gives in, but insists that Lucy should have the elder man's room so that, by avoiding connection between the two young people, at least some propriety might be preserved. Charlotte, exploring George Emerson's former room, finds pinned over the washstand a sheet of paper with a large question mark written on it. The final chapter finds the newly married Charlotte and George back at the *pension*, in the room Lucy took over from Mr Emerson. A circle is drawn and questions are resolved. The room has a view over the River Arno and to hills beyond.

Well, the pattern is actually not quite this simple. 'Passion requited, love attained', writes Forster in the book's closing paragraph. But the final sentence reads: 'The song died away; they heard the river, bearing down the snows of winter into the Mediterranean.' The rivers of spring are replenished by the snows of winter. One season depends on another. It cannot always be summer, even in fables. And Forster's writing, even in this relatively early novel, frequently has a quizzical, somewhat self-conscious air to it, as if hinting to us that there are more question marks around than we might at first sight be aware of.

During the novel's first spring, when water brings the current of living, the *pension* party visits Fiesole, in the hills above Florence. Lucy, guided by one of their Italian carriage-drivers, steps out of a wood onto an open terrace covered with violets:

> From her feet the ground sloped sharply into the view, and violets ran down in rivulets and streams and cataracts, irrigating the hillside with blue, eddying round the tree stems, collecting into pools in the hollows, covering the grass with spots of azure foam. But never again were they in such profusion; this terrace was the well-head, the primal source whence beauty gushed out to water the earth.

Forster's description converts earth metaphorically to water. It is a brief passage, restrained in length when compared with landscape descriptions by some more effusive writers. The passion of Forster's description lies not in extent but in concentration. He plays many linguistic variations on his metaphor; from his initial triad of 'rivulets and streams and cataracts' – each element intensifying its predecessor – to a sequence of present participles which convey the idea of movement, of nature in action: 'irrigating', 'eddying', 'collecting into pools', 'covering the grass with spots of azure foam'. These participial phrases draw the sentence out into a continuing process, rendering the syntax fluid as the element it describes.

Modernist writing, seeking to match its style to essential experience rather than surface appearance, adopts similar processes. Here is Virginia Woolf describing the painter Lily Briscoe, in *To the Lighthouse*, applying her brush to the canvas:

And so pausing and so flickering, she attained a dancing rhythmical movement, as if the pauses were one part of the rhythm and the strokes another, and all were related; and so lightly and swiftly pausing, striking, she scored her canvas with brown running nervous lines which had no sooner settled there than they enclosed (she felt it looming out at her) a space. Down in the hollow of one wave she saw the next wave towering higher and higher above her.

(Part three, 'The Lighthouse', chapter three)

Present participles convey continuity and repetition of action; co-ordinating conjunctions (those repeated 'and's) keep the sentence moving, linking one phrase or clause to another and even maintaining links between sentences; and the wave image adds a metaphor of fluidity and repeated process matching the liquidity of Woolf's syntax, expressing Lily's painting as in process of being composed, rather than as an object, a block of material.

Forster's prose is similarly 'painting' the landscape, expressing its unfolding to the eye of the beholder. Woolf is attempting to express the interior of her character, how it feels within to be caught up in a creative process which, in its elemental force, seems to take over from her own volition. So Forster is trying to describe not precisely, in any formally designed structure, what the view is, but how it feels to Lucy to receive this sudden overwhelming visual experience. The action, the power and the vitality are all within the landscape itself. She, Lucy, is swept up in that movement, as she has 'fallen' onto the terrace, and as the violets will 'beat against her dress in blue waves', and as George Emerson will then step quickly forward and kiss her.

Water is frequently associated in *A Room with a View* with femininity and creativity. Lucy has bought in a Florence art shop a photographic reproduction of Botticelli's *Birth of Venus*. This painting, in Florence's Uffizi gallery, depicts the goddess Venus floating ashore on a scallop shell over the waves of the sea. The goddess is a nude figure, but stands in a pose of modesty rather than eroticism. Love is chaste, feminine, natural, carried to earth on waves. The terrace onto which Lucy steps is metamorphosed into a sea of violets lapping at her feet and becomes the 'source', the spring, the 'wellhead' of beauty and love. It is the moment in the novel, the first impulsive kiss, at which love is born. George responds unthinkingly, instinctively to the natural, chaste image of femininity that flows into his sight.

3.6 Describing towns: Elizabeth Gaskell, *North and South* (1854–5), volume one, chapter seven; Charles Dickens, *Hard Times* (1854), book one, chapter five

The action of Elizabeth Gaskell's novel *North and South* is initiated by Mr Hale, an Anglican clergyman in the rural south of England, coming to believe that his conscience no longer allows him to remain in post. He takes up a position as a private tutor in the northern manufacturing town of Milton-Northern (based on Manchester). Leaving his wife at the seaside town of Heston, Mr Hale and his daughter Margaret go to Milton to look for a house. Here Elizabeth Gaskell describes their approach to the town:

> For several miles before they reached Milton, they saw a deep lead-coloured cloud hanging over the horizon in the direction in which it lay. It was all the darker from contrast with the pale grey-blue of the wintry sky; for in Heston there had been the earliest signs of frost. Nearer to the town, the air had a faint taste and smell of smoke; perhaps, after all, more a loss of the fragrance of grass and herbage than any positive taste or smell. Quick they were whirled over long, straight, hopeless streets of regularly-built houses, all small and of brick. Here and there a great oblong many-windowed factory stood up, like a hen among her chickens, puffing out black 'unparliamentary' smoke, and sufficiently accounting for the cloud which Margaret had taken to foretell rain. As they drove through the larger and wider streets, from the station to the hotel, they had to stop constantly; great loaded lurries [lorries] blocked up the not over-wide thoroughfares. Margaret had now and then been into the city in her drives with her aunt. But there the heavy lumbering vehicles seemed various in their purposes and intent; here every van, every waggon and truck, bore cotton, either in the raw shape in bags, or the woven shape in bales of calico. People thronged the footpaths, most of them well-dressed as regarded the material, but with a slovenly looseness which struck Margaret as different from the shabby, threadbare smartness of a similar class in London.

Milton is viewed principally through what it produces, beginning with a dark cloud seen from far off, the result, as Margaret and her father discover when they get closer, of smoke being emitted by factory chimneys. Initially the impact is visual, the appropriately industrial colour of lead being contrasted with a paler sky whose potential attractiveness is diminished by the first half of the hyphenated 'grey-blue' and the onset of winter. At closer quarters, the smoke can be tasted and smelt. That these sensory responses derive from deprivation of rural fragrance as much as they are distinctively industrial is a nod to the novel's underlying theme as conveyed in its title.

This is a townscape unfamiliar to its observers, as it would have been to many of its first readers when published as a serial in Dickens's *Household Words*. It was Dickens who proposed the title *North and South*, a phrase from chapter eight. Elizabeth Gaskell's working title had been 'Margaret' or 'Margaret Hale', the novel's principal character and agent. Uprooted from her comfortably middle-class southern home, she experiences this industrial landscape as strange and unaccustomed. Streets are straight, houses are identical and the factory is an unappealing oblong. Everything is rigid, lacking the natural curves and variety of landscape. Gaskell's striking simile of the factory as a hen among her young chickens views the unfamiliar through reference to what is familiar to her, conveying the strangeness, the foreignness of industrial architecture to a country-dweller.

The structure of the paragraph takes Margaret and her father closer to Milton, then into the town itself. Their lives are in the process of moving to a new and – at least at first – disconcerting environment. Gaskell's detailed account of the traffic and bustle of Milton's streets maintains contrast, now with the city of London. Earlier chapters have shown Margaret in the comfortable urban setting of Harley Street in London as well as in rural Helstone, where Mr Hale has his parsonage. Industrial activity in Milton has an obsessively single purpose which takes over everyone and disregards everything else, even Acts of Parliament. 'Unparliamentary' smoke refers to an 1847 Act which sought, but ineffectually, to control the emission of smoke.

Gaskell's account does contain explicitly judgemental elements which move beyond description and into the area of comment we shall examine in Chapter 6. Streets are not only regulation-straight, but also 'hopeless', an adjective conveying more a sense of despair than a purely visual record (though the two are, no doubt, related, the visual effect causing hopelessness in the viewer or, perhaps, the inhabitants). In the final sentence, it is explicitly Margaret who casts judgement on how the Milton pedestrians are dressed. Is there a touch of southern bias here? Milton people have money enough to buy good material, but not the style to wear it: brass but no class.

The narrative, then, is to begin with generally neutral, simply reporting that 'they saw'. But the descriptive details accumulate negative implications which build towards concluding explicit judgements. That Margaret is the principal observer indicates that it will be she whose responses to her new environment determine much of the novel's point of view. That contrasts – rural/urban; London/Milton; south/north – are at the heart of the description looks ahead to the novel's central and pressing concern: can conflicts between differing perspectives be reconciled or is division an inherent quality of modern society? Margaret will be the key figure in this question, her central significance indicated by Gaskell's original title.

Dickens's choice of the novel's eventual title reflects a concern for contemporary social developments prominently displayed in his own novel *Hard Times*, which immediately preceded *North and South* in *Household Words*. His description of Coketown, based on his experience of visiting Preston in Lancashire, makes an instructive contrast with Gaskell's of Milton:

> It was a town of red brick, or of brick that would have been red if the smoke and ashes had allowed it; but as matters stood it was a town of unnatural red and black like the painted face of a savage. It was a town of machinery and tall chimneys, out of which interminable serpents of smoke trailed themselves for ever and ever, and never got uncoiled. It had a black canal in it, and a river that ran purple with ill-smelling dye, and vast piles of building full of windows where there was a rattling and a trembling all day long, and where the piston of the steam-engine worked monotonously up and down like the head of an elephant in a state of melancholy madness. It contained several large streets all very like one another, and many small streets still more like one another, inhabited by people equally like one another, who all went in and out at the same hours, with the same sound upon the same pavements, to do the same work, and to whom every day was the same as yesterday and to-morrow, and every year the counterpart of the last and the next.

Dickens's account is altogether more dramatic and rhetorically expressed. Its pitch – Dickens entitles the chapter 'The Key-Note' – is heightened by syntax and language. The sentences are presented with simple but persistent anaphora: 'It was a town ... it was a town', 'It was a town', 'It had a black canal', 'It contained several large streets'. Uniformity of the environment is rendered through heavy repetition of 'like one another', 'the same', 'every'. The concluding sentence piles up its clauses as the streets and people jostle one another in replicated succession.

Gaskell's simile of the hen among its chickens applied the domestic, rural and known to a new sight. Whereas 'defamilarization' works by turning what is common into something new and strange, Gaskell's simile does the opposite: it accommodates the strange by making it something known to the Hales. The result is an inappropriate incursion of the familiar into the unfamiliar, showing that they are in a foreign place which does not operate in ways entirely normal elsewhere. Dickens's similes, by contrast, are outlandish and surreal, suggesting now a dangerous wildness in the scene ('like the painted face of a savage'), and then a bizarre unnaturalness ('like the head of an elephant in a state of melancholy madness'). These are not the sort of similes that would have occurred to Margaret Hale. Visual details are accordingly extreme and uncompromising – 'unnatural red and black', 'a black canal' – whereas Gaskell's are more delicate. Their judgemental quality is never in doubt and is supported by the strong and unambiguous 'ill-smelling dye'. In *North and South*, the description of the smell of smoke is more qualified. Throughout, Gaskell creates a sense of a thoughtful mind observing and judging, certainly, but judging on the basis of contrasting experience. There is no such observer in *Hard Times*. There is no Margaret, just the rhetorical, even strident voice of a committed narrator. The passage suggests a novel mainly concerned to drive home a message with the relentless power and persistence of a piston. Gaskell's indicates that social observation and commentary will be mediated through a character who is to be involved in the events as a woman rather than merely a voice for ideas.

The two descriptions do, however, share one sort of commitment. They both wish to confront the state of towns representative of increasingly significant sections of the British environment and British society at a particular time, broadly the 1840s and 1850s of a rampant Industrial Revolution. They are contemporary novels, concerned with what is happening now, at the moment of their publication. The committed journalist and social commentator in Dickens clearly saw in Elizabeth Gaskell a writer whose work shared enough of his interests to be a worthy successor in his magazine. Indeed, the success of her earlier novel, *Mary Barton: A Tale of Manchester Life* (1848), had already led Dickens to invite her to contribute to his new journal, and her story *Lizzie Leigh* was the opening item in the first number. *Hard Times*, *Mary Barton* and *North and South* are all examples of what has been termed the 'condition of England' novel, following the Victorian social analyst Thomas Carlyle's raising of the 'Condition-of-England' question.[8] The townscapes we have been examining represent a larger geographical area (the industrial 'north') and the economic and social condition of the whole nation, as well as being (with varying degrees of exactness or rhetoric) accurate descriptions of real places. They do not merely describe actual locations, but are also parts of a wider picture – a nation or society as an entity. They act as large-scale versions of synecdoche, that is, a figure of speech in which a part stands for the whole. In some theories of the novel, the term 'metonymy' is used to define this representational function of narrative. Metonymy is actually a figure in which an attribute (rather than a part) of something is substituted for the thing itself, so synecdoche is the strictly proper term.[9]

Such novels are not the product of just one crucial time in British history, though it is true that the mid-nineteenth century was a particularly fertile time for writers with such social concerns. 'Condition of England' novels – 'state of the nation' is a common alternative tag – continued to be written through the Victorian period. For example, Anthony Trollope's *The Way We Live Now* (1874–5) depicts, in an unfavourable light, aspects of late Victorian capitalism such as share dealing and stock exchange speculation. International finance and human greed combine to corrupt private and public integrity. Moreover, ambitious examples occurred throughout the twentieth century. For example, Margaret Drabble's trilogy *The Radiant Way*, *A Natural Curiosity* and *The Gates of Ivory* (1987–91) expands from a study of intellectuals living in Thatcherite England in the 1980s to a geographically wider engagement with issues of capitalism and violence.

In the present century, Ian McEwan's *Saturday* (2005) begins and ends with its central figure, the neurosurgeon Henry Perowne, looking out at night over his cityscape, the London square near the Post Office Tower where he and his family live. Both nocturnal scenes are shot through with images of violence and danger: the flashing lights of an ambulance, a plane on fire heading towards Heathrow airport, the prospect and fear of bombs in a post-9/11 world. The Saturday between the two nights is the day of London's 2003 anti-Iraq War demonstration and of sudden incursion of frightening violence into Henry's life. The public and the private, society and the self, share territory, intersect and reflect each other. McEwan enacts this at the level of plot: Henry's minor motoring accident, which initiates a threatening sequence of events, is partly caused by traffic restrictions resulting from the march through London, and then Henry later finds himself operating to save the life of the man who attacked him. The two nocturnal scenes, which frame the novel and the day, describe a circle, quiet reflective calm containing fear and violence. Like the cyclical

Goldberg Variations of Bach, which he has playing as background music while he is conducting the operation, Henry returns to where he began, but 'changed by all the variations that have come before'. Music is metonymic of living itself: it is a quality of existence, a key element of our experience as (like Henry) sensitive human beings; and its form represents the entire shape of the novel and of life. We begin in dark, live through the 'seven ages', or seven days, of man, and face the final darkness of the end of the week with mingled tranquillity and fear.

We live through, but also in, the fiction because McEwan writes in a historic present tense. For example, Henry watches the burning plane in a sequence of instant sensations – at first, vague and even misleading (he thinks it must be a comet), then taking clearer visual and aural form:

> The leading edge of the fire is a flattened white sphere which trails away in a cone of yellow and red .... The engine note gives it all away. Above the usual deep and airy roar, is a straining, choking, banshee sound growing in volume .... Something is about to give.

Most novelists use the past tense. Whether narrators are first person or third person, they look back on events that have occurred. By doing so, they convey reassurance to the reader that there will be progress to some kind of outcome, the point from which they are able to view the entire story. McEwan's present tense imbues the narrative with an edgier feeling: narrator and reader experience Henry's day in company with his own uncertainty of knowing where his life is going or how the day will end. This instability synecdochically infiltrates the novel's depiction of the state of the nation. There is unrest, there is a threat of violence and its uncontrollable consequences, in a country which is on the verge of war, manifesting disquiet about its direction.

Historical fiction more commonly deals with events whose outcomes are known and familiar to most readers. Its characters are not fictional, as are McEwan's, but real historical figures from a period earlier than *Saturday*'s still uncomfortable and contested 2003. A past tense is therefore natural and expected. However, Hilary Mantel's unfolding trilogy about the court of a real and famous Henry as seen through the eyes of Thomas Cromwell, Henry VIII's secretary and principal puppet-master, is also narrated in the present tense. A Tudor court obsessed by questions of royal succession, aristocratic influence and personal intrigues may be historically remote; but the feelings it engenders, notably fear, are shared by a Saturday in 2003 and, it may be, the present day. The superficial habits of living might change, but raw emotions do not; nor does the feeling that individuals are caught up in events taking place on a national stage, over which we have no control. Like Henry Perowne, Thomas Cromwell manages crises by his supreme skill. But his life is a continual present lived in an insecure place, on the edge of perpetually smoking fire.

4

Presenting Action

4.1 First-person action: Daniel Defoe, *Moll Flanders* (1722)

It was now a merry time of year, and Bartholomew Fair was begun. I had never made any walks that way, nor was the fair of much advantage to me; but I took a turn this year into the cloisters, and there I fell into one of the raffling shops. It was a thing of no great consequence to me, but there came a gentleman extremely well dressed and very rich, and as 'tis frequent to talk to everybody in those shops, he singled me out, and was very particular with me. First he told me he would put in for me to raffle, and did so; and some small matter coming to his lot, he presented it to me – I think it was a feather muff; then he continued to keep talking to me with a more than common appearance of respect, but still very civil, and much like a gentleman.

He held me in talk so long, till at last he drew me out of the raffling place to the shop-door, and then to take a walk in the cloister, still talking of a thousand things cursorily without anything to the purpose. At last he told me that he was charmed with my company, and asked me if I durst trust myself in a coach with him; he told me he was a man of honour, and would not offer anything to me unbecoming him. I seemed to decline it a while, but suffered myself to be importuned a little, and then yielded.

I was at a loss in my thoughts to conclude at first what this gentleman designed; but I found afterward he had some drink in his head, and that he was not very unwilling to have some more. He carried me to the Spring Garden, at Knightsbridge, where we walked in the gardens, and he treated me very handsomely; but I found he drank freely. He pressed me also to drink, but I declined it.

Hitherto he kept his word with me, and offered me nothing amiss. We came away in the coach again, and he brought me into the streets, and

by this time it was near ten o'clock at night, when he stopped the coach
at a house where, it seems, he was acquainted, and where they made no
scruple to show us upstairs into a room with a bed in it. At first I seemed
to be unwilling to go up, but after a few words I yielded to that too, being
indeed willing to see the end of it, and in hopes to make something of
it at last. As for the bed, etc., I was not much concerned about that
part.

Here he began to be a little freer with me than he had promised; and I by
little and little yielded to everything, so that, in a word, he did what he
pleased with me; I need say no more. All this while he drank freely too,
and about one in the morning we went into the coach again. The air and
the shaking of the coach made the drink get more up in his head, and
he grew uneasy, and was for acting over again what he had been doing
before; but as I thought my game now secure, I resisted, and brought
him to be a little still, which had not lasted five minutes but he fell fast
asleep.

I took this opportunity to search him to a nicety. I took a gold watch, with
a silk purse of gold, his fine full-bottom periwig and silver-fringed gloves,
his sword and fine snuff-box, and gently opening the coach-door, stood
ready to jump out while the coach was going on; but the coach stopping
in the narrow street beyond Temple Bar to let another coach pass, I got
softly out, fastened the door again, and gave my gentleman and the
coach the slip together.

Verbs, we are told when we learn about parts of speech, are 'doing'
words. Verbs are the essential parts of sentences, the words that turn
them into complete and meaningful utterances. Sentences are made
by the actions verbs contain.

In this incident in Defoe's *Moll Flanders*, Moll's concern throughout is to tell us what happened, what she did and what the gentleman
did. So verbs are the dominant grammatical forms, usually active,
simple and monosyllabic: 'took', 'fell', 'told', 'held', 'drew', 'found',
'kept', 'came', 'brought', 'made'. The occasional two or more syllable
verbs remain at a straightforward and familiar level of usage: 'carried', 'treated', 'declined', 'presented'. Moll tells her story in a very
direct, uncomplicated way. Defoe chose this kind of language for, no
doubt, a number of reasons. His first novel, *Robinson Crusoe*, proved
to be highly successful (see Section 2.1), and *Moll Flanders* is just one
of a series of more or less sensational stories he produced rapidly in
the years following the appearance of *Crusoe*. As a tried and hard-
ened journalist, he could recognize a popular and lucrative publishing

venture when he saw one. His style has a wide readership in mind; his
novels are an extension of his journalism.

The style of the novel also reflects the narrator. Moll, born in
Newgate prison, a victim of youthful seduction, passed from one
brother to another, serial wife and then (as in the episode we are
looking at) thief, comes from a social level where blunt speech was,
to say the least, likely to have been the norm. In his preface, the 'publisher' says that he has actually cleaned up Moll's prose to make it
more acceptable to a readership, but the Defoe who lies behind both
Moll and his 'publisher' knows enough to retain immediacy of expression. After all, he too was a child of London and was familiar with
prison and life at the bottom of society. He wrote from experience of
the world Moll inhabits.

An action-centred narrative, where people are too busy trying to
survive and prosper in a bustling city environment to have leisure
for fine style, strikes a chord with both his narrator and his readership. Verb-centred writing follows naturally. There is no time to
indulge in extensive descriptions of people or places. The reader of
Moll Flanders learns very little about the way people look: there is
no external eye to survey the figures, as there is in the openings of
Hardy's *The Mayor of Casterbridge* and Bennett's *Riceyman Steps*
(see Section 2.2). Indeed, it is important for Moll's survival that her
person should be as little observed as possible. When she goes out to
steal, she disguises herself as a respectable and so trustworthy woman.
In the entire narrative, she is, at a fundamental level, in perpetual
disguise: 'Moll Flanders' is a pseudonym for a true name we never
learn.

Moll stops to describe people only when their appearance is significant for her action. When adjectives are in short supply, the occasional
one or two make an impact. So the 'gentleman' who picks Moll out
in the first paragraph of our excerpt remains anonymous throughout
and is physically invisible. Is he tall or short or of middle height? Are
his eyes brown or blue or grey? If Moll notices, she does not tell us.
Instead, the adjectives she uses about him are 'well dressed' and 'rich';
and, just to push the point home, each is given an adverbial intensi-
fier: 'extremely', 'very'. That is all Moll, and we, need to know. These
adjectives rest dormant in the action that follows, until they burst out
with fresh elaboration in the last paragraph, when Moll exploits his
drunken slumber to subject him to a thorough search. Moll 'took this
opportunity' (she had, in the first paragraph, innocently taken 'a turn'

into the cloisters – that is, the arcades in front of the shops – at the fair as if preparing the linguistic ground for a more direct kind of taking), and she proceeds to take the items that, we now learn, justified her initial adjectives. The gentleman is indeed 'extremely well dressed and very rich': his watch is 'gold', his gloves are 'silver-fringed', his purse of gold is 'silk', his periwig and his snuff-box are 'fine'. The gentleman is not so much a human being as a mobile possessor of valuable items. This is so despite the intimately human contact which is central to the event but marginal to Moll's concerns. Moll passes over what is, presumably, the highlight from his point of view with a flip dismissal: 'As for the bed, etc., I was not much concerned about that part.' That non-literary abbreviation, 'etc.', registers both the irrelevance of sex for Moll and the narrative's almost comic refusal to be interested in anything of no consequence to her. The reader looking for the lubricious, lured in by the covers chosen for some paperback editions or by some film versions, will be disappointed – another victim of false promises, taken for a ride, treated as a function of the market-place.

Places, as well as people, are subordinated to action. Before launching into the story, Moll allows but the most perfunctory of initial scene-setting: 'It was now a merry time of year, and Bartholomew Fair was begun.' What would a writer fond of local colour make of this? Bartholomew Fair was an annual event which took place on the site now occupied by Smithfield market on St Bartholomew's Day, 24 August. Ben Jonson set a play there, revelling in its teeming life, its mingling of the classes, its untrammelled devotion to sensual indulgence and its criminal activity. Such was Bartholomew Fair's reputation for licence that it was eventually banned in the Victorian period. There would have been crowds of people; but Moll is interested in only one person, the gentleman. As far as her narrative is concerned, he and she might have been the only fairgoers. There would have been many varieties of stalls, selling all kinds of goods and offering all kinds of inducements to pleasure and expense. But only a raffling shop is mentioned. Life is a lottery when you are living on your wits or your looks (or both), as Moll is. Moll says that she 'fell' into a raffling shop, as if inadvertently, but she rather gives the game away by explaining that raffling shops are places where people talk to one another, so making conversation between strangers a normal activity. So there is no description of the shop. Defoe's eye is not on the environment, let alone future readers with an interest in social history. Like his narrator, he is focussed on the utility of place, its capacity to furnish opportunities for productive action.

Focus on action, and on selection of which actions are relevant and which may be omitted as inconsequential, results in economical narration. It takes Moll just these six paragraphs to give us this whole event. It is a self-contained story, with its own beginning and satisfying conclusion, as Moll's skill, adroitness and opportunism produce a successful outcome – successful for Moll, that is. The narrative bids goodbye to the story as Moll slips softly out, leaving the gentleman to continue his unconscious journey to (presumably) discovery and remorse. In this way, the event has the force of an episode: that is, one within a longer narrative from which it may be separated yet from which it does naturally arise.[1] Such narrative episodes or interpolations are often a feature of picaresque fiction – novels about low-life characters (*picaro* is Spanish for 'rogue') making their way rumbustiously and often comically through a lively or hostile society. A structure that takes protagonists on journeys from one incident to another – Cervantes's *Don Quixote* (1605; 1615) is the signal and most influential example – lent itself readily to novels centred on action. This structure can still be observed in novels that aspire to more elaborate and ethically aware aims. Henry Fielding's *Tom Jones* (1749), for example, is a sophisticated study of the problems of maintaining moral probity within a complex and deceptive world in which actions have causes and (often unforeseen) consequences (see Section 4.3). But it is also characterized by episodic set-pieces, such as a mock-heroic battle in a churchyard where Tom's lover Molly Seagrim is attacked by her vengeful peers. Fielding's novels, indeed, contain entirely interpolated stories – of Mr Wilson in *Joseph Andrews* (1742), of the Man of the Hill in *Tom Jones* – which arise from, and comment obliquely on, the main narrative, but with a different set of characters.

In fact, Defoe does make more of this incident with the gentleman. Moll takes her booty to her 'governess', a woman who acts as bawd and receiver of stolen goods. She persuades Moll to see the gentleman again, as a result of which Moll conducts an occasional affair with him for about a year, receiving payment for sexual favours but not a regular maintenance. The story of their relationship itself is narrated concisely: just nine paragraphs take us from the first time they meet again to his final departure. It is another episode before Moll resumes her 'old trade' of thieving. The whole novel is marked by economy of narrative, a quick turnover of incident. Defoe does not dwell or meditate, but sets a rapid pace from action to action.

Because Defoe habitually chooses first-person narrative, he does in any case rule out any possibility of authorial commentary and reflection on his fiction. He does make Moll herself reflect from time to time on what she has done and the life she is living; but this itself raises a problem which has preoccupied critical writing on Defoe. Immediately after our extract, Moll embarks on several paragraphs of moralizing on the folly and weakness of men who allow themselves to become so 'heated' by wine that they lose control of their actions and fall into immoral and dangerous behaviour. Think of the shame, Moll lectures us, with which the gentleman will look back on their liaison and reproach himself for associating with a whore, especially if – as is likely the case – he has a virtuous wife and innocent children.

How seriously does Defoe mean us to take Moll? It does, after all, take two to tango, and Moll seems happy enough to accept money from the gentleman during their intermittent relationship, money which might have gone to that honourable wife and those little children. Is Moll, in short, an inveterate and shameless hypocrite? Or is she performing one of the common functions of the picaresque protagonist: exposing the follies and vices of the society around her? Is she an agent of moral commentary or is she an example of the immorality she claims to despise?

These questions are present in the Bartholomew Fair episode itself. We noted Moll's claim that she 'fell', as if by accident, into a raffling shop. She takes care to tell us that it was the gentleman who 'singled' her out. She insists that he took the initiative: he 'held me in talk', he 'drew me out of the raffling place', he 'carried me to the Spring Garden'. He is repeatedly the subject of the active verbs, right up to the sexual encounter: 'he began to be a little freer with me than he had promised', 'he did what he pleased with me'. Moll's response, she says three times, is eventually to 'yield' to his importuning and insistence. 'Yield' is an intransitive verb and requires another party to force or at least encourage. To say 'I yielded' is to hover between agency and passivity, between being a controlling subject and a controlled object.

Further, there are parts of the narrative where Moll drops her guard. When asked to accompany the gentleman in a coach, she 'seemed to decline it a while' and 'suffered' herself to be importuned. Then, when being encouraged to go upstairs to a room with a bed in it, Moll 'seemed to be unwilling'. She is acting a part, feigning reluctance and so readily exposing herself to the accusation of hypocrisy and manipulation of the event. By the time the pair have returned to the coach, Moll is open enough to talk of her 'game' being secure. The gentleman is the object of her pursuit and her opponent in a contest for supremacy. The final paragraph is unashamedly triumphant in tone. Moll becomes the clear subject of active and transitive verbs which narrate her success, her victory. The gentleman persuades her into the coach, but who is taking whom for a ride?

Readers of a first-person novel can derive their interpretation only from the narrator's words. But those words are chosen and ordered by the novelist. Moll Flanders tells her story in a manner veering between self-justification and confession of guilt, between exposing others' faults and falling back on her own urgent, if intermittent, repentance. It is not, therefore, surprising that readers also veer between exasperation at Moll's hypocrisy and enjoyment of her triumph over adversity, between seeing her as the object of her creator's implicit irony and regarding her as a champion of feminism and individualism, between treating her as morally depraved and claiming that she successfully exposes the contradictions at the heart of a materialistic and competitive society. In Robinson Crusoe, Defoe defined an individual who constructs his identity as hero; in Moll Flanders he set up an inconstant narrator whose actions reflect our own, and our society's, uncertainties.

4.2 Decisive actions: Charlotte Lennox, *The Female Quixote* (1752), book nine, chapter nine; Joseph Conrad, *Lord Jim* (1900), chapter nine

Two principal characters find themselves at a critical point in their lives. The decision they make now will determine the course of their future. Should they take the leap?

The first is Arabella, daughter of a Marquis who, after years of enjoying effective power at court, has been the victim of plotting and has fallen from grace. Taking his new young bride with him, the Marquis retires to country seclusion where his isolation is increased by the death of his wife three days after giving birth to Arabella. Arabella grows up under the benign tutelage of her father, whose library supplies her with her chief pleasure. Unfortunately, she is particularly attracted to her mother's collection of romances, 'not in the original French, but very bad translations'. These romances prove to be not just pleasing entertainment for Arabella, but, in the absence of any real experience, the source of her notions and expectations of the world. The bulk of *The Female Quixote* is taken up by Arabella's comic attempts to apply the models of these romances to her life. She turns her world into the imaginary world of romance: gardeners become disguised noblemen, local horse races become modern versions of the original Greek Olympic games ('Do the candidates ride in chariots?'). Constantly buoyed up by her fertile imagination as she is, Arabella's encounters with reality never lessen her ardour for romance.

As the novel nears its close, Lennox provides her heroine with one final adventure. She and her female companions are taking a walk beside the river Thames when three or four horsemen come into view riding towards them. Lost as Arabella's mind is in 'the follies of romances', she at once decides that they intend to seize and carry off the ladies. She rushes to the riverside where, seeing no boat to save them, she addresses her companions:

> What that beauteous Roman lady performed to preserve herself from violation by the impious Sextus, let us imitate to avoid the violence our intended ravishers yonder come to offer us.
>
> Fortune, which has thrown us into this exigence, presents us the means of gloriously escaping: and the admiration and esteem of all ages to come, will be the recompense of our noble daring.
>
> Once more, my fair companions, if your honour be dear to you, if an immortal glory be worth your seeking, follow the example I shall set you, and equal with me the Roman Clelia.
>
> Saying this, she plunged into the Thames, intending to swim over it, as Clelia did the Tiber.

Comedy often works by exposing the gap between how someone sees the world and how it actually is. Cervantes's *Don Quixote*, the model for much eighteenth-century fiction, is the classic instance of this comic form. Charlotte Lennox's title, of course, declares her indebtedness. Arabella's excited and hyperbolic language habitually raises to absurd heights events we can see are perfectly ordinary. The reader has long been fully aware that a gardener turns out to be simply a gardener, and races events with cash prizes, bets and humdrum shady characters, and so has no expectation now other than that the intended ravishers are simply men riding horses. Arabella elevates an entirely common experience to a trial of her virtue devised by 'fortune'. Both the danger of the moment and the consequences of successful escape are magnified by (frequently alliterative and assonant) rhetoric: 'violation', 'violence', 'exigence', 'esteem', 'honour', 'glory'. Arabella's choice of words is consistently Latinate ('fortune', not 'luck'), a register of language on the level of its historical and fictional points of reference, as mediated and decorated by the elaborate and tireless pen of Madeleine de Scudéry. Published in ten volumes between 1654 and 1660, de Scudéry's *Clélie, histoire romaine* is set in classical Roman times, but displays the topics of romance and the narrative of fantasy. Arabella seems to have admired de Scudéry's best-seller more for its romance plot than for its serious discussion of emotion and psychology, which animated readers in fashionable French salons.

All of Arabella's elaborate attitudinizing and elevated language are being set up by Lennox for a crashing fall. With her plunge into the Thames, Arabella immerses herself in the cold reality of eighteenth-century England as fully as she has immersed herself in the glorious fantasies of romance. The Thames is not the Tiber, or, at least, not the Tiber of Scudéry's fiction in which 'deep and rapid river', as Arabella earlier related (book two, chapter three), Clelia threw herself and swam to the other side in order to preserve her honour from the sexually predatory Sextus. Arabella has to be pulled out of the Thames, and becomes dangerously ill with a fever until 'by a favourable crisis, and the great skill of her physicians' (book nine, chapter ten) she is restored to health. Lennox's finale ensures that this moment of crisis is not just physical. During her illness, Arabella is also tended by another sort of doctor, a doctor of divinity. Once she has recovered, Arabella and this doctor calmly and seriously debate the nature and value of fictional literature, its relationship to real experience and its application to human life. Arabella is not simply 'cured' in this discussion of her psychological disease: she reveals herself to be, beneath the brittle surface of acquired romantic delusion, a woman of sound and sensible character. This discussion lasts for just one chapter (book nine, chapter eleven; the penultimate), but it is where the novel's true meaning lies. Its very conciseness, as compared with the extensive romantic comedy preceding it, is the novel's equivalent of the brevity with which Arabella's elevated language is drowned in the simple clause, 'she plunged into the Thames'.[2]

Romance delusion can make for entertaining reading while it lasts, as long as it remains clearly distinguished from how the world actually is. The need for this distinction is a recurrent subject in eighteenth-century fiction. Jane Austen's *Northanger Abbey* (published posthumously in 1817, but written in the 1790s) exposes the fallacy of romance, or, given the specific reference of the novel, of late eighteenth-century 'gothic' fiction. In essence, the question is whether the world is how extravagant fiction depicts it or how common sense sees it. Catherine Morland, the heroine of *Northanger Abbey*, has, because of her reading of fiction, come to believe that people commonly act melodramatically by, for example, murdering their wives. She learns, painfully but productively, that such extremes of behaviour are exceptional. She also learns that many people do indeed behave cruelly, but in less exaggerated and all too real ways. Low-level spite and envy are more common among people than are extremes of gothic villainy, even when the suspect's name is General Tilney and his home is the beguilingly named Northanger Abbey.

The other danger of romance is that it trivializes serious things. Arabella's conviction that any random horsemen are threatening ravishers and that ladies can escape their clutches by demonstrating heroic behaviour on the grand scale can obscure the murkier reality that sexual violence does exist in society and that women sometimes cannot escape. Samuel Richardson's *Clarissa* (see Section 4.4) reminds us of these serious truths. Charlotte Lennox's comic novel, by debunking a myth, represents a significant stage in regularizing the way we think about ourselves and society, as well as in making the nature of honourable action a central theme of the novel form.

Our second character at a crisis point is a merchant seaman called Jim, at the time employed as chief mate of the *Patna*. His story is being told retrospectively to some after-dinner companions by Marlow, a fellow sailor who crops up regularly as narrator in Joseph Conrad's novels. Marlow encountered Jim at an inquiry into the actions of the crew of the *Patna*. In a calm sea at night the ship apparently struck something and was on the verge of sinking. The *Patna*'s German skipper and two engineers managed to launch a lifeboat in which they intended to leave the ship and the 800 pilgrims on board to their fate. They called out in the darkness to another member of the crew, a so-called 'donkey-man' named George, to jump from the ship and join them in the lifeboat. They did not know that George had died from a heart attack brought on by the emergency. It is not George who heard the cries to jump, but Jim. Should he desert the ship and save his life, or stay aboard and do his duty by the passengers in his care? Marlow recounts the moment of Jim's confession:

> 'He raised his hand deliberately to his face, and made picking motions with his fingers as though he had been bothered with cobwebs, and afterwards he looked into the open palm for quite half a second before he blurted out:
>
> ' "I had jumped..." He checked himself, averted his gaze.... "It seems," he added.

'His clear blue eyes turned to me with a piteous stare, and looking at him standing before me, dumbfounded and hurt, I was oppressed by a sad sense of resigned wisdom, mingled with the amused and profound pity of an old man helpless before a childish disaster.

' "Looks like it," I muttered.

Jim's five unsatisfactory words are hemmed in by description, subjected to Marlow's gaze, which he returns uncomprehendingly. There are three timescales in Conrad's complex narrative: the present moment, when Marlow is speaking to his companions; the past, when Jim spoke to Marlow; and the further past of the event itself. The first is indicated by speech marks; the second is reflected in the dominant tense, the preterite ('He raised', 'he looked', 'he blurted out', 'He checked', 'he added'). The third is obscurely rendered in the pluperfect (or past perfect) tense – 'I had jumped ...'. But this pluperfect is slippery. Marlow is here quoting Jim's words at the time of his statement to Marlow, so the tense should be preterite. What did Jim do? He jumped – so, telling his story, he should say, 'I jumped'. His use of the pluperfect distances the deed, detaches Jim from the event as if it were somehow an action which predates itself. His choice of tense (itself perhaps unconscious) reflects Jim's lack of consciousness (whether real or feigned) of jumping: his only awareness is of the action having taken place. Jim relates this key moment in his life – which will affect his perception of himself, others' judgement of him, and his determination with regard to his future conduct – as if from the lifeboat. Absence of consciousness of acting necessitates absence of motive: it precludes the obvious question, 'why did you jump?' Jim is, as it were, erasing from his narrative the opportunity for the question to be asked. Is this evasion on his part, or was the jump somehow unwilled, outside his control?

The impression Conrad creates of uncertainty and vagueness about the nature of Jim's action is strengthened by his use of aposiopesis, the breaking off of a sentence or speech before it has finished. Conrad does this twice: first, in implying that something is missing after Jim has said 'I had jumped', secondly, in Marlow's observation of Jim's avoidance of eye contact ('averted his gaze ...'). Both suggest evasiveness or shame on Jim's part: a refusal to complete a sentence with some kind of explanation, and a refusal of intimacy with Marlow. Marlow first appears in the novel when Jim's eyes, at the inquiry, 'rested upon a white man who sat apart from the others' (chapter four). In the same paragraph, Conrad narrates that Jim 'met the eyes of the white man' and then 'looked at him' before turning away 'as after a final parting'.

This motif of mutual contact is picked up by Marlow in his present account of Jim: 'His clear blue eyes turned to me with a piteous stare'. Throughout the novel, Marlow repeatedly calls Jim 'one of us'. They belong to the same trade, they are fellow craftsmen bound together by the honour of service. By failing in his duty of care to his passengers, Jim has betrayed that bond. He and Marlow look at one another as equal sharers in the honour of their occupation. As a French lieutenant who had been on board a gunboat which rescued the drifting *Patna* – for the absurdity of Jim's jump from the ship is savagely pointed up by the fact that the *Patna* did not sink after all – tells Marlow, honour is what is real, and 'what life may be worth when [. . .] the honour is gone – *ah ça! par exemple* – I can offer no opinion' (chapter thirteen).

So the looks between Marlow and Jim are those not of full equality and mutual understanding. They are incomplete, like Jim's sentences. Jim's vision is obscured: he acts as if cobwebs are gathering round his face which he vainly tries to clear away. When their eyes do meet, they are generations apart: Jim is a pathetically hurt child, Marlow an old man, sadder and wiser. The weight of the dishonour reduces Marlow, too, for Jim's action affects all who profess the code. He cannot respond with any clarity, his voice reduced to a mutter; and incomplete syntax infects his subject-less ' "Looks like it" '. There is no doctor of divinity to bring Jim round after his ill-omened leap. Instead, the action carries with it its own effects. As Conrad wrote in a letter to Marguerite Poradowska in 1891, *Chaque acte de la vie est final et produit fatalement ses conséquences* ('Every act in life is final and fatally produces its consequences').[3] If there is to be redemption, then it lies solely within the culprit to achieve it. Conrad's existentialist vision is much darker than Lennox's, where enlightenment is shown to be capable of producing a happy outcome to a comic novel. However, both authors share one belief, that the nature of ethical action is the novel's true subject.

4.3 Life-changing actions (1): Henry Fielding, *Tom Jones* (1749), book nine, chapter two

Jones stood for some minutes fixed in one posture, and directing his eyes towards the south; upon which the old gentleman asked, What he was looking at with so much attention? 'Alas, sir,' answered he, with a sigh,

'I was endeavouring to trace out my own journey hither. Good heavens! what a distance is Gloucester from us! What a vast tract of land must be between me and my own home.' 'Ay, ay, young gentleman,' cries the other, 'and, by your sighing, from what you love better than your own home, or I am mistaken. I perceive now the object of your contemplation is not within your sight, and yet I fancy you have a pleasure in looking that way.' Jones answered with a smile, 'I find, old friend, you have not yet forgot the sensations of your youth. – I own my thoughts were employed as you have guessed.'

They now walked to that part of the hill which looks to the north-west, and which hangs over a vast and extensive wood. Here they were no sooner arrived, than they heard at a distance the most violent screams of a woman, proceeding from the wood below them. Jones listened a moment, and then, without saying a word to his companion (for indeed the occasion seemed sufficiently pressing) ran, or rather slid, down the hill, and without the least apprehension or concern for his own safety, made directly to the thicket whence the sound had issued.

The two paragraphs point, like the two sides of the hill, in opposite directions. Looking towards the south, Tom Jones tries to map the path that has brought him to his present position. Banished from the Somerset home of Squire Allworthy, the guardian who brought him up after finding him abandoned as a baby in his bed, and accompanied by Partridge, the village schoolmaster wrongly accused of being Tom's father, he has made his way via Gloucester to an isolated house whose owner, a retired elderly solitary called 'the Man of the Hill', he rescues from two robbers. Tom's view from the hill (though Mazard, the name Fielding gives it, is fictitious, the geographical context points to a location in the Malverns) is back to his past, the place from which he has come, but the distance is now too great for him to trace. His past is another country; his journey has brought him to the present.

Walking round the hill to the north-west, Tom has no time to linger on a prospect which is in any case obscured by an impenetrable-looking wood. As soon as he and the old man reach this spot, they hear a woman screaming. Without a word, Jones rushes down the hill towards the woman in distress.

Fielding distinguishes between the two paragraphs in ways that complement the actions involved. Looking back to the past, Tom is motionless 'for some minutes'. On the other side of the hill, seeing is replaced by listening, which lasts but 'a moment'. Dwelling on what has happened can be indulged at leisure; the necessities of the present demand immediate action. This action, however, is restricted to the young Tom; his companion is abandoned by Tom and the narrative on, we assume, the summit. As the Man of the Hill has himself discovered, a world in which people being assaulted seems to be a common occurrence calls for youthful intervention. That is no country for old men.

Time for reflection also allows for conversation. The south-facing Jones has the leisure to exclaim on how far from home he is. The Man of the Hill is able to infer from Tom's sigh that more lies in the past than just a home. Old age might bring physical limitations, but it also brings wisdom. In the concluding chapters of book eight, the Man of the Hill has given Tom and Partridge an account of his life in order to explain why he has fled from society to his isolated house. His experiences have taught him cynicism, but he can still recognize the feelings of youth. Tom's exile from home brings with it banishment from his beloved Sophia.

But the exigencies of present distress leave no time for words: actions now speak. Fielding appropriately spends few words on his account, but they are carefully chosen. Tom's precipitate response to the woman's screams is, Fielding's parenthetical observation owns, both understandable and admirable, and his selflessness bears testimony to a concern for others without thought for his own safety already displayed when rescuing the Man of the Hill. But Fielding's correction – 'ran, or rather slid' – and Tom's disappearance into a thicket in the woods strike a warning note.

Fielding's characterization of his hero as a boy and young man has shown us an attractively warm-hearted figure, loving and full of ardour. But his good qualities have their accompanying weaknesses, notably a lack of discretion and a tendency to yield to the passions of the moment. Fielding has developed his portrait of Tom alongside a contrasting depiction of Master Blifil, son of Squire Allworthy's sister, with whom Tom has been brought up. Blifil is the opposite of Tom: a model of discretion, cool and controlled where Tom is warm and impulsive. As Fielding's contrasting pair grow up, so the difference between them grows troubling and sinister ramifications. One telling crisis, carefully set out by Fielding, occurs when Allworthy is taken gravely ill. The sadness of the occasion is exacerbated by the sudden death of Mrs Blifil, news brought by her son to the doctor tending Allworthy. The doctor strongly advises that Allworthy in his present condition should not be told of his sister's death, but young Blifil insists that his uncle has firmly and repeatedly instructed him never to keep any secret from him. Blifil insists that literal obedience to his uncle's wishes should override medical advice, a resolution in which he is supported by two hypocritical members of the household, a clergyman to whom has been entrusted the education of the two boys (called, with a pre-Dickensian flourish, the reverend Mr Thwackum), and a philosopher named Square who does not allow his professed Platonism to interfere with his pursuit of carnal pleasures. Tom only hears the news when Allworthy, on his sick-bed, tells him. Tom is furious that his guardian has been exposed to such distressing news when in a weakened state, but tries to repress his anger for fear of the consequences for Allworthy of further disruption.

The irony of this earlier event is that it is the impulsive Tom who controls himself at what he regards as Blifil's 'indiscretion' (book five, chapter nine). That Allworthy has by now gathered the household around his bed to give them details of his will and has confirmed young Blifil as heir to his whole estate (except for specific sums for Tom and others) prompts a reader to further consideration of Blifil's 'indiscretion'. Happily, Allworthy recovers. Unhappily, Tom celebrates the good news by taking rather too liberally to the bottle. His 'naturally violent animal spirits' are inflamed, so that a snide remark from Blifil about Tom's parentage provokes him to grab hold of Blifil's collar, leading to a scuffle between them. Worse is to follow. Seeking to cool himself by taking a walk in the open air on what is a pleasant evening in June, Tom rhapsodizes on his love for the absent Sophia only to encounter the rather earthier but distinctly accessible figure of Molly Seagrim, with whom he retires 'into the thickest part of the grove' (book five, chapter ten).

Tom Jones is the novel that most completely and successfully draws the newly emergent form (it was published only 30 years after Defoe's *Robinson Crusoe* launched modern fiction) into the complex world of moral contingency. Some of Fielding's names for his characters ('Allworthy', for example) recall the genre of allegory, where moral absolutes and abstractions are marshalled for the purpose of clear and uncomplicated instruction, as in *The Pilgrim's Progress* (1678), John Bunyan's highly popular and influential Protestant narrative of a Christian's struggle to attain the Eternal City. But 'Tom Jones' inhabits the ordinary everyday world in which human beings are neither idealized depictions of virtue nor irredeemable villains. In his hero Fielding presents a mixed picture. Tom is not perfect, nor is he a good man with a single weakness, as tragic heroes are often defined. Tom's failings are inextricably involved with his admirable qualities. He is

angry when he hears that Allworthy's dangerous illness may have
been worsened by the injudicious decision to tell him of his sister's
death. He celebrates Allworthy's recovery with the brio of one who
truly loves him and desires his well-being. His celebrations leave him
vulnerable to understandable, but rash and unhelpful, demonstrations
of his anger. These turmoils of emotion then leave him hopelessly
defenceless when exposed to sexual temptation. His rapid yielding is
not only deplorable and inexcusable given his (warm and heartfelt,
if naïve) exclamations of love for Sophia, but entails consequences
that lead to the banishment in which we have found him in book 9.
This is not a story of good and evil. It is a narrative in which terms
such as 'discretion' and 'indiscretion', and qualities such as warmth
of character and love for one's fellow man (and woman) are subjected to the confusing realities of imperfect people put into complex
situations.

When, therefore, we read that Tom, on hearing 'the most violent
screams of a woman, proceeding from the wood below them', without a thought for his own safety 'ran, or rather slid, down the hill'
and 'made directly to the thicket whence the sound had issued', we
recognize all his admirable ardour, his commitment to active moral
intervention. But will he keep his feet on the ground, or will he fall in
ways that thick woods and women seem to invite? Tom's precipitate
readiness to rescue people in trouble reflects the same hot-blooded
thoughtlessness that leaves him distressingly open to temptation when
the rescued woman later flirtatiously signals her gratitude over dinner
at an inn.

Tom Jones is constructed on a grand scale. It is Fielding's major
example of the 'comic epic-poem in prose' defined in his preface to
Joseph Andrews (1742) as the form he was creating. But its architecture is under firm control: the first 6 of its 18 books are set in
Somerset at Allworthy's estate; books seven to twelve contain Tom's
and Sophia's adventures on the road; and the concluding books are set
in London, where Tom experiences the darkest consequences of his
actions before a comic resolution restores him to Allworthy's favour
and Sophia's fidelity. It is a novel of the country and the city, and of
the roads linking them.

Book eight, which brings the novel towards its half-way point, ends
with the Man of the Hill's interpolated autobiography in which, as in
the larger novel, London is a place of moral crisis. His story shadows
Tom's own, but his misanthropy and chilling indifference (throughout Jones's courageous rescue of the woman, he sits at its summit

'with great patience and unconcern') are challenged and countered by Tom's vital engagement in moral action. Book nine pitches Tom into its most ethically complex areas, but the youth we have met in the first half is in essence the man who is painfully obliged to mature in the second. Youth and maturity are mutually reflective: like Tom's strengths and weaknesses, two parts of the same man, two sides of the same hill.

4.4 Life-changing actions (2): Samuel Richardson, *Clarissa* (1747–48), letter 257; Charles Dickens, *Great Expectations* (1860–61), volume one, chapter eighteen

Transitions in the action of novels can be effectively brief. Samuel Richardson's *Clarissa* is a vast work in which not very much happens. As Samuel Johnson said, 'if you were to read Richardson for the story, your impatience would be so much fretted that you would hang yourself. But you must read him for the sentiment, and consider the story as only giving occasion to the sentiment.'[4] Slow-moving, reflective and meditative *Clarissa* may be, but its structure hinges on one violent action: the rape of its heroine by Robert Lovelace, a handsome nobleman who ruthlessly pursues her. Like all Richardson's novels, *Clarissa* is epistolary in form, the story being told by means of exchanges of letters between the protagonists. These letters are usually lengthy, allowing plenty of space for correspondents to provide both full accounts of events, such as conversations, and extensive commentary on them. It is not what happens, but how protagonists react to what happens, that is the heart of the matter. But when it comes to announcing the rape itself, Lovelace does so in a letter of startling brevity:

> And now, Belford, I can go no farther. The affair is over. Clarissa lives. And I am
>
> Your humble servant,
> R. LOVELACE

All the psychological pressure on Clarissa to yield to Lovelace, all her staunch defence of her autonomy and right of self-determination end in these few words. All Clarissa's trauma and her willed self-destruction lead from them; and so does Lovelace's decline towards his own form of suicide, when he allows himself to be killed in a duel. In the brevity of Lovelace's words lie failure, disillusion and finality. The act has been committed, but in such circumstances (Clarissa has to be drugged, such is her determination never to submit) and – as Lovelace seems to recognize – with such consequences that he reports with neither triumph nor satisfaction. The 'aristocratic' code he represents (he shares his name with a seventeenth-century cavalier poet), in which male aggressive sexuality is deemed becoming, attractive and victorious, is defeated at the very moment of its nominal achievement. Clarissa's tragedy is also victory for the ideals she espouses.

Other transitions are dwelt on at length, the narrator appearing unwilling to let the past go and move on to its consequences. The key event in Dickens's *Great Expectations* is the moment when the narrator, Pip (the best his 'infant tongue' could make of his full name, Philip Pirrip, and a childish diminutive which tellingly remains with him into adulthood), is informed of his unexpected change of fortune. Pip is an orphan, brought up by Joe Gargery the village blacksmith and his wife, Pip's sister (habitually referred to as 'Mrs Joe'). A London lawyer called Jaggers arrives to tell Pip that he is in receipt of 'great expectations' from an anonymous benefactor, who has also lodged a sum of money with Jaggers for Pip's education and maintenance. In order to realize his 'great expectations', Pip has to leave the forge, where he is apprenticed to Joe, and move directly to London in order to undertake an education fitting for his altered social position.

Great Expectations was serialized in weekly instalments in Dickens's journal *All the Year Round* in 1860–1, before being published in three volumes in 1861. Dickens devoted an entire instalment to this moment of transition in Pip's life. In the book form, the instalment became a whole chapter, the eighteenth and penultimate of volume one, which Dickens called the first 'stage' of Pip's expectations. The event itself is of such immense significance that a full instalment/chapter feels appropriate. But Dickens does more with his chapter than spin it out to a length reflecting its importance. He uses the breadth of canvas available to him both to create a dramatically powerful scene and to approach the real meaning of his novel.

The movement Pip makes from remote forge to big city is both geographical and social. The social gap between the two environments is figured in the chapter's opening scene, where Jaggers (called at this stage a 'strange gentleman') appears out of nowhere in the Three Jolly Bargemen. Strangers have a habit of suddenly popping up from nowhere, as in the famous opening chapter when a mud-covered convict emerges from among the graves in the churchyard where the infant Pip is shivering and beginning to cry. The scene this time is more convivial, but also has crime as a motif. A group including Joe and Pip is gathered round the fire at the inn listening to Mr Wopsle, the church clerk, give a dramatic rendition – rather as Dickens himself did at his celebrated public readings from his works – of a criminal report of a 'highly popular murder' in a newspaper. Jaggers, with 'an expression of contempt on his face', interrupts and cruelly exposes Wopsle's lack of legal understanding, slapping him down with ruthless sarcasm. Jaggers has an 'air of authority', but his manner is unnecessarily superior and arrogant. He is deliberately and decisively emphasizing division between the social classes, between an educated London professional and provincial ignorance.

Having cowed his audience, Jaggers demands to know which of the company is Joe Gargery and which is Pip. Obedience is immediate and unqualified: Jaggers 'beckoned' Joe from his place, 'and Joe went'. Pip and Joe accompany Jaggers to the forge, where the lawyer sets up the scene: he seats himself at a table, draws a candle towards him, looks at entries in his pocket-book, and then peers out into the darkness as he announces his name and mission. His manner towards Joe is brisk, condescending and dominating, as with rhetorical questions he gains from Joe his agreement to release Pip from his apprenticeship: 'You would not object to cancel his indentures at his request and for his good?' Having announced that Pip has 'great expectations' (he repeats the phrase to allow its resonance to echo through the room and the narrative), Jaggers turns from Joe to Pip: 'I address the rest of what I have to say, to you.' Joe is excluded, the past now dismissed in favour of the future.

Great Expectations is a first-person narrative. Pip is telling us his story, like Robinson Crusoe relating his adventures (see Section 2.1). Many novels are about how people grow up from childhood or adolescence to adulthood. First-person narrative is often chosen: Charlotte Brontë's *Jane Eyre* (1847) and *Villette* (1853), for example. But others, such as D. H. Lawrence's *Sons and Lovers* (1913), adopt third-person narrative, often resulting in a greater distance between reader and character. These novels, in whichever form, are generically referred to as examples of the *Bildungsroman*, a German term meaning 'formation or picture novel'.

Pip narrates from the perspective of a man who has lived through the dramatic and painful events of his young life, notably the sudden violent appearance of the convict; through the tense and bizarre experience of becoming the victim of Miss Havisham's revenge on men for having been jilted and the plaything of Estella, her principal instrument of revenge; through (looking ahead from chapter eighteen) the unexpected arrival of his benefactor when Pip is established as a man of fashion in London.

The majority of Pip's autobiography is a chronological narration in the past tense, events being described as they occurred. Despite his knowledge of all that has happened, Pip generally tells his story as it appeared to him at the time of its happening. In chapter eighteen, Pip's response to Jaggers's announcement of his 'great expectations' is: 'My dream was out; my wild fancy was surpassed by sober reality; Miss Havisham was going to make my fortune on a grand scale.' Now the mature Pip telling the story knows that the young Pip's assumption will be disproved. The first-time reader is, however, left to accept the statement at face value, while the older Pip 'keeps back facts'.[5] At one level this is simply an exercise in the novelist's arts of suspense and surprise. But Dickens translates a writer's device into the substance of his meaning: the past is unchangeable and retrievable only through hopeless regret. Past and present are separate tenses, but both present in our consciousness and conscience.

So far the chapter has been dramatic in form, presented by direct speech and striking events and gestures: the sudden appearance of the 'strange gentleman', his forensic examination of Wopsle, his demand to be introduced to Joe and Pip. Pip deepens the mystery of the gentleman by not telling us at first that he recognized him as a man he had seen at Miss Havisham's house. The drama reaches its climax with Jaggers's description of the terms of Pip's 'great expectations'. Only after these have been fully explained does Joe come back into focus, as he proudly and nobly confirms his refusal to take money in recompense for the loss of Pip's services in the forge:

> Joe laid his hand upon my shoulder with the touch of a woman. I have often thought him since, like the steam-hammer, that can crush a man or pat an egg-shell, in his combination of strength with gentleness. 'Pip is that hearty welcome,' said Joe, 'to go free with his services, to honour and fortun', as no words can tell him. But if you think as Money can make compensation to me for the loss of the little child – what come to the forge – and ever the best of friends! – '
>
> O dear good Joe, whom I was so ready to leave and so unthankful to, I see you again, with your muscular blacksmith's arm before your eyes, and your broad chest heaving, and your voice dying away. O dear

good faithful tender Joe, I feel the loving tremble of your hand upon my arm, as solemnly this day as if it had been the rustle of an angel's wing!

Pip assumes control of the story, and Dickens's prose moves from dramatic to reflective. Pip steps back to tell us that Joe has often been in his thoughts between the time of the events being described and the present, when he is writing his life-story. He describes Joe in the manner of one who has had long to reflect on his value, his combination of the muscular strength of a blacksmith and the gentleness of a sensitive man. Pip's striking mechanical simile ('like the steam-hammer') is that of an adult writer, a touch of sophistication which, by its contrast with Joe's colloquial and incomplete speech, demonstrates how far apart they now are, even as Pip celebrates Joe's proper pride (his indignant refusal of Jaggers's financial offer) and his love for, and loyalty to, Pip himself.

The second paragraph frankly owns Pip's disloyalty, his boyish lack of emotional reciprocation. This self-awareness lies firmly in the present moment, as Pip recalls Joe's physical presence: 'I see you again'. His memory of Joe picks up on his preceding description: 'Joe laid his hand upon my shoulder' becomes 'I feel the loving tremble of your hand upon my arm'. Joe's strength and gentleness evoke the adjectives 'muscular' and 'tender'. Joe's pride is figured in his 'broad chest heaving'. Pip's elevation of Joe in his emotive phrase 'the rustle of an angel's wing' derives from 'with the touch of a woman'. At this supreme moment – as the mature Pip now reveals it to have been, despite (or because of) his ignorance of it at the time – Joe transcends his sex and even his humanity. Behind this picture of Joe lies the bitter contrast of how Pip has been raised by his sister, Mrs Joe Gargery. Her proud (in a less noble sense of the word) refrain is that she has brought Pip up 'by hand'. It is on this note that she is introduced, in the opening paragraph of chapter two, where Pip sardonically observes that he knows from experience that she has 'a hard and heavy hand' and uses it liberally on her husband as well as on himself.

Dickens is beginning to suggest something vital about the novel: that its key focus will become the effect of events on the maturing Pip, and how the mature Pip looks back on the past with regret and self-reproach. These emotions accompany the distressing realization that the past is another country, lost to everything but bitter-sweet memory.

The chapter now pursues this desolate self-awareness by dramatizing Pip's irreversible separation from the life he has known with Joe and

Mrs Joe. Central at this point is another character, a girl called Biddy. When younger she taught Pip to write. She now lives in the forge as housekeeper, since Mrs Joe has been incapacitated as a result of a violent physical assault. So Biddy is a key part of Pip's past and present life.

Pip narrates the moment when Joe tells Biddy of Pip's fortune in a series of short, sharp sentences: 'Biddy dropped her work, and looked at me. Joe held his knees and looked at me. I looked at both of them.' There are no elaborate similes, not even an adjective or adverb. There are just verbs: everything is in the action. These verbs set up a parallelism, which ought to unite the trio but actually divides them as securely as the full-stops between the sentences. Dickens uses 'looking' as a motif to convey both understanding and incomprehension, the gaze that meets and the gaze that reflects ignorance. As the evening proceeds, Pip increasingly feels Joe and particularly Biddy looking at him; but he himself sits 'looking into the fire' while Joe and Biddy talk about how they will live without him. The dynamic of the relationships is moving inexorably.

Dickens's narrative separates the characters physically as the triangle of their relationship breaks apart. At the end of the day, Pip, in a prefiguring of his departure from the forge, retires to his own small room. A 'mean little room', he calls it, 'that I should soon be parted from and raised above, for ever'. These, his sentiments at the time of the action, resound significantly across the spaces of time and place: 'mean', set against his new-found wealth, 'for ever' ominous in its hollow finality. From his open window – it is a warm evening – Pip sees Joe walking outside and then Biddy bringing Joe his pipe and lighting it for him. 'He never smoked so late, and it seemed to hint to me that he wanted comforting, for some reason or other.' At the moment of the action, Pip looks, but lacks the mature knowledge of the human heart needed to understand. Joe's sensitivity we have already seen. Biddy's actions now demonstrate her equivalent understanding and sympathy. Biddy does not extract herself from human relationships by elevating men to angels: she sees in Joe a lonely man requiring homely comfort and companionship. Pip is the truly isolated figure, solitary in his callow egocentricity. The last traces of Joe, and of his own ignorance, are all that are left to him:

> Looking towards the open window, I saw light wreaths from Joe's pipe floating there, and I fancied it was like a blessing from Joe – not obtruded

on me or paraded before me, but pervading the air we shared together. I put my light out, and crept into bed; and it was an uneasy bed now, and I never slept the old sound sleep in it any more.

This, Dickens's concluding paragraph in the chapter, is the culmination of the motif of 'looking'. Pip's sentimental interpretation of Joe's pipe smoke reflects his self-centredness. He wants or needs Joe to be blessing him, whereas a sensitive response would recognize it as Joe's signal of distress. Pip's verb 'fancied' captures the dual point: at the time he imagined the smoke to be a blessing, but now he knows that this was simply self-delusion. His actions, his extinguishing of the light and creeping into bed are truer; and his resonant final clause – 'I never slept the old sound sleep in it any more' – hammers a last nail into the coffin of his past. Chapter eighteen is an extensive transition because it is one long, final farewell.

4.5 Symbolic action: D. H. Lawrence, *The Rainbow* (1915), chapter seven

Will and Anna Brangwen, the second generation in D. H. Lawrence's study of the lives of a Nottinghamshire family, are visiting Lincoln Cathedral. Will is familiar with the building and approaches it in a state of ecstasy. 'He was,' writes Lawrence, 'to pass within to the perfect womb.' For Will, the gloom and twilight of the interior is a place free from the cycle of time, lying between east and west, dawn and sunset. It holds birth and death, its hush germinating a seed whose flower 'would be radiant life inconceivable, but whose beginning and whose end were the circle of silence'. 'Before' and 'after' are 'folded together', everything that is vital being created and also contained in an ultimate 'oneness'. Entering the cathedral is for Will a way of penetrating the twilight of both darknesses, that of the womb and that of the grave. The climax of his experience centres on a Gothic arch:

Here the stone leapt up from the plain of earth, leapt up in a manifold, clustered desire each time, up, away from the horizontal earth, through twilight and dusk and the whole range of desire, through the swerving, the declination, ah, to the ecstasy, the touch, to the meeting and the consummation, the meeting, the clasp, the close embrace, the neutrality, the perfect, swooning consummation, the timeless ecstasy. There his soul remained, at the apex of the arch, clinched in the timeless ecstasy, consummated.

Lawrence's account does recognizably follow the physical contours of the architecture. From the horizontal plane of earth the stone pillars leap up vertically then swerve inwards at the formation of the arch before meeting at its apex. To this extent, the passage retains a grasp on actuality. However, we would hardly confuse Lawrence's prose with a description of a church interior in one of Nikolaus Pevsner's *Buildings of England* series: 'The nave is seven bays long plus the odd bay between the towers.... The arches have no dogtooth. The piers all have stiff-leaf capitals of Lincoln stone.'[6] The language of the architectural historian is technical, precise and clipped, not adjectives one would apply to Lawrence's writing. The salient features of his paragraph are repetition, listing of nouns and asyndeton (that is, the omission of conjunctions). The words repeated render the experience as passionate, sexual: 'desire', 'meeting', 'ecstasy' and 'consummation' occur twice in the first sentence, 'ecstasy' and 'consummated' close the second sentence, and 'timeless' bridges the two, each time qualifying 'ecstasy'. The paragraph thus ends by bringing together three key words: 'timeless ecstasy, consummated'. This insistent repetition overflows into the surrounding text. 'Consummation' recurs once in the preceding paragraph and twice in the following paragraph; 'ecstasy' and 'apex of the arch' reappear in the next paragraph. Other examples of repetition add to the effect: 'womb' is repeated three times in the preceding paragraph, following on from the earlier statement that Will's entry to the cathedral is 'to pass within to the perfect womb'. Other groups of words in the extract are semantically close: 'twilight', 'dusk' and 'neutrality'; 'the touch', 'the clasp', 'the close embrace' and 'clinched'. Listing of words and phrases adds to the impression of relentlessness, one term following another in rapid succession; while the scarcity of co-ordinating conjunctions compresses the syntax. The convergence of these stylistic features produces an effect characteristic of Lawrentian prose, a simultaneous feeling of expansiveness and contraction. Like the cathedral itself, the prose contains and reconciles extremes.

Clearly, Lawrence is not merely describing the cathedral, nor is he simply describing Will's emotions in any ordinary sense. 'Will felt very happy as his eye followed the curve of the arch to its cusp' would be a risibly weak paraphrase. Lawrence's register of language is high-pitched and impassioned, despite the word 'soul' being the subject of the second sentence. Indeed, the juxtaposition of 'soul' and sexual language is another of the extract's yokings of extremes – physical and spiritual – into one entire expression. Lawrence is straining for some expression of what Will is: not so much his 'character' as his profound essence of being. Lawrence wrote in a letter:

> You mustn't look in my novel for the old stable ego of the character. There is another ego, according to whose action the individual is unrecognisable, and passes through, as it were, allotropic states, which it needs a deeper sense than any we've been used to exercise, to discover are states of the same single radically unchanged element.[7]

He is attempting to convey not emotions, which are transient and mutable, but something deeper in people, which is their hidden substance while external physical properties vary (that is the meaning of 'allotropic'). To express this substance, Lawrence reaches for a special style, something he calls in another letter the 'exhaustive method',[8] as opposed to 'pure object and story', the method, he says, of his earlier novel *Sons and Lovers*. In the exhaustive method, objects – here the cathedral's gothic arch – cease to be separate from the person who experiences them totally, not just at a superficial level of physical contact or emotional reaction. Will's whole being is engaged in the action of merging with the architecture: his consummation is achieved as the arch attains its apex. He is the cathedral, as the cathedral is the whole of experience. Lawrence's prose, rhythmic and incantatory, strives to be appropriately all-encompassing, merging extremes as the cathedral unifies opposites (horizontal and vertical).

Lawrence's exhaustive method is, at root, an attempt to embed symbolism essentially within narrative action. At their simplest, symbols are physical objects which stand for or represent something else, usually an abstract idea. A dove iconographically represents peace. A pair of scales stands for justice, as in the statue above the Old Bailey at the London Law Courts, where a blindfolded figure holding them represents freedom from prejudice.

Literary symbols combine an image, a described object or an event with a concept, a feeling or an abstract meaning. The link between public symbols of the scales-of-justice kind and literary symbols is most evident in drama, where they can retain their primary visual presence. For example, in the play-within-the-play in *Hamlet*, the poison his brother pours into the sleeping king's ear is both agent of murder and physical manifestation of the corruption permeating the court of Elsinore. The relationship between poison and corruption, between object and concept, is that of synecdoche: poison is part of a wider evil (cf. Section 3.6).[9]

In novels, objects can similarly represent ideas. In Henry James's *The Golden Bowl* (1904), flawed relationships centre symbolically on the purchase and breaking of an imperfect gilded crystal bowl. Lawrence also highlights symbolism by the title he chooses for his novel. Both the golden bowl and the rainbow have a biblical source, an indication of the high seriousness with which James and Lawrence endow their books.[10] Rainbows make brief appearances at stages of Lawrence's novel, including a passing reference in chapter seven. The gloom of the cathedral is 'spanned round with the rainbow', echoing the previous chapter where Lawrence, in his 'exhaustive' expression of Anna's relationship with her husband and her new child, Ursula, writes of dawn and sunset as being the 'feet of the rainbow that spanned the day'. This association between Anna and rainbow develops into her ultimate refusal to be drawn in to share Will's immersion in the cathedral. Despite acknowledging its power, Anna finds its roof to be confining, restricting. A rainbow is also an arch but a rounded one, rather than the cathedral's pointed gothic arch, and one formed of light and colour, not stone. It is translucent and fleeting, not static and heavy. It recurs when elements of air and water combine to make 'great architecture of light and colour and the space of heaven', as Lawrence writes in the novel's finale where Ursula, the next generation, sees a rainbow form over the landscape. The rainbow offers a vision of something greater and freer than a gothic arch, which is limited by its own converging shape, its desire for self-fulfilment and hence sterility.

Symbolist poetry – as opposed to poetry that simply includes a number of instantly recognizable symbols – gradually evokes its meaning by accumulating associations, which emanate from the symbolic object. In the purest forms of symbolist poetry, such as we find in the work of Stéphane Mallarmé, the associations actually displace the object, so that a state of mind or feeling forms itself without distraction. The poet goes through a process of transposition, whereby the physical object initiating the symbolism is obliterated and reconstituted in terms of its associations. Parts of Lawrence's account of Will's experience in Lincoln Cathedral approximate to this process. The object – the Gothic arch – is at times replaced by terms, such as 'neutrality' and 'ecstasy', which form Lawrence's meaning: the essential state of Will himself. However, Lawrence's substituted terms often (as here) shade into abstracts. Mallarmé works primarily through the concrete. His phrase 'le noir roc courroucé' ('the black rock angered') displaces the original image to which it is visually linked (a dark cloud) but retains a physical strength to act as a centre for the associations he accumulates around it: the solidity of a tombstone and the indelible quality of the man it and the poem commemorate (the poet Verlaine).[11]

Novelists can also follow a symbolist path without committing themselves to the simple and obvious equivalence of object and meaning, while at the same time avoiding abstracts with their potential for vagueness and uncertainty. Novelists deal in narrative, so that the object itself – the action, the event – is not displaced, even when diffracted through a stream of consciousness method (see Section 5.7). Rather, the meaning or emotion is integrated with the object: concept and image do not exist in separate spheres like the terms of an equation, but fuse into simultaneous expression. Actions remain real in themselves but, by the manner in which they are narrated, carry wider or more general significance.

When we looked at a passage from Thomas Hardy's *The Woodlanders* (Section 2.3), we saw how an episode in which Giles Winterborne, the novel's tragic hero, and Marty South plant saplings is used by the novelist to provide readers with insight into the characters of his protagonists. Giles's natural sympathy with, and understanding of, the young trees express his rapport with the natural world; while his neglect of his companion demonstrates the hopelessness of the young and vulnerable Marty's love for him. The saplings are, then, symbolic of the sphere of which they are a fragile part: a synecdoche, again. But, at a wider level, the whole event is reflective of a world in which human relationships are often thwarted by chance, by unforeseen consequences or by human blindness. Giles, having been promised the hand of Grace Melbury in an arrangement made by their fathers, is emotionally fixed on a course which diverts him from recognizing other people's emotions – despite their proximity to him – and draws him into a set of human interrelationships culturally and socially foreign to him. The potential for mutual understanding evident but frustrated in the planting scene continues to be thwarted until the novel's bleak conclusion, where Marty and Giles can only be 'together' when Giles is dead and so irreversibly blind to her devotion. Hardy makes no explicit point during the planting scene, but narrates it discreetly, allowing its significance to rest within the scene and echo quietly beyond, into the fabric of the whole novel.

Lawrence's account of Will Brangwen's response to the architecture of Lincoln Cathedral can hardly be described as discreet. His strongly rhythmic prose style imbues it with an emphatic and rhetorical energy which is insistent and, for some readers, quite overpowering. That is the very symbolic point. Will's experience overwhelms him, removes him from the area of common human feeling and hurls him into something deeper than 'character' and emotion, something elemental and expressive of the core of his being. Its sheer intensity is almost frightening, a pitch of experience reached by several Lawrence characters at times. It cannot last: Will's moment of ecstasy in the cathedral is broken by Anna's recalcitrance, and he never again attains such a vision. How can we live intensely and at the same time remain in ordinary human society? Lawrence's symbolic prose reflects and embodies his recurrent, pressing concern.

4.6 Coming up for air (1): George Orwell, *Coming up for Air* (1939), part two, chapter three

Symbolic actions in novels range from the obvious or intrusive to the subtle or integrated (see Section 4.5). Readers vary in the degree to which they can tolerate the more palpable forms. The intense urgency with which Lawrence presses his symbolism is for some a sign of his passionate commitment. Living is an act of such vibrant significance that the genteel laws of literary decorum should not be allowed to interfere by lessening the ardour of his vision. For others, Lawrence's 'exhaustive' writing confuses effective communication with straining for effect.

That events in novels may be entirely embedded within a realistic narrative and, at the same time, take on symbolic significance is perfectly understandable. This is especially so when those actions are viewed retrospectively. We do, after all, often look back on experiences we have had or events we have wholly or partly caused and find in them a significance which has strongly influenced our thinking about who we are and what we stand for. Perhaps this is why retrospective narrative is so common, whether in the form of occasional analepsis (flashback) or full-scale fictional autobiography.

George Bowling, the narrator of Orwell's *Coming up for Air*, is middle-aged (he is 45) and rather overweight ('fatty' is his nickname). He lives in a suburban house identical to all the other semi-detached houses in his long, faceless street. He works as an insurance salesman, earning about what his neighbours earn. He is in a joyless marriage with Hilda, and has two kids. He has forgotten what it is to do more than merely exist. His most intense memories of a time when he was not just alive, but living, are of going fishing as a boy in the country around the family home at Lower Binfield, in Oxfordshire:

> But the next moment there wasn't any doubt about it. The float dived straight down, I could still see it under the water, kind of dim red, and I felt the rod tighten in my hand. Christ, that feeling! The line jerking and straining and a fish on the other end of it! The others saw my rod bending, and the next moment they'd all flung their rods down and rushed round to me. I gave a terrific haul and the fish – a great huge silvery fish – came flying up through the air. The same moment all of us gave a yell of agony. The fish had slipped off the hook and fallen into the wild peppermint under the bank. But he'd fallen into shallow water where he couldn't turn over, and for perhaps a second he lay there on his side helpless. Joe flung himself into the water, splashing us all over, and grabbed him in both hands. 'I got 'im!' he yelled. The next moment he'd flung the fish on to the grass and we were all kneeling round it. How we gloated! The poor dying brute flapped up and down and his scales glistened all the colours of the rainbow. It was a huge carp, seven inches long at least, and must have weighed a quarter of a pound. How we shouted to see him! But the next moment it was as though a shadow had fallen across us. We looked up, and there was old Brewer standing over us, with his tall billycock hat – one of those hats they used to wear that were a cross between a top-hat and a bowler – and his cowhide gaiters and a thick hazel stick in his hand.

The style of this could hardly be more different from that of the extract from *The Rainbow* we looked at (Section 4.5). Orwell, through George Bowling, writes in a direct, immediate and concrete manner. Orwell's choice of both language and syntax creates these effects, together with his avoidance of any elaborate or literary devices. With two short and uncomplicated exceptions ('where he couldn't turn over', 'as though a shadow had fallen across us'), the sentences consist either of single clauses (twice contracted into a verb-less exclamation: 'Christ, that feeling!') or of two or three co-ordinated clauses linked by the simplest of all conjunctions, 'and'. There are 11 such uses of 'and'. Together with six uses of 'and' to link nouns, adverbs or participles ('a cross between a top-hat and a bowler'; 'up and down'; 'jerking and straining'), the result is a passage always about what happened next, with no time lost in extraneous explanation or reflection. Orwell employs the conjunction 'but' three times, on each occasion at the beginning of a sentence, a usage which might not please some purists but does further simplify the sentences. The only word used more frequently than 'and' is the simple definite article, which occurs 23 times.

'The' is linked five times to the word 'moment': 'the next moment' four times, 'the same moment' once. We move rapidly from one brief moment to the next. The passage is looking back to George's past, but its momentum is strongly forwards as the excitement carries the boys with it.

'The' and 'and' are both, of course, monosyllables, and the entire passage avoids unnecessary polysyllabic words. Particularly strong are monosyllabic verbs: 'felt', 'saw', 'gave' and so on. These verbs frequently convey direct sensory experience: 'felt', 'saw', 'grabbed' and so on. They are all active verbs, so that 'what happened' always relates immediately to the agent of the action: I, we, Joe, they, the fish.

Other linguistic forms are kept simple. There are relatively few adjectives, and these are mostly precise and unelaborated: 'red', 'huge', 'tall', 'thick'. Abbreviated forms convey a restrained level of colloquialism consistent with a speaking voice: 'wasn't', 'he'd', 'couldn't'. Orwell avoids abstract and even metaphorical language, which would have detached the passage from the concrete immediacy of objects. George's description of the carp's scales as glistening 'all the colours of the rainbow' is the closest he comes to writing of an object in terms of something else, and the phrase simply evokes a familiarly colourful scene to convey the fish's variegated colouring. There are no biblical or symbolic resonances about this rainbow. Joyously tactile experience is celebrated with youthful enthusiasm, and rendered with direct simplicity.

Orwell is, like any good writer, using language appropriate for the nature and context of the event he is narrating. This is the young boy's first experience of real fishing, an activity which George tells us earlier had always attracted him: 'the thought of fishing sent me wild with excitement'. He captures youthful desire for action and adventure by writing about it in terms of sensory pleasure, and youthful naivety by the comic disparity between the size of the fish – 'seven inches long at least' – and childish hyperbole – 'a great huge silvery fish', 'a huge carp'. This is how a boy would feel about it, and how an older man – one with enough understanding and ability – would attempt to convey the rush of childhood experience. George Bowling is both an eight-year-old boy on his first independent escapade, with no adults but only older lads for company, and a mature man thinking back and releasing his young, vital self. Inside the fat middle-aged man lurks his inner boy.

But we know that another George, Orwell himself, felt very strongly about maintaining clarity in all use of English. In his essay 'Politics and the English Language', published in the magazine *Horizon* in

April 1946, he highlighted a number of bad habits into which, he thought, contemporary writing had fallen. Among these he mentioned the use of phrasal verbs instead of simple verbs ('render inoperative' for 'break'); of the passive voice in preference to the active; of phrases such as 'with respect to' instead of simple conjunctions and prepositions; and of pretentious and inflated language. Such abuses, Orwell argued, not only made writing uglier, but also obscured meaning and corrupted thought.

The power of language to misrepresent truth is relentlessly displayed in Orwell's famous dystopian novel, *Nineteen Eighty-Four* (1949). Winston Smith works in the Ministry of Truth, where he rewrites past newspaper articles to fit current party propaganda, and is tortured into confessing his dissident activities in a building which houses the Ministry of Love. The prime function of the political system portrayed so chillingly in *Nineteen Eighty-Four* is to subjugate personal will to authoritarian control. By distorting language to serve its ends, the party suppresses any capacity for individual expression and thought. This is why Winston's act of writing down his real feelings about the political state cannot be tolerated. Nor can his relationship with his lover Julia be allowed to continue. Their love is an expression of authentic feeling, of emotional and tactile engagement. To love and make love to another human being accord individual experience a value above the collective will of the system. The ultimate defeat of Winston is that he is tortured and brainwashed into loving not a real woman but the fabricated image of 'Big Brother'.

Our extract from *Coming up for Air* is about authentic, sensuous experience. George realizes he has caught a fish when the float dives down beneath the surface and 'I felt the rod tighten in my hand'. His elliptical exclamation 'Christ, that feeling!' repeats the keynote word, which resonates before and after the event itself. His older brother, Joe, has excited his interest by telling him 'how your float gives a bob and plunges under and you feel the rod bending and the fish tugging at the line'. Now George is feeling all this for himself. This memory has never left him. It's strange, he muses, 'the feeling I had for fishing – and still have, really'. It's not something you can 'explain' or 'rationalize', he writes. The experience is not to be rendered into abstract terms, to be coated with the gloss of fake philosophy. That would, at best, neutralize the experience itself, and, at worst, distort and destroy it. It would convert Julia into Big Brother. Orwell's account conveys immediacy of direct action through simple, active verbs. He does not convert feeling into abstractions, elevate it metaphorically into the spiritual, or enhance it with Latinate language and complex syntax. He keeps it at the level of solid reality which George finds reassuringly actual in the names of English coarse fish: roach, rudd, dace, bleak, barbell, bream, gudgeon, pike, chub, carp, tench. These words are largely monosyllabic, and begin and end with strong consonants. As George says, they are 'solid kind of names'.

Orwell narrates the event with such uncompromising directness that he does not permit his narrator to succumb to nostalgic sentimentality. George recalls the event with pleasure and excitement, but does not shrink from its cruelty. 'The poor dying brute' is the mature man's phrase, not that of an eight-year-old. His, too, is the open acknowledgement of the children's insensitivity: 'How we gloated!' 'How we shouted to see him!' The boys' exultation in capture and destruction of the carp has something barbarous and primitive about it. The fish is hauled up into the air to die. The incident is about breathing the air of active living; but it is also about children behaving as, in George's later words, 'savage little animals, except that no animal is a quarter as selfish'.

Another shadow falls across the childhood scene, that of 'old Brewer'. The adult world in the form of an authority figure looms over the boys, ending their idyllic adventure. The last sentence of the paragraph is by a considerable distance its longest: it stretches out, extinguishing joy as Brewer's distinctive, a touch comical, appearance defines his difference from youthful spontaneity. In his hand is not a fishing-rod but a threatening hazel stick (with which he will manage to land some 'good swipes' before the boys escape).

George Bowling in the next chapter explicates what he feels his childhood and, specifically, fishing represent. For him, they mean the civilization in which he grew up and which he thinks is now close to its end. Sitting beside a quiet pool belongs to another age, one 'before the war, before the radio, before aeroplanes, before Hitler'. *Coming up for Air* is imbued with fatalism, a feeling that everything is changing for the worse. When, in the second half of the novel, George decides to take a visit back to Lower Binfield, he finds that his pool and what it means have gone. Like the fish, he comes up for air but encounters only his own mortality.

The fishing scene is thus, in terms of how it ripples out into the whole novel, considerably more than an exercise in nostalgia. Looking back on it, George Bowling certainly recalls a boyhood of instinctive joy, of 'glad animal movements'.[12] But George Orwell is the last writer to allow his hero to become sentimental. Those glad animal movements found their outlet in acts of savagery, and fishing-rods were weapons of destruction for the poor fish. Lower Binfield was a pre-war, pre-adult world, but it contained the elements of a later and more starkly destructive society. The scene represents something ominous about human instinct as well as the passing of time. Nonetheless, the event itself is narrated in a way that is equally uncompromising in its depiction of vital, sensory experience. It demonstrates Orwell's commitment to the significance – however complicated – of the object itself, of actions which demonstrate that human beings live in a tactile world. As George Bowling says when reflecting on the day's adventure, no matter how much punishment he took for it and how much the other boys might have lied about it afterwards, he had 'felt the fish tugging at the line' and 'they couldn't take that away from me'.

4.7 Coming up for air (2): William Golding, *The Spire* (1964), chapter six

Dean Jocelin has had a vision: he has been called on to build a spire on the tower of his cathedral. Others call it Jocelin's Folly. His master builder, the aptly named Roger Mason, tries to dissuade him at each stage of the spire's construction from continuing further. The cathedral – clearly based on Salisbury – was built on next-to-non-existent foundations, and the pressure of the spire's additional weight is dangerously close to destroying the whole building. Jocelin, however, remains committed to his faith in the project, despite all practical objections and the severe human cost incurred as both clergy and artisans come under their own strain, physical and emotional. As the building work slowly and painfully proceeds, Jocelin climbs up to the summit on a cold and foggy December day:

> On such a day, he passed through the close from the deanery to the west door, hardly able to see his feet for fog; and though the nave was clear of it, like a sort of bubble, it was near enough pitch dark. He climbed, and came out of the corkscrew stair on to the beams, and in a blinding dazzle. For up here, the sun was shining; and even those rays that pierced the chamber were faint against another light that blazed upwards, lit lead and glass and stone, lit the underside of the beam roof, so that the very adze marks were visible. Then when he climbed through this dazzle to the upper chamber, up the ladders and levels to where men were working with blue hands and came at last on the ragged top – then he was pained and blinded indeed, and had to press his palms to his eyes. For there was downland visible all round but nothing else. The fog lay in a dazzling,

burning patch over the valley and the city, with nothing but the spire or
the tower at least, piercing it. Then he was strangely comforted, and for
a time, almost at peace.

The paragraph follows the contours of Jocelin's ascent. In the first sentence Jocelin is at ground level, walking from his deanery to the nave
from which the tower and spire rise. The second sentence narrates
his climb to the first level of the constructions, where the paragraph
pauses before (at Golding's repetition of 'he climbed') the fourth
sentence takes Jocelin to the upper chamber where building work is
currently going on.

At each stage, the paragraph describes the light. At ground level
everything is obscured: outside by fog, inside the cathedral by darkness. The two levels of Jocelin's ascent bring him out of darkness
and into increasingly bright light, first as reflected from beneath and
shining on the underside of the roof, then the full refulgence of the
sun above the fog. His trajectory is through darkness to light, the
journey of theological and secular comedy, of Dante's *Divine Comedy* (*Inferno, Purgatorio, Paradiso*), Mozart's *The Magic Flute*, and
Fielding's *Tom Jones*.

William Golding's vision, however, resists such a simple and
straightforward description. He achieved public recognition with his
first novel, *Lord of the Flies* (1954), which remains his best-known
work. In it, a group of boys are marooned on an island in the best
traditions of adventure stories. The boys organize themselves into
a miniature society for the common good, their survival and prosperity. They are, after all, British, and so the products of a mature
civilization and a well-established education system. Unfortunately,
dissension and then violence break up the concord, with the result that
order collapses and something appallingly like evil takes over. Onto
the comic pattern of a belief in the innate goodness of human beings
which will resolve difficulties and end in harmony, Golding places a
counter-pattern that reverses the process. When, at the end of *Lord of
the Flies*, the adult world arrives in the form of a rescuing white-suited
naval officer, the little boys who have turned into manifestations of
darkness suddenly revert to being just little boys. The two patterns
converge painfully and uncomfortably.

So, in our extract from *The Spire*, Golding counterpoints one
structure – that of ascent, of coming up for air and light – with
another. He does this by weaving into the fabric of his prose an alternative thread. When Jocelin attains the first stage of his climb, he

has risen from the floor of the cathedral where it is 'near enough pitch dark' to a place where 'the sun was shining'. But his initial experience when he emerges from the stair is of 'a blinding dazzle'. The light, suddenly encountered, is so strong that its effect is to make him blind. This phrase, 'blinding dazzle', resounds through the paragraph. The reflected light that has such a powerful effect 'blazed' upwards, the word combining the consonantal opening of 'blinding' with a lengthened version of the vowel and following consonant in 'dazzle'. Tellingly, the sun is not the sole source of this intense light. 'The sun was shining' is innocuous and pleasant enough; but, when reflected off the cathedral's lead, glass and stone, it is transformed. A human construction converts benign sunlight into blinding fire.

Jocelin's ascent to the upper chamber is through this 'dazzle' (the word is simply repeated) and up ladders and platforms, the means by which men are enabled to build the spire. At this level Jocelin is 'pained and blinded indeed'. The present participle 'blinding', used adjectivally, turns into its past participle: process becomes the completion of that process, intensified by 'pained' and 'indeed'. The fog, through which the mounting spire and Jocelin have pierced and which obscures the city below, lies 'dazzling, burning', the third use of 'dazzle' now juxtaposed with the metaphorical fire encountered in 'blazed'. At the foot of the cathedral fog covers the land so that it cannot be seen; at this temporary summit, fog still obscures the city in which the cathedral has its roots. Jocelin has risen from darkness to light, but a light whose intensity is painful and forces him to press his hands to his eyes in a gesture of blindness.

How, in view of these paradoxes, do we read the final sentence of the paragraph? It conveys, clearly, a sense of serenity attained: it closes on the word 'peace'. The pain Jocelin experiences is, after all, temporary. His eyes will become accustomed to the light. Indeed, this sentence's quietness suggests that they already have. But there is the oddity of the adverb 'strangely', which Golding does not explain. What is 'strange' about Jocelin's state? And 'at peace' is qualified by 'almost', and is itself, it seems, temporary: 'for a time'. The sentence manages to be simultaneously restful and uneasy.

In its fusion of aspiration and painful experience, the paragraph acts as a microcosm of the whole novel. Jocelin suffers from a recurrent pain in his back. He interprets this as an angel punishing him or, when it relents, comforting him; but it is actually a wasting disease of the spine which will kill him. Agony, felt temporarily in blinding light, accompanies Jocelin's body remorselessly and finally. Is it, then, mere delusion to represent a physical illness in spiritual terms? Can attempts to rise to ethereal heights shake off the infirmities and pains of the body? 'No man', thinks Jocelin, 'can live his life with eagles', and, in a prayer on the spire's platform, he acknowledges that 'I bring my essential wickedness even here into thy air' (chapter five). The mentally painful recognition forced on Jocelin, as he pursues his ambition with a single-mindedness all the greater the more isolated he becomes in his belief that the spire will stand, is that all aspiration to good is ineluctably entwined with, and founded upon, corruption and evil.

The cathedral itself is evidence of this paradox. When the earth beneath it opens, its foundations are revealed to be not solid stone but rotting corpses. As the spire grows, Jocelin's vision of its erection becomes shamefully entangled in his half-recognized obsession with the red-haired Goody Pangall, wife of a cathedral servant. Worst of all, Jocelin uses his discovery that Roger Mason is having an affair with Goody to exercise control over him, and force him to stay and continue to build the spire even after all the evidence indicates that they have reached the highest point at which the building's weak foundations can possibly stand the pressure. Jocelin succumbs to the temptation to use sin and human weakness to ensure the creation of what he believes to be for the good. Can you not recognize a miracle all about you, Jocelin demands of Roger: 'Can't you feel it? Can't you get strength from it, learn from it, see how it changes everything?' It has changed things all right, replies a bitter Mason, 'can't you see what you've done?' (chapter five).

Jocelin cannot see: he is 'pained and blinded indeed'. The light that dazzles him is also the source of his 'burning', a vision of something infinite but mediated through, reflected by, corrupt humanity. And yet the spire stands and Jocelin is 'almost at peace'; as he will finally be at the end of the novel when his pain, accompanied by nightmarish visions, has killed him. And yet the spire stands.

4.8   The significance of actions: Penelope Fitzgerald, *The Blue Flower* (1995), chapter thirteen

Most writers give prominence to significant actions by dwelling on them, highlighting them and writing them up. For others, transitory events eventually or retrospectively achieve significance.

Penelope Fitzgerald's *The Blue Flower* tells the story of Friedrich von Hardenberg, known as Fritz, and Sophie von Kühn, whom he meets when she is 12 years old and with whom he instantly falls in love. These are historical figures. Fritz will become famous, after the events of the novel, as the German romantic poet Novalis. His gold ring bearing the inscription 'Sophie be my Guardian Spirit' survives in the Municipal Museum at Weissenfels. His *Hymnen an die Nacht* (Hymns to the Night) are high points in European Romanticism, passionate and ecstatic prose poems entwining life and death, light and dark, as twin spirits and principles of human existence. In the course of Fitzgerald's novel, Fritz twice reads aloud the beginning of a story he is writing about a young man lying in bed at night, remembering a stranger who told tales of a blue flower. Novalis left unfinished at his death in 1801 a fragment of a novel, *Heinrich von Ofterdingen*, in which the young Heinrich is absorbed by his vision of blue flowers as emblems of metaphysical striving for the infinite. The historical Sophie died two days after her fifteenth birthday. *The Blue Flower* concludes with Sophie half awake on her death-bed after a long agonizing illness and with Fritz arriving home after his final departure from her house.

Fritz meets Sophie in the course of his work with Kreisamtmann Coelestin Just, a magistrate and area tax collector, to whom his father sends him to learn administration and office management. Fitzgerald presents Fritz's arrival at the Just household largely through speech, as she does much of the novel's action:

> Once in the parlour, he looked round him as though at a revelation. 'It is beautiful, beautiful.'
>
> 'It's not beautiful at all,' said Rahel. 'You are more than welcome here, I hope that you will learn a great deal and you are free, of course, to form whatever opinions you like, but this parlour is not beautiful.'
>
> Fritz continued to gaze around him.
>
> 'This is my niece by marriage, Karoline Just.'
>
> Karoline was wearing her shawl and housekeeping apron.
>
> 'You are beautiful, gracious Fräulein,' said Fritz.
>
> 'We expected you yesterday,' said Rahel, dryly, 'but you see, we are patient people.' When Karoline had gone out, as she very soon did, to the kitchen, she added, 'I am going to take the privilege of someone who met you so often when you were a student, and welcomed you, you remember, to our Shakespeare evenings, and tell you that you ought not to speak to Karoline quite like that. You did not mean it, and she is not used to it.'

'But I did mean it,' said Fritz. 'When I came into your home, every-thing, the wine-decanter, the tea, the sugar, the chairs, the dark green tablecloth with its abundant fringe, everything was illuminated.'

'They are as usual. I did not buy this furniture myself, but –'

Fritz tried to explain that he had seen not their everyday, but their spiritual selves. He could not tell when these transfigurations would come to him. When the moment came it was as the whole world would be when body at last became subservient to soul.

The setting is a very ordinary parlour with common trappings detailed with economical precision: table, chairs, fringed tablecloth, tea, sugar, wine-decanter. We have walked into the living quarters of myriad north-European paintings of domestic interiors, whose dull plainness is echoed in Fitzgerald's avoidance of elaborate detail and colour: even the green of the tablecloth is suppressed by 'dark'. But Fritz has apparently entered a place of light and beauty, the common world translated into a visionary gleam. Explicitly religious language both introduces the scene ('revelation') and runs through Fritz's attempted explanation of his exalted response ('spiritual', 'transfigurations', 'soul'). For the Romantic poet, such visions simply come upon him unbidden, unannounced and unexpected. There is no apparent cause, nothing that justifies or explains. Explanations belong to the mechanical world of tax collection and office management. Poets, when they experience what Friedrich's English contemporary Wordsworth called 'spots of time',[13] enter a noumenal sphere tangential to, but rising above, quotidian normality. The next time Fritz has such an experience, it is of Sophie looking out of a window. This moment in the Justs' parlour is a prefiguration of the supreme moment, which changes Fritz's life for ever.

But we are not all Romantic poets. Fitzgerald counterpoints her idealistic young poet with the very different attitude of his hostess. Rahel is Coelestin Just's second wife and widow of a professor at the university where Fritz has been schooled in the kind of German idealist philosophy that sits uneasily alongside the practical necessities of making a living. Fritz's father is hoping that his time at the Justs' will bring him down to earth; his receptivity of transformative visions suggests that Fritz will prove a reluctant apprentice. Frau Rahel, despite her former life as a professor's wife and hostess of Shakespeare evenings (Shakespeare was German Romanticism's favourite foreign writer) at Wittenberg (Hamlet's university, too), takes a starkly down-to-earth view of her room. Her response to

Fritz's ecstatic 'It is beautiful, beautiful' is to knock his repetition back at him, qualified by equally emphatic negatives ('It's not beautiful at all'; 'this parlour is not beautiful') and separated by a distinctly sardonic welcome and invitation to exercise his freedom of judgement. Frau Rahel has encountered Fritz 'so often when you were a student': a wealth of meaning lies in that guarded but weary 'so often'. She has seen not just his type, but himself, before.

The scene encapsulates the novel's central conflict. Life in the dreary normality of its various domestic interiors is about the need and the will to survive. Disease and untrustworthy medical practice stand ready to strike, as poor Sophie discovers most painfully. Alongside, in the lives of the professors Schlegel and Fichte and their precocious students, thought dominates, with its airy agreeable notions such as that all nature is one and indivisible. When those worlds intersect, the results are frequently comic.

However, these intersections have their victims too, as agonizingly felt in their way as by those enduring operations without anaesthetic. Speech has the power to cut, and idealism has the potential to wound. It is only a moment in time, a brief few words and a short exit. The key event in the current scene passes by so quickly that we may miss it. Fritz certainly does. So overcome is he by the radiant illumination, which elevates Frau Rahel's parlour and everything it contains to the heights of visionary idealism, that he cannot see the obvious. Karoline Just, Coelestin's niece, has been his housekeeper for four years. She is 27 and unmarried. Her working clothes ('her housekeeping apron') are just other ordinary objects transfigured by Fritz into their spiritual selves: 'You are beautiful, gracious Fräulein'. Her rapid departure is scarcely noted. Even the narrative reports it after the event: 'When Karoline had gone out'. Rahel tells Fritz that he ought not to speak to Karoline as he did because she (unlike Rahel who knows all about students of idealist philosophy) is 'not used to it' and will therefore not be able to see through it as unsentimentally as Rahel does. It is telling that, in his list of the items in the room 'illuminated' by transfiguration, Karoline, her shawl and apron do not signify. She has passed out of his mind as rapidly and quietly as she left the room.

5

Speaking

5.1 Direct speech: Frances Burney, *Cecilia* (1782), book two, chapter six

Guardians in literature are a mixed bunch, offering mixed blessings. The heroine of Frances Burney's second novel, *Cecilia*, is the lucky ward of not one but three guardians. All three live in London, though at very different, but equally suggestive, addresses. Mr Harrel lives in Portman Square, a new and fashionable development in the west end, built between 1764 and the 1780s. He enjoys an accordingly modish and expensive lifestyle, but one that is paper-thin, incurring continual debt. Mr Briggs lives in the city of London. He is the opposite of Mr Harrel: an eccentric curmudgeon and source of much of the novel's humour. Being shuffled between these two is disconcerting enough for a young woman, but worse follows. In our example, Cecilia is admonished by her third guardian, Mr Delvile, who boasts an aristocratic house in St James's Square by St James's Palace. To accompany this elevated address, Delvile evinces a belief in the traditional appurtenances of high social status: family, a treasured name and frigidly decorous manners. Such manners are reflected in the way he speaks to Cecilia:

'I have received information, from authority which I cannot doubt, that the indiscretion of certain of your admirers last Saturday at the Opera-house, occasioned a disturbance which to a young woman of delicacy I should imagine must be very alarming: now as I consider myself concerned in your fame and welfare from regarding you as my ward, I think it is incumbent upon me to make enquiries into such of your affairs as become public; for I should feel in some measure disgraced myself,

should it appear to the world, while you are under my guardianship, that
there was any want of propriety in the direction of your conduct.'

Delvile here raises with Cecilia the behaviour of 'certain' of her
admirers – she clearly has many – in the public space of Covent Garden opera house, a place of fashionable resort and social, as well as
cultural, pleasures. However, the 'indiscretion' of Cecilia's male companions is not his chief concern. His speech modulates from their
unspecified behaviour to the nature of her 'conduct' (the final word
in the paragraph). As befits a man of breeding, Mr Delvile is not
so indelicate as to cast any direct aspersion on his ward. His modus
operandi is much more serpentine, but its purpose in its way is clear
enough. The phrase, 'a young woman of delicacy', is carefully placed
and measured: it implies 'and you, of course, are a young woman
of delicacy, as who would not wish to be, or at any rate to be so
esteemed'. It therefore follows, does it not, that the 'disturbance' –
again unspecified – occasioned by the event must be of considerable
concern to her: 'alarming', indeed, is Delvile's strong word. And why
should the behaviour of others be of such concern to Cecilia? The
answer is that it might indicate, or be seen as deriving from, some
'want of propriety' in her 'conduct'. Thus Delvile reveals the basis of
his view (or perhaps his society's view, which he endorses or accepts)
of public impropriety. It is, of course, the woman who is to be blamed,
or, at least, who exposes herself to censure.

   However, we have not quite reached the heart of Delvile's ethical
position. He tells Cecilia that he is 'concerned in your fame and welfare', a statement which appears unexceptionable until one notices the
preposition. Prepositions and verbal forms with prepositions are, as
most foreign learners of English will painfully admit, the most slippery
and ambiguous of grammatical structures. The passive construction of
the verb 'concern' has a range of meanings: to be interested, to care, to
be troubled, to have a part, to be implicated, to be involved. The relevant meaning will be indicated partly by the context, but mostly by
the preposition that follows. One can be concerned 'about', 'for', 'in',
'with', and each changes the meaning of the verb. In Delvile's case,
there is a difference between being concerned 'in' Cecilia's 'fame' and
being concerned 'for' Cecilia's welfare. Whereas the latter would indicate care for his ward's well-being, the former suggests that he feels
implicated in her reputation.

   Prepositions slide around in usage and over time, and Delvile's col-
location of 'fame' and 'welfare' is an additional complicating factor.

However, the later part of his speech makes his drift clear. His concern is that any perceived impropriety in his ward's behaviour will reflect adversely on him. It is not her possible disgrace, but his, that is of significance. Nothing must be allowed to harm his status. The linguistic marker of Delvile's egocentricity is the prominence in his speech of the first-person pronoun. This short extract contains no fewer than 11 uses of its various forms: six 'I's, two 'my's, one 'me' and two 'myself's.

Delvile's speech also has a stiff formality, as reflected in its circumlocution and choice of elevated register. He tells Cecilia that he has 'received information', not that he has learnt or heard. The event in question 'occasioned a disturbance'. He thinks 'it is incumbent upon me', not that he should or ought to. He addresses Cecilia as if she were a public meeting rather than a young woman. His language distances him from his ward, asserting his authority and superiority over her. It is the language of control, not the language of intimacy. Cecilia will find here no friendliness or genuine concern for her well-being.

It is perfectly possible to combine decorum and deference. Burney demonstrates this at once and, at the same time, points ahead to plot developments by introducing to the scene Delvile's son, Mortimer, who has previously encountered Cecilia at a masked ball:

> 'Mortimer,' said Mr Delvile, 'I understand you have already had the pleasure of seeing this young lady?'
> 'Yes, Sir,' he answered, 'I have more than once had that happiness, but I have never had the honour of being introduced to her.'

Mortimer's response is politely formal but concise, and he subordinates himself to his new acquaintance, according precedence to her. Whereas his father's speech dominates and subdues, Mortimer's is respectful and open. Through these distinctions in the use of speech, Burney delineates not merely tension between father and son but an active shift in attitudes to the furtherance of social relationships.

Connection between speech, manners and respect for other people lies at the heart of the social dramas presented in Burney's novels, and in those of her admirer, Jane Austen (and then of those novelists who followed her). Austen frequently makes abuse of language a source of comedy. Here, for example, Mrs Elton, the snobbish *arriviste* in the social world of *Emma*, magnificently converts a ball for Mr Weston's son Frank Churchill into a reception in her honour:

> 'Nobody can think less of dress in general than I do – but upon such an occasion as this, when everybody's eyes are so much upon me, and in compliment to the Westons – who I have no doubt are giving this ball

chiefly to do me honour – I would not wish to be inferior to others. And I see very few pearls in the room except mine.'

(Volume three, chapter two)

Mrs Elton appears determined to outdo her predecessors in ego-centricity, her speech spiralling into a celebration of her own status. The words 'I', 'me' and 'mine' run glistening through her language like pearls on a necklace, equally enriching and setting off their owner.

Direct speech is the unmediated presentation of the words spoken (or thought) by a person. In most novels, direct speech operates by a convention which allows a person's actual words to be set out in grammatically formed and complete sentences. In reality, most of us speak in less assured and more hesitating structures. Disparity between speech in a novel and a more likely version of it seldom distracts a reader. We all understand the convention, and, in any case, it is easy to imagine that many characters are indeed well able to speak in thought-out sentences – including the formal Mr Delvile and Mrs Elton, who, one suspects, has rehearsed her speech carefully. Direct speech is a powerful means of portraying the character of the speaker. People reveal themselves through their actions, as in the case of Jim's leap from the ship he thinks is sinking (see Section 4.2); but novelists such as Burney and Austen show that how we speak can be just as cogent an indication of who we are and how we view our relationships with other people.

5.2 Dialogue: Samuel Richardson, *Sir Charles Grandison* (1753–4), volume one, letter seventeen; Henry Green, *Nothing* (1950)

In this scene from *Sir Charles Grandison*, Harriet Byron rejects the unwanted addresses of Sir Hargrave Pollexfen:

I told you, Sir, that you must not expect anything from me but the simplest truth. You do me an honour in your good opinion; and if my own
heart were not, in this case, a very determined one, I would answer
you with more politeness. But, Sir, on such an occasion as this, I think
it would not be honourable, it would not be just, to keep a man in an
hour's suspense, when I am in none myself.
And are you then (angrily) so determined, Miss Byron?
I am, Sir.
Confound me! – And yet I am enough confounded! – But I will not take
an answer so contrary to my hopes. Tell me, madam, by the sincerity

which you boast; Are you not engaged in your affections? Is there not
some one happy man, whom you prefer to all men?
I am a free person, Sir Hargrave. It is no impeachment of sincerity, if a free
person answers not every question that may be put to her, by those to
whom she is not accountable.

This is indeed a 'scene'. Richardson presented much of *Sir Charles Grandison* textually in the form of drama. Harriet's dialogue with Sir Hargrave is like a script, without even those conventional markers of speech to which we are accustomed when reading novels: 'she said', 'he replied' and so on. The extract contains one, as it were, direction to the actor, the bracketed word 'angrily', but otherwise consists solely of the words spoken.

This dramatic form enables Richardson to present directly and forcibly Harriet Byron's articulate assertion of her autonomy and integrity. All her speeches begin with a clear statement of her freedom and self-determination, each time tempered by politeness which contrasts with the anger that marks Sir Hargrave's loss of self-control: 'I told you, Sir', 'I am, Sir', 'I am a free person, Sir Hargrave'. The third of her speeches, her response to a characteristic claim of the wooer or seducer that no woman could possibly be without a male attachment, extends clear statement into resounding assertion of human, not just female, liberty.

Harriet's rational self-control is marked, too, in the balance between her polite, respectful, but firm acknowledgement of the 'honour' she feels in his good opinion of her, and the counterweight of the honour she does him in replying honestly to his advances. This is admirable delicacy and respect coupled with forthright rejection. The very clarity of my response, Harriet says, is a tribute to the honourable character of your address. Sir Hargrave's irate and self-important manner suggests, a reader may feel, that Harriet's attribution to him of principled conduct confers too great an honour on him. Future events will confirm such a suspicion in the strongest terms. Harriet's superior command of her language and principles will be matched not by the importunate Pollexfen, but by Sir Charles Grandison himself.

The novel form's common reliance on speech and dialogue as a means of delineating character, advancing action and presenting conflict reflects its profound relationship with drama. As Mark Kinkead-Weekes observes in his definitive study of Richardson, the 'more dialogue there is, and the less interruption by the narrator, the more dramatic the scene becomes'.[1] Richardson's adoption of epistolary method was a means of making the events and, more importantly,

characters' feelings and thoughts immediate to the reader. Throughout his novels, he places the reader in as close a relationship to the
action as possible. Epistolary form was in time found too cumber-
some. Even such an obvious admirer of Richardson's work as Frances
Burney began in epistolary mode (the form of her first novel, *Evelina*),
but soon forsook it for third-person narration. The dramatic method
so compellingly created in, above all, *Sir Charles Grandison* remained
his lasting legacy to future writers.

The most imaginative novelists make creative use of their inheri-
tance. Henry Green is best known for novels that reflect his own experience of industrial activities in the inter-war years of the twentieth
century (see Section 5.5). In his later work he developed a more dramatic and less descriptive manner in which direct speech occupies
centre stage. *Nothing* (1950) and *Doting* (1952) are largely composed
in a series of dialogues, like tableaux in a play. These dialogues are
confrontations, but not in the overt manner of Harriet Byron's rejection of Sir Hargrave Pollexfen. Green's characters do not inhabit a
world of moral certainty and declared principles: their motives are
obscure, sometimes because they lack full understanding of a situation
or of what has led to it, and sometimes because they wish to ensure
that their companion remains in ignorance of what they know. Dialogues are therefore often teasingly oblique, their polite, even trivial
surface playing over something less sure and darker beneath.

In *Nothing*, Jane Weatherby and John Pomfret are former adul-
terous lovers, each now in a new informal and impermanent
relationship – Jane with Richard Abbot and John with Liz Jennings.
Jane has a son, Philip, and a young daughter, Penelope; John has a
daughter, Mary. The first half of the novel has ended with Philip's
21st birthday dinner, hosted by Jane in a hotel where a number of
the scenes take place. During the dinner, Philip and Mary announce
that they are engaged, then escape from the mainly middle-aged dinner party to a night club where they dance in 'a state of unthinking
happiness perhaps'.

Green opens the second half – the novel is carefully structured, and
his manuscript indicates a half-page break at this point – with a dialogue between Jane and John which begins a process through which
that word 'perhaps' is explained and exposed. Jane has invited John to
dinner in her flat:

'And how is dear Liz?' she enquired as she brought the man a glass of
    sherry.

'Quite well I trust.'

'Aren't you seeing so much of her now then John?'

'But of course,' he said. 'The fact is this news about our respective children has rather thrown me out of my normal gait.'

'So it's become a question of striding between you and Liz,' Mrs Weatherby commented. Her look on him over the decanter was one of sweet compassion. 'Oh my dear,' she continued 'you must be careful. Don't let it end as our love did in great country walks.'

'Really Jane when do I ever get away?' he cried. 'All my work in town here, and now this engagement! Philip and Mary are going to keep us pretty well occupied you know. Lot to arrange and so on.'

'I'm sure,' she agreed. 'Just sit back and relax.'

'And how is little Penelope?' he enquired.

She made a beautiful flowing gesture of resignation. 'Oh my dear,' she said. 'Sometimes I bless Providence I have a man like you can share my problems.'

'Isn't Richard much use then?'

'I don't know what I should do without him but he has that failing John of the absolutely true, true to one I mean, of being almost completely unimaginative poor dear.'

Mr Pomfret laughed. 'I see,' he said. 'Sometimes I have just wondered what you found in Richard.'

'Loyalty,' she breathed and smoothed her skirts.

'Which you never came across in me?'

'Don't let's rake up the past darling. What's over's over.'

'Enough's enough you mean?'

She let out a gentle peal of laughter, leaning back on the sofa.

'Oh John aren't you horrid!' she cried.

'Good sherry you have here,' he said.

Their conversation apparently unfolds as smoothly as Jane's skirts, but is actually entirely managed by her: like her dress, its sleekness results from her careful arrangement. As hostess, she takes the initiative, covering her polite enquiry about Liz by bringing him a glass of sherry, an aperitif as defining of class in 1950 as the servants the people employ and the hotels they frequent. John's qualifying 'I trust' opens the door for her more searching question about his current relationship. The engagement between Mary and Philip has disturbed John's life, but it also necessitates more intimacy between Jane and John. However, Jane maintains an air of concern for Liz, John's metaphor ('my normal gait') enabling her to raise their own earlier affair as a warning of what can happen if relationships are allowed to cool. Jane's 'sweet compassion' appears unexceptionable.

John's polite inquiry is about Jane's young daughter, but she at once diverts it towards a comparison between John and her present lover, Richard. She manages to be at the same time loyal to Richard – this, indeed, is the quality she says she admires in him – and to use him to convey her high valuation of John's capacity for sympathy and support. Her compassion for Richard looks more condescending ('poor dear') than 'sweet'.

Their conversation has ensured that such comparisons must be brought to mind. 'Don't let's rake up the past darling', says Jane after she has done precisely that by referring to their past relationship, its decline and demise together with the qualities which would appear once to have temporarily sustained it. Jane's language has become both socially polite and intimate ('darling'), and her manner bantering ('Oh John aren't you horrid!'). John, however, appears keen to change the conversation: his *non sequitur* in praise of Jane's sherry returns us to the beginning while maintaining social etiquette.

Authorial contributions to the scene are more frequent than in our extract from *Sir Charles Grandison*, but mostly remain at the level of speech indicator ('she said') or stage direction ('leaning back on the sofa'). There is no overt narrative comment or evaluation. However, there are moments when actions take on a degree of suggestion: Jane's 'beautiful flowing gesture of resignation' in response to John's inquiry about Penelope has the florid quality of one prone to self-dramatizing. Smoothing her skirts as she breathes the word 'loyalty' again draws attention to the studied artificiality of tone and action. We are conscious of being in the presence of an actor.[2]

How conscious of this is John? Green gives us little to suggest what he is thinking. His praise of Jane's sherry may indicate a desire to prevent the dialogue from becoming more familiar. It may reflect embarrassment. Or it may simply show that he has nothing more imaginative to say. Does he talk about sherry because he does not know where the conversation is going, or because he knows all too well? His remark seems to inhabit a comedy of manners, the novelist/dramatist observing humorously, even a touch satirically, the awkward and slightly absurd ways in which society people behave. John's glass of sherry becomes a repeated point of reference in the several pages of dialogue which follow, suggesting one possible reason for his gradual loss of control to his dominant partner.

Direct speech brings the reader into immediate contact with the character. In the case of Richardson's Harriet Byron, there is no doubt that her words are a true representation of her feelings and

her principles. Her moral value in the novel resides in her authenticity, the fidelity of her words and actions to her judgement and beliefs.
Green's characters, rather than declaring principles, raise questions
about motivation, about their real meaning and intention. His may be
a less violent world than that of Sir Hargrave Pollexfen, but it contains
its own duplicities and its dangers. From the time of its publication,
Nothing has divided readers. Some have found it trivial and indul-
gent towards a post-war society concerned only with its own round of
affairs and petty jealousies. Others have detected beneath its glittering
surface Green's exposure of an ethical void: nothing.

5.3   Debate: Samuel Johnson, *Rasselas* (1759), chapter twenty-eight

Prince Rasselas and his sister Princess Nekayah discuss the desirability
of marriage:

> 'I know not, said the princess, whether marriage be more than one of
> the innumerable modes of human misery. When I see and reckon the
> various forms of connubial infelicity, the unexpected causes of lasting
> discord, the diversities of temper, the oppositions of opinion, the rude
> collisions of contrary desire where both are urged by violent impulses, the
> obstinate contests of disagreeing virtues, where both are supported by
> consciousness of good intention, I am sometimes disposed to think with
> the severer casuists of most nations, that marriage is rather permitted
> than approved, and that none, but by the instigation of a passion too
> much indulged, entangle themselves with indissoluble compacts.'

> 'You seem to forget, replied Rasselas, that you have, even now, repre-
> sented celibacy as less happy than marriage. Both conditions may be
> bad, but they cannot both be worst. Thus it happens when wrong opin-
> ions are entertained, that they mutually destroy each other, and leave the
> mind open to truth.'

> 'I did not expect, answered the princess, to hear that imputed to false-
> hood which is the consequence only of frailty. To the mind, as to the eye,
> it is difficult to compare with exactness objects vast in their extent, and
> various in their parts. Where we see or conceive the whole at once we
> readily note the discriminations and decide the preference: but of two
> systems, of which neither can be surveyed by any human being in its
> full compass of magnitude and multiplicity of complication, where is the
> wonder, that judging of the whole by parts, I am alternately affected by
> one and the other as either presses on my memory or fancy? We differ
> from ourselves just as we differ from each other, when we see only part

of the question, as in the multifarious relations of politics and morality: but when we perceive the whole at once, as in numerical computations, all agree in one judgment, and none ever varies his opinion.'

Princess Nekayah's two speeches apply an elevated linguistic register to remarkably flexible and varied syntax. Her first, terse sentence sets up a proposition, that marriage might simply be one of the many ways in which people experience unhappiness. Nekayah does not declare herself clearly in favour of this theory: she introduces it guardedly ('I know not') and in the subjunctive mood to express possibility rather than certainty ('whether marriage be'). However, she proceeds to elaborate it forcibly, adducing a disturbing list of the ways in which married people make one another unhappy. Her command of rhetoric – the art of persuasive speaking – is, indeed, apparent from the outset. 'Innumerable modes of human misery' employs an impressive register of language, enhanced by resonant alliteration deriving from the stressed syllable of her subject, 'marriage'.

This alliterative technique – more commonly a feature of poetry than of prose – continues in Nekayah's second sentence, where forceful language ('violent', 'obstinate', and so on) is complemented by interweaving patterns of consonantal repetition, of softly voiced 'v' ('various', 'diversities', 'violent', 'virtues', 'severer', 'approved') but also of the harder 'c' and 'd': 'connubial', 'unexpected causes', 'discord', 'rude collisions', 'contrary desire', 'contests', 'disagreeing', 'consciousness', 'disposed', 'casuists', 'indissoluble compacts'. Nekayah sets this percussive language within complex and rhetorical syntax. She defers the main clause ('I am sometimes disposed') until nearly two-thirds of the way through a long sentence, consisting of 91 words. The reader wonders when the sentence will get to its resolution, such are the innumerable modes of unhappiness. Nekayah may say she is careful not to rush to judgement – even after the list of miseries she declares herself only 'sometimes disposed' to the rather cynical conclusion that marriage is merely a means by which sexual passion can be contained – but she is proving a pretty strong advocate. Indeed, she comes across like a skilful barrister trenchantly pleading a case while professing reluctance – a familiar rhetorical ploy: 'I am sorry about where this argument is taking us, but I can't in all honesty deny the evidence.'

The formality of Nekayah's speech is reinforced by her choice and arrangement of words. She invests her speech with formality and resonance by repetition of the same phrasal pattern, with or without adjectival pointing: 'innumerable modes of human misery', 'various forms of connubial infelicity', 'the diversities of temper', 'the oppositions of opinion'.

As for her choice of words themselves, she would sometimes seem to open herself to an objection often made against Samuel Johnson's language generally, that she never chooses a simple word where a complicated one will do, especially if it is derived from a Latin rather than Anglo-Saxon root. Why, for example, does she say 'connubial infelicity' rather than, perhaps, 'marital unhappiness', which, though using more familiar words, is scarcely colloquial? The answer is twofold. First, Nekayah, like her creator who had published his celebrated *Dictionary* four years before *Rasselas*, is aware of fine nuances of meaning. Both 'connubial' and 'marital' are used to mean 'related to marriage'; but the etymology of the former is from Latin for 'marry' (*nubere*), while 'marital' derives from the Latin word for 'husband' (*maritus*). Nekayah is talking about marriage, not the behaviour of husbands specifically. Does it matter, since the words in English are commonly used as synonyms? Perhaps not, but, given the existence of two words, why not use the one whose history makes it more exact for the context? Secondly, since 'connubial' is derived from Latin, there is linguistic and historical harmony in the use of a Latinate noun ('infelicity', from *felix*) rather than an Anglo-Saxon one ('unhappiness', from 'hap' meaning 'chance', 'luck').

These are, indeed, fine nuances; though they would have been apparent to more readers in the eighteenth century, when knowledge of Latin (if not of Anglo-Saxon) was commoner than today. But, taken as a whole, Nekayah's choice and arrangement of language, organization of sentence-structure and use of rhetorical and phonetic techniques build up a massively consistent effect. She is speaking in a dignified and respectful manner, one appropriate to her status as a character, her regard for her brother, and, above all, the seriousness and importance of her subject. How should people live their lives? Can we attain happiness? How can we maintain moral dignity in a world where our intentions and desires appear so often to be frustrated by the contingencies of existence and our own failings? These are the questions underlying not just the dialogue between Nekayah and Rasselas about marriage, but the novel as a whole. It is right and harmonious to apply to subject-matter a level of discourse which matches and respects it. There is a decorum to effective communication.

If Nekayah's first speech smacks of the law courts, Rasselas's reply
and her riposte make it clear that the contest between them is really a
philosophical debate. Rasselas objects on the grounds of her inconsistency. Nekayah has earlier argued that being unmarried is a less happy
state than being married. He is referring to chapter twenty-six, where
Nekayah says that her observations of single people have shown them
to suffer from the melancholy of loneliness, and concludes that 'Marriage has many pains, but celibacy has no pleasures'. Her argument,
then, is illogical, which Rasselas concisely expresses through antithesis: 'Both conditions may be bad, but they cannot both be worst'.
Nekayah has been aiming her considerable rhetorical skills at a state,
marriage, which she earlier set above its opposite.

However, Rasselas has failed to recognize the theoretical context
underlying both Nekayah's sets of comments. She began her long
sentence 'When I see and reckon the various forms of connubial infelicity'. Their debate on marriage has grown out of their decision –
made in chapter twenty-three – to divide between them the task of
examining how people behave in various stations of life. They are conducting experiments based on observation of individual instances and
reckoning up what they see. Nekayah's pessimistic view of marriage is
a result of her recognition of the 'various forms', the different ways, in
which married people are unhappy. In her reply, she first knocks back
Rasselas's neat antithesis with an alliterative one of her own ('false-
hood'/'frailty') – another debating ploy: anything you can do, I can do
better. She then picks up the language that conveyed her philosophical perspective and that Rasselas, she implies, has missed or ignored.
Just as, 'to the eye', it is difficult to compare objects of great extension, so we cannot intellectually encompass ideas 'various in their
parts', constituted of many different elements. They are discussing
marriage; but marriage is an abstract noun which, in reality, comprises
a 'vast' number of individual instances. Because the siblings have been
observing examples of people living in a married or unmarried state,
it is only natural that they will tend to be more strongly affected by
whichever types they have most recently seen. This is what Nekayah
means by 'frailty'. It is beyond human capacity to observe a whole
'system' (marriage, so all married people) at once. It is only 'numerical computations' that permit such a total comprehension: there, once
we understand the concepts, we all agree and never vary. But marriage
is not like this: it cannot be reduced to a number or equation.

There is, then, a further ground for Johnson's use of formal language in this dialogue. The debate between brother and sister is not

only about its ostensible topic, marriage. It is also about the appropriate kind of philosophical basis for discussing the subject. Because the
abstract noun 'marriage' consists of many instances, only an empirical
method is valid. This, however, means that examples can be viewed
only one at a time, so that an overview cannot be attained and we
are likely to be more affected by what is most immediately before us.
A debate about philosophical method demands consistency of method
and its linguistic equivalent, decorum of expression.

Rasselas is very clearly a 'novel of ideas'. It is often noted that,
as our extract shows, Johnson makes no attempt to differentiate his
characters by how they speak. They all sound alike. Indeed, critics
have questioned whether we should regard it as a novel at all – the
fate, as we shall see, of many a novel of ideas (see Section 6.4) –
and have looked to classifications such as 'moral fable' or the French
conte philosophique ('philosophical short story'). It is striking that
Rasselas should have been published in the same year as the most
famous of *contes philosophiques*, Voltaire's *Candide*. Other critics go
further and view *Rasselas* as a series of essays strung together on a
tenuous plot. But it is worth noting that 1759, the year of *Rasselas* and
Candide, is also when the first volumes of *Tristram Shandy* appeared
(see Sections 2.1, 6.8). In its way, Johnson's work is as challenging
to novelistic orthodoxy as Sterne's. *Tristram Shandy* is a novel without an ending; *Rasselas*'s final chapter is entitled 'The conclusion, in
which nothing is concluded'. Johnson employs an appropriate form,
dialogue, to present the marriage debate. The overall form of *Rasselas*
refuses to say that everything has been said. Perhaps critics should
follow its lead and conclude that the debate is not over about what
constitutes a novel, at least until they can plausibly claim to have sur-
veyed in its entirety the genre of prose fiction, vast in its extent and
various in its parts.

5.4 Comic dialogue: P. G. Wodehouse, *The Code of the Woosters* (1938), chapter nine; Evelyn Waugh, *Men At Arms* (1952), book one, chapter one; Ronald Firbank, *Valmouth* (1919), chapter eight

Stephanie ('Stiffy') Byng, niece of Sir Watkyn Bassett, wants to
marry Harold ('Stinker') Pinker, an old chum of Bertie Wooster and
presently an impecunious curate. Jeeves, Bertie's peerless manservant,
has proposed a scheme to persuade Sir Watkyn to give his blessing to
the marriage and provide Stinker with a vicarage, the first step, Stiffy

is confident, on his way to a bishopric. Bertie and Sir Watkyn are on somewhat difficult terms, the latter being convinced that Bertie is an untrustworthy kleptomaniac currently eyeing up his latest acquisition, a silver cow-creamer – a cream-jug in the shape of a cow, his first sight of which takes Bertie into 'a different and dreadful world' (chapter one). Jeeves's plan is that Bertie should ask Sir Watkyn for permission to marry Stiffy himself. Jeeves judges (correctly) that Sir Watkyn will be so appalled at the idea that, when Stiffy announces that she is already engaged to Stinker, he will readily agree to all she asks.

Bertie is, to put it mildly, reluctant to submit himself to a tête-à-tête with the fearsome Sir Watkyn, but, as usual, is cajoled into it by Stiffy's entreaties, not to say blackmail. It is Bertie's fate to have his gentlemanly principles – the code of the Woosters – exploited by all manner of unscrupulous females, from bossy aunts to drippy blondes. 'Kipling was right. D. than the m. No getting round it' (chapter eight). Well, you can't go into a request to become Sir Watkyn Bassett's nephew without 'a few preliminary *pourparlers*', so Bertie decides to approach the topic with his customary subtle indirection:

'Have you ever thought about love, Sir Watkyn?'

'I beg your pardon?'

'About love. Have you ever brooded on it to any extent?'

'You have not come here to discuss love?'

'Yes, I have. That's exactly it. I wonder if you have noticed a rather rummy thing about it – viz. that it is everywhere. You can't get away from it. Love, I mean. Wherever you go, there it is, buzzing along in every class of life. Quite remarkable. Take newts, for instance.'

'Are you quite well, Mr Wooster?'

'Oh, fine, thanks. Take newts, I was saying. You wouldn't think it, but Gussie Fink-Nottle tells me they get it right up their noses in the mating season. They stand in line by the hour, waggling their tails at the local belles. Starfish, too. Also undersea worms.'

'Mr Wooster –'

'And, according to Gussie, even ribbonlike seaweed. That surprises you, eh? It did me. But he assures me that it is so. Just where a bit of ribbonlike seaweed thinks it is going to get by pressing its suit is more than I can tell you, but at the time of the full moon it hears the voice of Love all right and is up and doing with the best of them. I suppose it builds on the hope that it will look good to other bits of ribbonlike seaweed, which, of course, would also be affected by the full moon. Well, be that as it may, what I'm working round to is that the moon is pretty full now, and if that's how it affects seaweed you can't very well blame a chap like me for feeling the impulse, can you?'

Who was it said that innocence is a tender plant; touch it and the bloom is gone? Or was it ignorance? Jeeves would know. Perhaps it's the same with comedy. But, still, here goes.

Relations between Sir Watkyn and Bertie exist in a permanent state of mutual incomprehension, and this is a dialogue between two men living in different worlds. Sir Watkyn's brief contributions are limited to three unavailing questions and one hopeless attempt to stem the Wooster tide. Bertie fails to understand, treating 'Are you quite well?' as a question about his physical rather than mental health. Whereas Sir Watkyn approaches speechlessness, Bertie becomes more and more effusive as he warms to his theme. He is blithely unaware of the spiralling absurdity of his accounts of aquatic ardour. As his trawl through marine creatures descends the tree of life, so his explanations mine a ludicrously solemn and anthropocentric (as Jeeves might say) vein. Humour often derives from incongruity, the collision between two comically ill-suited objects or actions. Here we have newts lining up in a seductive fashion show, and ribbonlike seaweed hearing the voice of Love and pressing its suit. Bertie's earnest attempts to gauge Sir Watkyn's responses ('That surprises you, eh?') and confiding asides ('It did me') add to the non-meeting of what passes for minds.

Throughout, Bertie displays his customary devotion to confused registers of language and mixed metaphors. Talk of love has birds and bees skulking somewhere in the depths of his subconscious, only to emerge in the idea of newts buzzing along. Newts suggest themselves to Bertie because keeping them is Augustus ('Gussie') Fink-Nottle's hobby. They are, of course, small-tailed amphibians allied to the salamander (Jeeves would know), though that they get it right up their noses in the mating season is perhaps less common knowledge among zoologists. Much of Bertie's language is the slang of the contemporary idle man about town, cultivated among his fellow members of the Drones Club (Gussie is one), where throwing bread-rolls around is about as intellectual as things get. 'Rummy' is an example, though it had actually been around since the 1820s. Alongside his occasionally odd – rummy, even – descents into pedantry ('be that as it may'), it contributes to the farrago of mixed registers that embellishes the sublime coloratura of Bertie's aria of love.

Comic dialogue commonly works by these kinds of incongruity – disparity between participating speakers, between their intellectual and social worlds, between registers of language, between parts of metaphors. Guy Crouchback, hero of Evelyn Waugh's *Sword of Honour* trilogy (see Section 6.7), is in a train on the way to join his regiment, when his fellow-traveller, another new recruit called Apthorpe, engages him in conversation:

> 'This is my new pair of porpoises. I expect you wear them too.'
> Guy looked from Apthorpe's boots to his own. They seemed very much alike. Was 'porpoise' Halberdier slang for 'boot'?
> 'I don't know. I just told the man I always go to, to make me a couple of pairs of thick black boots.'
> 'He may have given you cow.'
> 'Perhaps he did.'
> 'A great mistake, old man, if you don't mind my saying so.'
> He puffed his pipe for another five minutes, then spoke again: 'Of course, it's really the skin of the white whale, you know.'
> 'I didn't know. Why do they call it "porpoise"?'
> 'Trade secret, old man.'

Like Sir Watkyn Bassett and Bertie Wooster, Guy and Apthorpe are living in different *milieux*. Guy represents the ordinary, the normal, while Apthorpe is a figure from off-centre. When he needs a pair of boots, Guy goes to a boot-maker and asks for them. Apthorpe turns boot-making into a mysterious art, whose secrets are known only to few. Guy understands language as it is conventionally used. For Apthorpe, language is a means of demonstrating one's difference from the norm: it slides around, defying its usual definition. Bertie Wooster is sublimely unaware of the effects his account of watery love is having on his interlocutor. Apthorpe is gloriously secure in his own world, puffing contentedly and complacently on his pipe and patronising Guy ('old man') while expressing himself in odder and odder speeches.

Another shared feature between Bertie Wooster and Apthorpe is obsessiveness. Once Bertie's imagination has been fired up by his vision, there is no stopping him, despite Sir Watkyn's attempts to do so. Apthorpe clings like a limpet to his *idée fixe*, unaware of his own peculiarity even when it ought to be apparent. He continues to find it funny that Guy doesn't wear porpoises, while the only criticism that his superior officers make of his appearance on parade is that his boots aren't properly polished. Waugh develops this combination of obsessiveness, obstinacy and blindness in the longest comic set-piece in *Men at Arms*, Apthorpe's efforts to hold on to his 'thunder-box', his portable lavatory. Crouchback acts throughout as his straight man, unable to stop himself teasing and prodding Apthorpe into greater and greater absurdity, with eventually explosive results.

Dialogue is formed by juxtaposition; comic dialogue exploits the potential for juxtaposition to sheer off into incomprehension resulting from gradually or rapidly diverging views of reality. Taken to its extreme, such comedy ends up close to the surreal, loosening our hold on rationality.

Ronald Firbank's *Valmouth* is set in a resort whose wonderful climate enables its inhabitants, mostly female, to live to vast ages, and to indulge in distinctly (or more often quite indistinctly) outrageous, or at least odd, activities. The scene in chapter eight is one of the regular social gatherings of the centenarians of Valmouth, at which new members are welcomed. As the hubbub of the party grows, so dialogues fragment:

> There uprose a jargon of voices:
> 'Heroin.'
> 'Adorable simplicity.'
> 'What could anyone find to admire in such a shelving profile?'
> 'We reckon a duck here of two or three and twenty not so old. And a spring chicken *anything to fourteen.*'
> 'My husband had no amorous energy whatsoever; which just suited me, of course.'
> 'I suppose when there's no more room for another crow's-foot, one attains a sort of peace?'
> 'I once said to Doctor Fothergill, a clergyman of Oxford and a great friend of mine, "Doctor," I said, "oh, if only you could see my – " '
> '*Elle était jolie! Mais jolie! . . . C'était une si belle brune . . . !*'
> 'Cruelly lonely.'
> 'Leery . . . .'
> 'Vulpine.'
> 'Calumny.'
> 'People look like pearls, dear, beneath your wonderful trees.'

'Jargon' is a complex word. Today it is generally pejorative in meaning, referring to a mode of language created and nurtured by a special group, class, trade or profession to mark out its difference from the rest of us and so create a closed shop. It implies a use of language that most people find rebarbative. This sense, which dates from the seventeenth century, derived from earlier meanings: unintelligible discourse and a debased form of speech constructed from mixing together two or more languages. The original meaning, used in Chaucer and revived in the nineteenth century, was the twittering of birds. Firbank may have had this more attractive sense in mind, but is using 'jargon' mainly in a further sense, dating from the eighteenth century, of a medley or babel of sounds. Dialogue is loosened into unattributed fragments of speech arising from the crowd. Some form whole sentences, some are partial sentences broken off, others are just single words. It is as if these female centenarians are tropical birds in the hothouse of Valmouth society, warbling inconsequentially or to uncertain purpose.

Some of Firbank's humour derives from his use of risqué aposiopesis in the manner of Laurence Sterne: ' "Doctor," I said, "oh, if only you could see my – " '. Some is concentrated in whole sayings that hover between the absurdly pathetic and the humorously self-aware, taking the form of proverbial statements: 'I suppose when there's no more room for another crow's-foot, one attains a sort of peace?' Words and phrases suggest the habits or pleasures of a certain class at a certain time ('Heroin'), or faintly hinted cattiness ('shelving profile', 'Leery'). Running through the sequence is a subdued or self-conscious eroticism eventually expressing itself in the decent obscurity of a foreign language: *Elle était jolie!*

The overall effect is of random voices which nonetheless seem to form, through juxtaposition, some kind of tantalizing medley, now teetering on the verge of meaning, now pulling back into opacity. The final line in our extract defines this: each individual item is a pearl – gleaming, polished yet enigmatic – strung on a thread which holds it in attractive but ambiguous proximity to its fellows. Like the structures of Firbank's short, jewelled novels, the jargon of voices escapes from normal narrative forms of cause and effect, and substitutes for them another kind of pattern, one created by suggestive placing, whether happy congruence or teasing incongruity.

5.5 Indirect speech: Charlotte Brontë, *Villette* (1853), chapter twenty-two; Henry Green, *Living* (1929), chapter seven

> He asked me, smiling, why I cared for his letter so very much. I thought, but did not say, that I prized it like the blood in my veins. I only answered that I had so few letters to care for.

Had Charlotte Brontë written this passage in direct speech it would have run something like this:

> 'Why do you care for my letter so very much?' he asked me, smiling.

I thought, but did not say, 'I prize it like the blood in my veins.' But I only
answered, 'I have so few letters to care for.'

In order to convert these direct speeches and thoughts into indirect
speech, the tenses are changed from present to past: 'care' to 'cared',
'prize' to 'prized', 'have' to 'had'. The speeches are reported rather
than given as if they were immediate utterances. 'Reported speech'
indeed, is a term often used of indirect speech specifically, although
some grammarians use 'reported speech' to refer to both direct and
indirect forms when given as past events. Further, because Brontë
gives us the man's words from her female narrator's point of view
his 'you' and 'my' become 'I' and 'his'. In indirect speech, the deixis –
that is, the way in which terms in an utterance are related to a specific speaker, addressee, time and place – reflects the perspective of
the reporter, not of the original speaker.

Why use indirect rather than direct speech? Many writers employ it
for variety's sake, simply in order to avoid lengthy stretches of direct
speech of the kind we regularly meet in the novels of Ivy Compton-
Burnett[3] and Henry Green. Indirect speech does, however, slightly
reduce the dramatic impact of a scene. The speaker's words merge
into the narrative, and so are more evidently under its control. When
as in *Villette*, there is a first-person narrator, she is just a shade more
dominant than the original speaker, whereas in a direct speech version
both characters would be given equal status to speak for themselves.

Villette is narrated by its heroine, Lucy Snowe. She has received a
letter from Dr John, a man to whom she has begun to feel attraction, and is cheered by its kindness and his evident pleasure in writing
about their recent times spent in each other's company. She loses the
letter in frightening, even melodramatic, circumstances, but is rescued
and reassured by Dr John himself, who has been called in to treat
the elderly mother of Madame Beck, governor of the boarding school
where Lucy is teaching. She is obliged to admit to Dr John that the
missing letter is his, and her extreme distress at having lost it puts her
in an embarrassing position. The answer she gives to his question is
her attempt to deflect attention from the value she accords the letter
on account of its sender and which she confesses to the reader in her
intense, unspoken simile.

By rendering the dialogue in indirect speech, Charlotte Brontë
makes Lucy's perspective the focus, so reflecting the fact that the letter's significance derives from her feelings for Dr John. These feelings
Lucy wants to keep from him, conscious as she is that they are intimate

and powerful. She contains Dr John's immediate words within her narrative as her veins hold her blood. This effect is striking because direct speech is far more common, in this scene and in *Villette* generally, than indirect speech: the latter's sudden appearance here is an artist's touch, allowing the reader to experience Lucy's momentary desire to conceal her emotions.

We have seen that Henry Green's later novels rely heavily on direct speech in dialogue form (Section 5.2). His earlier novels mix the narrative modes more freely, but do so in a highly idiosyncratic manner. His second novel, *Living*, is primarily about the men who work in a Birmingham iron foundry and the women who are trapped in their own factories, the small terraces where they keep house for the men. Films, romance and – for the men – football matches offer the only, delusory, escape. Here Lily Gates, who cooks and cleans for her widowed father, her grandfather and a lodger, has spent a Saturday afternoon taking a bus trip with Bert Jones, a vice hand in the foundry tool room, to see his uncle and aunt, lodge-keepers at a big house outside the city. This is the beginning of their relationship:

> After supper they had started back for bus terminus towards ten o'clock. They had talked. Lily thought Bert Jones was great on talking. She had said what kind of a life did they live up in the big house which his uncle was gatekeeper of and he said there was three young ladies, daughters of the house, but were no sons, father employed a lot of men in Birmingham he said. She said when they married, those three, would the eldest come with her 'usband to live in the house so it would stay in the family, and he said he couldn't tell and she said she wondered what kind of lives they did live there.
>
> She said it seemed a pity there wasn't a man the house wouldn't come to though girls were as good as men but still. She said they'd go out to dances every night probably and have a high old time. He said perhaps he kept his daughters in and didn't let them out much but she said that class never did that, the girls were free as the fishes in the sea and as slippery, using words her father would have used. And more than that she said, she had asked his aunt and she'd seen them come out of an evening scores of times, so she said.

The very first sentence demonstrates an apparent oddity of Green's style. Why has he left out the definite article, which correct grammar demands before 'bus terminus'? Various attempts have been made by critics to explain the recurrent peculiarities of his expression. Does the omission of articles bring the reader into immediate collision with the solidity of objects, particularly the factory machinery that rules and sometimes threatens the men's lives? Is he conveying the materiality and brutality of working conditions? This is the favoured line of politically engaged critics. Or, alternatively, is the fractured syntax a modernist technique, breaking up our secure hold on writing as a smooth representation of reality in favour of a more awkward, but truer, version of how we see the world? This is the favoured line of aesthetic critics. Both interpretations seek to accommodate the novel to preconceived critical models. If we read our passage as a whole, rather than extract its opening sentence, a different perspective is opened up by the rhythm of Green's writing.

Lily has been walking out with the lodger, Jim Dale. But she finds his lack of liveliness and conversation irritating. While she claps hands and hums along to music in cinema, Jim can't join in. 'It's 'ot in 'ere' is the limit of his chat (chapter three). Jim and Lily are not getting along. So when Bert Jones and she 'talked', it's worth repeating: 'Lily thought Bert Jones was great on talking'. So what did they talk about? Green tells us in a torrent of repetitions of the simplest marker of indirect (in this case) speech, 'he/she said'. From the fourth sentence of the first paragraph onwards, every sentence begins like this, some add one or two in the middle, and some end with it. Twelve times in six sentences we are hit over the head with it ('she' wins eight to four). The paragraphs are great on talking, so much so that commas are frequently omitted in order to render the breathless rush of speech.

So Lily gets what she wants, a man who matches – well, nearly – her own enthusiasm for headlong speech. The topic of their conversation is the three daughters of the big house where Bert's uncle is gatekeeper, and the lives they live. Lily imagines them as independent and free women; Bert, more conservatively, suggests that the father might not let his daughters out much. The owner of the big house is an employer, of a 'lot of men in Birmingham': as he orders the lives of his male workers, so, perhaps, he keeps his women under control. *Living* has a strong class strain running through it. But, no, Lily won't have this: 'the girls were free as the fishes in the sea'. Bert's aunt has confirmed that they often went out in the evening: the women agree, and override Bert's reservation.

The outpouring of speech expresses Lily's desire for her own freedom. She wants a man who will take her away from Birmingham, the stifling and cramped city where she is trapped. Her enthusiasm is naïve and artless, even rather absurd, and yet touching in its very simplicity and open delight. Bert's capacity to join in and even to take the initiative (it is his uncle and aunt they visit) is encouraging, but, ultimately, he cannot advance as far as she does in her vision of female emancipation. Being 'great on talking' may turn out to have its limitations.

Much the larger part of the extract is given in indirect speech, so that both Lily's and Bert's words are incorporated into the narrative while maintaining their own strong idiom. Tenses are changed from the present of direct speech to the past of indirect. Lily would have said: 'It seems a pity there isn't a man the house won't come to though girls are as good as men but still.' Green alters this to its indirect equivalent: 'She said it seemed a pity there wasn't a man the house wouldn't come to though girls were as good as men but still.' At the same time, he allows the breathlessness of Lily's speech to remain. He doesn't tidy it up by adding the punctuation that formal syntax would require but Lily's excitement brushes aside. Nor does Green sort out the characters' grammar: he allows Bert's 'there was three young ladies' to remain. This is how two people such as Lily and Bert would talk when chatting and gossiping together. The comic rush of 'he said/she said' is the narrator's own touch of the gossip.

Before launching into their speeches, Green briefly sets up the context in report mode, telling us where and when the conversation took place. By employing indirect, or reported, speech, he brings the two narrative modes more closely together than would have been the case had he used direct speech. His omission of the definite article before 'bus terminus' allows a touch of colloquialism, of appropriate speech rhythms, to enter his report. This peculiarity of syntax Green reserves for his narrative, as he tends to throughout the novel. It is the reporter's own oddity of expression, his contribution to a narration which is often idiosyncratic, but engagingly idiomatic and authentic.

5.6 Soliloquy to free indirect style: Eliza Haywood, *The History of Miss Betsy Thoughtless* (1751), chapter eighty-two; Frances Burney, *Cecilia* (1782), book six, chapter one; Jane Austen, *Emma* (1816), volume one, chapter sixteen

The heroine of Eliza Haywood's *The History of Miss Betsy Thoughtless* reflects alone on the deficiencies of her past behaviour:

In fine, she now saw herself, and the errors of her past conduct in their true light: – 'How strange a creature have I been!' cried she, 'how inconsistent with myself! I knew the character of a coquet both silly and insignificant, yet did everything in my power to acquire it: – I aimed to inspire awe and reverence in the men, yet by my imprudence embold- ened them to the most unbecoming freedoms with me: – I had sense enough to discern real merit in those who professed themselves my lovers, yet affected to treat most ill those, in whom I found the great- est share of it. – Nature has made me no fool, yet not one action of my life has given any proof of common reason.'

'Even in the greatest, and most serious affair of life – that of marriage' – added she, with a deep sigh, 'have I not been governed wholly by caprice! – I rejected Mr Trueworth, only because I thought I did not love him enough, yet gave myself to Mr Munden, whom at that time I did not love at all, and who has since, alas, taken little care to cultivate that affection I have laboured to feel for him.'

Drama commonly uses the device of the soliloquy to enable charac- ters to retreat to their innermost heart and mind. That which cannot be said to others may be spoken to oneself. This dramatic conven- tion allows an audience privileged access to a character's real thoughts and feelings. We, as it were, eavesdrop on them. In our extract, Eliza Haywood – herself in her younger days a playwright and actor – translates soliloquy into the novel form. Betsy's speech is an act of self-analysis. It enables her to look with new clarity upon contradic- tions in her conduct, which have brought her to a state of personal and matrimonial unhappiness.

Betsy expresses awareness of her perverse behaviour by means of a repeated pattern of statement (for example, 'I knew') followed by the qualifier 'yet'. This structure is employed five times. An obvi- ous objection is that Haywood thereby renders Betsy's thoughts more ordered and organized than would have been the case had she really been in a state of emotional turmoil. But soliloquies sel- dom attempt to imitate the disordered reflections of a disturbed mind. Hamlet's famous 'To be or not to be' speech suggests, by, for example, its use of mixed metaphor ('take arms against a sea of troubles'), some degree of agitation. But the contours of Hamlet's exploration of the temptations and fears of suicide are clear enough. He maintains his grip on reason, even though under extreme pres- sure. Soliloquy provides a formalized representation of emotions in order that we, the audience, can recognize and identify them. The careful structure of Betsy's soliloquy shows she is now taking con- trol of her life by acknowledging her own past inconsistency. This is the key moment in her development of intellectual maturity: the turning-point in her life, a confession of error which clears the way for future change. The formality of her speech both objectifies her thought processes and marks her new-found capacity to shape, to order her life.

In terms of novel form, the most obvious extension of the soliloquy is found in epistolary fiction. Letters, especially those written to a confidant(e), such as the heroine's to Anna Howe in Samuel Richardson's *Clarissa*, provide a vehicle for organized articulation. Because we readers are given access to private correspondence, we can follow how the writer arranges her perception of her experiences and her responses to them.

Frances Burney wrote her first novel, *Evelina*, in epistolary form, but changed to third-person narrative for her second, *Cecilia* (see Section 5.1). Like Haywood, Burney wishes to express her heroine's responses with immediacy, but she does so without resorting to the theatrical device of soliloquy. As Cecilia's relationship with Mortimer Delvile develops, she is suddenly disconcerted to observe the sister of a poor man befriended by Delvile privately kissing a letter and then hiding it from view. Cecilia cannot but think that the letter is from Delvile:

> And why should he write to her? what was his pretence? That he loved her she could now less than ever believe, since his late conduct to herself, though perplexing and inconsistent, evinced at least a partiality incompatible with a passion for another. What, then, could she infer, but that he had seduced her affections, and ruined her peace, for the idle and cruel gratification of temporary vanity?

Burney here takes a further step in the development of narrative method, which has far-reaching consequences for the novel form: she identifies the narrative voice with Cecilia's thoughts. The questions Cecilia asks are running through her mind. If she spoke them in soliloquy, she would say, 'And why should he write to her? what is his pretence?' Burney transfers these questions directly into the narrative, signalling the move by a change in tense from present to past ('what was his pretence?') because she is reporting Cecilia's thoughts. But Cecilia's words are otherwise unchanged, and there is no marker of indirect speech of the 'she thought' form. Narrative and soliloquy merge, bringing the former (and so the reader) into direct contact with the character's thoughts. The narrator and reader share Cecilia's perspective and, therefore, the painful conclusions to which she – wrongly – leaps. This technique is called free indirect style, a translation of the French *style indirect libre*. The effect is akin to empathy: Burney projects her narrative into Cecilia's mind, so identifying herself with her heroine. The result is an act of comprehension by which the character is brought into an intimately close relationship with the narrator (and so the reader).

It is sometimes claimed that Jane Austen was the first novelist in English to use free indirect style. This, as we have seen, is wrong; but it is perhaps in Jane Austen's work that we first encounter a sustained usage of the technique within the context of novels fundamentally about how human beings understand and misunderstand each other. *Emma* is the outstanding example. Emma has decided that her protégée, Harriet Smith, should marry Mr Elton, the newly-arrived vicar of Highbury. She draws Harriet's portrait in order to bring her beauty to his attention, and is encouraged by his fulsome praise of the picture. Later Mr Elton delivers a charade whose solution is 'courtship', and Emma interprets this as confirmation of his admiration for Harriet. However, when Emma is unexpectedly trapped alone in a carriage with him, she is disconcerted to find herself the object of his ardent declaration of love. Emma reflects on her dreadful error:

> How she could have been so deceived! – He protested that he had never thought seriously of Harriet – never! She looked back as well as she could; but it was all confusion. She had taken up the idea, she supposed, and made everything bend to it. His manners, however, must have been unmarked, wavering, dubious, or she could not have been so misled.

> The picture! – How eager he had been about the picture! – and the charade! – and an hundred other circumstances; – how clearly they had seemed to point at Harriet. To be sure, the charade, with its 'ready wit' – but then, the 'soft eyes' – in fact it suited neither; it was just a jumble without taste or truth. Who could have seen through such thick-headed nonsense?

Austen here mingles narrative modes. 'She looked back as well as she could' is narrative report. 'She had taken up the idea, she supposed' is indirect speech, or, rather, thought. But the dominant mode is free indirect style. Thinking back to her portrait of Harriet, Emma's reflection is 'how eager he was about the picture!' Conversion to free indirect style requires a change in tense. Had Jane Austen used direct speech, Emma's verb would have been past tense, 'was', as she is thinking of Elton's past behaviour. Now that the narrator is reporting her thoughts, she requires the verbal form that expresses an action prior to a specified past time: this is the pluperfect tense (or past perfect, as it is also termed), 'had been'. Otherwise Emma's own words are retained: 'How eager he had been about the picture!'

The passage provides the reader with intimate access to Emma's thoughts, while at the same time Jane Austen's narrative embraces and participates in Emma's reactions. We follow her from puzzled annoyance ('How she could have been so deceived!'), to reflection on how she must have fallen into error ('His manners, however, must have been unmarked, wavering, dubious'), to indignant self-justification ('how clearly they had seemed to point at Harriet'), to outrage at Elton's inadequacy ('Who could have seen through such thick-headed nonsense?'). Emma is confused and upset, and so someone who evokes the reader's and narrator's understanding. We feel with her, as we too could have been similarly deceived. Yet the narrator also holds her slightly at arm's length, so that we can observe an element of absurdity, albeit very human absurdity, in, for example, the way she translates her mistakes into someone else's fault. Emma is, at the same time, someone about whom we can feel compassionately and someone whose faults are frankly and often embarrassingly exposed. The narrative's combination of detachment and proximity is the sophisticated means by which Austen depicts her infuriating yet endearing heroine.

5.7 Stream of consciousness: Virginia Woolf, *Mrs Dalloway* (1925)

Quiet descended on her, calm, content, as her needle, drawing the silk smoothly to its gentle pause, collected the green folds together and attached them, very lightly, to the belt. So on a summer's day waves collect, overbalance, and fall; collect and fall; and the whole world seems to be saying 'that is all' more and more ponderously, until even the heart in the body which lies in the sun on the beach says too, that is all. Fear no more, says the heart. Fear no more, says the heart, committing its burden to some sea, which sighs collectively for all sorrows, and renews, begins, collects, lets fall. And the body alone listens to the passing bee; the wave breaking; the dog barking, far away barking and barking.

Going and coming, beckoning, signalling, so the light and shadow, which now made the wall grey, now the bananas bright yellow, now made the Strand grey, now made the omnibuses bright yellow, seemed to Septimus Warren Smith lying on the sofa in the sitting room; watching the watery gold glow and fade with the astonishing sensibility of some

live creature on the roses, on the wall-paper. Outside the trees dragged
their leaves like nets through the depths of the air; the sound of water
was in the room, and through the waves came the voices of birds singing.
Every power poured its treasures on his head, and his hand lay there on
the back of the sofa, as he had seen his hand lie when he was bathing,
floating, on the top of the waves, while far away on shore he heard dogs
barking and barking far away. Fear no more, says the heart in the body;
fear no more.

The first paragraph appears about a fifth of the way into
Mrs Dalloway. Clarissa Dalloway sits on a sofa to repair her green
dress, which she intends to wear at a society party she is hosting in
the evening. The second extract occurs about three quarters of the
way through the novel. Septimus Warren Smith, who is suffering from
post-traumatic stress disorder after his experiences in the First World
War, sits on a sofa, while his wife, Rezia, sits at a table sewing. *Mrs
Dalloway* is written without chapter divisions, small breaks in a page
occasionally marking shifts of scene.

Clarissa Dalloway and Septimus Warren Smith have never met, and
never will. Their lives are very different: she is a privileged politi-
cian's wife living in luxury in Westminster, he a poor shell-shocked
former soldier. But they exist simultaneously on this single June day
in London, like millions of others having time and place in common.
They share much more than this, however: they breathe through similar forms of language and similar images, so that they appear somehow
coexistent or complementary within their class and gender differences.

The syntax of both paragraphs is largely energized by present participles. Clarissa's paragraph builds them up gradually, beginning with
the action of her needle 'drawing' the silk of her dress together,
and culminates in a pattern of phonic and verbal repetition, 'breaking ... barking ... barking and barking', as words gathered together
in one sequence. Septimus, as it were, begins where Clarissa ended,
with a sequence of present participles, and moves towards a literal
repetition of the phrase 'barking and barking'. Present participles
denote continuation, things in the process of happening and moving
through time. Reiteration of the form sustains a rhythmic pulse, like
the beating of life.

Liquidity of movement blends the two paragraphs, folding one over
the other. Images of water run through both, particularly waves, which
are water in continual motion, ebbing and flowing. In both paragraphs,
'waves' are explicitly linked to present participles, sewing syntactically
together a noun indicating movement and a verbal form representing

continuum: 'the wave breaking', 'through the waves came the voices of birds singing'.

The two paragraphs are not, of course, identical. Clarissa and Septimus retain their individuality. For example, each passage also contains its own pattern of verbal repetition. In Clarissa's, the words 'collect' and 'fall' combine her gathering the folds of fabric in the action of sewing with the breaking and re-gathering of waves. Variant forms of 'collect' combine reiteration with process: 'collected', as when the sea is prepared to release its next wave; 'collectively', an adverb applied to the sea's sighing sound. Synonyms and shades of meaning also join variation to repetition: 'quiet', 'calm', 'content', 'gentle', 'lightly'. Septimus's paragraph has its distinctive synonyms ('beckoning', 'signalling') and verbal repetition ('now...now'; 'far away...far away'), and a more varied palette than Clarissa's green: 'grey', 'yellow', 'gold'.

However, these are variations within a pattern. A further striking repetition across the paragraphs is the resonant chorus 'Fear no more, says the heart'. Clarissa had first encountered this expression when, walking towards Bond Street to buy flowers for her party, she passed Hatchards' bookshop on Piccadilly and saw a book in the window open at the lines 'Fear no more the heat o' the sun/Nor the furious winter's rages'. These lines are from Shakespeare's *Cymbeline*, part of a lyric sung over the supposedly 'dead' body of Imogen. They express the finality, but also the comfort, of death, as the conclusion of life's hardships. For Septimus, suffering mental disturbance exacerbated by the clumsy and unsympathetic attentions of ignorant and arrogant doctors, the quotation is particularly apposite. In his paragraph it occurs at the very end, after the phrase 'barking and barking far away' has reflected as a mirror Clarissa's 'far away barking and barking'. Whereas Clarissa's application of the quotation to a burial at sea (thus linking the element that stands for eternal repetition to the ending of life) is, as it were, buried in the heart of her paragraph, in Septimus's paragraph it is placed as a finale, pointing to his death by suicide, which follows soon after.

The *Cymbeline* line, 'Fear no more the heat of the sun', recurs right at the end of the novel, where Clarissa retires temporarily from the throng at her party to contemplate death, and the young man – Septimus, though she does not know even his name – who has embraced it violently but defiantly. For, although Mrs Dalloway and Smith never meet, their paths through life do meet at a remove. Sir William Bradshaw, the Harley Street specialist who has been treating

him, and whose unwanted arrival to take him away to a nursing home
precipitates his suicide, is a guest at her party. Lady Bradshaw explains
that they are late on account of the young man's death. As Woolf's
elaborate interweaving of language, syntax and image between our
two paragraphs expresses, Clarissa and Septimus – so different, yet
so alike – share sensitivity, a responsiveness to the rhythms of living
and the vision of death. But, where Septimus has committed himself
in his final act, flinging life away, Clarissa has only thrown a shilling
into the Serpentine, a euphemistic yet self-consciously miniature and
inadequate image for drowning. Clarissa's internal world is realized
through another person, at a distance. She returns to her guests.

Mrs Dalloway is written in the third person. The Clarissa paragraph
begins as 'Quiet descended on her', and it is 'her' needle that draws
the silk. The Septimus Warren Smith paragraph names him, and follows up with 'his' and 'he', three times each. These are not interior
monologues like Molly Bloom's in the final section of James Joyce's
Ulysses (1922). In an interior monologue, a character's thoughts are
presented directly in the order and form in which they are supposed
to occur to him or her. As with a dramatic soliloquy, we – the audience, the reader – are overhearing private thoughts. Virginia Woolf
herself approaches this kind of writing in the monologues she gives to
her characters in *The Waves* (1931), though she sets them in inverted
commas and repeats the tags 'said Rhoda', 'said Bernard', without any
further authorial commentary. Joyce cuts out even these perfunctory
tags, removes punctuation and presents Molly's thoughts in an apparently random order. Both soliloquies and interior monologues are, of
course, literary conventions: audiences know they are in a theatre listening to Hamlet's lines as written by Shakespeare, and readers know
they are reading a book written by an author. It is not by chance that
Molly's monologue begins and ends with 'Yes'.

However extensively or minimally mediated by the author, such
attempts to express the flow of a character's inner thoughts and feelings, from Betsy Thoughtless (see Section 5.6) to Clarissa Dalloway
to Molly Bloom, are varieties of what is commonly termed 'stream of
consciousness', a phrase coined by William James, brother of the novelist Henry James, in his *Principles of Psychology* (1890). As we recognize in Virginia Woolf's recurrent use of waves as an image, James's
liquid metaphor is apposite, indicating continuity and naturalness.

In the case of our *Mrs Dalloway* extracts, the narrative drifts into
a condition of inwardness as the character does. The first sentence
of Clarissa's paragraph maintains a clear hold on her physical task

and ends with a solid noun, 'the belt'. From that point, the action and rhythm of sewing, regular and repeated, are gradually transferred to language and images suggestive of interior feeling. The narrative takes over as the agent of 'sewing' elements which, taken together, represent a mind reflecting on buried ideas, random objects and remembered fragments, all marked by rhythmic, mesmerically repetitive prose. The Septimus paragraph opens in rhythmic mode, moves outward to the literal figure of Smith lying on his sofa and then drifts back to mingled images in the mind (water, birdsong). The narrative thus, as in free indirect style, engages with the characters themselves, making itself at one with them, joining them in their reverie. The passages, when read together, become parts of a single fabric, which in turn connect with other areas of the novel. *Mrs Dalloway* is, like Lily Briscoe's painting in *To the Lighthouse* (see Section 3.3), composed, its scenes, images and characters sewn together into the fictional fabric. The novel itself shares the sensitivity and vision of its principal characters: narrative and character are as one.

6

Commenting

6.1   The authorial voice: Anthony Trollope, *Framley Parsonage* (1861), chapter four; Arnold Bennett, *The Old Wives' Tale* (1908), book two, chapter five

In his *Autobiography*, Trollope described his aim in creating Mark Robarts, the central character of *Framley Parsonage*, as being the depiction of 'an English clergyman who should not be a bad man, but one led into temptation by his own youth and by the unclerical accidents of the life of those around him'.[1] Robarts is the vicar of Framley, in the diocese of Barchester, the fictional setting for Trollope's series of novels that began with *The Warden* (1855) and concluded with *The Last Chronicle of Barset* (1867). While on a visit to Chaldicotes, seat of Nathaniel Sowerby, Whig MP for the Western Division of Barsetshire, Robarts has received an invitation from the grand Duke of Omnium to join a party at Gatherum Castle. He has been told that the bishop will be there, furnishing an attractive opportunity to develop an acquaintance and so enhance his career prospects. Mark has gone to bed, determined to resist temptation. However, his 'first thoughts' on waking 'flew back' to the invitation. Trollope precedes his hero's reflections – so really his second thoughts – with a general comment on human vulnerability to the vice of ambition:

> And there is nothing viler than the desire to know great people – people of great rank I should say; nothing worse than the hunting of titles and worshipping of wealth. We all know this, and say it every day of our lives. But presuming that a way into the society of Park Lane was open to us, and a way also into that of Bedford Row, how many of us are there who would prefer Bedford Row because it is so vile to worship wealth and title?

I am led into these rather trite remarks by the necessity of putting forward some sort of excuse for that frame of mind in which the Rev. Mark Robarts awoke on the morning after his arrival at Chaldicotes. And I trust that the fact of his being a clergyman will not be allowed to press against him unfairly. Clergymen are subject to the same passions as other men; and, as far as I can see, give way to them, in one line or in another, almost as frequently. Every clergyman should, by canonical rule, feel a personal disinclination to a bishopric; but yet we do not believe that such personal disinclination is generally very strong.

The first paragraph is a condensed essay, or perhaps a résumé of an essay, on the subject of ambition. It emerges directly and unambiguously from the authorial voice, openly declaring his opinion. His language is strongly committed ('nothing viler'). His social attitudes are evident in his correction of 'great people' to 'people of great rank' – social and moral greatness are different and not necessarily reconcilable qualities – and in the phrases 'hunting of titles' and 'worshipping of wealth'. The short middle sentence of the paragraph rhetorically binds the reader to the author's point of view. The third sentence performs a turn common in essay writing: having made and confirmed his universal moral point, he questions our ability to put our money where our mouth is. Which of us, given the opportunity to enter the fashionable society of Park Lane in Mayfair, would renounce it in favour of the socially less grand society of Bloomsbury? He even follows a common stylistic path of repeating earlier words in his final clause ('vile', 'worship', 'wealth', 'title') to emphasize the contradiction between what we all say and what most of us actually do, so bringing his brief essay full circle. We have, in miniature, a paradigm of one essay format: assertion of principle, assumption of reader's assent, qualification of principle by appeal to common practice.

In the second paragraph, Trollope explicitly applies this essay to his novel, explaining why he has devoted time to what he confesses are commonplace observations. In so doing, he treats his character as a real person, for whose state of mind he needs to apologize. His argument is a syllogism: all human beings are subject to the temptations of ambition; clergymen are human beings; therefore clergymen are subject to the temptations of ambition. This logic involves a further example of human actions being contrary to principles, in this case as applied to the special case of *nolo episcopari* ('I do not wish to be made a bishop'), the required formal response to an offer of a bishopric. The conclusion of Trollope's syllogism – clergymen are as fallible as the rest of us – receives the support of his own experience: 'as far as I can see'.

Trollope's open, indeed insistent, use of the authorial voice serves three main purposes. First, it enables him to establish clearly the novel's central moral and psychological concerns. By adopting the roles of essayist and commentator on his own fiction, Trollope can do this with clarity and economy. There is no Henry James-like slow and oblique approach to the grey areas of human conduct. Trollope simply says what he means and then returns to the story. Other novelists might tentatively shine a weak and probing torch into the darkness of human motivation; Trollope, as it were, switches on an overhead light. Secondly, he ensures that his reader will assess his hero's weakness with understanding and sympathy. There are characters in Trollope's world who invite a reader's stern judgement, but the youthful and attractive Mark Robarts is clearly not going to be one of them, however serious a situation he may find himself in. Judge him harshly and we judge ourselves. Trollope here establishes a rapport with his reader and fellow member of the frail human race. Thirdly, the boundaries of Trollope's social world are defined with geographical precision as stretching from London opulence to provincial reflections of the same class structure. Within this world, the church – and for Trollope this means the established Church of England – plays a central and piquant role as the ideal test of his thesis that we all deplore ambition and yet none of us can resist its lures. The Church of England is both guardian of the nation's conscience and representative of its worship of class.

Trollope was writing at a time when strong and influential novelistic voices deprecated any kind of intrusive author. The artist, Gustave Flaubert famously wrote in a letter in 1857, ought to be in his work like God in creation, omnipotent but invisible. Great art, he later wrote (1866), is scientific and impersonal.[2] The appropriateness or otherwise of the author's overt presence within his or her own novel had been a bone of contention from the novel's earliest days. The eighteenth-century battle between the respective followers of Samuel Richardson and Henry Fielding was largely one of ethical judgement about the relative merits of Pamela's prudential morality and Tom Jones's reckless vivacity (see Sections 6.2 and 4.3, respectively). But the authors' different narrative methods were part of the issue: Richardson's epistolary method enables the character herself, in her role as letter-writer, to present, declare and defend her entrenched positions; whereas Fielding's jovial, hail-fellow-well-met narrative presence invites us, as it were, to share a pot of ale with him and Tom next time we're passing the inn at Upton.

Both types of narrative, of course, have their strengths and have produced their masterpieces. The absence of Ford Madox Ford from *The Good Soldier* (see Section 2.5) leaves the reader no hiding place from Dowell's fractured and disturbed vision of emptiness. But part of the pleasure and profit in reading *Middlemarch* (see Section 2.4) is that we feel we are encountering a thoughtful and sympathetic observer of the frail human condition (even if one somewhat less likely than Henry Fielding to buy us a drink). George Eliot and others fulfil one of the valid and enduring purposes of novel writing: to enable us readers 'to enlarge our knowledge and understanding of the world'.[3] Victorian novelists took particular delight in adopting roles on their own stages. It is part of the audience's pleasure to watch such different actors as the essayist-author of *Framley Parsonage* and the sardonic commentator on human folly of *Vanity Fair* (1848), who brings out from and puts back in their box his cast of puppets. William Makepeace Thackeray, author of *Vanity Fair*, clearly saw in his fellow novelist one he was pleased to have amongst his narrative dramatis personae: he invited Trollope to supply the lead item in his new *Cornhill Magazine*, and there it was that *Framley Parsonage* appeared in 1860.

Considerable effect can be gained by judicious mingling of narrative methods. Arnold Bennett may still have the reputation in some quarters of being a provincial *petit bourgeois*, a journalist among authors, a simple man from the Potteries down if not out in London; but he approached the art of novel-writing with not only the professionalism of a man who earned his living through his pen but also the sophistication of a writer aware of, and to a considerable degree involved in, the literary cross-currents of his age. After several years of hard work in London, he moved in 1903 to Paris, where he met Turgenev and pursued his interest in the French realist school of Flaubert, Maupassant and Balzac. He wrote *The Old Wives' Tale* in France, avowedly on the model of Maupassant's *Une Vie*, a study of the provincial life of a woman from convent school to old age. Bennett doubled the number of heroines so that he could trace the divergent, yet ultimately convergent, lives of a pair of sisters.

Constance and Sophia are the daughters of John Baines, owner of a draper's shop in Bursley, one of the 'Five Towns' which are Bennett's fictional version of the Potteries towns. Constance remains at home, marrying her father's dull but efficient and reliable shop assistant, Samuel Povey, who takes over the business after John's death. The restless Sophia elopes with Gerald Scales, an attractive but untrustworthy travelling salesman, who carries with him all the exotic allure of one who works for the biggest wholesale firm in Manchester. Sophia goes with him to France, where she learns about human – especially male – fallibility and how to fend for herself. As she and her sister, now a widow, enter their later years, Sophia returns home. The lonely, bleak, yet noble deaths of the sisters represent, as Bennett puts it in the title of the fourth and final book of *The Old Wives' Tale*, 'what life is'.

The young Samuel Povey cuts a somewhat gauche figure, and is the butt of Sophia's sense of humour and mischievous behaviour. The mature man grows in stature, notably through his dedication to the cause of his cousin Daniel, a respected member of the community who kills his drunken and irresponsible wife. Daniel is tried and condemned to judicial hanging. Samuel attends the trial assiduously and then organizes a petition against the execution, which gains considerable but futile local support. His efforts take their toll on his health, and, after visiting Daniel in Stafford prison the day before the execution, he returns home in a hysterical state, walks through icy rain to see the rector about a demonstration planned for the day of the hanging and then takes to his bed with a cough and a fever. Constance, concerned at Samuel's rapid deterioration, summons a doctor.

> The venerable Harrop pronounced the word 'pneumonia'. It was acute double pneumonia that Samuel had got. During the three worst months of the year, he had escaped the fatal perils which await a man with a flat chest and a chronic cough, who ignores his condition and defies the weather. But a journey of five hundred yards to the Rectory had been one journey too many. The Rectory was so close to the shop that he had not troubled to wrap himself up as for an excursion to Stafford. He survived the crisis of the disease and then died of toxaemia, caused by a heart that would not do its duty by the blood.

Medical precision, particularly about deaths and their causes, had been a feature of realist prose since Gustave Flaubert – the son of a Rouen surgeon – meticulously and extensively traced the agonizing death of Madame Bovary from arsenic poisoning. Examination of 'what life is' necessitates an unblinking gaze at its ending. Bennett will supply such a gaze when, later in the book, Sophia views the

pallid, thin and brittle body of Gerald Scales. Here, Bennett maintains a more detached and economical descriptive account of the final
event in Samuel's life. His 'flat chest' and 'chronic cough' form a
backcloth to the lengthy and intensive activities of his tireless jour-
neying and activity on behalf of Daniel, and to the brief final stage
which has brought on his acute ending. The presence and status of
the 'venerable' doctor inform Bennett's factual account, his writing
adopting the exactness and brevity of a death certificate. As is the
case in by far the larger part of *The Old Wives' Tale*, Bennett keeps
the narrator at a distance, allowing the doctor and the facts to speak
for themselves. But then, suddenly, he changes key for the chapter's
conclusion:

> A casual death, scarce noticed in the reaction after the great febrile
> demonstration! Besides, Samuel Povey never could impose himself on
> the burgesses. He lacked individuality. He was little. I have often laughed
> at Samuel Povey. But I liked and respected him. He was a very honest
> man. I have always been glad to think that, at the end of his life, destiny
> took hold of him and displayed, to the observant, the vein of greatness
> which runs through every soul without exception. He embraced a cause,
> lost it, and died of it.

The first sentence is perhaps the kind of reflection on Povey's death
that any sensitive novelist might have made. It does, however, quietly link the great commotion of the demonstration to the lone man's
death through the adjective 'febrile': the public display of communal
distress and the private ending of the life of the man who has done
most to generate that event are both kinds of fever, an agitation which
shakes a crowd or an individual.

The dramatic moment comes when Bennett qualifies his unsenti-
mental summary of Povey's limitations – his greatest achievement had
been altering the labelling system in his shop – by suddenly stepping
out from behind the canvas of his portrait to declare that he actually
knew and liked Povey. Like Trollope and Mark Robarts, Bennett and
Samuel Povey exist, it seems, on the same layer of reality. Bennett's
art has been as scientific as Flaubert would wish in the first half of
the paragraph, but he is far from invisible in the second. How those
who believe in a withdrawn and detached author would be shocked.
The author reveals himself as part of a community, which his own
novel depicts. Bennett clearly intends his intervention to be unexpected. This is the only occasion in the novel when the author speaks
in the first person as an intrusive narrator; and comment of any kind

is rare. When, by contrast, the narrator of Samuel Butler's *The Way of All Flesh* (1903) says after the death of his godson's mother, 'With all her faults I had always rather liked Christina' (chapter eighty-three), his comment is naturally embedded in his consistently frank but sympathetic voice, and so comes as no surprise.

This, then, is the moment for Bennett to add his weight to the meaning of his novel. Human life may be ultimately bleak, and its humble participants absurd (he admits that, like Sophia and most of his readers, he has so far found Samuel Povey slightly ridiculous), but this ordinary little man has shown himself capable of one great act. He was also a decent human being. Honesty may not be the most strikingly heroic of virtues, but it may be one of the most admirable and useful – as Jane Austen's Emma Woodhouse learns from George Knightley. This common man, Samuel Povey, deserves a fanfare.

Bennett is also fully aware of the place of this event in his larger narrative. A sardonic view is seldom far away in his work. He notes, for example, that the execution of Daniel Povey was the most riveting event in Bursley since the shooting of an escaped elephant; and he observes how, when the demonstration comes to an end, the public houses do a roaring trade. Human beings do not always behave with decorum. But 'decorum' is exactly the word for Samuel Povey, and Bennett's prose now matches it. His language is simple, the sentences short and restrained: 'But I liked and respected him. He was a very honest man.' Nevertheless, Povey merits a quiet flourish: the conceit that something as grand as 'destiny' may have taken hold of him. The final sentence is not a bad epitaph to have and is set out with the simple dignity of unadorned language and triadic form: 'He embraced a cause, lost it, and died of it.'

The Old Wives' Tale shows us that we can all attain, in our own ways, a comparable integrity. Povey's widow Constance achieves, in the novel's final chapter, her own version. Old, ill and frail, she staggers to the town hall in icy rain, which seems to be semi-permanent in Bursley, to vote against the Federation of the Five Towns. Like her husband's walk to the rectory, this precipitates her death. She catches a chill which, a doctor is on hand to report objectively, brings on acute rheumatic fever. There are values, causes which, however hopeless (the anti-Federationists win the day, but not the whole campaign), can ennoble through their capacity to give purpose and dignity to an otherwise humdrum life. By connecting his characters – here husband and wife – through such acts of selfless commitment, Bennett demonstrates that there is a 'vein of greatness' running through us.

By stepping out from his own book to deliver an elegy on Samuel Povey, the author takes his stand for human worth. The objectivity of so much of his narrative ensures that a spotlight illuminates his sudden entry onto the stage. Authorial comment in a realist narrative can carry extraordinary weight.

6.2 Action: Henry Fielding, *Joseph Andrews* (1742), book four, chapter eight

As *Joseph Andrews* draws near to its happy conclusion, its hero is keen to hasten his wedding to his beloved Fanny Goodwill. Both the young lovers' paths to eventual union have been crossed by exposure to several sexual predators, some outrageously comic, some dangerously threatening.

The novel's gambit is an inversion of the conventional depiction of women as subject to unwelcome male advances. Samuel Richardson's first novel, *Pamela* (1740), had become the publishing sensation of its time by extending this single plot-line to combine narrative suspense with psychological acumen and, eventually, a happy and morally acceptable outcome. Pamela Andrews is the young and inexperienced servant of Lady B____. When her mistress dies, she is flattered, propositioned and virtually imprisoned by her ardent and infatuated new master, Squire B____. Pamela withstands all his advances, and the treachery of other members of the household. The novel's resolution comes when Squire B____ sees the error of his ways, and preserves moral propriety at the expense of fidelity to class norms by asking Pamela to marry him. Wedding bells ring out and, as the novel's subtitle puts it, 'virtue' is 'rewarded'.

Pamela's success generated numerous criticisms, parodies and spin-offs by 'pro-' and 'anti-Pamelists'.[4] Not everyone thought that 'virtue' was something to be 'rewarded' in quite such a material way, or that Pamela's behaviour was quite so morally acceptable. Henry Fielding's short burlesque *Shamela* (1741) presents a very different heroine whose 'virtue' is nothing but pretence. The much more substantial *Joseph Andrews* invents for Pamela a brother. His situation begins as a parody of Pamela's: his master, Sir Thomas Booby, an uncle of Pamela's B____, dies, and the innocent young servant is sexually assailed by the widow Lady Booby and, for good measure, her comically grotesque servant Mrs Slipslop. However, Fielding soon develops the narrative into a much wider and deeper depiction of how difficult it is not just to preserve one's virginity in a sexually rapacious society, but to trace a path of active virtue in a world governed by other and more insidious vices, notably hypocrisy.

Sexual violence does remain a threatening element in the vicious landscape through which the protagonists have to tread their way towards union and happiness, the proper rewards of their true virtues. In the seventh chapter of book four, Fanny has been propositioned by a preening beau, and then physically assaulted by his servant. Joseph is fortunately on hand to rescue Fanny by fighting off the intended rapist. These dangerous events explain the urgency with which Joseph then begs Parson Adams to expedite the marriage he is to conduct for his young friends. Only by becoming man and wife as soon as possible can their apprehensions be alleviated.

However, Adams attributes Joseph's eagerness to sexual desire and unreasonable fear. He subjects Joseph to an impromptu sermon on the sins of carnal appetite and failure to trust in God's care for his creatures. Both sins, Adams says, are passions – strong feelings – and excessive indulgence in them amounts to criminality. Adams warns Joseph that he is too much inclined to yield to his passions. Even love when over-indulged may blind us to our duty. Adams, in the set manner of sermonists, cites biblical precedents: Matthew's gospel for the evils of lust, and the Old Testament story of Abraham and Isaac for the need for us to submit to God's will in everything.[5] Adams moves to his peroration:

> 'Now, believe me, no Christian ought so to set his heart on any person or thing in this world, but that whenever it shall be required or taken from him in any manner by Divine Providence, he may be able, peaceably, quietly, and contentedly to resign it.' At which words one came hastily in and acquainted Mr. Adams that his youngest son was drowned. He stood silent a moment, and soon began to stamp about the room and deplore his loss with the bitterest agony. Joseph, who was overwhelmed with concern likewise, recovered himself sufficiently to endeavour to comfort the parson; in which attempt he used many arguments that he had at several times remembered out of his own discourses both in private and public, (for he was a great enemy to the passions, and preached nothing more than the conquest of them by reason and grace) but he was not at leisure now to hearken to his advice. 'Child, child,' said he, 'do not go about impossibilities. Had it been any other of my children, I could have borne it with patience; but my little prattler, the darling and comfort of my old age, – the little wretch to be snatched out of life just at his entrance into it; the sweetest, best-tempered boy, who never did a thing to offend me. It was but this morning I gave him his first lesson in *Quæ Genus*. This was the very book he learnt; poor child! it is of no

further use to thee now. He would have made the best scholar, and have been an ornament to the church; – such parts, and such goodness, never met in one so young.' 'And the handsomest lad too,' says Mrs. Adams, recovering from a swoon in Fanny's arms. 'My poor Jacky, shall I never see thee more?' cries the parson. 'Yes, surely,' says Joseph, 'and in a better place, you will meet again never to part more.' I believe the parson did not hear these words, for he paid little regard to them, but went on lamenting whilst the tears trickled down into his bosom. At last he cried out, 'Where is my little darling?' and was sallying out, when, to his great surprize and joy, in which I hope the reader will sympathize, he met his son in a wet condition indeed, but alive, and running towards him.

The chief characteristic of this episode is its economy of means. By this stage, Adams's sermon has – it must seem to the ardent Joseph, who knows from recent experience that some situations demand immediate action rather than words – gone on quite long enough. When the narrator cuts off Adams's flow, it is with a single sentence, consisting of two co-ordinated clauses linked by the simplest conjunction, 'and', together with one subordinate noun clause: 'At which words one came hastily in and acquainted Mr. Adams that his youngest son was drowned'. Emphasis is on action: 'came in', 'acquainted ... that', 'was drowned'. Fielding does not give us the actual speech of the messenger, so that narrative event displaces 'words'. The only descriptive word is the adverb 'hastily', a minimal and appropriate indication of urgency. The messenger's identity is hidden in the anonymous 'one': the message matters, not who delivers it. 'Acquainted' perhaps also strikes a somewhat distant note, though this may be partly because the transitive use of 'acquaint' in the sense of 'inform' is now less common than it was in Fielding's time.[6]

The incident is also quickly, and happily, resolved: 'he met his son in a wet condition indeed, but alive, and running towards him'. Between the false report and the real encounter, in which two simple but essential adjectives ('wet ... but alive') are contained within verbal action ('met', 'running towards him'), Fielding allows space for Adams's strong responses. But these are again handled with economy. A single sentence is enough to convey the power of his emotions: 'He stood silent a moment, and soon began to stamp about the room and deplore his loss with the bitterest agony'. A moment of shock gives way to entirely natural violent physical action and strong feeling.

The longest sections of the episode are allocated to Joseph's efforts to comfort Adams, and then to the parson's lament for his 'lost' son; and it is in these that Fielding poses clear but discreet questions about his character's consistency and justification in claiming moral high ground. Joseph uses 'many arguments' taken from Adams's own sermons. Fielding does not give examples so that the scene is not unnecessarily stretched out, and, no doubt, so that the reader is not diverted into wondering about Joseph's possible lack of tact. Fielding clearly wants the emphasis to be on Adams himself and his inability to apply to his own present condition the lessons with which he has spent so long 'acquainting' others. The parenthesis is the most trenchant contribution, its abstract vocabulary ('passions', 'reason', 'grace') sitting uneasily alongside the physical actuality of the event and Adams's reactions.

Adams's own words are also pretty damning, if understandable in human terms. He is patronizing to Joseph: 'Child, child'. He makes a morally dubious distinction between his youngest and his other children, whose sudden deaths would, it seems, have been more bearable. I suspect it occurs to most readers (if only at a second reading) that Adams's partiality is probably transferable: 'Had it been any other of my children ... but my sturdy eldest boy/my darling beloved daughter ...'. Extreme emotion heightens the value of its object. Adams's account of his son is couched in superlatives: his 'sweetest, best-tempered boy' would have 'made the best scholar'. He lapses into self-indulgence in imagining for the boy a dazzling ecclesiastical career on the basis of an elementary lesson in Latin grammar,[7] and there is a touch of dramatic rhetoric in his gesturing towards 'the very book' from which the lesson was taken and his declaration that 'it is of no further use to thee now'. Adams is guilty not only of failing to execute his own sermons, but of self-indulgent partiality.

However, the scene remains short and is rapidly defused, before the disparity between Adams's comically self-contradictory and weak behaviour and the seriousness of the supposed event can get out of hand.[8] For Adams, though the temporary butt of the comedy, behaves entirely naturally. Fielding's broader target is facile moralizing divorced from human truth. Adams is, indeed, one of the heroes of *Joseph Andrews*, the wielder of (at times very) muscular Christianity. He is a fearless and valiant protector of people in distress, and a good-hearted innocent abroad. He has two not unattractive failings: a naïve trust, contrary to all his experience, that those who call themselves Christians will behave as true Christians, and a self-indulgently high estimation of his own capacity as a sermon writer. This pride is his, relatively harmless, version of the hypocrisy pervading the society depicted in *Joseph Andrews*.

The brevity of the scene, and the way in which it suddenly appears in the narrative and as quickly recedes, lend it the quality of a parable, that is, a short story, set within a longer narrative, which illustrates a moral or theological idea. Like the novel's opening conceit of male virtue being laid siege to, this parable is an inversion of the convention. It illustrates not how a good Christian should behave, but how a man whose calling is to instruct others in obedient and moral conduct actually does behave when he is put to the test. Its lesson is not theological doctrine but human nature. It teaches us that people's emotions are more subject to the power of immediate events than their rational discourse might suggest, and that any humane account of the world needs to take into sympathetic account such weakness. Fielding's vision is essentially comic. We are all of us frail and blind to our shortcomings. But some shortcomings are more endearing than others. Even Joseph, meek and mild as he is, loses his patience when, after duly celebrating the health of his son, Adams coolly reverts to his sermon ('No, Joseph, do not give too much way to thy passions'), as if nothing had happened. Neither Joseph nor Fielding can let Adams get away with this flagrant inconsistency. When Adams goes on to warn Joseph that it is sinful to love even his future wife excessively, Joseph protests that he cannot but love Fanny immoderately, and is praised and encouraged to do so by Mrs Adams, who interrupts her husband with a sturdy common-sense defence of married love: 'Don't hearken to him, Mr. Joseph, be as good a husband as you are able, and love your wife with all your body and soul too.' Mrs Adams's forceful contribution, which appropriately concludes the chapter and her husband's cross-examination of the good Joseph, reminds us that she has played a brief part in the parable, her cry that her 'drowned' son was 'the handsomest lad' illustrating that human partiality, if not taken to absurd lengths, is both a natural and admirable expression of love for our dear ones. Fielding's commentary on human affairs is channelled through such humble but touchingly authentic characters.

6.3 Conversation: Jane Austen, *Persuasion* (1818), volume one, chapter eleven

While Captains Wentworth and Harville led the talk on one side of the room, and, by recurring to former days, supplied anecdotes in abundance to occupy and entertain the others, it fell to Anne's lot to be placed rather apart with Captain Benwick; and a very good impulse of her nature

obliged her to begin an acquaintance with him. He was shy, and disposed to abstraction; but the engaging mildness of her countenance,
and gentleness of her manners, soon had their effect; and Anne was well
repaid the first trouble of exertion. He was evidently a young man of
considerable taste in reading, though principally in poetry; and besides
the persuasion of having given him at least an evening's indulgence in
the discussion of subjects, which his usual companions had probably no
concern in, she had the hope of being of real use to him in some sug
gestions as to the duty and benefit of struggling against affliction, which
had naturally grown out of their conversation. For, though shy, he did not
seem reserved; it had rather the appearance of feelings glad to burst their
usual restraints; and having talked of poetry, the richness of the present
age, and gone through a brief comparison of opinion as to the first-rate
poets, trying to ascertain whether *Marmion* or *The Lady of the Lake* were
to be preferred, and how ranked the *Giaour* and *The Bride of Abydos*; and
moreover, how the *Giaour* was to be pronounced, he showed himself
so intimately acquainted with all the tenderest songs of the one poet
and all the impassioned descriptions of hopeless agony of the other; he
repeated, with such tremulous feeling, the various lines which imaged
a broken heart, or a mind destroyed by wretchedness, and looked so
entirely as if he meant to be understood, that she ventured to hope he
did not always read only poetry; and to say, that she thought it was the
misfortune of poetry, to be seldom safely enjoyed by those who enjoyed
it completely; and that the strong feelings which alone could estimate it
truly, were the very feelings which ought to taste it but sparingly.

The extensive conversation between Anne Elliot and Captain
Benwick is narrated entirely from the perspective of Anne. No word
of direct speech, either from Anne or from Benwick, is given, and it is
not presented in indirect speech, which would have conveyed a near
verbatim account (see Section 5.5). The paragraph instead provides
a summary and summation of the conversation, as mediated through
Anne's perception and growing understanding of a young man whom
she has only recently met.

It is Anne's lot throughout *Persuasion* to be separate from the main
group. She is almost openly despised by her father and elder sister, and
she is treated by her married younger sister as a useful child-minder
On social occasions, Anne plays the piano while others dance. Her
new sailor acquaintances at Lyme will prove to be a much healthier
and more upright set than her own self-regarding family; but, for the
moment, her relationship with one, Captain Wentworth, is strained
and awkward because they have only recently resumed social con
tact after she had broken off her engagement to him several year

earlier. Further, conversation among them is bound, as the opening sentence of the paragraph acknowledges, to be dominated by shared male experiences.

Anne therefore is drawn towards the other outsider in the group. Captain Benwick had been engaged to Captain Harville's sister, Fanny, who died the preceding summer while Benwick was at sea in search of promotion and financial competence, which would have enabled their marriage to go ahead. Benwick is, according to Wentworth (whose estimation of character is as sound as anyone's when not affected by personal sentiments), a man of strong feelings and 'quiet, serious, and retiring manners', and so vulnerable to the emotional effects of his affliction. The generous Captain Harville has taken Benwick into his family and, though no reader himself, has set up shelves for Benwick's books in their cramped living quarters.

Benwick's conversation with Anne is reported in two sentences, the first of moderate length ('He was evidently a young man . . .'), the second of much greater length ('For, though shy . . .'). These complex but lucid sentences unfold as Benwick opens up in response to Anne's kindly and sympathetic attention. Benwick is, we are twice told, 'shy', but he proves to be not 'reserved': a nice distinction between his natural diffidence and timidity on the one side, and coolness of disposition on the other. Indeed, Anne's sympathy soon evokes warmth in Benwick, which confirms Wentworth's opinion of his strong feelings.

The initial clause of the first of those sentences sets up the premise, that Benwick is a man of taste and sensitivity, and leads to two consequences. The first is conveyed in a long prepositional construction: 'besides the persuasion of having given him at least an evening's indulgence in the discussion of subjects, which his usual companions had probably no concern in'. Anne provides for Benwick what his bluff sailor colleagues cannot: a shared pleasure in, and knowledge of, books. One imagines that there was not very much chat about poetry on the quarter-decks of warships, particularly during the Napoleonic wars, recently brought to a temporary end by the Treaty of Paris of 1814. *Persuasion* is explicitly set at this time, which explains the presence back on land of so many sailors. Like many a sensitive woman, Anne is able to identify and engage with an aspect of Benwick's nature which purely male companionship frustrates and suppresses.

However, though a sympathetic conversationalist and fellow poetry-lover, Anne is also clear-headed and rational. Jane Austen, ever alert to fine distinctions of language, places the word 'indulgence' carefully and tellingly. As used here, it has its primary and original

meaning as identified by the *Oxford English Dictionary*: the willing gratification of another person's desire or humour. Anne allows
Benwick to share with her an otherwise private love. But another
meaning of 'indulgence' had crept into its meaning as early as the
seventeenth century: the action of yielding oneself to a desire or
propensity. The former sense is a beneficent act by one person to
another; the latter turns the process inward and begins to shade
into 'self-indulgence', giving way to one's inclinations to a possibly
excessive or even dangerous degree.[9]

Anne is as prone as any of us to giving way to her own feelings.
But she also has a hard-headed side, which renders her fully aware
of universal shortcomings. Jane Austen will end the chapter with
Anne's reflection that, like many a moralist, she has been eloquent
in her advice to another person on a point in which her own conduct would not bear examination. Thus the prepositional construction
('besides...') is checked by a full clause expressing a more pragmatic
response: 'she had the hope of being of real use to him in some sugges-
tions as to the duty and benefit of struggling against affliction'. 'Duty'
and 'benefit' are the abstract language of ethics, not the metaphorical
or hyperbolical flights of poetry. 'The duty and benefit of struggling
against affliction' sounds like the title of a moral essay or an improving
sermon.

The last sentence in the paragraph is another of those *tours-de-force*
of Austen's prose which demonstrate her total command of expression
(see Section 3.2). Its form is created first by the repeated deferral of
its main clause until the topics of conversation have had time to 'burst
their usual restraints'. Poetry itself as a generic whole; the richness
of the present age of poetry writing (all the poems named are recent
publications, from Scott's *Marmion* in 1808 to the two Byron poems,
The Giaour and *The Bride of Abydos*, in 1813); the relative merits of the recent works of the two most famous contemporary poets,
Walter Scott and Lord Byron; and – with a nice touch of deflating
humour – how *The Giaour* should be pronounced (answer: to rhyme
with 'power') pass by as topics that each, no doubt, occupied a good
few minutes.

Austen then checks the flow of ideas by a sequence of three clauses
which demonstrate that Anne is not only taking part in the conversation but also taking stock of her companion. These clauses also, by
means of the adverb 'so' and the adjective 'such', give notice of a
consequence whose significance builds up as it is deferred. Benwick
'showed himself *so* intimately acquainted with all the tenderest

songs...'; he 'repeated, with *such* tremulous feeling...'; and he 'looked *so* entirely as if he meant to be understood' that.... These clauses are about the strong emotional force of Benwick's relationship with his beloved poetry. He is 'intimately' acquainted with Scott's 'tenderest' songs and with Byron's 'impassioned descriptions of hopeless agony'. The lines he chooses to recite reflect a 'broken heart' or 'a mind destroyed by wretchedness'. Such is his ardour that he is confessionally opening himself up to Anne's understanding: these are not, for Benwick, fictions, but channels for his own intense love and suffering.

However, the syntax of the sentence is under careful management because these are not Benwick's actual words but Anne's summary of their emotive content. Austen sets each statement in its place, and resolves the syntax by switching from Benwick as subject to Anne: '...that *she* ventured....' Anne delicately but firmly takes control of the sentence as she endeavours to rein in Benwick's poetic ardour with the cooler language of prose. Anne has three prosaic warnings: she hopes Benwick does not read only poetry; she says that poetry is perhaps most dangerous to those who love it most; and she observes that 'the strong feelings which alone could estimate it truly, were the very feelings which ought to taste it but sparingly'. A triad of warnings matches the earlier triad of clauses summarizing Benwick's reactions.

Jane Austen's commentary is oblique, sensitive and complex. Indeed, the very word 'commentary' strikes a crudely discordant note, that of the mere literary critic stumbling to write in tune with the finest art. There are so many lines of music that Austen is here blending into her counterpoint. Poetry is a powerful medium for the expression of feeling. Male society, particularly male professional society, perhaps does not encourage or even allow its more sensitive members means of self-expression. Human sympathy, one woman's recognition of one man's needs, is also a powerful agent, and for good. Self-expression and self-indulgence are near allied, and thin partitions do their bounds divide. The former is necessary and healthy, but the latter is inward-looking and dangerously obsessive. Benwick does not just identify with the suffering heroes of Scott and Byron; he is relishing the process of self-identification. Anne is aware of this, and ensures that she is able to stand back from the intensity of the emotion. It is, she goes on ruefully to acknowledge, so much easier to do so when someone else's emotions are on display. This is not to cast doubt on the authenticity of Benwick's distress, but to say something about the sheer complexity of our human emotions: distress can coexist with pleasure.[10]

Further, conversation, the art of sympathetic human discourse, is therapeutic and healthy. Conversation is the acknowledgement of other people's thoughts and feelings. An element of humour helps (how do you pronounce 'Giaour'?). Poetry may be powerful, but so too is prose. Jane Austen's sentence gives full expression to Benwick's feelings, but always within the effortlessly balanced judgement of complex yet lucid syntax. A good sentence holds together its constituent elements and shapes them to a satisfying conclusion. This is precisely what Anne is doing as she responds to Benwick with mingled sympathy and objectivity. Jane Austen's sentence is itself the expression of its meaning: it enacts itself.

Still further, this passage is not just about Benwick. Anne, too, has lost a beloved – not tragically, as Benwick has, nor, it will prove, finally. But she is additionally suffering from the recognition that she has ultimate responsibility for her own loss: if she had not listened to well-intentioned persuasion, she would have now been married to him. Wentworth's presence – his is the first name in the paragraph – is thus a source of simultaneous and continuing agony and pleasure for her. Her love for him will actually prove deeper and more lasting, if not more intense, than Benwick's for Fanny Harville. Indeed, in the precise economy of Austen's plotting, the two relationships are intimately linked. Anne's agony has been increased by signs of a growing relationship between Wentworth and Louisa Musgrove, sister of Anne's brother-in-law. The sudden and unexpected news of an engagement between Benwick and Louisa ('of course they had fallen in love over poetry', muses Anne in volume two, chapter six) frees up the pathway towards the reunion of Anne and Wentworth. As significantly, the Benwick story underlies the celebrated discussion between Anne and Captain Harville about the relative constancy in love of women and men (volume two, chapter eleven).

Finally, Jane Austen's commentary on the complexity of human emotions is distanced from the authorial voice by being dramatized through Anne Elliot. Its wisdom and perception are not, as it were, imposed from without, but are implicit within the texture of the heroine's own story. Its sentiments have been arrived at through suffering and alienation. Its ethical profundity is not easily donned, but is heroically won. Its testimony to the soothing power of sympathetic but clear-minded conversation is shown by one who is relentlessly excluded by others. Its mature and measured sentence structure demonstrates how command of language can order all but the most disruptive of feelings and experiences. It marks a key stage in the empowerment of Anne as agent of her own destiny rather than object of others' persuasion. Anne's oblique declaration of continuing love for Wentworth in the course of her later conversation with Captain Harville, which prompts from Wentworth the most spontaneous and powerful love-letter in Jane Austen, is *Persuasion*'s conclusive comment on the relationship between language and autonomy.

6.4 Satirical narrative: Jonathan Swift, *Gulliver's Travels* (1726), part four, chapters five and eight

Dissatisfaction with the present state of society and belief in the possibility of an ideal society have long inspired the human imagination. Plato's *Republic* set the classical model. In pursuit of a proper definition of justice, Socrates there describes a hierarchical model of a sustainable state, an intellectual aristocracy benignly directed by a philosopher-king and integrating the diverse orders of human society. Many later writers have taken their cue from Plato, their visions reflecting different historical circumstances and philosophical positions. In the renaissance, Thomas More's *Utopia* (1516) is the most celebrated, its combination of critique (of private property and monarchism) and counter-ideal (communism and social integration) a trenchant commentary on the present, a noble vision of the future and a summation of humanist ideals. Written in Latin, the intellectual *lingua franca* of the period, it transcends national boundaries in favour of European enlightenment, and its title (from the Greek, meaning 'not-place') has become the generic name for projects of political and social organization.

Such works belong to a philosophical rather than novelistic tradition, but their fictional nature and imaginative ambition have attracted novelists with an interest in how societies function and how they fail to fulfil ideals of human aspiration. We have seen George Orwell, in *Coming up for Air*, setting his narrator's dissatisfaction with his dreary suburban life against a vision of a fuller, organic mode of living (see Section 4.6). Orwell employs a common novelistic procedure of balancing unattractive reality and tempting ideal, though he is far too level-headed a writer to allow the former to operate simply as an uncriticized excuse for the latter. The fundamental dichotomy between observable human poverty and imagined (or recollected) ideal does, however, provide a productive fictional model for many writers, such as, in the Victorian period, Samuel Butler, whose *Erewhon* (1872: the title an anagram of 'nowhere')

envisages a (flawed) utopia to set questioningly against the constric-
tions of the contemporary world. Orwell's most famous narratives are,
of course, his fable *Animal Farm* (1945) and his searing vision of political and psychological totalitarianism, *Nineteen Eighty-Four* (1949).
These, together with Aldous Huxley's *Brave New World* (1932), represent what is commonly referred to as 'dystopian' literature, that is
to say fictional visions of an unattractive, even nightmarish, society.

Whether the world described reflects a writer's aspirations or fears,
the narrative strategy remains similar. Readers are invited to make
comparisons between the society with which they are familiar in their
everyday experience and that described in the fiction. As Lemuel
Gulliver, narrator of *Gulliver's Travels*, says when confronted by the
giants of Brobdingnag after living among the miniature Lilliputians,
'philosophers are in the right when they tell us, that nothing is great or
little otherwise than by comparison' (part two, chapter one). Jonathan
Swift's procedure in the first two parts of *Gulliver's Travels* is to subject his narrator to a process of defamiliarization (see Section 3.6)
whereby his belief in the human form as standard, the norm against
which all other creatures are measured, is undermined by discover-
ies of recognizably human beings of sizes so much lesser, and then
greater, than himself. Once admit a process of comparability and
the process is potentially open-ended: 'who knows but that even this
prodigious race of mortals might be equally overmatched in some distant part of the world, whereof we have yet no discovery?' (part two,
chapter one).

Gulliver's Travels consists of four separate voyages undertaken
by its narrator to strange and outlandish parts of the world where
such relativity obliges him to reconsider his relationship, and his
society's, to unexpected alternatives, which may invite favourable or
unfavourable comparisons. Differences in size are the obvious, and
most immediately disarming, observations Gulliver makes. But it is
behavioural differences that are ultimately the most disturbing aspects
of the increasingly kaleidoscopic experiences to which Gulliver is
exposed. Such differences do not simply displace the human form
as physical standard: they oblige us to question the validity of our
cherished perceptions of our own values.

Part four, Gulliver's voyage to the country of the Houyhnhnms,
is the climax of an increasing process of defamiliarization. These
Houyhnhnms are horses in form, but possess the power of speech,
the capacity to organize themselves into a stable and sustainable society, and command over a race they call yahoos, who are savage and

violent in their behaviour but disturbingly human-like in outward appearance. Such is the gap in behaviour and understanding between Gulliver and his society on the one side, and the Houyhnhnms on the other, that extensive descriptions of both are required to enable a full comparison. Swift first has Gulliver, in chapter five, give an account to his Houyhnhnm master of common practices back home. Of these, warfare is particularly difficult for the Houyhnhnm to understand, particularly as the Houyhnhnms lack the technological capacity for advanced forms of mutual destruction.

Here are two excerpts from Gulliver's explanation of why human beings go to war:

> Sometimes the quarrel between two princes is to decide which of them shall dispossess a third of his dominions, where neither of them pretend to any right. Sometimes one prince quarrelleth with another, for fear the other should quarrel with him. Sometimes a war is entered upon, because the enemy is too strong, and sometimes because he is too weak. Sometimes our neighbours want the things which we have, or have the things which we want; and we both fight, till they take ours or give us theirs....

> Alliance by blood or marriage is a sufficient cause of war between princes, and the nearer the kindred is, the greater is their disposition to quarrel: poor nations are hungry, and rich nations are proud, and pride and hunger will ever be at variance. For these reasons, the trade of a soldier is held the most honourable of all others: because a soldier is a yahoo hired to kill in cold blood as many of his own species, who have never offended him, as possibly he can.

The primary quality of Swift's prose here is its cool logic. Anaphora – beginning each sentence with 'sometimes' – conveys both careful detachment and steady accumulation. Gulliver is not getting carried away, but is nonetheless free and frank in his commentary. Yet, as one 'sometimes' follows another, then another, then another, the impression is increasingly built up that there are so many possible situations that one or other of them is likely to apply to any international relationship.

A bizarre conclusion emerges from the remorseless logic of individual examples. 'Sometimes one prince quarrelleth with another, for fear the other should quarrel with him.' This sentence pivots on its comma, each half the mirror-image of the other: prince A fights prince B/prince B fights prince A. The chiasmus, the crossed syntax, conveys the inescapability of the closed and self-destructive logic. Prince

A declares war on prince B because he is afraid that prince B will declare war on him. Prince A's actions therefore precipitate the very thing of which he is fearful. Violence can only be avoided by violence.

'Sometimes a war is entered upon, because the enemy is too strong, and sometimes because he is too weak.' Both possible conditions, set out in parallel adverbial clauses, precipitate war. Can there ever be complete equality of opposing forces? Therefore there is no condition that is not itself a *casus belli*, a situation which justifies war.

'Sometimes our neighbours want the things which we have, or have the things which we want'. Chiasmus again locks in the logic: 'want . . . have'/'have . . . want'. The absurdity of this proposition lies in its being self-perpetuating. The result of war will be either that our neighbours will take from us the things they want or that we will take from them the things we want. The outcome will be the same situation, an inequality between having and wanting. The cycle will therefore be repeated endlessly.

Swift's language remains on a general level. No specific wars are referred to. This was not the case in the earlier parts of *Gulliver's Travels*. For example, in part one a war takes place between the island of Lilliput and its close neighbour Blefuscu. Gulliver makes himself a hero among the Lilliputians by capturing the bulk of the Blefuscan fleet and hauling them to Lilliput. This war is a thinly-veiled analogy with the War of the Spanish Succession (1701–13) and the hostilities between England and France. So not all the alternative societies Gulliver visits are as peace-loving as the Houyhnhnms. Swift's satire in the earlier sections of the book is more specific, evident and limited. By depicting events at home in the miniature form of Lilliputians, Swift makes both appear ridiculous and contemptible. The Lilliputians are small and mean-minded. Are we any better?

But in part four, Swift's canvas is broader. In our paragraph, Gulliver lists various other justifications for waging war before drawing his desolating general conclusion. If it is the case that any condition will provoke war, then no change can take place: 'poor nations are hungry, and rich nations are proud, and pride and hunger will ever be at variance'. There is, it seems, something unchangeable, endemic, in human nature which produces continual warfare. Utopian solutions, such as equal distribution of wealth among nations, appear hopelessly unattainable, contrary to the observable realities of human societies.

It is often the case that Swift reserves his sharpest remarks for the conclusions of paragraphs. Here his final sentence stands out from the

rest by its sudden shift in argument, allied to a particularly savage sarcasm. He maintains the language of logic ('for these reasons'), but
moves the focus from the causes of war to a cultural cliché. Since war is
so profound and unalterable a part of how we function as social beings,
those who propagate war on our behalf are the most 'honourable' of
us. Military heroism is a deeply embedded cultural notion. A hint of
the mercenary in the word 'trade' perhaps strikes a warningly discordant note, but scarcely prepares us for the sheer force of the second
part of the sentence. Swift's description of a soldier is remorseless in
its accretion of defining criteria: 'hired [a consequence of "trade"] to
kill in cold blood as many of his own species . . . as possibly he can'.
Each phrase and clause twists the knife: soldiers kill not out of passion but coolly and deliberately; they kill their own species, not others
for the purpose of feeding; they have no personal motivation for their
actions; and the more they kill the higher they are regarded. The key
and most disturbing word is, again, the logical indicator: 'because'.
It is not that these defining characteristics of a soldier are even necessary evils. No, they actually constitute what we term 'honour'. Human
society is marked by a value-system in which virtue is defined by our
capacity to kill as relentlessly as possible.

  Swift even slips in the word 'yahoo' as part of his definition, thus
disarming, as it were, those who argue (and many critics do) that
the yahoos are perversions of human beings, human beings with all
the good bits omitted and the bad bits exaggerated. Well, soldiers
have already committed themselves to that omission and exaggeration; which is why they are honoured. I write of 'Swift' here, not
'Gulliver', for it is very difficult not to conclude that the strident savagery of this conclusion breaks through the mould of a 'persona' –
that is, the Lemuel Gulliver who is the notional narrator. To try
to escape from Swift's *saeva indignatio*[11] ('savage indignation') by
claiming that this is only his persona's view, feels too like a shifty
deflection of an uncomfortable truth. In his standard account of the
connections between satire and novel, Ronald Paulson makes the
point that the novel as it emerges in the eighteenth century shares
with satire a concern to depict a recognizably actual world, one
containing actions and people akin to those we have experienced
ourselves. Satire needs 'to convince, at least momentarily, that its
world is real and that the evil it shows really does exist.'[12] Otherwise, we might add, why bother to satirize it? *Gulliver's Travels* is
scarcely a 'realist' novel, its satirical journeys taking on the air of
fantasy and fable as they accumulate. But its subject is not so much

the alternative societies on display, but our society. That is where the satirical realism lies.

When describing the Houyhnhnms' alternative society in chapter eight, Swift's commentary on us is more oblique than when he is letting Gulliver describe warfare, but it is nonetheless sharp and uncomfortable:

> Friendship and benevolence are the two principal virtues among the Houyhnhnms, and these not confined to particular objects, but universal to the whole race. For a stranger from the remotest part is equally treated with the nearest neighbour, and wherever he goes, looks upon himself as at home. They preserve decency and civility in the highest degrees, but are altogether ignorant of ceremony. They have no fondness for their colts or foals, but the care they take in educating them proceeds entirely from the dictates of reason. And I observed my master to show the same affection to his neighbour's issue that he had for his own. They will have it that nature teaches them to love the whole species, and it is reason only that maketh a distinction of persons, where there is a superior degree of virtue.

The tricky word in this paragraph is 'fondness'. A modern reader may well conclude too hastily that a species with 'no fondness' for its offspring sounds unattractively cold. But the original meaning of 'fondness' was 'foolish, excessive affection', as when King Lear refers to himself as a 'foolish fond old man' (IV.vii.60).[13] The dominant note in the paragraph is the Houyhnhnms' universal benevolence. This is stated unambiguously in the first sentence, in the antithesis of 'not confined to particular objects, but universal to the whole race'. The second sentence exemplifies the general point by asserting that the horses treat all strangers as they do their nearest neighbours. The central word is 'equally', which follows up 'universal' and contrasts with 'particular'. This is a society of equals, one devoid of discrimination. The final sentence reiterates the argument: their love is for the 'whole' species. Should reason observe a moral superiority in any individual, then that is acknowledged. But there is no natural aversion or preference shown on the basis of, let us say, colour. One of the Houyhnhnms whom Gulliver first encounters in chapter one is a grey, the other is a bay; but they treat each other with equal respect.

In this context of respectful equality Gulliver observes that the horses have no fondness for their own colts or foals, adding that his master shows 'the same affection to his neighbour's issue that he had for his own'. They do not lack true affection; love is given equally to all members of the species. Swift tells us how to interpret 'fondness' two paragraphs later, when Gulliver describes how a married pair of Houyhnhnms show to each other the 'same friendship and benevolence' they bear to 'all others of the same species' when they meet, 'without jealousy, fondness, quarrelling, or discontent'. 'Fondness' is one item in a list of the ill effects of partiality and discrimination from which their guiding virtue of universal benevolence protects them.

Repetition within our paragraph of the word 'neighbour' strikes a note which would not have escaped Jonathan Swift, Dean of St Patrick's Cathedral, Dublin, nor eighteenth-century readers in general, nearly all of whom would have been familiar with biblical texts. A resonant commandment in the gospels is the injunction to 'love thy neighbour as thyself', a reiteration of God's command to Moses that 'thou shalt love thy neighbour as thy self'.[14] If we find the Houyhnhnms' impartiality and universal benevolence uncomfortable, then we are demonstrating that we have problems in implementing biblical commands. Many critics have argued that the Houyhnhnms cannot be taken as ideals. But, at least in this instance, it is difficult to avoid the conclusion that the principles by which they live are not only natural, but Christian.

Gulliver's description of the Houyhnhnms' society is cool and dispassionate. It proceeds through observations and statements. Adjectives are generally confined to abstracts, such as 'particular' and 'universal'. The even tenor of his sentences endows the occasional striking word or phrase with considerable force. The word 'fondness' may strike at least the modern reader in this way. A phrase such as 'in cold blood' in Gulliver's description of a soldier surely explodes fittingly like a grenade.

But these are not, generally speaking, narratives which engage a reader in the way that most novels, whether realist or modernist, do. To adopt Samuel Johnson's observation about John Milton's epic poem *Paradise Lost*, the 'want of human interest is always felt'.[15] Lemuel Gulliver himself, the one constant in a stream of diverse journeys, is given at the outset a *curriculum vitae* after the manner of *Robinson Crusoe* – he was the third of five sons of a Nottinghamshire family, studied for a short time at Cambridge, was bound apprentice to a London surgeon, and so on – but does not develop into the central figure in his narrative as Crusoe does.

Gulliver's Travels is not a novel of character; rather, it is a novel – or perhaps a sequence of short narratives – of ideas. The American novelist and critic Mary McCarthy wrote of the comic novels of Thomas Love Peacock, an early nineteenth-century commentator on the excesses and foibles of Romantic lives and attitudes, that they rest on one joke, that 'the ordinary stuff of life is swept away to make room for abstract speculation'.[16] Peacock's characters talk, dispute and sometimes pose outrageously, but they exist outside human relationships and domestic normality. Lemuel Gulliver does have a wife and children, but spends precious little time with them, being ever eager to set out on fresh voyages to alternative societies which furnish increasingly disruptive comparisons with our own. When he returns from the country of the Houyhnhnms, he is affectionately greeted by his long-suffering wife, at which, 'having not been used to the touch of that odious animal for so many years, I fell in a swoon for almost an hour' (part four, chapter eleven).

Instead of calling for a marriage guidance counsellor – one fears that Gulliver is beyond hope – it is more helpful to see *Gulliver's Travels* as part of what another American novelist and critic, Gore Vidal, has called 'a brilliant line of satirical narratives' stretching from 'Aristophanes to Petronius to Lucian to Rabelais to Swift to Voltaire to Thomas Love Peacock'.[17] The point of these narratives, Vidal argues, is that they serve as places where counter-establishment ideas can be pursued. Establishments want people to be positive and so supportive of their norms or assumptions. Subversive ideas, as Winston Smith, the defeated hero of *Nineteen Eighty-Four*, discovers, must be vigorously suppressed in order to preserve the status quo. Perhaps this is why narratives that do not fit into conventionally accepted novelistic categories usually find themselves marginalized. Is *Gulliver's Travels* even a novel in any meaningful sense? Or can it be quietly banished to a niche marked 'eighteenth-century satire'?

6.5 The sense of an ending (1): Anne Brontë, *Agnes Grey* (1847), chapter twenty-five

Endings are seldom easy. Even in the best novels, they can seem perfunctory or rushed, as if the writer has said all there is to say and wants to conclude as rapidly as possible. Henry James wryly observed that some readers want from a good novel a happy ending with 'a distribution at the last of prizes, pensions, husbands, wives, babies, millions, appended paragraphs, and cheerful remarks.'[18] Some novelists are content to supply these requirements and leave it at that.

However, conclusions also provide an opportunity for writers to make their final comments on the work their readers are about to close. Such commentary may be more or less direct or oblique; finales can be more or less conclusive or open-ended. Anne Brontë's ending of her first novel, *Agnes Grey*, published together with the now better-known *Wuthering Heights* by her sister Emily, is a miniature master class in how to provide a conclusion which, though conventional in outline and much of its content, embodies the essence of the novel's significance:

> Here I pause. My diary, from which I compiled these pages, goes but little farther. I could go on for years; but I will content myself with adding, that I shall never forget that glorious Summer evening, and always remember with delight that steep, rugged hill, and the edge of the precipice where we stood together watching the splendid sun-set mirrored on the restless world of waters at our feet – with hearts filled with gratitude to Heaven, and happiness, and love – almost too full for speech.
>
> A few weeks after that, when my mother had supplied herself with an assistant, I became the wife of Edward Weston, and never have found cause to repent it, and am certain that I never shall. We have had trials, and we know that we must have them again; but we bear them well together, and endeavour to fortify ourselves and each other against the final separation – that greatest of all afflictions to the survivor; but, if we keep in mind the glorious heaven beyond, where both may meet again, and sin and sorrow are unknown, surely that too may be borne; and meantime, we endeavour to live to the glory of Him who has scattered so many blessings in our path.
>
> Edward, by his strenuous exertions, has worked surprising reforms in his parish, and is esteemed and loved by its inhabitants – as he deserves – for whatever his faults may be as a man (and no one is entirely without) I defy anybody to blame him as a pastor, a husband, or a father.
>
> Our children, Edward, Agnes, and little Mary, promise well; their education, for the time being, is chiefly committed to me; and they shall want no good thing that a mother's care can give.
>
> Our modest income is amply sufficient for our requirements; and by practising the economy we learnt in harder times, and never attempting to imitate our richer neighbours, we manage not only to enjoy comfort and contentment ourselves, but to have every year something to lay by for our children, and something to give to those who need it.
>
> And now I think I have said sufficient.

Anne Brontë's first-person narrator, the Agnes Grey of the title, begins and ends her finale with frank acknowledgement of her role as teller of her own story. She pauses for breath, refers to her source,

tells us she has many years of her life still to live even though
her diary runs out at this point, but says she will content herself
with observing that she will never forget the scene her narrative has
reached. This scene, conventionally enough, is of Agnes's acceptance
of Edward Weston's proposal of marriage, which she has narrated with
remarkable restraint and economy, bluntness even:

> 'You love me then?' said he, fervently pressing my hand.
> 'Yes.'

As if anticipating Henry James's recipe for keeping readers happy,
Agnes then remembers to tell us briefly about her husband, their
children and their modest but adequate income – far from James's
'millions', but then James preferred to write about heiresses and
the moneyed classes, what Mary McCarthy tartly termed the 'piano
nobile' of society,[19] for whom hard times means needing to marry
someone rich enough to maintain their villa in Florence. Within her
more modest circumstances, Agnes even manages something akin to
James's 'cheerful remarks': 'we manage . . . to enjoy comfort and contentment'. Having done what is required, Agnes then brusquely signs
off like someone not wanting to outstay her welcome or make a fuss.
    Agnes's conclusion does its duty unshowily, with a decorous ret-
icence which may appear dispassionate. These characteristics are
precisely those by which she lives her life. Her one-word response to
Edward's fervent desire for her love is typical. It is simple, honest,
straightforward, if perhaps slightly comical (some readers may feel)
in its avoidance of romantic rhetoric. Anne Brontë has provided a
conclusion sufficient on its own for readers to draw her heroine's character. Because the content and manner of this conclusion resemble
Agnes herself in unassuming modesty, it would be all too easy to over-
look the novelist's artistry. Brontë creates a microcosm of Agnes's life
in a series of stages, each marked by a paragraph, from 'I shall never
forget . . .' to 'Our modest income . . . .'. These paragraphs are of varying lengths, reflecting the degree to which explanation is required of
the process described and the achievement defined, but none is excessive or self-indulgent. That each is restricted to one or two sentences
demonstrates Agnes's capacity for measured and rational control of
her actions. All is in its place; everything is neat and complete.
    The first stage is that which the story has reached, the moment of
romantic fulfilment as Agnes accepts Edward Weston's proposal. She
here allows herself a moment of narrative luxuriance absent from

the preceding dialogue. She and Edward have walked together to the outskirts of the seaside town to which she and her mother have moved in order to set up a small school. The novel identifies this town merely as 'A____', but commentators agree that it is clearly based on Scarborough, which Anne Brontë knew well and where, less than two years after the publication of *Agnes Grey*, she would stay during her final illness. Agnes and Edward climb a hill in order to watch the sun set over the sea. This hill now becomes 'steep' and 'rugged', even a 'precipice' from which the sunset is 'splendid'. Her description shares its territory with the dramatic landscapes popularized by Ann Radcliffe's novels (see Section 3.4). All nature combines appropriately on this 'glorious' summer evening. The sentence is rich in adjectives, a common and often repeated effect in Ann Radcliffe's descriptions, but rare enough in *Agnes Grey* to make it shine out with exceptional force. The sea is elevated by a resonantly alliterative phrase, 'world of waters', which Brontë has borrowed from Milton's *Paradise Lost* (book three, line eleven: 'The rising world of waters dark and deep'), where it describes the creation of the world. Agnes and Edward are entering a new world, one that is both beautiful and, as God's creation, theologically approved. Their hearts are filled with gratitude to Heaven, happiness and love, in that order. Edward, whom Agnes first met when he was only a curate, has recently acquired the living of a village two miles from A____, together with a house and 300 pounds a year. These are not riches, but sufficient to enable him to offer a 'respectable' (the adjective Edward himself used in chapter twenty-four to describe the house) life for his wife and family. Agnes's devotional language ('gratitude to Heaven') locates the scene in not just a romantic but also a socially and theologically approved context.

The novel has been much concerned with the relationship between financial comfort and moral principle. It has set Agnes, a serious, plain young woman with dark brown hair, against Rosalie Murray, beautiful, carefree, flirtatious, with light brown hair 'strongly inclined to yellow' (chapter seven). The contrast is similar to that between the heroine and Blanche Ingram in Charlotte Brontë's *Jane Eyre*, which had been published just two months earlier than *Agnes Grey*. Rosalie marries, becomes Lady Ashley and lives in an elegant mansion surrounded by a spacious park; but her marriage is loveless and all her beauty has not secured her happiness. The measured ardour achieved by Agnes shines out by contrast as secure, merited and lasting. The moment of romantic intensity is itself but an evening, brief and transitory, but its power will keep it alive in the memory ('I shall never forget . . . .') while its foundation in respectable, solid values will ensure its survival.

Survival is the subject of Agnes's next paragraph ('A few weeks after that . . . .'). She narrates the marriage very briefly, with an absence of ceremony which no doubt reflects the event itself. Her emphasis is, rather, on her certainty of its rightness, in marked contrast to Rosalie's regret and open detestation of her husband. But the second sentence of the paragraph, and the longest in the entire conclusion, is about the reality of living. It is a complex sentence, its stages marked by semi-colons and the commonest of conjunctions which convey addition ('and') and qualification ('but'). Characteristically, Agnes's emphasis is on life's hardships, its 'trials' and 'afflictions', and its conclusion is devotional. This is the sentence of a realist. The compensation for the knowledge that life has brought, and will bring, its trials is the assurance that wife and husband bear them together. Life is difficult, but it is shared difficulty. Agnes is silent about what these trials may be: illness, loss of children (common enough in the period)? The details are less important than the general message about life. One affliction, however, is specified, since it is universal and unavoidable: the death of husband or wife. It is not the death itself that is viewed as the affliction, but the surviving partner's sorrow. Death is firmly set in the context of belief, which makes it not just bearable for the survivor but itself the pathway to greater happiness. The key clause is the conditional 'if we keep in mind the glorious heaven beyond'. That sonorous adjective strikes a rare, but here repeated, note of assertion. One 'glorious' summer evening brought wife and husband together, and 'glorious' heaven will be their reward for a life well lived.

What a life well lived consists of is the subject of the two following paragraphs. For Edward, in his capacity as minister to his people, it is to strive to improve his parish and gain the esteem and love of his parishioners. Agnes sets his role as pastor first in her list. For Agnes herself, the good life is motherhood and the education of their children. Education has been the central concern of Agnes's narrative. Her ambition throughout has been to be a governess – that common female role in the nineteenth century – and eventually to run her own small school. Her experiences have been arduous in the extreme, for she has encountered supremely spoilt and even violent children, the products of undisciplined and over-indulgent upbringing. Examples of poor parenting and Agnes's struggles have established a realistic context for what we may take to be her exemplary education of her own children. She makes a point of insisting on her own responsibility for them.

Finally, Agnes turns to the modesty of their income and lifestyle. They live a humble life, one devoid of envy towards those financially better off (the example of Rosalie lies silently in the background), but one of independence. Prudence ensures not just survival but contentment, and their care extends not only to their own children but to others in need. Charity is the duty of all, and their manner of living shows that charity lies within the capabilities of even those of modest means.

The vision of living that Anne Brontë provides is restrained, realistic and of its time. A more cynical age may find it repressed, excessively respectful of hierarchy, or pietistic. But of its integrity and moral earnestness there can be no doubt. It convinces because of its consistency with the character of the narrator, its studious reflection of her experience of the destructive results of other styles of life, and, above all, the patient, quiet and measured style in which Agnes describes it. The conclusion is, in every sense, resolution.

6.6 The sense of an ending (2): Thomas Hardy, *Tess of the d'Urbervilles* (1891), chapter fifty-nine

Anne Brontë concludes her first-person novel by channelling the narrative modes of description and action through the character of her narrator. Character and narrative modes are mutually reinforcing: Agnes writes her finale in the way she does because of who she is, and the way she writes her finale contributes to how we see her character. The values and beliefs implied in the novel are those embedded within her narrative. When we turn to a third-person novel such as Thomas Hardy's *Tess of the d'Urbervilles*, we find direct and explicit commentary sitting more or less easily alongside narrative and action:

> The prospect from this summit was almost unlimited. In the valley beneath lay the city they had just left, its more prominent buildings showing as in an isometric drawing – among them the broad cathedral tower, with its Norman windows and immense length of aisle and nave, the spires of St. Thomas's, the pinnacled tower of the College, and, more to the right, the tower and gables of the ancient hospice, where to this day the pilgrim may receive his dole of bread and ale. Behind the city swept the rotund upland of St. Catherine's Hill; further off, landscape beyond landscape, till the horizon was lost in the radiance of the sun hanging above it.

Against these far stretches of country rose, in front of the other city edifices, a large red-brick building, with level grey roofs, and rows of short barred windows bespeaking captivity, the whole contrasting greatly by its formalism with the quaint irregularities of the Gothic erections. It was somewhat disguised from the road in passing it by yews and evergreen oaks, but it was visible enough up here. The wicket from which the pair had lately emerged was in the wall of this structure. From the middle of the building an ugly flat-topped octagonal tower ascended against the east horizon, and viewed from this spot, on its shady side and against the light, it seemed the one blot on the city's beauty. Yet it was with this blot, and not with the beauty, that the two gazers were concerned.

Upon the cornice of the tower a tall staff was fixed. Their eyes were riveted on it. A few minutes after the hour had struck something moved slowly up the staff, and extended itself upon the breeze. It was a black flag.

'Justice' was done, and the President of the Immortals, in Æschylean phrase, had ended his sport with Tess. And the d'Urberville knights and dames slept on in their tombs unknowing. The two speechless gazers bent themselves down to the earth, as if in prayer, and remained thus a long time, absolutely motionless: the flag continued to wave silently. As soon as they had strength they arose, joined hands again, and went on.

Direct authorial commentary is one defining characteristic of the mainstream nineteenth-century novel (Dickens, Thackeray, Eliot, Trollope), so in this respect *Tess* is conventional. However, Hardy's conclusion is in most other ways highly unconventional. 'Fulfilment' (Hardy's ironic title for the final phase of his novel) for Tess lies not in marriage, children, financial stability and assurance of future happiness, but in the last action of her life, her execution for the murder of her seducer, Alec d'Urberville. The black flag raised over the tower of Wintoncester (Hardy's transparent fictional name for Winchester, based on its original name of Wintonceastre) jail flies over Tess's body and fictional happy endings. Prizes are distributed not by a benign novelist but by a sinister 'President of the Immortals'.

The first two of the final four paragraphs of *Tess* are in descriptive mode. Angel Clare, Tess's husband, who deserted her after learning of her seduction by Alec and with whom she fled after killing Alec, and Tess's younger sister 'Liza-Lu have emerged from a gate in the prison wall (they have presumably visited her for a final time) and climbed up the West Hill from which they gain a prospect of the city. The description is in two parts, divided between the paragraphs.

The first looks across the city, in a hollow between West Hill and St Catherine's Hill, to the south-east. The features of the view are either medieval (the extensive cathedral and the hospice of St Cross) or in the medieval tradition (Winchester College, a mixture of medieval and more recent architecture, and St Thomas's church, an early Victorian replacement – in fourteenth-century style – of an earlier medieval church). The city is imbued with a sense of the past.

This is not just incidental topography. The events of the novel are set off when John Durbeyfield, Tess's father, is told that he is lineally descended from a Norman knight called d'Urberville, who came over to England with William the Conqueror. The family vaults, replete with effigies under Purbeck-marble canopies, are at Kingsbere (Hardy's fictional name for Bere Regis, whose church contains the Turberville Chapel). Winchester cathedral's Norman windows reflect the long-lost grandeur of Tess's family. Like so much of Hardy's writing, this novel sets present action within a large historical sweep expressive of both social decline and the littleness of individual lives. Winchester's buildings are also mainly ecclesiastical and so representative of a Christian ethic. Hardy picks out in particular the hospice of St Cross, noting that 'to this day the pilgrim may receive his dole of bread and ale'. This perhaps reads as if taken from a Winchester tourist board pamphlet: Hardy does have a tendency to annotate his descriptions in a somewhat pedantic manner – what critics have sometimes termed his 'local historian' style. But it is there for a reason. Its simple but active charity contrasts strongly with how contemporary society has treated Tess. Hardy famously and provocatively subtitled his novel 'A Pure Woman'. Tess is condemned for her failings, but in each case – her seduction, her illegitimate child, and even her killing of Alec – the novel indicates that she is the victim of circumstances, male subjection and hypocrisy, and social stigma. Charity may continue at St Cross, but it is profoundly lacking in society at large.

Of this inhumanity, the prison is the emblem. Its red-brick modernity contrasts with the stonework of the medieval buildings, and, as Hardy explicitly states, its grim uniformity distinguishes it from Gothic irregularity. Hardy's description becomes increasingly direct and condemnatory as it narrows in on the tower from which the black flag will be viewed. The tower is 'ugly' and 'flat-topped', and is twice called a 'blot' on the beauty of its surroundings. The description carries a clear value judgement, suggested even in the ugly monosyllabic and plosive word 'blot'. The legal code by which a 'pure' woman is hanged is as harsh and unfeeling as Hardy's language.

Even before the final paragraph, then, authorial commentary is unmistakable. However, by channelling it through the scene as viewed at a distance by the silent figures of Angel and 'Liza-Lu, Hardy detaches the event from sensationalism. There is no final scene between Tess, her sister and her husband, simply the statement that Angel and 'Liza-Lu emerged from a gate in the prison wall. What would Dickens have made of such a parting? Arnold Bennett devotes several pages of *The Old Wives' Tale* to an account of a public execution in Auxerre (book three, chapter three), filling it with noise, spectacle and garish horror. Bennett provides ample dramatic colour, though he scrupulously admits in his preface that he had never actually witnessed a public execution and relied for his material on articles in a Paris magazine. His purpose, however, does extend further: to see an execution is the ambition of Gerald Scales, with whom Sophia has eloped. The bloodthirsty brutality of Bennett's imaginative rendering of the event and, particularly, of the crowd's enthusiasm reflects savagely on Gerald. Sophia's revulsion marks a significant stage in her separation from Gerald and the values he represents and endorses. The whole event is also a powerful contribution to *The Old Wives' Tale*'s exploration of the human capacity to range from gross conduct to individual dignity (as in Samuel Povey's sacrifice on behalf of his cousin: see Section 6.1).

Tess's execution is, of course, not conducted in public. But it is nonetheless striking that Hardy marks the event only by its public symbol, and does so with narrative restraint: 'It was a black flag'. His two witnesses remain silent throughout, their grief contained within: their restraint matches that of the narrative. Where Bennett shows how a man's death can be met by disgusting displays of human vulgarity, Hardy describes dignity and humility in Angel's and 'Liza-Lu's silent kneeling in a gesture of reverence. Human beings can act with a nobility which shames the social ethos of their age.

In this context, the first sentence of Hardy's last paragraph strikes a note which some readers find troubling or disruptive. Bennett also uses the clause, 'Justice was done', when the crowd's shrieks tell the horrified Sophia, who has collapsed on her hotel floor in 'terror and loathing', that the execution has taken place. But he does not enclose the word 'justice' in the ironic inverted commas Hardy uses. These convert the expression into overt authorial commentary, giving voice, as it were, to feelings and judgements which, if they are shared by his characters, remain unspoken by them. Bennett's highly dramatic scene is judged through Sophia's anguished reactions.

Hardy's quieter scene is judged by the author's typographical intrusion.

What, then, do we make of the appearance of a 'President of the Immortals' who has 'ended his sport with Tess'? Hardy's phrasing is doubly literary. That touch of pedantry emerges again in his explanation, 'in Æschylean phrase' ('President of the Immortals' is a literal translation of Aeschylus's *Prometheus Bound*, line 169); and behind the rest of the sentence lie Gloucester's lines in *King Lear*: 'As flies to wanton boys are we to the gods – They kill us for their sport' (IV.i, 37–8). Hardy's phrasing and allusions suddenly elevate the narrative level to that of dramatic tragedy, a world apart from social critique, which seems to be the earlier focus in this conclusion.

However, the action has sometimes been viewed from a cosmological rather than social perspective. Worse the wear from celebration of his newly discovered knightly ancestry, John Durbeyfield is unable to drive his cart to Casterbridge in time for the Saturday market. Tess and her young brother Abraham undertake the journey, despite its being the middle of the night. Abraham gazes on the stars in the night sky, and asks if they are worlds like ours. Tess ponders that, like the fruit of their apple tree, they may be a mixture of sound and blighted worlds. Which do we live on, asks Abraham, to which Tess replies 'a blighted one' (chapter four). When a drowsy Tess's waggon is then in collision with a noiseless mail-cart, as a result of which their horse Prince is fatally gored, Tess's gloomy conviction appears to be corroborated. Later, after her seduction by Alec and the death of her infant child, Tess heads out to the Froom valley in search of work and a new life. In descriptive mode, Hardy gives an extensive account of its meadows, river, flowers and cattle. Then he suddenly pulls back to view the scene from an angle far above human perspective: Tess is 'like a fly on a billiard-table of indefinite length, and of no more consequence to the surroundings than that fly' (chapter sixteen).

These shifts in perspective strike many readers as disconcerting, for good or ill. Like Tess herself, who speaks two languages, local dialect at home and standard English to others, the narrative seems to have different voices depending on how the action is being viewed. Critics have frequently noted this, but disagree about whether the result is disruptive confusion or defamiliarizing tension.[20] Is Tess a plaything of antagonistic universal forces, or is she a victim of current social and ethical attitudes? Can the novel not make its mind up, or does its kaleidoscopic point of view destabilize glib or conventional conclusions in favour of a radical uncertainty or agnosticism?

As suddenly as he has shifted his frame of reference, Hardy reverts to his preceding narrative manner. Reference back to those d'Urberville ancestors in their marble tombs at Kingsbere quietly reminds the reader of how the sorry events all began, and further isolates past from present. After the silent gesture of Angel and 'Liza-Lu – all the more potent for its restraint – Hardy concludes with a sentence of telling, measured simplicity, its three main verbs ('they arose, joined hands again, and went on') presented sparely and without commentary. Hardy's allusion to the concluding lines of Milton's *Paradise Lost*, where Adam and Eve 'hand in hand with wandering steps and slow,/Through Eden took their solitary way', is altogether more discreet than his invocation of Greek tragedy and emerges naturally from the context. What the future holds is unknown and unspoken. In chapter fifty-eight, Tess expressed to Angel her wish that he would marry 'Liza-Lu after her death. The narrative now respects Angel's refusal to look beyond the sorrow of the present ('If I lose you I lose all' is his response to Tess), while joining the living together in a final gesture of companionship, mutual comfort and stoicism. We may be expelled from paradise, but we can still act with dignity and even nobility. That human beings demonstrate their highest qualities when acting with restrained and simple harmony is the novel's final note, shown in the characters' actions. But the same paragraph has also told us something different, that human beings are insignificant victims. Are both points of view equally truthful?

6.7 The sense of an ending (3): Evelyn Waugh, *Unconditional Surrender* (1961), 'Epilogue'

In 1951, to celebrate the opening of a happier decade, the government decreed a Festival. Monstrous constructions appeared on the south bank of the Thames, the foundation stone was solemnly laid for a National Theatre, but there was little popular exuberance among the straitened people and dollar-bearing tourists curtailed their visits and sped to the countries of the Continent where, however precarious their condition, they ordered things better.

This paragraph opens the epilogue (entitled 'Festival of Britain') to the final part of Evelyn Waugh's trilogy, *Sword of Honour*. The first volume, *Men at Arms*, saw the hero, Guy Crouchback, enlist in the Royal Corps of Halberdiers at the beginning of the Second World War; the second, *Officers and Gentlemen*, has as its principal action Guy's part in the disastrous allied campaign in Crete;

and *Unconditional Surrender* concludes with Guy contributing to partisan struggles in Yugoslavia towards the end of the war. The epilogue moves six years ahead, to 1951, when Waugh was writing *Men at Arms*.

Our two sentences are at the same time strongly contrasted and mutually supportive. The first is short and simple, the statement of an event and its purpose. Taken out of context, it contains no overt value judgement. That the 1950s would be a 'happier' decade than the 1940s, a time of war and its aftermath, appears self-evident and unobjectionable. Someone who has reached this epilogue after reading the three parts of the trilogy proper would, however, have an ear attuned to Waugh's habitual ironic manner. It is no accident that the campaigns in which Crouchback takes part all end chaotically and leave him with little or no credit. A narrative that has shown most aspects of government and state organization to be incompetent, and those in charge to be serial bunglers if not certifiably insane, hardly sets the scene for a reader's confidence in a government's capacity to implement successfully its decree of a festival. State-organised jollity sounds something of an oxymoron.

The second sentence, longer and marked by syntax of qualification ('but'), casts an explicitly jaundiced eye over the simple facts. The south bank of the Thames was the centre of the Festival of Britain. The subsequently restored Royal Festival Hall to the west of Waterloo Bridge remains as its legacy – a concept much trumpeted by modern manifestations of the same impulse to organized national celebration. The concrete bunkers of the rest of the South Bank, including the National Theatre whose opening would have to wait until 1976 (25 years after the laying of its foundation stone), represent and enshrine the triumph of modernist ideals of post-war architecture. At the time of the Festival, the most spectacular building was the Skylon, a 300-foot vertical sliver of steel discreetly carried by cables held by steel beams. Apparently a contemporary joke was that the Skylon, like the British economy, had no visible means of support.[21]

It is difficult for commentary on Waugh's paragraph not to adopt the cynicism his prose invites. The adjective 'monstrous' does not even attempt to hide authorial judgement, exposing 'solemnly' to ironic reading. The second half of the sentence explains and justifies Waugh's dyspeptic tone. The government's decree runs counter to the real state of the populace. Their poverty ('straitened') blights the celebration, and has the unlooked-for effect of sending visitors from the United

Kingdom's richer ally, whose dollars were meant to inject life into its dormant economy, fleeing to mainland Europe. Those countries may be in no better economic shape than the UK, but – as Laurence Sterne's sentimental traveller had told us 200 years before – they order things better over there.[22]

A wealth of cynicism is rendered economically, in a single paragraph, with no authorial 'I' figure, but by sardonic presentation of a series of events. Waugh's attitude passes an oblique comment on the whole state of post-war Britain: the people are poor, the buildings are ugly, authority and the populace are disconnected, and a wide gap separates the UK from the rest of Europe. Why is this epilogue imbued with such sourness? The answer is that Waugh's tone emerges naturally out of the preceding novels, where in a manner veering between hopeless despondency and hilarious farce, he has narrated the death of idealism.

At first, the outbreak of war appears to give Guy Crouchback a sense of purpose, of meaning in a life which has lost its direction. Halfway to his three score years and ten, Guy is at the classic point for a mid-life crisis, as was Dante when he began the most famous of all Italian poems, his *Divine Comedy*:

> *Nel mezzo del cammin di nostra vita*
> *mi ritrovai per una selva oscura,*
> *chè la diritta via era smarrita.*
> (In the middle of the journey through our life I found myself in a dark wood where he straight path was lost.)

The Italian parallel is geographically apposite. As *Men at Arms* opens, Guy is living in a villa in Italy built by his grandfather. Broome, his family home in the west of England, is let to a convent. Guy is displaced and doubly rootless, for he is tolerated but not fully accepted in his Italian residence. He is also emotionally barren. His wife Virginia left him years before, and she is now in the process of separating from her third husband, an American called Troy. Virginia's restlessness and sexual selfishness are recurring strands in the novels, representing much that is unsatisfactory in personal relationships in the modern world. Guy is a Roman Catholic, which renders him isolated both personally (he cannot re-marry while his wife is living) and socially (Catholics in England are still living under the shadow of historical exclusion). Hearing the news of the Molotov-Ribbentrop Treaty in 1939, Guy finds his purpose: 'The enemy at last was plain in view, huge and hateful, all disguise cast off. It was the Modern Age in arms' (*Men at Arms*, prologue, section one). He now belongs. He now has an ideal to fight for.

But Guy's attempts to realize this purpose end in failure and ignominy. He never succeeds in becoming one of the men. He is older than most and gets called 'uncle', like the few other older officers, notably the egregiously eccentric figure of Apthorpe, one of Waugh's sublime comic creations (see Section 5.4). His association with a fellow uncle who cannot be taken seriously – even by Crouchback himself – rubs off on Guy. *Men at Arms* ends with the decline of Apthorpe from an illness acquired in his African days. Trying to be kind to him, Guy smuggles a bottle of whisky into Apthorpe's hospital room. The whisky finishes Apthorpe off, and Guy finds himself in disgrace.

Everything he touches, in spite of his good intentions, goes horribly wrong. So Guy is charged with leading a minor military manoeuvre in Dakar, only to find that a mad senior officer called Ritchie-Hook (whose response to any military situation is that it provides an opportunity to 'biff' the enemy) stows away, flouts orders and commits the grisly act of cutting off a native's head (he calls it his coconut). Guy is subject to official censure for the appalling incident, taking the rap for the actions of one supposedly his superior. Guy's personal life, meanwhile, is no less unsuccessful. On leave, he attempts to make love to Virginia in Claridge's Hotel, but she mockingly spurns him. His Catholicism, which deems Virginia his only legitimate partner, is another hierarchical institution which leaves him open to derision and shame.

In *Officers and Gentlemen*, the Cretan episode exposes the book's title to savage irony, as Guy experiences the fallibility, selfishness and criminality of his fellow soldiers. The politics of the war is confused for him by the UK's alliance with Bolshevik and atheist Russia. The great cause is over, and all that is left is the pursuit of personal honour. As *Unconditional Surrender* draws to a close, Madame Kanyi, whom Guy befriends in the course of his attempts to ensure the escape of a group of Jews during the partisan struggle in Yugoslavia, tells him that the war was desired not just by the Nazis. Others wanted it for their own purposes. There was, she says, 'a will to war, a death wish, everywhere. Even good men thought their private honour would be satisfied by war. They could assert their manhood by killing and being killed'. Did people in England feel this, she asks? 'God forgive me', says Guy, 'I was one of them' (*Unconditional Surrender*, book three, section four). On his return to Italy, Guy discovers that most of the

Jews had been successfully evacuated, but that the Kanyis had been taken away and tried by the partisans because they had been seen associating with a British Liaison Officer.

The delusion from which Guy has suffered now leaves him lost amid forces greater and more destructive than himself. The modern novel began with one man cast away on a desert island. But whereas Defoe charts the triumph of Robinson Crusoe over his circumstances and his environment, Waugh delineates defeat, disillusion and the advent of a bleak new world. His hero is cast away on an island now alien to him. Welcome to the Festival of Britain.

6.8   The sense of an ending (4): Julian Barnes, *The Sense of an Ending* (2011), section two; B. S. Johnson, *Albert Angelo* (1964), *House Mother Normal* (1971)

You get towards the end of life – no, not life itself, but of something else: the end of any likelihood of change in that life. You are allowed a long moment of pause, time enough to ask the question: what else have I done wrong? I thought of a bunch of kids in Trafalgar Square. I thought of a young woman dancing, for once in her life. I thought of what I couldn't know or understand now, of all that couldn't ever be known or understood. I thought of Adrian's definition of history. I thought of his son cramming his face into a shelf of quilted toilet tissue in order to avoid me. I thought of a woman frying eggs in a carefree, slapdash way, untroubled when one of them broke in the pan; then the same woman, later, making a secret, horizontal gesture beneath a sunlit wisteria. And I thought of a cresting wave of water, lit by a moon, rushing past and vanishing upstream, pursued by a band of yelping students whose torchbeams criss-crossed in the dark.

There is accumulation. There is responsibility. And beyond these, there is unrest. There is great unrest.

The closing two paragraphs of Julian Barnes's Booker Prize-winning novel, *The Sense of an Ending*, are carefully, even rigorously, formal. The first, longer paragraph is constructed of two sentences beginning 'You', followed by seven statements beginning 'I thought of'. The last of the seven is given the syntactically expected variation of 'And I thought of': it is the final item in a list, even if some style directives would frown on a sentence beginning 'And'. The second, very short paragraph contains four observations taking the form 'There is' followed by abstract noun; with the 'And' variation again, this time linking the second statement to the third, which is, in a sense, the final statement since the fourth sentence is an intensified repetition of the third. The controlling stylistic device in these paragraphs is anaphora, the repetition of words or phrases at the beginning of successive sentences. This is ordered, measured writing. We are in the hands of a narrator who knows exactly what he wants to say, an educated and literary man.

But the contents of this highly controlled writing are fragmentary, disparate and despairing. The first sentence locates the novel's ending as conterminous with a sense of the end of living as a process of learning and improvement. Sadder even than contemplating the close of life is the recognition that we have reached a point beyond which no change, no progress is possible. The 'You' construction, an informal version of the non-specific 'one' (as in 'one gets towards the end of one's life'), includes all of us, narrator and reader. The second sentence fills the void – if we cannot look forward, what can we do? – with a despairing retrospective question: not 'what can I be pleased about, proud of?' but 'what else have I done wrong?'

The narrator's answer to this question is the series of seven thoughts. These are mostly images from his past, memories of scenes, incidents and words, which appear to have little or nothing connecting them. Who are the kids in Trafalgar Square? Is one of them the same person as the young woman dancing, or Adrian, or Adrian's son? There are variations among the thoughts. The third is different from the others, as it refers not to a specific person or scene but to a general sense of all that is unknowable, beyond our comprehension. These fragments are, then, but a selection of a mass of possible unknowns, just a few to get us started on a desolating review of the unchangeable past. There is some sense of progression in the thoughts, at least in terms of length of description (and so, possibly, of importance?). The sixth, that concerning a woman (is this the same as the earlier 'young woman' or is the dropping of the adjective a mark of differentiation?), consists of two memories and is consequently the longest in words. But length does not bring clarity. Are the two images, of the woman frying eggs and making a secret gesture, related? The first seems trivial, the second mysterious. Or are we meant to attribute meaning to a broken egg? The final thought does at least reflect something of a phenomenon: a wave rushing preternaturally upstream, but, again, any meaning it might have is omitted, left to our free association and the vague feeling that its position and prefacing conjunction ('And') ought to confer on it some significance, as the climax of the paragraph.

If we look to the very last paragraph for indication of some significance, which has so far eluded us, we shall be disappointed. Its
abstracts are no more meaningful to us than the earlier concrete
images. 'There is accumulation'. Does this refer to the seven thoughts?
If so, to what do they accumulate? Or is it a more general statement:
that experiences or memories merely pile up randomly? This is the
root meaning of 'accumulate', from Latin *accumulare* meaning 'to add
to a heap'. Or is there some more specific meaning lurking in the word,
as in the specialized financial sense of the addition of interest to a principal sum? But, if so, how does 'responsibility' fit in? And how does it
all lead to 'unrest', the book's final note emphasized by repetition and
addition of 'great'?

Such uncertainties constitute the lineaments of one strand of post-
modern fiction. The belief sustained and assumed in most earlier
narrative is that events are connected in a causal chain, of which each
link is the consequence of the last and the cause of the next, and which
moves towards a clear, explicable and satisfactory conclusion. The
good end happily and the bad unhappily: that is what fiction means.
Or, to put it another way, the prizes are distributed, the babies listed
and outcomes assumed.[23]

But, at some point in the twentieth century, we lost our confidence in such linearity and concatenation of events, such moral clarity.
When this happened differs according to the account you're reading.
Virginia Woolf's celebrated, if perhaps over-interpreted, assertion that
human nature changed in 1910 is used by those wishing to locate the
transformation in the early twentieth century.[24] This suits a history
which calls in, or accumulates, such diverse events as the exhibition in
London of post-impressionist paintings and Einstein's special theory
of relativity. Well, Einstein's theory was published in 1905, but that's
near enough. And his general theory of relativity, which extended
the theory from observers moving relative to one another at constant
velocity to non-inertial frames of reference, is later (1916), by which
time we were in the First World War, another favoured event in the
narrative of the twentieth century as destruction of the old order.

Other versions of a similar narrative place the key date later in
the twentieth century, more in 'postmodernism' than in 'modernism'.
The most significant distinction between these slippery and, again,
probably over-interpreted terms is that modernism re-examines artistic conventions and explores stylistic experimentation in order to
reflect changes in views of what human nature is; whereas postmodernism subjects these very modernist processes to a self-conscious,

self-questioning scrutiny. The postmodernist novel does not simply re-examine experience by questioning established stable ideas; it includes itself in a process of radical disintegration, undermining its own pretensions to represent advanced theories. It is inherently self-reflexive, perhaps ultimately self-destructive.

We referred earlier to B. S. Johnson's experimentation with narrative in his novel *Albert Angelo* (see Section 2.2). In the second part of this novel ('Exposition'), he goes through all six forms of the verb as ways of narrating. The fourth part, 'Disintegration', takes a further radical step. It explicitly questions the validity of the first-person narrator himself, undermining his pretensions to produce an authentic narrative. Instead, we have a series of disjointed remarks about telling stories, telling the truth and telling lies. The novelist confesses that his novel is deceitful, in, for example, substituting fictional for real names. But how do we know that the claimed 'real' name is 'real'? The narrative is, in this way, epistemologically regressive: the possibility of truth and meaning retreats indefinitely. The prose begins to implode under the weight of its own agonized 'truthfulness': ' — — Is about the fragmentariness of life, too, attempts to reproduce the moment-to-moment fragmentariness of life, my life, and to echo it in technique, the fragmentariness, a collage made of the fragments of my own life, the poor odds and sods, the bric-à-brac, a thing composed of, then'.

Later novels by B. S. Johnson push more and more at the existential boundaries of coherence and fragmentation. *The Unfortunates* (1969) was published in 27 unbound sections, separately paginated, in a box. Two were marked 'First' and 'Last' – fixed, like birth and death – but readers were permitted to assemble the others however they liked. In his penultimate novel, *Christie Malry's Own Double Entry* (1973), Johnson delays a description of Christie until chapter six, where he exclaims that the reader's imagination is surely stronger than the writer's and so tells us to make of Christie what we want, which will probably be an image of ourself. If writing is self-reflexive, then perhaps reading is, too.

House Mother Normal, subtitled 'A Geriatric Comedy', is perhaps the logical climax of Johnson's oeuvre. Eight patients in a geriatric home are each allocated 21 pages, starting and ending at the same point in an evening, to express their own present thoughts and memories of the past. Each character is in turn more senile than the last. Johnson supplies explanatory tables for the characters, detailing their physical and mental conditions, as the disembodied voice of medical science. As the book 'progresses' (it is in the form of a series of regressions to the same point), incoherence and blank spaces increasingly break up the surface narratives. A further surprise awaits the reader, in the form of a final section from the House Mother herself, whose 'normality' takes the form of psychotic domination. All the patients end towards the top of their page 21 with 'No, doesn't matter', except for the last, whose final five pages are all blank. House Mother's page 21 is different: she closes with a jingle about death coming to all and then adds a line at the bottom: 'And here you see, friend, I am about to step', followed by an extra page: 'outside the convention, the framework of twenty-one pages per person. Thus you see I too am the puppet or concoction of a writer (you always knew there was a writer behind it all? Ah, there's no fooling you readers!)'.

Johnson's novel thus incorporates its own implosion into incoherence and silence. Yet, at the same time, it delineates a desolate view of aging as exactly that: implosion into incoherence and silence. The increasingly fragmentary nature of the narrative is both self-destructive and an agonizing representation of its subject(s). The narrative seeks its own end, but, in so doing, maintains an expressive form. An impulse to disintegration meets an impulse to re-integration. And, if the writer goes as far as he can not to re-integrate, readers will always be ready to do his work for him by seeing the characters as images of themselves (or of what they hope are not themselves) and being clever enough to see what he is up to. There's no fooling us. Even if we are left to organize the novel for him, we know he's there behind it all. The paradox Johnson's novels challenge, yet acknowledge, is that, whatever form his pursuit of disintegration takes, it still has a form.

That is one narrative of how the twentieth-century novel challenged its predecessors' demonstration of linear form and logical, complete conclusions. Here's another.

The beginnings of *Robinson Crusoe* and *Tristram Shandy* point in different directions: one to an external world of events and facts, the other to an interior world of ideas and opinions. But, just as much of eighteenth-century philosophy is about how body and mind are connected, so these two novels actually demonstrate the intersection of body and mind.[25] Both are subject to the dominant givens of all human experience, time and space.

In chapter thirteen of book four, Tristram Shandy breaks off in mid-sentence to observe that it has taken him a whole year to get to the point in his autobiography at which he is one-day old. A lot of things have needed explanation, and these things take time.[26] So, Tristram observes, he now has 'three hundred and sixty-four days more life to write just now, than when I first set out'. Whatever progress the narrative has made has been outweighed by an increase in the amount that remains to be narrated. If this goes on (and why should it not, why should every day of his life not be as busy as his first?), then 'the more I write, the more I shall have to write'. The novel's material is accumulating more quickly than he can write about it, and so it seems to be going backwards. But, of course, it is not. We may be in book four, but Tristram has managed to get himself born. That is some progress. The paradox is that Tristram the narrator and Tristram the subject are moving at different relative speeds. From the point of view of baby Tristram, the story is advancing, although very slowly. From the point of view of adult Tristram, the story is regressing, and at quite a rate: 364 days in 365. From the point of view of the author, Laurence Sterne (we always knew there was a writer behind it all – there's no fooling us readers), both timescales are simultaneously present. His novel is going backwards and forwards at the same time.

Each patient in *House Mother Normal* has time to fill 21 pages. Time is a constant for all of us. But each narrative varies greatly in the amount of material it contains within this space, depending on the patient's alertness to the present and recall of the past. Time is experienced more fully by some than by others. On page 15 of each narrative, the patients reminisce. Sarah Lamson (patient number one) remembers catching a trolleybus up the Edgware Road. Charlie Edwards (patient number two) looks back on wartime experiences. The equivalent space for George Henbury (patient number seven) is a blank. Memory decays as age withers us, and one person's time for recollection occupies personally significant space while another's is emptiness, or, even worse perhaps, senile incoherence.

The history of the novel is one of progress through time. Language changes with the changing conditions of everyday life. The narrator of *The Sense of an Ending* writes of 'a bunch of kids in Trafalgar Square'. Laurence Sterne would not have used this phrasing, and Trafalgar Square did not exist when he was writing. Someone in *Tristram Shandy* could not have crammed his face into a shelf of quilted toilet tissue, as Adrian's son did to avoid Barnes's narrator (Tony Webster is his name). Yet, from another perspective, the novel keeps looking back, picking at life's recurrent questions, such as the relativity of time. It is a commonplace of literary criticism to label *Tristram Shandy* the first modernist (or should that be postmodernist?) novel. Literary criticism does tend to repeat itself. Even books of literary criticism have been known to repeat themselves.

Tony Webster confesses at the outset of his narrative that time puzzles him. Clocks and watches confirm that time is a regular progression. But, from another perspective, it seems to speed up or slow down, sometimes even to disappear altogether.

Tony ends *The Sense of an Ending* with a series of seven thoughts. The images he recalls have all appeared during the course of his memoir, though not in the order in which he lists them. They are lodged in his present memory, fragments of a past he has been doggedly chasing to try to make sense of it. His pursuit has led him to these and other fragments, some unexpected and decidedly unwelcome. But they still don't add up. He never does 'get it', as an old girlfriend keeps telling him.

What does become apparent, even to Tony, is that time repeats itself in all kinds of distressing ways, ways we'd rather not know about. Perhaps there is something he doesn't remember, when he writes the final two sentences of his book. His first recounted memory is of a history lesson at school, which brought Adrian's superior intelligence to Tony's attention. Another boy acted unwittingly as warm-up man for Adrian's class act. In response to the teacher's request for a description of Henry VIII's reign, the boy proffers the suggestion that there was 'unrest'. Asked to elaborate, he expands his insight to 'great unrest'. This boy Tony describes as a 'cautious know-nothing who lacked the inventiveness of true ignorance'. So do the final words of Tony's narrative imply that his earlier dismissal of his schoolboy contemporary might more truthfully be applied to himself? Or has Tony's story shown that there may actually be something more to such a vague and seemingly banal conclusion than meets the eye? Is this all that can be said about anything in the past? Now Tony is divorced, retired and bald, and he spends some of his time as a volunteer at his local hospital, meeting sick and dying people. He'll know his way around the hospital when his turn comes, he observes sardonically.

We may be sure of one thing. Julian Barnes is fully aware of the repetition of 'unrest', 'great unrest'. *The Sense of an Ending* is a highly organized and densely structured novel. Words, phrases, scenes resonate across Tony's memoir, now suggesting meaning, now resisting it. Repetition, the narrative version of memory, tantalizingly hints at significance (why else do these images remain lodged in our mind?), but, much as time might reverse its customary forward movement like the Severn Bore, its echoes drown in incomprehension. The novel's intricate texture, woven by Barnes's lucid, economical and precise writing, comes to an ending which makes absolute artistic sense while expressing the infinite relativity of sensory experience.

Flaubert's Parrot (1984), the book which first brought Barnes to wide prominence, and his analysis of Géricault's painting *The Raft of the Medusa* in *A History of the World in 10$^1/_2$ Chapters* (1989) testify to his fascination with, and understanding of, the complex, shifting relationship between art and life. Criticism by itself, including literary criticism, can only accumulate; but the critical spirit, when ennobled by the creative impulse, can result in a new work of art. Perhaps that is what fiction means.

Notes

1 Introduction

1. William Hutchings, *Living Poetry: Reading Poems from Shakespeare to Don Paterson* (Basingstoke: Palgrave Macmillan, 2012).
2. The Latin aphorism means that life is short whereas art lasts for a long time. I hope Latinists will forgive my play on 'longa'.
3. See Helmut Bonheim, *The Narrative Modes: Techniques of the Short Story* (Cambridge: D. S. Brewer, 1982).

2 Describing People

1. Lewis Carroll, *Alice's Adventures in Wonderland*, chapter twelve.
2. *OED*, 'merchandise', sb. 1 and 2.
3. *Selected Writings of Daniel Defoe*, ed. James T. Boulton (Cambridge: Cambridge University Press, 1965), p. 120.
4. Ibid., p. 227.
5. Ibid., p. 52.
6. See Descartes' sixth *Meditation* (1644).
7. See Ian Watt, *The Rise of the Novel* (London: Chatto & Windus, 1957), chapter three, on *Robinson Crusoe*.
8. See F. B. Pinion, *A Thomas Hardy Dictionary* (Basingstoke: Macmillan, 1989), entries for 'Wessex' and 'Weydon-Priors'.
9. See James Wood, *How Fiction Works* (London: Vintage Books, 2009), p. 64.
10. Thomas Hardy also makes significant use of prolepsis and analepsis. At the end of *The Woodlanders*, Marty, alone at Giles's grave, whispers that she will never forget him and, when she plants young larches, will remember that no one could plant as he did. As in their tree-planting scene (see Section 2.3), Marty and Giles are both eternally separate and yet together – now in the memory of the woman who has endured in her suffering, isolation and fidelity.
11. George Eliot, 'The Natural History of German Life', *Westminster Review*, July 1856; in *George Eliot: Selected Essays, Poems and Other Writings*, ed. A. S. Byatt and Nicholas Warren (Harmondsworth: Penguin, 1990), p. 110 [pp. 107–39].
12. Essay on 'Impressionism', *Poetry and Drama*, 2.6 (June–December 1914), quoted in *Ford Madox Ford: The Good Soldier*, ed. Martin Stannard (New York: Norton, 1995), pp. 261–2.

13. In the eighteenth century, 'country houses became a prominent and familiar part of the landscape for the leisured, mobile middle classes – not
just imposing spectacles to be glimpsed from a distance but attractions
to be entered and viewed in the course of their travels'. (Ian Ousby, *The
Englishman's England: Taste, Travel and the Rise of Tourism*, Cambridge:
Cambridge University Press, 1990, p. 65).
14. 'The approbation of moral qualities most certainly is not deriv'd from
reason, or any comparison of ideas; but proceeds entirely from a moral
taste, and from certain sentiments of pleasure or disgust, which arise upon
the contemplation and view of particular qualities or characters.' (David
Hume, *A Treatise of Human Nature*, ed. L. A. Selby-Bigge, 2nd ed. revised
P. H. Nidditch, Oxford: Clarendon Press, 1978, p. 581, Book III, Part III,
Section I).
15. Hume, *Treatise of Human Nature*, ed. Selby-Bigge, p. 575.
16. J. L. Mackie, *Hume's Moral Theory* (London: Routledge, 1980), defines
'sympathy' in Hume's ethics as signifying 'a tendency to share what one
takes to be the feelings of another' (p. 120). Eva M. Dadlez, *Mirrors
to One Another: Emotion and Value in Jane Austen and David Hume*
(Chichester: Wiley-Blackwell, 2009) cogently relates Austen's fiction to
Hume's moral philosophy.
17. Hume, *Treatise of Human Nature*, ed. Selby-Bigge, pp. 575–6.

3 Describing Places

1. See James Wood, *How Fiction Works* (London: Vintage, 2009), p. 34.
2. *Jane Austen's Letters*, ed. Deirdre Le Faye, 3rd. ed. (Oxford: Oxford University Press, 1997), p. 203. In her letter to her sister Cassandra (4 February
1813) Austen uses ampersands for 'and'.
3. Henry James, 'The Art of Fiction', in *The Art of Criticism: Henry James on
the Theory and the Practice of Fiction*, ed. William Veeder and Susan M.
Griffin (Chicago: University of Chicago Press, 1986), p. 173.
4. 'Modern Fiction'; 'Mr Bennett and Mrs Brown', in *Collected Essays by
Virginia Woolf*, ed. Leonard Woolf (London: The Hogarth Press, 1966),
pp. 105, 330.
5. 'George Eliot'; 'Jane Austen', in *Collected Essays*, pp. 201, 148.
6. Both essays were collected in Roger Fry's *Vision and Design* (London:
Chatto and Windus, 1928), pp. 239; 51–2.
7. *Wordsworth: Poetical Works*, ed. Thomas Hutchinson, revised Ernest de
Selincourt (London: Oxford University Press, 1936), p. 536.
8. In Carlyle's tract *Chartism* (1839). *Thomas Carlyle: Selected Writings*, ed.
Alan Shelston (Harmondsworth: Penguin, 1971), p.154.
9. See David Lodge, *The Modes of Modern Writing: Metaphor, Metonymy,
and the Typology of Modern Literature* (London: Edward Arnold,
1977).

4 Presenting Action

1. *OED*, 'episode', 2.
2. A nineteenth-century critic proposed that the debate between Arabella and the divine is so different in style from the rest of the novel that it must be by another author, Samuel Johnson, who knew and admired Lennox's work. There is no evidence for such an attribution, which is both patronizing and unimaginative: the change in manner is deliberate, the novel's plunge into a saner, if less funny, style.
3. Letter to Marguerite Poradowska, 15 September 1891, *The Collected Letters of Joseph Conrad*, ed. Frederick R. Karl and Laurence Davies, vol. 1, 1861–97 (Cambridge: Cambridge University Press, 1983), p. 93.
4. *Boswell's Life of Johnson*, ed. George Birkbeck Hill, revised L. F. Powell, vol. 2 (Oxford: Clarendon Press, 1934), p. 175.
5. John Mullan, *How Novels Work* (Oxford: Oxford University Press, 2006), p. 47.
6. Nikolaus Pevsner and John Harris, *Lincolnshire*, 2nd ed. revised Nicholas Antram (Harmondsworth: Penguin, 1989), p. 460.
7. *The Letters of D. H. Lawrence*, II, p. 183, eds George J. Zytaruk and James T. Boulton (Cambridge: Cambridge University Press, 1981).
8. Ibid., p. 142.
9. On symbolism and synecdoche/metonymy, see David Lodge, *The Art of Fiction* (London: Secker and Warburg, 1992), chapter thirty.
10. Ecclesiastes, 12:6: 'or the golden bowl be broken'; Genesis, 9:13: 'I do set my bow in the cloud, and it shall be for a token of a covenant between me and the earth.'
11. Stéphane Mallarmé, 'Tombeau', *Collected Poems and Other Verse*, ed. and translated E. H. Blackmore and A. M. Blackmore (Oxford: Oxford University Press, 2006), pp. 210–3.
12. William Wordsworth, 'Lines composed a few miles above Tintern Abbey', l. 74.
13. *Wordsworth: Poetical Works*, ed. Thomas Hutchinson, revised Ernest de Selincourt (London: Oxford University Press, 1936), p. 577.

5 Speaking

1. Mark Kinkead-Weekes, *Samuel Richardson: Dramatic Novelist* (London: Methuen, 1973), p. 402.
2. Michael North calls Jane 'the finest actress in a pageant of acted emotions'; see Michael North, *Henry Green and the Writing of His Generation* (Charlottesville: University Press of Virginia, 1984), p. 205.
3. From her second novel, *Pastors and Masters* (1925), Ivy Compton-Burnett developed her own highly individual use of dialogue as the main vehicle of communication.

6 Commenting

1. Anthony Trollope, *An Autobiography*, ed. Michael Sadleir and Frederick Page (Oxford: Oxford University Press, 1980), p. 142.

2. *L'artiste doit être dans son oeuvre comme Dieu dans la création, invisible et tout-puissant; qu'on le sente partout, mais qu'on ne le voie pas* (letter to Mademoiselle Leroyer de Chantepie, 18 March 1857) (Flaubert, *Correspondance,* ed. Jean Bruneau (Paris: Gallimard, 1980), II, 691); *Je crois que le grand art est scientifique et impersonal* (letter to George Sand, 15 December 1866) (*Correspondance,* ed. Jean Bruneau (Paris: Gallimard, 1991), III, 579).

3. David Lodge, *The Art of Fiction* (London: Secker & Warburg, 1992; Vintage, 2011), p. 10.

4. Bernard Kreissman, *Pamela-Shamela: A Study of the Criticisms, Burlesques, Parodies and Adaptations of Richardson's Pamela* (Lincoln: University of Nebraska Press, 1960).

5. *Matthew*, 5: 28; *Genesis*, 22: 1–18.

6. David Lodge finds 'acquainted' a coldly formal word in the course of his excellent examination of this incident as an example of 'showing', not 'telling' (*The Art of Fiction*, p. 123).

7. 'Quae genus' is a section (on irregular nouns) in the Eton Latin grammar, then a standard textbook.

8. Lodge sees Fielding as playing a 'risky game' and also points to the rapidity with which the misunderstanding is cleared up (*The Art of Fiction*, pp. 123–4).

9. It is noteworthy that this sentence also includes the word 'persuasion', whose range of senses, from being argued out of a view by external pressure (*OED* 1) to conviction, self-belief (*OED* 2), are central to the novel's psychological and moral examination.

10. I am indebted throughout this section to the excellent discussion by Eva M. Dadlez, *Mirrors to One Another: Emotion and Value in Jane Austen and David Hume* (Chichester: Wiley-Blackwell, 2009), pp. 16–18.

11. The phrase he famously included in his own epitaph.

12. Ronald Paulson, *Satire and the Novel in Eighteenth-Century England* (New Haven: Yale University Press, 1967), p. 19.

13. Cf. William Hutchings, *Living Poetry: Reading Poems from Shakespeare to Don Paterson* (Houndmills, Basingstoke: Palgrave Macmillan, 2012), p. 37.

14. *Matthew*, 19, xix; 22, xxxix; *Mark*, 12, xxxi; *Leviticus*, 19, xviii.

15. Samuel Johnson, 'Life of Milton', *Lives of the Poets*, ed. Roger Lonsdale (Oxford: Clarendon Press, 2006), I, 290.

16. Mary McCarthy, *Ideas and the Novel* (London: Weidenfeld and Nicolson, 1980), p. 13.

17. Gore Vidal, 'Thomas Love Peacock: The Novel of Ideas', *The New York Review of Books*, 4 December 1980; in *The Essential Gore Vidal*, ed. Fred Kaplan (London: Little, Brown and Company, 1999), p. 908.
18. Henry James, 'The Art of Fiction', in *The Art of Criticism: Henry James on the Theory and the Practice of Fiction*, ed. William Veeder and Susan M. Griffin (Chicago: The University of Chicago Press, 1986), p. 168.
19. Mary McCarthy, *Ideas and the Novel*, p. 14.
20. See, for example, David Lodge, *The Language of Fiction* (London: Routledge, 1966), chapter four; Linda M. Shires, 'The radical aesthetic of *Tess of the d'Urbervilles*', *The Cambridge Companion to Thomas Hardy*, ed. Dale Kramer (Cambridge: Cambridge University Press, 1999), pp. 145–63.
21. 'The Reunion: Festival of Britain', BBC Radio Four, 24 August 2003.
22. Laurence Sterne, *A Sentimental Journey* (1768) opens: 'They order, said I, this matter better in France'.
23. See Section 6.5.
24. 'Mr. Bennett and Mrs. Brown', in *Virginia Woolf: Collected Essays*, ed. Leonard Woolf (London: The Hogarth Press, 1966), I, 320.
25. See Section 2.1.
26. 'In this novel the serial order of *narration* is continually invaded by the order of *explanation*.' A. D. Nuttall, *Openings: Narrative Beginnings from the Epic to the Novel* (Oxford: Clarendon Press, 1992), p. 158.

Index of Literary and Grammatical Terms

Note: Page references are to sections of the text where principal discussion or use of the term may be found.

allegory: a narrative that operates on two levels: the literal story and characters, and a further level of meaning as represented by the story and characters, 79

alliteration: repetition of consonants, particularly in stressed syllables, 72, 113, 115, 161

analepsis: retrospect or flashback to an earlier event or passage, 24, 92, 180n10

anaphora: repetition of a word or set of words in successive clauses, 26, 60, 153, 173

antithesis: contrasting ideas by balancing words of opposite or different meaning, 49, 115, 156

aposiopesis: breaking off in mid-sentence, 75, 121

assonance: repetition of vowel sounds, 72

asyndeton: omission of particles, usually conjunctions, 88

Bildungsroman: novel which narrates the development of the hero or heroine from youth to adulthood [German], 83

chiasmus: reversal in a second phrase or clause of the main elements of the first phrase or clause, 153–4

clause: a set of words forming a subject and predicate, 13, 45, 49, 57, 60, 87, 93, 113, 135, 143, 148, 149, 154, 155, 162, 166

closure: degree to which a narrative comes to a satisfactory conclusion or is open-ended, 158–63, 163–8, 172–9

comedy of manners: genre in which social manners and behaviour are humorously represented, 111

condition of England novel: novel describing, usually critically, the social or political state of England (cf state of the nation novel), 61–2

conte philosophique: a short fiction dealing with ideas [French], 116

cultural materialism: location of texts within contemporary cultural practice, particularly with regard to the implicit and explicit political nature of a society

decorum: consistency in relationship between form, language and content, 92, 106, 114, 116, 140, 160

defamiliarization: turning something common into something new or strange by viewing it in an unfamiliar way, 60, 152, 167

deixis: the way in which the terms in an utterance are related to a specific speaker, addressee, time and place, 122

diegesis: in narratology, the way in which a story is told; an extradiegetic narrator tells the story from outside the events; an intradiegetic narrator tells the story from within, as a participant in or observer of events (cf focalization)

direct speech: presentation of the actual words spoken by a character, 84, 101, 104–7, 107–12, 112–6, 116–21, 121–3, 146

dramatic irony: a situation in which the audience or reader understands what a character does not; or when a character's words or actions rebound on him or her, 19

duration: the time over which a story takes place; or the time given to the story by the text

dystopia: depiction of an imaginary society that is flawed or nightmarish, 95, 152

ellipsis: omission of a word or words in a sentence, 95

episode: an event narrated within a longer narrative; or a section of a serialized work, 69, 143

epistolary: fiction told in letters, 81, 108–9, 127, 136

fable: short narrative conveying a moral, 55, 116, 152, 155

fictional autobiography: an account of a character's life as written by himself or herself, 5, 92

first-person novel: a novel narrated by a character within the action or by a character observing the action (cf. third-person novel), 4–10, 11, 20, 63, 65–71, 83, 122, 139–40, 159, 163, 175

focalization: perspective from which a story is told (cf diegesis)

free indirect style: rendering a character's thoughts in reported format (as with indirect speech, q.v.), but without formal tags ('she thought' etc) and retaining language appropriate to the character, 127–9, 133

gothic: an extreme form of romance (q.v.), marked by horror and mystery, 73–4

historical fiction: fiction dealing with events and characters from a particular historical period, 63–4

historic present: narration of past events in the present tense, 63

hyperbole: exaggeration, 53, 72, 94, 148

indirect speech: speech as reported by a narrator, with the deixis (q.v.) made appropriate to the reporter's point of view, 121–5, 127, 128, 146

interior monologue: the thoughts of a character rendered directly to the reader, 132

intrusive narrator: narrator who breaks into the narrative with comment on an action or a character, 28, 136, 139–40, 167

irony: discrepancy between ostensible and real meaning of words, or between intended and actual outcome of actions, 34, 47, 79, 164, 166, 169, 171

melodrama: originally a stage-work mixing drama and music; later used of works of a sensational kind, 122

metaphor: figure of speech in which one thing is described in terms of another, 53, 56–7, 94, 95, 99, 110, 132, 148

metonymy: figure of speech in which an attribute of something represents the thing itself, 62–3

mixed metaphor: a metaphor in which the elements of the comparison are incongruous, 118, 126

modernism: a movement of early twentieth-century thought, characterized by re-examination of, or departure from, established artistic conventions; in literature frequently involving stylistic experimentation to reflect changes in perception of human nature, 47, 56, 124, 157, 169, 174, 177

narratology: the study of narratives from a strictly narrative point of view (as opposed to, for example, their social context)

novel of ideas: fiction in which philosophical, political or cultural ideas are presented, debated or criticized, 116, 157

omniscient: 'all-knowing'; a narrator outside the story, able to see and interpret the action and characters' thoughts and feelings, 11–12, 15, 22, 29

oxymoron: combination of two apparently contradictory elements, commonly an adjective and noun, 169

parable: very short narrative with a distinct and pointed moral (cf fable), 145

paradox: an apparently self-contradictory statement that actually contains truth, 99, 176, 177

persona: the speaker in a novel or poem, not to be identified with the author, 155

phrase: a combination of words not containing a predicate or main verb, 13, 38–9, 44, 56, 57, 95, 114, 130, 131, 155, 157, 161

picaresque: fiction narrating the adventures of rogues or low-life characters, 69–70

point of view: the perspective from which the story is seen; the relation in which the narrator stands to the story, 20–3, 59–60, 63, 146, 150

polysyndeton: repetition of conjunctions, 26

postmodernism: a movement in late twentieth-century thought in which modernism (*q.v.*) was subjected to self-conscious scrutiny, 174–6, 177

present participle: verbal form denoting a continuing, incomplete action, 39, 41, 56–7, 93, 99, 130–1

prolepsis: anticipation of a future event, 24, 180n10

realism: portrayal of real life in a truthful manner, 13, 18, 40, 47, 62, 92, 141, 155–6, 157

register: level of language and syntax with reference to their context, 113, 118

rhetoric: the art of persuasive writing or speaking, 45, 53, 60–2, 72, 92, 113–5, 144, 160

romance: originally, a medieval tale of chivalry or love; later used of fiction with events and scenes remote from those of everyday life, usually with a love element, 40–2, 71–4, 160–1

satire: a work exposing folly or vice to ridicule, 111, 151–8

simile: figure of speech in which one thing is likened to another, 59–61, 85, 86, 122

soliloquy: a speech in which a character is alone and utters her or his thoughts and feelings, 126–7, 132

state of the nation novel: novel describing the condition of a country (cf condition of England novel), 62–3

stream of consciousness: rendering of the flow of a character's internal experiences, 91, 129–33

subjunctive mood: form of verb expressing wish or condition, 113

symbol: object that represents an abstract meaning or concept, 89–92, 94, 166

synecdoche: figure of speech in which a part stands for the whole, 62–3, 89, 91

tense: form of a verb denoting the time of the action, 39, 63, 75, 84, 122, 125, 127–9

third-person novel: a novel narrated in the third person ('he', 'she', 'they'), rather than by a character within the action (cf first-person novel), 10–16, 20, 63, 83, 109, 127, 132, 163

unreliable narrator: narrator whose understanding and interpretation of characters and action cannot be trusted, 25–30

utopia: depiction of an imaginary ideal state, 151–2, 154

General Index

Note: Page references with letter 'n' followed by locators denote note numbers.

Addison, Joseph, 54
Aeschylus
  Prometheus Bound, 167
Aristophanes, 158
Austen, Jane, 47, 106, 128
  Emma, 106–7, 128–9, 140
  Mansfield Park, 1, 42–7, 49, 50–1
  Northanger Abbey, 52, 73–4
  Persuasion, 145–51
  Pride and Prejudice, 30–6, 40, 54

Bach, Johann Sebastian, 63
Balzac, Honoré de, 137
Barnes, Julian
  Flaubert's Parrot, 179
  A History of the World in 10½ Chapters, 179
  The Sense of an Ending, 3, 172–9
Behn, Aphra, 9
Bell, Vanessa, 42, 50
Bennett, Arnold, 47
  The Old Wives' Tale, 137–41, 166
  Riceyman Steps, 14–15, 67
Bonheim, Helmut, 180n3
Botticelli (Alessandro di Mariano dei Filipepi)
  Birth of Venus, 57
Brontë, Anne
  Agnes Grey, 158–63
Brontë, Charlotte
  Jane Eyre, 55, 83, 161
  Villette, 83, 121–3
Brontë, Emily
  Wuthering Heights, 51, 55, 159

Brookner, Anita
  Hotel du Lac, 2, 37–42
Bunyan, John
  The Pilgrim's Progress, 79
Burke, Edmund
  A Philosophical Inquiry into the Origin of our Ideas of the Sublime and Beautiful, 54
Burney, Frances
  Cecilia, 104–7, 127–8
  Evelina, 109, 127
Butler, Samuel
  Erewhon, 151–2
  The Way of All Flesh, 140
Byron, George Gordon, Lord, 149
  The Bride of Abydos, 148
  The Giaour, 148, 150

Canaletto (Antonio Canal), 39
Carlyle, Thomas, 61
Carroll, Lewis
  Alice's Adventures in Wonderland, 4
Cervantes, Miguel de
  Don Quixote, 9, 69, 72
Chaucer, Geoffrey, 120
Compton-Burnett, Ivy, 122
  Pastors and Masters, 182n3
Conrad, Joseph
  Lord Jim, 74–6, 107
  Nostromo, 37–8

Dadlez, Eva M., 181n16, 183n10
Dante (Dante Alighieri)
  Divine Comedy, 98, 170

Defoe, Daniel
  *The Complete English
    Tradesman*, 6
  *The Farther Adventures of
    Robinson Crusoe*, 5
  Moll Flanders, 65–71
  A Review, 6
  Robinson Crusoe, 3, 4–10, 12, 16,
    20, 66, 71, 79, 83, 157, 172, 176
  Roxana, 5
  The True-Born Englishman, 7
Descartes, René, 9
Dickens, Charles, 59, 164
  All the Year Round, 82
  Bleak House, 1
  Great Expectations, 82–7
  Hard Times, 60–1
  Household Words, 59, 60
Doyle, Arthur Conan
  A Study in Scarlet, 13
Drabble, Margaret
  The Gates of Ivory, 62
  A Natural Curiosity, 62
  The Radiant Way, 62

Einstein, Albert, 174
Eliot, George, 36, 164
  Middlemarch, 11–12, 16, 19–25, 29,
    30, 36, 47, 137
  *The Natural History of German
    Life*, 25
Epictetus, 8

Fielding, Henry, 136–7
  Joseph Andrews, 9, 69, 80, 141–5
  Shamela, 141
  Tom Jones, 28, 69, 76–81, 98, 136
Firbank, Ronald
  Valmouth, 120–1
Fitzgerald, Penelope
  The Blue Flower, 100–3
Flaubert, Gustave, 136, 137, 139
  Madame Bovary, 138
Ford, Ford Madox
  The Good Soldier, 25–30, 137

Forster, Edward Morgan
  Howards End, 55
  A Passage to India, 55
  A Room with a View, 55–7
Frith, William Powell, 39
Fry, Roger, 50

Galsworthy, John, 47
Gaskell, Elizabeth
  Lizzie Leigh, 61
  Mary Barton, 61
  North and South, 58–62
Géricault, Théodore, 179
Golding, William
  Lord of the Flies, 98
  The Spire, 97–100
Green, Henry, 122
  Doting, 109
  Living, 123–5
  Nothing, 109–12

Hardy, Thomas
  Far from the Madding Crowd,
    12–13
  Life's Little Ironies, 19
  The Mayor of Casterbridge, 1,
    10–16, 20, 38, 67
  The Return of the Native, 38, 51
  Tess of the d'Urbervilles, 163–8
  The Woodlanders, 16–19, 20, 91,
    180n10
Harris, John, 182n6
Haywood, Eliza
  *The History of Miss Betsy
    Thoughtless*, 125–7, 132
Hume, David, 33
  A Treatise of Human Nature, 35
Hutchings, William, 180n1, 183n13
Huxley, Aldous
  Brave New World, 152

James, Henry, 43, 132, 136, 158, 160
  The Golden Bowl, 90
James, William
  Principles of Psychology, 132

Johnson, Bryan Stanley
  Alberto Angelo, 10, 175
  Christie Malry's Own Double Entry, 175
  House Mother Normal, 175–7
  The Unfortunates, 175
Johnson, Samuel, 81, 157
  Dictionary, 114
  Rasselas, 112–6
Jones, Robert, 54
Jonson, Ben, 68
Joyce, James
  Ulysses, 132

Kinkead-Weekes, Mark, 108
Kipling, Rudyard, 117
Kreissman, Bernard, 183n4

Larkin, Philip, 43
Lawrence, David Herbert, 55, 92
  The Rainbow, 87–92, 93
  Sons and Lovers, 83, 89
Lennox, Charlotte
  The Female Quixote, 71–4
Lodge, David, 181n9, 182n9, 183n3, 183n6, 183n8, 184n20
Lucian, 158

McCarthy, Mary, 157–8, 160
McEwan, Ian
  Saturday, 62–4
Mackie, John Leslie, 181n16
Mallarmé, Stéphane, 90–1
Mantel, Hilary, 63–4
Maupassant, Guy de, 29, 137
  Une Vie, 137
Milton, John
  Paradise Lost, 157, 161, 168
More, Thomas
  Utopia, 151
Mozart, Wolfgang Amadeus
  The Magic Flute, 98
Mullan, John, 182n5

Nashe, Thomas, 9
North, Michael, 182n2
Novalis (Friedrich von Hardenberg), 100–1
Nuttall, Anthony David, 184n26

Orwell, George
  Animal Farm, 152
  Coming up for Air, 92–7, 151
  Nineteen-Eighty-Four, 95, 152, 158
  'Politics and the English Language', 94–5
Ousby, Ian, 181n13

Paulson, Ronald, 155
Peacock, Thomas Love, 157–8
Petronius, 158
Pevsner, Nikolaus, 88
Pinion, F. B., 180n8
Plato
  Republic, 151
Poradowska, Marguerite, 76

Rabelais, François, 158
Radcliffe, Ann, 55, 161
  The Mysteries of Udolpho, 51–5
Richardson, Samuel, 136
  Clarissa, 74, 81–2, 127
  Pamela, 136, 141
  Sir Charles Grandison, 107–9, 111–2
Rousseau, Jean-Jacques, 51
Rubens, Peter Paul, 28

Scott, Walter, 149
  The Lady of the Lake, 18
  Marmion, 148
Scudéry, Madeleine de
  Clélie, 73
Shakespeare, William, 102
  Cymbeline, 131
  Hamlet, 89, 102, 126, 132
  King Lear, 156, 167
Shires, Linda M., 184n20

Sterne, Laurence, 121
   A Sentimental Journey, 170
   Tristram Shandy, 7–10, 116, 176–7
Swift, Jonathan
   Gulliver's Travels, 151–8

Thackeray, William Makepeace,
   137, 164
   Vanity Fair, 137
Trollope, Anthony, 164
   Autobiography, 134
   Framley Parsonage, 134–7, 139
   The Last Chronicle of Barset, 134
   The Warden, 134
   The Way We Live Now, 62
Turgenev, Ivan, 137

Verlaine, Paul, 91
Vidal, Gore, 158
Voltaire (François-Marie
   Arouet), 158
   Candide, 116

Watt, Ian, 180n7
Waugh, Evelyn
   Men at Arms, 118–9, 168–9, 170–1
   Officers and Gentlemen, 168, 171
   Unconditional Surrender, 168–72
Wilde, Oscar
   *The Importance of Being
     Earnest*, 42
Wodehouse, Pelham Grenville
   The Code of the Woosters, 116–9
Wood, James, 180n9, 181n1
Woolf, Virginia, 42, 174
   'Modern Fiction', 47
   Mrs Dalloway, 2, 129–33
   To the Lighthouse, 47–51,
     56–7, 133
   The Waves, 51, 132
Wordsworth, William, 54
   'Lines composed a few miles
     above Tintern Abbey', 182n12
   The Prelude, 54, 102